AVID

READER

PRESS

TO THE

MOON

AND

BACK

A NOVEL

Eliana Ramage

AVID READER PRESS

New York   Amsterdam/Antwerp   London   Toronto   Sydney/Melbourne   New Delhi

AVID READER PRESS
An Imprint of Simon & Schuster, LLC
1230 Avenue of the Americas
New York, NY 10020

This book is a work of fiction. Any references to historical events, real people, or real places are used fictitiously. Other names, characters, places, and events are products of the author's imagination, and any resemblance to actual events or places or persons, living or dead, is entirely coincidental.

Interior design by Ruth Lee-Mui

Manufactured in the United States of America

ISBN 978-1-6680-6585-3

A NOTE TO THE READER

While one character's background is inspired by a case involving the Indian Child Welfare Act, this is a novel. Its characters, action, and dialogue are wholly fictional and not intended to portray any real person or represent any real events. All the novel's characters, and any details about them, are the author's invention.

For my parents

"When you first came to us
we did not have an Ojibwe name
to know the sky beyond
the sky beyond the sky

How were we to know
he was she was
they are
you

How were we to know who?"

—From "How It Escaped Our Attention," by
Heid E. Erdrich

REMOVAL

June 1987

I imagine her terrified. Our mother. Two children in the back seat. She drove like a woman followed, even after we left him at the foot of that tall hill. There was blood there, back in Texas, and tiny shards of glass still covered my sister. She sat beside me, her small body glittering in passing lights—the brights of cars, the moon.

I remember our mother pulling off the highway into dark towns, buying biscuits at the drive-through with small bills in a rubber band, pulled from under the driver's seat. Kayla slept and I ate three biscuits, hers and mine and our mother's, too. Our mother, who cried silently behind the steering wheel from Dallas to Plano to Sherman to McAlester. I practiced reading highway signs. Our mother helped me sound them out, until she didn't.

I was in my school clothes. My underwear said *Tuesday* in cursive. A long time later, we passed a blue sign with a buffalo-skin shield and eagle feathers and little brown crosses. *Oklahoma*. Our mother corrected me, *oh* not *ah*, but she was talking again. She was alive. She pulled off the highway at the first rest stop past the blue sign and she took one giant breath, in and out with her eyes closed. I copied her. Kayla wiggled against the straps in her booster seat. She started to sing, happily and to herself.

I would grow up with stories in Tahlequah, though never the kind I asked for. There were no stories for what had happened, for why we'd left Texas and when we might return.

Instead, this: "When I was a little girl," our mother said, "my mother and my father got into some trouble and my mother took us to spend the summer with my grandmother in Oklahoma. There weren't any movie theaters, and we had to walk a long way to fill up jugs of water in the mornings, but my arms got strong, and I read a lot of chapter books, and it was peaceful, all the way to August."

Instead, this: "When your great-grandmother was a girl, she was a student at the Cherokee Female Seminary, which was very special before it burned down. Your great-grandfather was a scholar, too, at the Cherokee Male Seminary. They learned there and then taught there, and even before that their parents had been educated there, too. One of them was a superintendent! People will tell you all kinds of things about Indians, all your life, but I'll tell you this. You girls come from people who studied Greek and Latin. Who studied philosophy and astronomy. Steph! *Astronomy!*"

Instead, this: "When your great-*great*-grandmother was a girl, she had to go all the way from Georgia to Indian Territory. Not Tahlequah, but close, along the Arkansas River. To this land, for sure—it's all ours—and on the way all sorts of people got sick and died. And after all that, Stephanie, no, for the love of God, I do not see the point in us moving again."

Our mother took my sister and me, and she drove through the night to a place she felt a claim to, a place on Earth she thought we might be safe. I stopped asking questions. I picked little glass pieces from my sister's hair. I watched the moon.

PART

ONE

1995–2000

ALL THAT IS OR EVER WAS OR EVER WILL BE

June 1995

Eight Years Later

I was thirteen years old in Oklahoma. Eight years now in the house in Tahlequah to which our mother had brought us. I wanted, more than anything, to be gone.

To outer space. To a better school than my own, that could help me get to outer space. And before that, to Space Camp. *At least* to Space Camp! The one thing that could hold me over while I waited for the rest of my life.

At Space Camp, I'd heard, you could take turns sleeping in a pod modeled after the real ones. You could zip yourself into a sleeping bag tethered to the wall, strap yourself down and close the hatch like it was real. Like if you didn't do these things, you'd float away.

I used to get this feeling sometimes, where everything would stop, and it would be like I was flying above myself, watching, remembering the moment I was in but from years ahead. It happened in moments when I most believed that maybe my life would take the shape I wanted it to. I felt that so many nights, with my sister breathing softly in the bunk below. My sister, content. Me sitting up, shivering and wrapped in an old blue quilt, ordered piles of papers spread around me. Flashlight waving over PSAT scores and essays. Financial aid forms filled with numbers, from pay stubs I had slipped from our mother's purse.

Whenever I started to think about how Phillips Exeter Academy might not let me in, and then how hard it would be to impress NASA without Phillips Exeter Academy, I'd switch off the flashlight. I'd lean back and look up at the glow-in-the-dark stars that Brett, my teacher but also my mother's boyfriend, had stuck to the ceiling.

I enclosed a letter with my application. I told them I was "on track" to become an astronaut, which meant I'd done very well in middle school science and would likely attend Space Camp in Huntsville that summer.

Then I waited for my Exeter acceptance letter. And I waited for my Space Camp application. My mother had said she would call to request it.

On the phone they said camp costs a thousand dollars. She said thank you and hung up.

She spent the next four weeks changing the subject when I asked about it, and then in April (still no word from Exeter) she sat down me and Kayla and said she had a surprise. (Brett was apparently excused from this family meeting, as he'd gone out to the country. He was visiting his ancient parents, and I wished he'd brought me with him.)

There wasn't money for Space Camp. It wasn't happening.

Kayla said, "Got it, okay, can I please be excused?" She'd been calling it "nerd camp" since Thanksgiving.

"No, you listen," our mother said, "both of you. You're not going to *the* Space Camp, but you are going to *a* Space Camp!"

"Oh no," Kayla said.

"Huh?" I said.

"I'm *running* it!" our mother said.

"Oh *no*," Kayla said.

"Kayla, watch it," our mother said, but she looked at me. Her hands gripped the couch cushion under her, tight. Her eyes were bright, wide, daring me not to be thrilled. I watched the clock above the couch, unwove the woven baskets on the bookshelf with my eyes.

Our mother explained that she and Brett had spent the last month staying up late, typing a grant proposal on the computer they'd bought together. "I even had a meeting with an astronomy professor, at his office," she said, clearly having waited days to tell me that.

"You're gonna make Cherokee Culture Camp all spacey," Kayla said, "aren't you?"

Our mother looked down at her hands, raw and rough but sweet-smelling from the bread factory where she worked. I used to press her palms to my face, used to breathe in the strange mix of rising dough and sharp-smelling machinery.

"You'll like Space-Culture Camp," she said.

I said we should try again for *Space* Camp. The real one, for next year. I could save up. Sometimes Exeter let kids have jobs on campus. I could see myself standing behind a tall marble desk in a library, getting paid to explain things to my fellow students. Maybe I'd wear my hair in a low bun.

Our mother looked like I had hit her. She was quiet and careful, opening her mouth and then closing it, and then she looked at me like, *Is this really who you are?*

She said, "This is the best that I could do."

All that was left was to pretend. We nodded and said great, thank you, can't wait.

We did the dishes. I washed and Kayla dried. I tried to look out the window over the kitchen sink, tried to find the night sky, but the lights were too bright. All I could see was the two of us reflected in the glass. Kayla played the Top 40 countdown on the radio and sang along.

Nothing stuck to her. The way she'd flit through the hallways at school— from class to class, friend to friend—it was incredible to me, and alien. My sister belonged, happily, like she'd sprouted out of the ground behind this house. I was something like a refugee, from a time and place my sister had forgotten. I wished I could have just a little of all that Kayla was.

At Space Camp, you strap into a multi-access trainer—like a spinning cage inside a spinning cage—and are rotated in every direction, no more than two turns the same way in a row, to keep the inner ear fluid from disrupting your balance. Astronaut candidates (they're called "ascans!") use something very similar in training, only with a joystick, so they can practice stabilizing a shuttle on reentry if it starts to spin out. Without stabilization, a real astronaut could experience g-forces so strong they die.

Space-*Culture* Camp was held in the middle school gym. It smelled like boys, and the lights overhead glared bluish green on our skin. Our words clapped off the walls and rushed back loud and harsh.

On the bleachers, which were folded against the wall, our mother had taped cutout paintings of planets and stars. She'd made them herself the night before, on the backs of old protest signs. *Moms Against Nukes* on the back of Venus. *Della Owens Belongs with Her Tribe . . . Support the Indian Child Welfare Act!* on the back of the moon. Our mother was never good at protest slogans and gave too much of herself to other people. When things didn't go as she had hoped (when, for example, Della Owens was taken from her family and sent back to the adoptive couple in Utah), our mother saw it as evidence of her own powerlessness. Like she alone had let down the world.

After snack time, our mother and Brett stacked everyone into the bed of a truck and drove us to the top of a low hill behind the cemetery. They then brought out a new, clean garbage can with Styrofoam duct-taped to the inside, and tipped it over. One at a time, we put on a helmet and climbed in.

Our mother did a countdown from ten—she was working from a limited base of knowledge, and for near everything we did, she had to say "blastoff"— and pushed us down the hill.

When everyone had gone, we sat in a circle in the grass and talked about how it had felt. How we thought astronauts might feel in *the same scenario.* "This circle time is just like a mission debrief!" is what she would have said, probably, if she even knew about mission debriefs. Most people didn't.

"They'd maybe be scared at first," said Meredith. She was new in town, and had wide-set, blue-green eyes. She had a look to her that was serious and a little spooky to me, but also made me want to stare at her when she wasn't looking.

"They'd get used to it, though," I said. "If you can't handle the vomit comet, then you can't handle space!" I was proud to know that nickname— "vomit comet."

Brett laughed. "Doyu hadvneliha," he said. It was nice sometimes, having words and phrases in Cherokee as our own language.

"Anyone else?" said our mother. "How would astronauts *feel*?"

"Nauseous," said Daniel. He'd lingered in the trash can at the bottom of the hill, before throwing up inside it and ending the activity for everyone. Kayla helped him climb out and brought him water and rubbed circles on his back with her hand. Kayla was always taking care of people. Even our own mother when she was sad, which was often. Kayla was so good at looking good, I sometimes looked bad in comparison.

"Nauseated," I corrected. Brett scrunched up his eyebrows and cocked his head at me, like he did at school or at home whenever I "got in my own way." That's what he called it when I was a show-off or a know-it-all or a bad friend. "Tsaneldodigwu awaduli," he'd say in the living room, the lunchroom, the carpool line. *I just want you to try.* Whenever he said that, whenever he made that face like he was worried about me, like I was the kind of child one had to worry about, I felt alone. I felt thrown out of the air lock, suited up without a tether. *Do you see me?* I wanted to say. *Do you see me at all?*

At Space Camp, there's a twenty-three-foot-deep neutral buoyancy lab for mission training. At the bottom of the pool is the pretend wall of a pretend space station with loose screws and deep tears and faulty supply tanks. A death trap—but pretend! You swim down with a scuba tank on your back, and they give you a problem and you fix it. There's an underwater countdown clock and a siren that gets louder and faster as you work, because it's space, and in space you're always one second from death. A red light flashes through the water, your white suit turning from swimming pool–blue to danger-red, and then blue, and then red red red, system failure like in Starfleet when the captain calls blue alert and it's dark and quiet and time to focus or else. And you're in your space suit, a hundred-pound mock space suit with the boots and everything, and with your clumsy, padded, white-gloved hands you're trying to turn a small screw back in place with a silver wrench, your wrist turning and your legs flailing out behind you—you're weightless, almost, you're almost there.

We didn't have that. We were driven to the creek behind Brett's friend Beth's house. Beth sat up high on her porch in a pink bikini and sunglasses like Barbie, and every so often she'd wave down to us. She held a cocktail with an umbrella in a tall glass, and I wondered again why my mother lived her life like fun was illegal. Why she was so downtrodden. Sometimes at church, back when we'd been new to town and had gone more often, I used to see charity posters of poor people in other countries, staring into the distance with everything they owned wrapped in blankets on their backs. In my mind I'd swap in my mother's face.

"Ma, there's a scuba park at Lake Tenkiller," I said.

"Camp is free," she said, and slapped a snorkel in my hand.

I laid my towel out neat on the grass and put on sunscreen, which no one else had bothered with even though skin cancer kills. I moved slowly down to the creek, keeping an eye out for sharp rocks and snakes, making contingency plans for if I cut myself or got poisoned. I only had about a decade or so to rid myself of every fear I still had. In the place of all those old fears I would put a more honorable kind of fear, which I called (and which NASA called) awareness and preparedness and disaster response protocol.

By the time I made it up to my shoulders in the water, most of the group was downstream. I hurried to catch up to them. John, a fellow almost ninth grader who had been mean to me when we first moved here, said he was Irish. Gracey, an almost seventh grader who was consistently kind and boring, said English and Polish and Scottish. Daniel said *full*-blood, the "full" sound like *fool*. His accent was country, like my father's had been. My mother tried to correct us away from it.

It was a weird ritual, the listing of fractions. But you had to be a tribal citizen to go to camp, which required having ancestors on a list of Cherokees the government had made a hundred years ago. That left a lot of room for working out what now set us apart. Meredith waved me back over to the group—I had been swimming away from them, inches at a time.

I smiled and shook my head and cupped my hands in the water, pretending to catch tadpoles.

When people asked "what are you," they meant what was my mother and what was my father. My father was white and dead. My mother refused to talk about him, except to say there'd been a car accident. She wouldn't talk about her parents, either, but that was because they'd kicked her out of their house.

Meredith shouted my name. Everyone turned and looked at me. I gasped in as much air as I could hold, pinched my nose, and sank underwater.

My eyes squeezed shut. My toes dug into the muddy creek bed. I made myself small.

. . .

My father was shouting about the universe again. The memory pushed into me like cold water on all sides.

"It's like *this*," he said. The two of us, left alone together. The last few days had been bad ones. Soon I'd see him crumpled over the wheel.

My father stepped away from me, into the woods behind the house in Texas, and I was afraid. I was cold. I thought of my purple coat on its low hook by the front door but knew he wouldn't let me leave. If I did, he'd chase me.

The white beam of a flashlight shone in my eyes, and a wall of black pushed toward me. I heard the heaviness of his boots on the ground. The crush of sticks and leaves.

"Can you see me?" he said.

I shook my head and turned away. Across the yard, through the bathroom window, I saw my mother bent over the bath. When my father had announced it was time for an astronomy lesson, she had let him take me.

I was getting too old to do bath time with Kayla. I missed our little boats with sails and our Marine Biologist Barbie. Our shark, toothy and open-mouthed. With a few turns of a crank, our father could make his fins move.

"Steph!" he said. "Try again! *Can you see me?*"

He turned my head back toward him and shook the light in my face. I closed my eyes.

"No, sir," I said, careful. I needed my coat, the toilet, whatever my mother had saved for me from dinner. It would be a long time before my turn in the bath.

"Exactly. Quasars are supermassive black holes, feeding on gas in young galaxies. They're like flashlights! So bright you can't see what's around them, or behind them—none of the whole rest of the galaxy."

I nodded, eyes still closed, and my father continued to talk. He held the light steady in my eyes and told me to be tough. Earth was tiny and unprotected. The universe was big, deadly, not known well enough to trust. It didn't matter who you were or where you came from. This part mattered because my mother was "part-Cherokee and stuck-up about it."

Whoever you were when the end came, you had to be ready to run.

"I am," I said. But he never believed me.

"I'm trying to protect you," he said, when my eyes filled with water. "To teach you. It could be an asteroid! A super volcano. Nuclear war. Whatever it is, there's gonna be a battle for resources. You gotta run before that, Steph. To the moon and back, if you've gotta."

"I know," I said.

My father nodded. With one hand, he brought the flashlight closer to my eyes. With the other, he counted out options for the end of the world. The Big Freeze, the Big Rip, vacuum decay.

I felt the wet on my cheeks. My eyes hurt so, so bad.

"Don't tell me you forgot what those are?"

"No, sir," I said, but it was a lie. I was five.

I came up for air.

Meredith spat water out her snorkel, dangerously close to Gracey's face. Gracey laughed good-naturedly. I climbed out of the creek, unsure where I was supposed to go now, and Meredith called my name again.

"Um, I've got cramps!" I shouted, running toward the woods. When I looked back, Meredith nodded slowly and swam away from where I'd stood in the water. John stared at me, forehead creased, like I had broken a rule.

Creek Day, I knew, would stretch well into the afternoon. My suit was too tight, a one-piece with bright yellow fabric pinching at my bottom, and the sun was hot on my back. I sat at the foot of a tree and closed my eyes. I remembered the mosquitos and opened my eyes again. I wanted to yell out in frustration. I wanted to be somewhere else.

I slapped a mosquito on my leg, and blood shot across the surface of my skin. My thighs were heavy now, and therefore more often covered, and lighter-colored than the rest of me. The line where my suit hit my legs had hairs peeking through, a new and humiliating problem that I might never solve. I pulled my legs up to my chest and held myself, covering my thick thighs and pointy knees and oily face. *You can't be the kind of person who cares about this*, I told myself. I was better than other girls, better than Brittany and Gracey and even—especially—Kayla. Kayla took a lot of pride in what she looked like. Because of that she had many burdens, like having to brush her hair every day. But I was different. I was a scientist.

I heard a laugh, high and fast, and then "hey, shut up!" Another laugh, deep or trying to be. I stood up and tiptoed forward.

The voices started up again, fast, excited. "You don't think she got in?"

"Nope."

"Why not?"

"Daniel, please, it's June! She can't keep waiting at the mailbox. It's sad."

The air was hot and humid, my skin wet from the creek or sweat or both. Quietly I stood up. Every step hurt the soft bottoms of my feet, not used to the twigs and rocks and cracked acorns strewn across the ground. The trees overhead made pretty patterns on my arms, surprising me, the sun passing through them to print a hundred little leaves against my skin. My arms were strong, even if they didn't look it, and my fingers were long, thin—just right, I imagined, for fixing mechanical errors on a ship.

I was just observing, I thought to myself. Observe, orient, decide, act. They do that in the air force. A lot of astronauts start out in the air force.

I saw a foot sticking out behind a tree, a bare shoulder leaning against the bark.

"I mean, hasn't she always been like that? Like, kinda *off*?"

That was Daniel.

"No! She's fine. Normal. But sometimes it's just like, *we get it!* You know a lot of shit about space!"

My sister.

Daniel laughed. He made his voice go up high and dumb and ridiculous, like a girl. Like me. "Excuse me," he said, "but I feel like the aerodynamics of this stickball game are highly problematized. If you'd simply anticipate the coordinates of this dimension . . ."

Kayla snorted. Daniel stood and reached out a hand, pulling Kayla up beside him.

She saw me. Her face fell.

"Wait, wait, wait," Kayla said. "Steph. Can we talk alone for a second?" She stepped toward me, and Daniel stepped toward her. She shook him off. Daniel reached for her again.

I caught the way Daniel draped his hand over her shoulder, his fingers dangling a few inches above her chest like it was nothing. The bow on her bikini had been tied and retied, haphazardly. Loose strings dangled over her belly. She was twelve years old.

"Steph, we were just—"

"Being mean to me?" I said. "Or letting Daniel *molest* you in the woods? Which is it?"

"Shut *up!*" she said, gripping her own shoulders. Then, softer, "Please, quiet down. Let's go talk somewhere."

"Let's talk about this *logically*," said Daniel.

"Shut up," said Kayla, and me. Daniel held his hands up and stepped back. He ran a hand through his hair. It was thick and black and wavy. No, *disheveled*. I wanted to hit them both, but I had to keep Kayla safe. I yanked her by the arm and pulled her body behind mine.

"We're supposed to be at swim time," I said. I was looking at Daniel but talking behind me, to my sister. My younger sister. I felt her breath just under my neck. She was shorter than me.

"You're just jealous," she said.

That was unkind. Hadn't she been a toddler on my lap, hiding in a closet? When our father locked us outside the house, I'd sat with her by the door. I would have taken her away with me, if I'd been older and known where to go. Now I really could run, soon, to Exeter—they were wrong, I still had time. But it was sad to know I'd be leaving her behind.

She seemed fine with that, though. She didn't remember what had happened to us.

I could barely believe what had happened to us. The fact that it *had*, the unthinkable part on the night we ran, made nothing that could come after it unthinkable. Our planet and everyone on it, sucked into darkness in the space of a breath.

"Kayla, don't be gross," I said.

I didn't know what I meant by that—if I was taking aim at her attitude or her body. It was true that I was jealous. Not of how her body looked, but of how freely she used it. How at home she was in it, how unafraid. She had, unlike me, no memory of what could go wrong.

I left Kayla and Daniel in the woods. Back at the creek, I sat down next to Brett. He had black hair and brown eyes and pink skin. He wore rolled-up blue jeans and a gray T-shirt with a tiny rip by the neck. Beth gave it to him, because she worked at the mall and got things free if there was something wrong with them. She was always giving us presents with something wrong with them. Once she gave me a purple water bottle that said *Shoot for the moon! Even if you miss, you will land among the staIrs.*

I looked down at our feet in the water, wishing our legs would look broken like a spoon in a cup because of refraction. It was the wrong angle, and the water was a kind of green that looked black. I listened to the kids swimming, far-off sounding in the echo of shrieks and splashing water. The snorkels were muddy, tossed in a pile on the bank. I wondered if my mother would drive to Walmart and try to return them that weekend. I could already see her standing over the bathtub, scrubbing them down, laying them out on a towel to dry in the yard. At Exeter, I thought, you can take scuba diving for PE.

Kayla was right; my acceptance letter had still not arrived.

Brett turned his whole self to look at me. He was smart, and he thought I was, too. He let me use his telescope whenever I wanted.

"Ahnawake," he said. It was my Cherokee name, though only he used it. His mother had given it to me since my mother couldn't.

"Mhm?" I said.

"What's going on, Ahnawake?" he said. "Why aren't you speaking proud in our camp language lessons? You know all this—it's baby stuff for you."

"Yeah," I said. "No need to show off."

Brett took one foot out of the water and folded it under him. He knew I loved to show off. "Are you sure that's it?"

I thought about telling Brett the truth. How I was terrified I hadn't gotten into Exeter, with the first day of school in just ten weeks. Shouldn't I have heard from them by now?

I thought about telling him how Space-Culture Camp was humiliating to me. How the things he and my mother cared about were not going to get me to space. How they were irrelevant outside this town, which would make my life small and unimportant.

Brett put his hand on the top of my head. "Ahnawake?"

Sometimes Brett said my Cherokee name so many times in a conversation it was like he was maybe trying to tell me something. He'd been the first person to treat us like we belonged when we got here. Our mother in the early days had no friends, and no local close relations, so she would do things like show up at events and name-drop our more famous Cherokee ancestors. "Nancy Ward's Cherokee name was Nanyehi!" she'd say. "We're related to her!" So were forty thousand other people. Seven years in, though, and Brett was still clearing out a space for us. Kayla took it, like our lives in Texas had never happened. Her life, her Cherokee life, was the only one she knew, and she had nothing to prove.

"I'm fine, Brett."

"Tsalagiha hniwi," he said. *Say it in all-Cherokee.*

I rolled my eyes. "Tohigwu."

In the early days of their relationship, our mother had asked Brett to cover our house in labels, bright pink index cards taped to every surface. Galohisdi. Gasgilo. Digohweli. Ganihli. They worked, to a point. Kayla quickly realized how happy her learning these words made our mother, and how important they were to our people's continued existence. She set about being the most enthusiastically Indian child our family had seen in generations. Our mother learned almost a hundred words in Cherokee, but they were all nouns in a language of mostly verbs. Still, she asked Brett to speak it to us on whatever level we'd understand. If it was frustrating—this wall of language she built around herself—she didn't let on. She'd say, "Keep going, I like to hear y'all talk."

Once, when I was ten or eleven, I heard them fight about it. I was on the floor of the bedroom I shared with Kayla, my ear pressed to the cold metal grate of the air vent. I heard "sure" and "fine" and "what do you mean" and "what do you *mean* what do you mean."

"Hannah, come on. Just say it's 'cause I'm traditional," Brett said.

The heave and jerk of a drawer on bent runners slammed shut. The snap of air caught under a sheet. My mother was making the bed. It was a Friday, and she did laundry on that day ever since learning the Cherokee word for it: tsungilosdi. *Wash day.*

"Just say that's why I'm here," Brett said. "If it's really just for the girls, heck, if that's all you want—*Hannah, stop, listen to me*—we could figure something out. I wouldn't leave them."

Water shot through pipes in the walls. I imagined her standing at the mirror, tapping lotion onto her cheeks with the tips of her fingers. I imagined her flossing, rinsing, taking her time.

I was almost asleep when she spoke again. "I'm not with you because you're traditional," she said. "I love you."

Brett said something I couldn't hear. I could almost see my mother, sitting up in bed, the way she'd let out a breath and close her eyes and hold up the palm of her hand. "But it's not *not* that you're traditional. I like what you give my girls."

"*Our* girls, Hannah," he said, and my heart broke open. Then he said, "Language practice."

"*Grounding*," she said.

Kayla came in and caught me then, said didn't I promise I'd stop? Didn't I know nothing good could come of this? I climbed onto the top bunk, and she flicked off the light. I fell asleep to the bright green patterns of glow-in-the-dark stars I could reach with my fingertips, to the low hum of my mother's voice through the grate. I used to think my mother was self-conscious and shallow, that she would stop at nothing to belong. Not realizing—not for a very long time—the strength it takes to say what you want. The ambition of wanting a certain life, of demanding it.

After camp that day, I sat on the ground by the mailbox with a book. The mailman came an hour later, sweating like crazy even in the shorts version of his blue uniform. My mother brought him out a plastic cup of water, as she always did in the summer. There was no letter for me.

I barely spoke on Tuesday. Only Meredith noticed. She touched my arm in the hallway, gentle, and looked at me with so much kindness. She smelled good, like the chlorine from pool time. I could stay here, I thought. I could swim in this.

"I told you, I'm *fine*," I said, pushing past her to go cry in private about Exeter. But I couldn't find anywhere that wasn't taken over by other people. Meredith didn't follow me like Brett would have, like—maybe?—my sister, and against all reason my feelings were hurt.

After lunch, Brett asked my mother to teach us what a solar eclipse and lunar eclipse were. Despite practicing at the dinner table the night before, she struggled through her explanation. Then Brett told us a traditional story about a frog eating the sun or moon—the word is the same for both, nvdo, which offended me—and how *that's* what an eclipse is. Nvdo walosi ugisgo translates directly to *sun/moon the frog eats it the round thing habitually.* Kayla already knew the story from her visits with Brett's father, our sort-of grandfather, and she decided to show off.

"If an eclipse happens," she said proudly, "we have to get out pots and pans and whatever, and make noise to scare the frog away." Brett nodded. Our mother beamed.

Brett gave us watercolors to paint pictures of a frog with a sun or a moon in its mouth. Kayla's frog was so realistic that a small line of campers asked her to paint portraits of them during our lunch break, her first work on commission. I painted a regular moon, all set to tell my mother that the frog was there, but it was frozen and suffocated and dead, its body too small to see on the moon at this scale. But Brett got to me first. He tugged at the collar on his unbuttoned button-down and leaned over my shoulder to pass Daniel a clean paintbrush. "I'm painting the frog next," I said quickly, "after the moon."

On Wednesday Kayla put her head on Daniel's shoulder during the basketweaving demonstration, and I thought about what it might feel like—his cheek warm against my hand, my hand tight around his waist. Our mother stood very still by the pile of dried hickory bark, her arms crossed, watching them. We weren't allowed to have boyfriends till we were sixteen. Kayla knew that. It was kind of our family's only rule.

I was surprised that Kayla wasn't in trouble, because she and Daniel were so obvious! When it was quiet, they laughed. When the rest of us laughed, they touched their noses together and whispered seriously into each other's mouths, eyes closed. At craft time, Daniel ran a dry paintbrush across the back of her neck.

On Friday, the last day of camp, I decided to tell my mother about Kayla and Daniel. How they were dating, which was against the rules.

I told myself I was worried about Kayla. Tattling would protect her. The very little I had understood of our life before Tahlequah colored everything in this new life worse than it was. There was no telling what a boy could do to her, if Kayla decided to let him.

I asked my mother if we could talk alone. "Sure," she said, "when we get to the climbing gym in Tulsa."

At the climbing gym in Tulsa, Brett and the gym staff set up our activity. Our mother explained the rules. "It's like an extravehicular activity simulation," she said. "Astronauts call it an EVA."

I already knew what that was, from all but memorizing the brochures for real Space Camp. You hang from a rope outside a pretend-leaking ammonia tank outside a pretend space station and repair the tank. Your legs stretch out behind you as you work, like you're flying.

"We're going to do something like it," my mother said, because the whole point of camp seemed to be to do our own, lesser version of everything. I leaned back in my chair and looked up at the ceiling. It was popcorned and yellow. I'd always pictured the training facility in Houston to be made mostly of glass.

My mother said we were going to be working in partners, and all up and down the rock-climbing wall we'd find index cards taped there by the staff. "One of you collects the English cards and one of you collects the Cherokee cards, and you match each Cherokee card with its translation. When you get to the top, let go of the wall and stick your legs out behind you a few seconds. So you can feel exactly what it's like to be in an EVA."

Exactly? Really?

Daniel said, "This sounds overly complicated?"

My mother shrugged. "Figure it out or lose."

I asked her if now was a good time to talk, and Kayla grabbed my arm. She looked at me hard, pleading.

Kayla knew I planned to tattle. The day before, when the mailman again delivered nothing but bills, I'd told Kayla that there were good reasons we weren't allowed to date at our age. "You know boys only want one thing," I said. (I'd heard that on television, though I suspected I, too, might want what boys want.) Kayla had told me to stop waiting for the mailman because my Exeter letter was never going to come. "You're, like, obsessed," she said, "and when you get like that, you get mean."

My mother said now was fine. "Just get me a Coke first, okay?" She handed me two quarters and dropped her purse on a bench.

The vending machine was different from the ones I was used to. Newer, with light-up square buttons and higher prices. I needed another ten cents.

I ran back to the bench and tore through my mother's bag. We were running out of time to talk.

Her purse was heavy, motherish. An empty box of Band-Aids, Neosporin, crushed pretzel sticks, an apple, and a little tube of ChapStick melted into the lining. There were four bottles of children's over-the-counter medicine, surely expired by now. There was a stack of unpaid bills she carried everywhere, as if waiting for inspiration. To better rummage for change on the bottom, I pulled out the bills and placed them on the bench. Water, electric, credit.

Phillips Exeter Academy.

I opened my fist. A few coins rolled across the floor.

Hands shaking, I unfolded the letter.

At the top was a golden embossed seal. Finis origine pendet. *The end depends on the beginning.*

Dear Miss Stephanie Harper,

It is with great pleasure that I write to offer you admission to Phillips Exeter Academy, with a full annual scholarship award of $22,590. Congratulations! Your thoughtful application convinced us that you would thrive at our academy. We sincerely hope that you will accept our invitation and inform us of your decision to accept your place no later than April 12.

The letter went on for a page, detailing the few expenses my family would be responsible for and how to browse the course catalog and when to speak on the phone with my adviser to plan my courses. My own adviser. My own courses.

April 12. It was June.

I burst into tears.

They had wanted me. And she had stolen that. She couldn't have hurt me better.

I stood in a corner and sobbed against a wall. A teenage receptionist asked if I was okay, and I stopped mid-cry to say no, and she said, "Do you need me to go get your mom or something," and I said, "*Hell* no!!!" and then I ran, wailing, into the women's restroom.

I only took a minute there, catching my breath behind a closed stall door. Then I stopped. I held my palm against the wall and focused.

I needed to be taken seriously. I needed to stick up for myself. I washed my face with cold water and patted it dry with a brown paper towel. Finally, shoulders back and jaw set, I returned.

"Where's the Coke?" my mother said.

"I forgot it."

She looked puzzled, then waved it away. "What did you wanna talk to me about?"

"Nothing."

"Okay," she said, which was infuriating. "Everyone paired up already, so you and me are a team."

"Ha," I said.

She gave me a confused look, but didn't push it. I knew she thought I was just being weird, like kids can be, and I hated her for it.

There were four slabs of rock-climbing wall lined up together, and we had reserved three of them. My mother and I were stationed at the end, strapping into our stupid harnesses that made a V-shape at the crotch. The fourth section was for the birthday party of a girl in a necklace that said HEATHER. She wore a glow-stick crown on her twisted-back, butterfly-clipped hair. It was a boy-girl party with a CD player and pizza and many family-size bags of chips. I had lost my spot at Exeter. I felt like I was melting inside my body.

I pulled up beside Kayla. "We need to talk about Mom," I said.

We leaned against the base of the wall, in our matching orange Space-Culture Camp T-shirts, our harnesses bunching our shorts. My head hurt.

"I know," Kayla said. "Please, please don't tell her about me and Daniel. If I have an official boyfriend, you know she'll make us break up."

"No—" I started.

"Hey," said Birthday Girl Heather, swaying over to us with one hand on a flat hip. Brittany, Kayla's most annoying friend, followed. She was hooked to the other end of my rope, ready to belay.

"What's your shirts say?" said Heather. She pointed at the Cherokee words printed across our backs, the same as were on my baseball hat. The characters looked close to English but not quite. A poster of a painting of Sequoyah, the man who'd invented the Cherokee syllabary despite his wife at one point setting fire to his life's work, lived in a large wooden frame in our living room.

I looked at Kayla and Kayla looked at Brittany. I tried to remember what I had been doing on April 12, the decision deadline. Had the admissions people even once tried calling the house? Had they called during work hours? Back in December, when I was applying to Exeter, I should have asked for an answering machine for Christmas. I should have brought the mailman hot chocolate and told him what kind of letter I was waiting for.

"Really," Heather said, when no one had answered her, "what do they say?"

"They say 'camp,'" said Kayla. Brittany laughed. We were all bad, slow readers in the syllabary. Cherokee was hard.

Heather smiled tightly. "So y'all are here with the Indian group?" She reached for an open bag of Cheetos Puffs, bigger than a toddler, and held it out to us.

Kayla rolled her eyes, which was rude and embarrassing. She was sensitive about Cherokee stuff with non-Cherokees, like she was scared they'd make fun of something precious to her. It was weird to witness. An hour from here, at home, she didn't care what people thought.

Kayla turned her back on Heather and started her climb.

"Oh my God," Heather said, "I was just being friendly."

"Yeah, that's the group we're with," I said. I sighed apologetically, like being affiliated with Cherokee mean girls was my cross to bear. Heather gave me a small smile and a wave and a single Cheeto Puff. I pulled myself up the wall after Kayla.

"You're supposed to say 'on belay,'" snapped Brittany.

"On-freaking-belay."

Brett was belaying my mother, but he was overinvested. He cheered non-stop for everyone. A very tall staff member, the scruffy blond man who'd done the safety talk when we first arrived, asked him to quiet down.

I climbed ahead of my mother, just a few feet from the ground. Careful. I felt the grainy fake rock, coated in sweat and dirt and chalk. I pressed my forehead to it and closed my eyes. It occurred to me that I could unhook myself and fall, the way it sometimes occurred to me on bridges that I could jump off them.

I pushed the thought from my mind. I gripped the wall. My mother had, somehow, nearly caught up to me.

"*I know about Exeter*," I said.

"Oh God. Honey," she said, "I had to." She reached up and touched my ankle.

I jerked away. "That's bullshit!"

She opened her mouth to correct me, maybe to say something about cussing, but she didn't. Maybe she knew how weak that sounded, that she'd *had to*.

I actually did *have to* be an astronaut. And to get there, I *had to* make it to places like Exeter and Harvard. I was going nowhere in Tahlequah. Where my mother had chosen to plop me down.

"It's *my life!*" I said.

"Not really," she said quietly. "Not yet."

Around us came the bangs and shouts of campers. The slap of a hand on paper and John yelling. EARTH! Another slap. Meredith. ELOHI! Slap. MARS! Slap. MASI! They were loud and fast and laughing, and the laughing told me that they *knew* the game was weird, and they were not ashamed.

My mother was breathing hard, trying to pull herself up to face me. "I left where I was from," she said. "My mother did, too. Even my grandmother. All you need to know is it nearly killed us. I have to watch out for you girls, even if you can't understand why."

This was old news to me. My mother had gotten pregnant with me as a high schooler, and her parents locked her out of the house. She and my father left Little Rock for Dallas, where she had always wanted to be. She'd been totally alone, cut off from her parents, her Applebee's tips taken from her each day by my father. It took six years for her to get us out of there. The first time she told me about losing her parents—in her own terrifying version of the sex talk—I'd had nightmares of being pregnant, or lost, or locked out of the house. Now I thought, *her* wildest dream *was to live in Dallas.*

"This is literally the opposite of that," I said. "It's the best school in America. It changes people's lives, and they thought I was smart enough to go there!" I began to climb again, quickly, determined to leave her behind.

"GO team, GO!" shouted Brett from the ground.

I made it halfway up the wall, collecting index cards. Astronaut, gravity, oxygen, solar system. My mother fell even farther behind me, grunting with each pull of her arm.

"We're not done here," she said.

I pulled myself up higher, maybe forty feet from the ground. She huffed and puffed and pulled herself to the halfway point. I hadn't expected her to make it this far. She was afraid of heights.

"I *love* that you're ambitious!" she shouted behind me.

Her voice carried up and across the wall. What would Birthday Girl Heather think? She was standing under us with all her friends. They were eating pizza on bright paper plates, looking up.

"Kayla and I are ambitious, too," my mother said. "You can do important things right here, where you'll be celebrated and appreciated and safe. Where no one will make you feel less-than."

"*Please,*" I said, catching my breath. "*Stop. Yelling. About our Private. Business.*"

To my left, Kayla made it up to my height. She shouted, "What are you two talking about?"

"Nothing," I said.

"You got this, Steph!" Brett said cheerily from below.

"Kayla, talk to your sister," our mother said. Her eyes were closed. She didn't want to see how high up she was.

"I'm leaving anyway in four years," I said. "At that point I'll be in competition with people whose mothers sent them to Exeter and Choate and Taft. Whose mothers *know* how college works!"

"That's *enough*." She was sweaty and heavy and awkward, her arms shaking below me. Eyes still closed, she motioned with her head at the wall beside us, at the campers chasing one another to the top, screaming out Cherokee space words.

"I'm switching teams," I said.

"But the cards won't match up!" my mother gasped.

I raced up the wall.

"Steph! Wait!"

I made it nearly to the top, desperate to get away from her. When I looked down, I saw there'd been no need. She was curled into a ball, palms covering her face, all her weight released onto the rope. She shook her head in refusal as the scruffy staffer yelled for her to rappel by pushing out with her legs.

Brett told the staffer to please lay off. He pulled my mother down by the rope, inches at a time. At the bottom, he caught her in his arms. He had no idea what she'd done to me.

I yelled for Kayla.

"*What* do you *want*," she said.

"Forget the game. I need to tell you what Mom did."

Kayla stared at the grips above her and pulled herself up to meet me. "After what-all you did to me?"

"Oh my God. I didn't tell her about your little boyfriend!"

"Right." Kayla swung her rope to the side and banged into me. "Whoops," she said.

Brett yelled up at us. "Kayla Harper, that better be an accident!" He was unhooking himself from the ropes, stepping out of his harness now that our mother was safe beside him. She rushed past him to the restroom. Her head was down, her hands still covering her face.

Kayla tried to kick me. I pushed off the wall, making Brittany hold all of my weight ("*God* how much do you *weigh*!"). My rope crossed over Kayla's.

The staffer ran over, blowing his whistle. "DOWN! NOW! This is how folks get strangled!"

Brett hurried to him, talking fast and low. He put his hand on the staffer's back, gentle, like settling a horse.

I landed mostly on the wall, kicking Meredith in the leg by mistake. It couldn't have hurt much, but she was tired of me being so rude to her.

"I am *tired* of you being so *rude* to me!" She swung her body into mine, pushing me into Kayla. Kayla shrieked and pulled my braid.

The staffer whistled again and again, summoning his boss to whistle alongside him. The birthday party was enthralled. One of the boys waved his pizza triangle sideways over his head like a pennant flag and said, "Fight! Fight! Fight! Fight!"

Daniel swung over to me. "You shouldn't have told on Kayla," he said. "What are you, jealous?"

"I didn't tell on her!" I said.

Meredith reached out to slap me, and I took both her wrists in my hands. I held her against the wall. She stopped struggling. She looked at me strangely, her eyes spooky-beautiful. Her lips parted in surprise. I thought, stupidly—what if we kissed?

Kayla tore me away by my hair. Without me to hold her body up with mine, Meredith fell a couple of feet. Her rope caught her. She dangled in the air, dazed. The birthday party cheered.

"This isn't fair, Steph," called Brittany from below. "You're so, *soo* heavy."

A third staff member had joined the first two, and he flashed the lights on and off while he blew his whistle. "GET DOWN," he said, shouting into a megaphone. "GET DOWN IMMEDIATELY."

Someone turned off the music. The room was quiet, and everyone stared at us. In their hands were sad slices of pizza, cut too thin. Was this, I thought, what it was like for astronauts? To look down in disappointment at the people of the Earth?

Brett switched to Cherokee, speaking slow so we'd understand. "My girls," he said. "They know you're Cherokee. I'm embarrassed."

Kayla watched me, breathing hard. Meredith and Daniel swung in slow circles, untangling themselves from each other before the slow drop down.

Someone at Heather's party turned the music back on, louder than before. They talked and laughed and somebody called out, "Guess they're on the warpath." Somebody's palm skipped fast against their lips. *Howowowowowowowowow.*

Daniel froze, one arm outstretched, forehead down.

Meredith swung around to face the party below. "*FUCK* off," she said. Loud and then quiet.

I saw my mother holding me back, so afraid of her own past that she'd force on me a small life. I saw my sister growing up faster than me, leaving me alone in the world. I saw the laughter in Heather's eyes, the confirmation that we were small-town and silly, that nothing I could do in Tahlequah would be enough to make me matter. I felt surer than ever that I would one day leave— that I wanted too much, too hard.

Our mother returned from the bathroom. Her face washed, her eyes red, her voice high and bright and weak. She said it was time to go home. The second group, which was supposed to get to climb after belaying the first group, didn't complain. We all wanted to leave and never come back.

Brittany yanked on my rope, signaling that I should move. I looked at Kayla. We were the last two left to rappel down.

"I got into Exeter," I whispered. "Months ago. Mom didn't tell me, and now it's too late."

Kayla nodded. She cupped her hand over my hand, over the faded plastic grip that held me to the wall. She said, "Let's go."

She swung past me, brushing her lips against my calf as she passed. She didn't want anyone to see.

People talk about wanting to be anywhere but here, but that wasn't it for me, not ever, not at all. It was wanting, needing, to be somewhere specific. Like I was all my life at a bus stop, reading the schedule again and again, checking my watch. I knew where I was supposed to be.

I closed my eyes and stretched my legs out high in the air behind me. I felt myself wrapped in thick, insulated material, given air to breathe, heated and cooled and protected. I felt my fingers tracing along the rock wall, and it wasn't a rock wall but an ammonia tank, a leaking ammonia tank. I was unscrewing the hatch, gripping sparkling silver tools in my space suit gloves, and I was a professional, my hands were still and expert and I had been born for this.

My crew was inside the shuttle and I was outside. On my own up here as I had been on Earth, but tethered tight with a short umbilical cable. I looked away from the crew, and down, in absolute wonder at the Earth below.

STEPH

SECRETS OF THE
EARLY UNIVERSE

Despite everything that had happened in Tulsa, we still had all the parents waiting for our performance at the closing ceremony back home. Camp was ending. We lined up on the edge of the stage and sang our pop song in Cherokee like a funeral dirge. Kayla and Daniel held hands through the whole thing, taking a stand for their love. We were still in our orange shirts. Mine had a small tear at the sleeve, and I worried no one could see it. No one would know how much I was hurting.

Everybody clapped, and my mother hurried away from me. Brett gave me a long, hard look from his place behind the podium, like he sensed something was wrong but didn't know enough to take sides. Only Beth came up to me after the performance. She gave me a tight hug, and a small, smooth rock, about the size of a quarter. She said it was called a moonstone. I wished it were a moon rock.

"What's wrong with it?" I asked. I didn't mean to be rude. That was just how she got free stuff at her job. There had to be something wrong.

"Nothing!" Beth said, like she'd surprised even herself. She laughed, saying she'd almost forgotten how to buy things the regular way. And then she stopped mid-sentence. She saw me, my eyes, how hard I'd been trying not to cry. Beth took a step back and lowered her voice. "There is *nothing* wrong with this stone, Steph," she said. "It's perfectly fine, just like you."

She squeezed my hands in hers, once, firmly, and nodded at me. Like

* 29 *

sending a soldier into battle, or one grown woman to another. I swallowed and nodded back at her. She left to find Brett and squeezed his hands, too.

Alone in my room, no one checked on me. The air conditioner broke. I was wet with sweat and miserable. No one seemed to notice my absence, except Kayla, who brought me a plate after dinner. We stayed up late trading stories about what a jerk our mother could be. Our mother had skipped Kayla's end-of-year art showcase at school because it was held at one p.m. and she was at the factory. I thought that was fair, but didn't say so to Kayla.

In the morning I heard Brett's voice. Up the walls, the floors, and through the grate at the foot of the bottom bunk.

"Hannah, are you *serious* right now?" he said. "How could you do that to her?"

My scholarship. So she'd kept it from him, too. I hurried down to the grate. I wanted to find out if she'd decided to confess on her own that morning, or if he'd had to push her into it.

But it didn't matter. I had lost my spot. Soon, the academic year at Exeter would begin without me.

In the popular but scientifically inaccurate understanding of the many-worlds theory of quantum mechanics, some other version of myself might be getting ready for boarding school. I was tired enough—sweaty and dirty and sore from the day before—for that to be a comfort. Brett and my mother yelled at each other while my sister slept through the morning with a pillow over her head and my stomach tightened up, waiting for something bad.

And then the sound of footsteps. The front door, the car door, wheels turning over gravel.

I put on my bathing suit. It smelled like mildew, from snorkeling in the creek two days before. I had forgotten to wash it.

The air-conditioning was still broken. I took a Coke from the fridge and lay on the cool kitchen floor with a book. The can felt good on my forehead and neck.

My mother lay down next to me in her stretched cotton nightgown. On the floor in front of her she set a red chipped mug of coffee. It was steaming, even in the heat.

She picked up my book. *The Big Bang: Secrets of the Early Universe.*

She gave me a nudge. "Well? What are the secrets of the early universe?"

I shook my head. She had thrown a whole thread of my life away.

She lowered her voice. "I wasn't making fun of it, honey. I'm really curious."

I tore my book out of her hands. She hadn't asked if she could see it. I went back to reading.

My mother moved her mug onto a folded magazine, protecting the floor. "What was there before the Big Bang?"

I snapped my book closed. She jumped a little. Good.

She was never going to apologize for Exeter. And this was rare, her interest. I wanted to know where she thought she was going with this shit.

I edged toward it. "What do you want to know?"

I thought she was a creationist. She had, in her more desperate years after Texas, taken us to church. But she liked the Cherokee story of creation more, the one with the water beetle and the mud. Everything suspended from four ropes in the sky, which will someday break.

She smiled tentatively. "The Big Bang is supposed to be the beginning of the universe. How could anything come before that?"

"The inflation period," I said, with enthusiasm. I couldn't help myself. "Maybe a bunch of repetitions of the Big Bang and then the Big Bounce and then the Big Bang. A cyclical universe, where it maybe goes bang, bounce, bang, bounce? The singularity. Um, everything ever—like future galaxies and everything—was the size of a peach."

The peach was a quadrillion degrees, I wanted to add. What a fun, weird fact. But I was embarrassed. It felt like she'd asked me about God, my deepest and most personal thoughts about God. And I was still mad at her.

My mother nodded. At first, I thought she just didn't get it. Then I thought, maybe she saw me struggling.

In truth, this was my third time reading *The Big Bang: Secrets of the Early Universe.* It had been my goal to understand the origins of Earth, the universe, and everything in it by my fourteenth birthday. I was behind schedule.

She moved closer to me and leaned her head on my shoulder. I stiffened. She stayed. "When was the Big Bang?" she asked.

An easy question. A gift.

"13.8 billion years ago!" Most people my age didn't know that.

"Huh."

I could almost feel her smile.

My mother said, "Do they bother with time before all that?" She circled her hand in the air, gesturing at the expansion of the universe from a highly compressed state to *this*—her hand, the floor, and the broken air conditioner.

"It's *actually* a controversy!" I had been too starved for her approval, for this brief feeling that I was okay. "There's some people who say that time *started* with the Big Bang, and you can't go further back in time than when time *started*."

"Oh?"

"Like, they say time didn't exist. But then *other people*, they say that where you put the zero is arbitrary. We happened to set the clock where we did, and like—you have to start counting from somewhere."

I had, it seemed, forgiven her.

"But what was there?" she said. "If there wasn't time?"

I had thought she was humoring me. Saying sorry in her own way. But her voice was different, hollow and sad, and the questions kept coming. All morning and into the afternoon, when the thick, wet heat pushed down to the floor and Brett had still not come home.

The questions came one after another, falling onto us, pressing us together. Each, one step closer to fear. How did it happen? Why did it happen? When will the stars burn out? What will happen to us then?

STEPH

OBSTACLES ON THE ROAD
TO IMMINENT DISASTER

May 1997

I bought an ornate gold-colored frame for my Exeter acceptance letter and nailed it to a wall in our living room. Surrounding it were Kayla's oil paintings, depicting elders in buckskin outfits harvesting corn. And elders in colonial outfits, freezing to death on the Trail of Tears. Kayla's paintings had helped her win Junior Miss Cherokee. She wore a crown and rode through town on a float. My Exeter letter, framed, couldn't even get me an apology.

I wouldn't make it to NASA, not without Exeter. The least I could do, on my way to dying a nobody in Oklahoma, was guilt my mother. But I never once saw her look at it.

Two years passed, two years when I could have been at Exeter. In that time, I gave up.

You wouldn't have known it from looking at me. My Cherokee improved. I received excellent grades. I went out to the country with Brett most weekends to help his parents with the struggles of being old. I read constantly, mostly sci-fi, and wrote some, mostly observations in what I called my geojournal, about the soil and rock in our part of Oklahoma. Since I'd never get to study other planets, I was trying to figure out this one.

In the spring of my sophomore year, I decided to audition for the school play. It's good to be well-rounded, I thought, when you are a person with no dreams. Also, Meredith was auditioning. She rarely spoke to me. But, in a play, she would have to.

The play was written by the senior class, following a Cherokee family on the Trail of Tears.

Kayla had no interest in auditioning, but she always lit up at the stories of our ancestors. To her they were like Bible stories, only true. At breakfast on the morning of my audition, once Brett had poured coffee for himself and our mother, Kayla pounced. Who in our family had been on the Trail of Tears? How many months had they walked? Barefoot, yes? Did they all die on the way?

"That far back, you've got a heck of a lot of ancestors to account for," our mother said. "Not all of them Cherokee. And if all your ancestors had died on the way, do you really think you'd be sitting here?"

"Well. Do you know, like, any stories about them? Just the Cherokee ones?"

"If you're interested, there are researchers who can help with that at the Heritage Museum," Brett said. "I could take you over there, maybe after school?"

Kayla asked three more versions of the same question, even though Brett had just offered to help. His help required research and work, though, like when I wanted to look at the moon and he made me calculate its angular size. Kayla just wanted a story.

Our mother kept looking at Brett and then back down at her cereal bowl, increasingly uncomfortable, but I wasn't sure why. Brett leaned back in his chair, arms crossed.

"All right, all right," our mother said. "The only people I know a Trail of Tears *story* for—you have to have *done something* to get remembered as special that far back—well, those people I know about did Removal in their own way."

"What's that mean?" said Kayla.

"They went west, same as everybody! But they went a little early, by steamboat."

"Jesus, Hannah, you're kidding," Brett said. Something must have flown over our heads.

"Steamboats were dangerous back then! A lot of them sank or exploded. People died."

Brett sighed. "Did your family's steamboat explode, Hannah?"

Our mother ignored him. She told us the reason for the steamboat. Her great-great-grandfather John, and nineteen other Cherokee men, had signed a treaty to sell what remained of Cherokee land. Otherwise it would have been taken by force, she explained, and people would have died. The treaty-signers chose the people over the land. That took moral courage.

Brett said people *did* die, thousands of them on the Trail. A full one-quarter or more of our tribe, dead.

Brett said, turning to face only me and Kayla, that it was okay to admit the stuff our family once did was selfish and cruel. That didn't mean *we* were selfish and cruel. We were strong, smart, Cherokee women. (Kayla sat up straighter at this. I tried not to roll my eyes.)

"Your ancestors were put in an impossible position," our mother said.

Kayla nodded, gravely.

"Hannah, they got paid," Brett said.

Our mother stood abruptly. She poured orange juice all the way up to the rim of my glass, and it almost spilled. "Don't share this stuff with people outside the family," she said. She gestured back at Brett with her chin, though I'd thought he was inside the family. "You see? They wouldn't understand."

I ate my cereal and thought about the Earth dying someday. We'd have to go to another planet, to choose humanity over our home. The people over the land. I could understand that.

Brett drove us to school. As a teacher he had to get there early, which meant we did, too.

He said, "I don't think you girls have been taught about the Cherokee Freedmen. Is that right?"

I said no. In the back seat, Kayla rolled down her car window.

"They're people descended from people," he said, "who were enslaved by Cherokees."

I was quiet but alert, looking to Kayla to make sense of this. She wouldn't meet my eye.

"After the end of slavery," Brett said, "many of them stayed here in Cherokee Nation. They were put on the rolls—a segregated part of the rolls. Then later, maybe ten years ago, they lost the right to vote in Cherokee elections. Because they don't have CDIBs, which means they can't be citizens."

Kayla said *oh*, almost brightly, like *now* this made sense. CDIBs meant Certificate of Degree of Indian Blood. Anything to do with CDIBs had to do with being colonized, and being colonized was something she thought about all the time. She'd probably already filed slavery under *things caused by colonization*.

I didn't have her confidence. CDIBs were just cards, one of two that we each had.

The light blue card, paper with a perforated edge, came from the Cherokee Nation. It declared our tribal citizenship, which was determined by our constitution. If I had babies with a non-Cherokee, and then that pattern continued for one thousand years, all my descendants would still be Cherokee.

The white laminated card was a CDIB, which came from the federal government. It kept track of "how Indian" every Indian was in the country, which in my family was Not Very, as the fraction halved each time one of my Indian ancestors had children with a non-Indian. (That had happened plenty, even before Removal.)

Watching the trees pass by on the side of the road, I tried to work through what Brett had said about Cherokees. About slavery. My mother told us stories about our ancestors because she said those stories—what our ancestors had lived through—made us who we were today. But now I knew Freedmen had Cherokee stories, too. What degree of Indian blood did I have over them, to make me real?

The car slowed and stopped. We were at school, in Brett's faculty parking spot. He waited to open the door. "It's not gonna be in your school play, I bet, that some Cherokees forced slaves to walk the Trail with them. But I think that's something you girls need to know about. Okay?"

"Okay," I said.

By lunchtime, I'd managed to shrug off the shadow of Brett's story. What did it matter what I thought about Freedmen, when I didn't make the laws on who could vote? That was the business of people on the tribal council, like Brett and Beth.

After school, almost no boys auditioned. I was cast in the role of Meredith's husband. This I could work with!

In preparation for the role, Brett took me to his barber. I asked him to give me the haircut of "a hardworking, middle-income, Cherokee family man in the late 1830s," which he interpreted to mean "short," which was good enough.

Together, Meredith and I were the most tragic, godforsaken couple in the world. We held hands a lot. Our first time, I felt panicked and sweaty but also good.

At our first rehearsal after my haircut (which had made my mother cry in the kitchen), Meredith improvised a gesture during the scene where she was taken from the house I'd built for her. As our classmate in a soldier costume pulled her away from me, Meredith pressed her forehead to mine and cried out, catching a fistful of my hair at the back of my neck. It hurt. My heart, metaphorically, fell out my butt and slammed on the stage.

When we were on the Trail together, I took care of Meredith. Her chest was in constant movement, her breaths deep and labored. She acted her heart out, the bundled-up red-haired American Girl doll that was our baby pressed against the many shining buttons of her shirt.

In the second act, I broke the neck of a mockingbird with my bare hands—which was a metaphor, because you're not supposed to kill them—and I gave the whole thing to Meredith to eat. In turn, Meredith did whatever she could for our children.

Our two oldest, twins, died in the stockades in Georgia. Our third child died of scarlet fever in Alabama. When a soldier in Tennessee threatened to shoot our crying baby, Meredith accidentally smothered it.

After we buried it, just past intermission, Meredith blocked the whole third act so that her head lay against my chest as we walked. *She* had chosen that, not the drama teacher. *It's possible she loves you*, I told myself. I bought a chicken sandwich from Chick-fil-A and zipped it into the outside pocket of her backpack after our second performance. No note. It wasn't a mockingbird, but it was something.

At the end of the Trail, when our once-rowdy family had been reduced to the two of us, I took my first steps into Indian Territory with an inconsolable Meredith in my arms. She sobbed real tears, all three nights in our school auditorium, and grasped at my chest and my tattered collar as I held her like the baby she had accidentally smothered.

After each performance Meredith would kiss me, the first three kisses of my life. Each kiss was longer than the kiss the night before. The two of us were wrapped in the heavy black cloth of a backstage curtain, like a burrito, while the audience waited for us outside.

On the third night she took my hand in hers and pulled it under her mud-crusted trade shirt, under her bra even, and made the softest sound in the back of her throat, and I thought I'd *die* to hear it again—I thought *this* is the meaning of life, making someone make a sound like that, everything I'd done before this had been a *waste*—and then she left to collect her bouquet of grocery store flowers from fucking *Daniel*.

I felt downtrodden, like I'd just watched my children all die one by one before my wife ran off with someone else. Hadn't we been a team? Meredith and I were like the only survivors in a world of regular people. Who could understand the horrors we had seen?

After the play, when we were back in high school and barely spoke to each other except for times like when I, for example, dropped my most sophisticated choice of book on the floor in front of her so she'd stop walking and get down on her knees and hand it back to me, it was like the anguish of our shared past had ruined us and now we were divorced.

I tried to talk about it with her, once. *We* were worth talking about! We were breaking down the sets.

When Meredith reached for a hammer I reached for it, too, and held my hand so gently over hers. I looked at her with the saddest eyes I could muster. Eyes like, *Did you love me? Do you? Will you again? Will anyone?*

Meredith laughed and let go of the hammer. "You can have it; I'll go do props." Like that was what I wanted from her. A hammer.

"I'll miss you," I whispered, "with the play over and all."

She was supposed to say she'd miss me, too. Then we'd kiss. I had planned this all out in my head.

She said, "Yeah, it was fun!"

Maybe she didn't realize the chicken sandwich had been from me? Maybe she didn't get that a chicken was like a bird, which was like a mockingbird— which was a metaphor? I would kill all kinds of animals for her, not just birds, if she ever needed me to.

I tried again. Even quieter, though everyone else was working backstage and being loud. "I like you a lot," I said. "Might I take you to Chick-fil-A sometime?"

Meredith looked stricken.

"Or, um, to somewhere you pick? Somewhere more expensive? I have twenty dollars."

It was already a compromise, a far cry from us making out. But it took years to get to the moon landing. Some people worked toward it for so long that by the time it happened they were dead.

I had wanted to ask her to be my girlfriend. Daniel, her boyfriend, would meet her in the parking lot in an hour.

Meredith sighed. She cocked her head like I should follow her, which I did gladly. Down the red-carpeted aisle to the auditorium double doors, like it was our wedding, only we were walking *away* from the altar, not toward it. I followed her out of the auditorium and into our empty classroom, hammer still in hand.

"I think there's been a misunderstanding," Meredith said.

It was weird to be in a classroom alone together, and thrilling. She sat on the teacher's desk. I sat in a chair at my same front-row desk from the school day, regretting immediately that Meredith was in charge. In our theater curtain burrito life, which did feel now like a whole separate life, Meredith had mostly let me lead.

"I have a boyfriend," Meredith said. "Daniel. You know that. You sit behind him in math."

I nodded.

"And you're a girl."

I raised an eyebrow. I thought, *Wasn't I a girl last week?* And also, weirdly, *What about everything we've been through?*

"I don't want to talk to you at school," Meredith said. "I get it, you were a boy for the play and you did the method acting thing. As a fellow artist, I respect that."

I wanted to throw up. I said, "But why did you put my hand on your—"

"*Steph!*" she snapped. "I am *not* going to tell anyone what you did. But— as someone who cares for your well-being? I think there's something wrong with you."

For months afterward, I remembered the play in my dreams.

At bedtime it was like I could put a VHS tape in my brain and fall asleep to an exact depiction of when I had almost been happy. When I had really thought, or had at least almost thought, that I might belong here. On Earth, even. I had tried. I could remind myself of that.

It looked like this:

Meredith fell to her knees at the very edge of the stage and looked out into the darkness of an audience she couldn't see, into a new life waiting for her in Indian Territory.

"Hold my hand," she said.

I wiped Meredith's tears with the end of her woven shawl, the only warmth she'd had through the long, hard winter, and her eyes shone in the spotlight that my sister, dressed in all-black, beamed down on her from the balcony. "Let us have a child in this new land. Let us put our suffering behind us, and start again, and rebuild a proud nation for the generations to come."

I knelt beside her. I dropped my forehead to her shoulder, and she held my head and rocked me gently, like I was her baby. I had no shoes, no jacket, no vest—I had given our children all that I had. Still, they had died. "My beloved wife," I cried out. "Do you really believe we can live again?"

"My beloved husband," Meredith said. "I *do* believe that, with all my heart. In fact, it reminds me of a song my dead mother used to sing . . ."

And then the stage lights went out, and the houselights came on, revealing our classmates and our families come to see us, and the whole ensemble was onstage again, even our three older children resurrected, even the soldiers with their guns stowed backstage, even Andrew Jackson, even our American

Girl doll, back safe in Meredith's arms, and we held hands and sang "Amazing Grace" in Cherokee, and the audience sang along to whatever words they knew, Kayla singing loud, shining the lights bright across the room onto everyone, from way up high in the back, while our mother, alone in the front row, cried in her best dress.

THIS DREARY EXILE OF
OUR EARTHLY HOME

A month later, when school was out, Brett took the family to Cherokee, North Carolina. It was the first time there'd ever been a Tri-Council meeting, the first time the three bands of Cherokees had been united in our homelands since the Trail of Tears. I was secretly still heartbroken about Meredith and didn't want to go. My mother promised me that, so long as we didn't miss the mound-building ceremony at Kituwah, on the second day she would drive me the four hours to Duke University. Dr. Lars Carson, my second-favorite astrophysicist, would be speaking there.

The last part of the drive to Cherokee had us winding up and down mountains, and I didn't want to put away my Dr. Carson book. We pulled over twice for me to throw up. When I got back in the car the second time, Kayla and my mother were holding hands. Brett was beaming. All three of them looked out at rolling forested mountains in every direction. "It's like we've finally come home," our mother said.

"I can feel them with us," Kayla said.

I turned around, leaned out the window, and threw up again.

The next morning, we sat in an elementary school auditorium. We were late and had missed the kids from the United Keetoowah Band. According to the program, they had opened the meeting in prayer.

Five Cherokee Nation kids shuffled onto the stage. The girls pulled at their tiny tear dresses, and the only boy fiddled with a black-and-red finger-woven sash worn tied over basketball shorts and a wifebeater. He tugged the ends around his neck and looked like he'd strangle himself. A teacher yanked it from his grip and ran back off the stage, while the children sang a short song about a baby bear.

Then it was the Eastern Band's turn—this was their school, full of grown-up visitors. Their girls were in tear dresses, too, but their boys went all out with little bandolier bags and shirts and leggings, even finger-woven garters. They sang the Cherokee song "Orphan Child" and skipped no verses.

The announcer said, "We will now move to our first item on the agenda. Are the council members prepared to vote on Resolution 101-A?"

The morning passed slowly. People talked too close to or far from the microphone about motions to petition the Library of Congress to digitize its Cherokee language texts, and to further fund a summer biking trip for youth that would trace the path of the Trail of Tears. Someone onstage would motion for a second and they'd get it, then the nays and yeas—mostly yeas—and then on to the next one. Each decision, painstakingly noted and debated and voted into law, felt small to me. What if we got hit by an asteroid? What could the three councils of Cherokee bands, even finally united for a weekend, do about that?

I was relieved to have my geo-journal, the thick, heavy sketchbook I bent over as the hours dragged on. "It's my get-into-college project," I often told people. If I was feeling petty, which I often was, I said that my stepfather had bought it for me after my mother forced me to turn down my full-ride scholarship to Phillips Exeter Academy, one of the oldest and most prestigious secondary schools in America. This was true, and it was also the reason Brett had promised to pay for and drive me to an SAT prep course in Tulsa.

To Kayla, though, my geo-journal was more than that. She knew it tied me to my life, to the one I was meant to have on another planet. I collected soil and rock shavings, and had Brett laminate them in the teachers' lounge at school. I labeled them and studied them and indexed them and slipped them into little envelopes I'd glued to each page of the journal. I surrounded them with notes in thick, black ink—classification, observations, whatever I could find on the area's geological history. Kayla, on a good day, would lie next to me on my bed and prop a pillow under her arms and sketch an image from memory of almost anywhere I described. My geo-journal was for geological maps of the fourteen counties in our tribal jurisdictional area, a place my sister felt complete belonging. If I asked her to draw somewhere she'd never been, like Oologah or Catoosa or Chelsea, she'd find an older boy with a car to drive us out there on a Sunday.

Finally, it was time to break for lunch. We filed through a line in the school cafeteria, elders first, and sat at big, round tables.

Our mother sat on Brett's right, Beth on his left. Our mother touched his elbow with her free hand, but mostly kept quiet and ate. I watched the adults, the easiness between Brett and Beth. Their parents were the same kind of country people, the same kind of poor. One of the things I knew about my own ancestors was that they'd wanted to be different from Cherokees like that. "Upwardly mobile," my mother had said once about her family, "until they weren't."

Brett and Beth leaned into each other, laughed, told jokes in the kind of Cherokee that was impossible for me. The kind that came from parents instead of worksheets, where the grammar might not follow what we'd memorized, and the speaker sometimes couldn't say why.

Our mother took Brett's and Beth's empty paper plates and piled them over her own. She dropped Brett's arm and stood there for a minute—three plates, three forks, three cups in her hands. Brett said something to Beth, and she laughed.

At afternoon recess on the first day of Tri-Council, our mother took Kayla back to the hotel to get changed into her tear dress and moccasins and etched-copper crown. Kayla was near the end of her reign as Junior Miss Cherokee, which she had won with her language skills (such as they were), her platform (Raising Awareness of Cyberbullying), and a talent portion that centered on her Trail of Tears paintings. She'd gotten a six-thousand-dollar grant she could only use toward college, which she wasn't sure she wanted to go to unless it were a fine arts conservatory in Italy or the Institute of American Indian Art.

It took a long time for Kayla to get dressed. Every time she wore her tear dress she added a little something that she'd made herself—a beaded hair clip, copper cuffs, finger-woven garters tied at her knees. Beth's aunt was teaching Kayla to make a turkey feather cape. I knew this because Kayla had a blog with one hundred and three subscribers, and regularly posted photos of her works in progress.

I was bored and tired. I reread a few pages of an article on quasars by Dr. Lars Carson, which I kept folded into a little square in my wallet. He described quasars—he described all elements of the universe—as simply what they were. His articles were nothing like how my father had described the universe, which I still remembered as terrifying. I went looking for Brett.

I started with the higher grades' classrooms and worked my way down the hall. The fourth grade had diagrams of photosynthesis on its classroom door, and the third had hand-drawn family trees.

I turned a corner, passed the first-grade classroom and on down the hallway. I looked through the window in the door of the kindergarten classroom.

Brett and Beth sat side by side on the teacher's shining wooden desk, ankles dangling, their feet knocking lightly against each other. They were reading from Beth's gray binder, her council notes open in her arms. Brett held her thigh in his hand. Beth pressed her forehead to his shoulder.

I touched the door handle. It was cold, and I felt suddenly afraid. His fingers slid higher, and closer, and up past the hem of her skirt, and I turned away.

At Kayla's meet-and-greet that afternoon, I stood beside our mother. Close, our arms touching. I watched her take photos of Kayla in her regalia beside children in a park. The Eastern Band version of Miss Cherokee was there as well, in a beautiful cape of brown turkey feathers. "Ma, it took her sixty hours!" Kayla shouted between photos, turning back to continue interrogating her fellow pageant princess.

I thought, *What happened to the turkey?* I thought, *I have to tell my mother what I saw.*

I said nothing that afternoon, or evening, or night. In the bed beside the bed I shared with Kayla, my mother and Brett lay side by side.

When Brett first came to us, I'd been afraid of many things. But he sat beside me with a telescope and let me look. He showed me the moon close-up. Every night we'd sit together on the roof and search for things in the sky, shivering in the cold or burning the bottoms of our feet on still-hot shingles. Every night my mother watched us from the window.

Brett was my one ally on the journey to space. I couldn't lose him.

The next morning was Duke Day! Dr. Lars Carson Day!

There was one last morning council session, which Brett couldn't miss. The mound ceremony at Kituwah, the only part of the weekend that mattered to my mother, would happen two hours earlier that evening than originally scheduled. I could tell my mother wanted to take back her promise, to not risk her one shot at a traditional ceremony in the homelands.

"Mom, we can't be late for the lecture," I said, standing beside an open car door. She looked at me, silent, then drove to Duke as if at gunpoint.

It was summer, but there were still students on campus. Young people were everywhere, cutting bare-legged across the grass, shoulders slumped under bright-colored backpacks. A few wore bikinis and swim trunks, nowhere near water. A tattoo-sleeved boy sat bare-chested on a bench and wrote in a notebook, heavy and thick-papered like my own.

Kayla stared down at her sketchbook. I looked out the window and saw who I could be. Walking home from the library late at night. Bent over a long black table, hands reaching for beakers and Bunsen burners, protective goggles pressing circles in my skin. Sitting cross-legged in cold, damp grass outside the observatory shed where they stored the five Schmidt-Cassegrain telescopes, waiting my turn to see the Cassini division in Saturn's rings.

Our mother parked outside the Richard White Lecture Hall. She hurried around to the trunk. We had only twenty minutes, and still had to find good seats.

"Kayla," she started. Her voice was quiet, strained. I thought maybe she'd found out about Brett and Beth touching each other. Or worse—she'd found out I hadn't told her. "Did you pack clothes for you and me last night?"

"You didn't tell me to," Kayla said.

Kayla and I had gotten into bed early, her with her sketchbook and me with my geo-journal. I wrote a sonnet about Meredith betraying me and Brett betraying my mother, and how love will always break your spirit. We had just finished a unit on poetry in school, and—though I hadn't admitted it—my geo-journal had long since stopped being for college admissions.

Beside me in bed, Kayla had sketched out her next project. She carried fancy German watercolor pencils everywhere she went, her most prized of Beth's defective gifts (in this case, every pencil was labeled a different, wrong color). Instead of a traditional turkey feather cape, she now wanted a peacock feather cape. I told her the drawing was pretty, and our mother told her it was historically inaccurate. Peacocks were from "India or maybe Africa," she said, "not from our traditional homelands." If people saw photos of Kayla in peacock feathers, as an official Cherokee Nation junior ambassador, what would they think? They fought, hard, and Kayla cried. "I'm sorry you don't feel, like, authentically Indian enough," Kayla said, "but that's *your* problem! Not mine! I don't have to prove anything to anyone!"

As I patted her on the shoulder with the flat of my hand, I was secretly grateful for the excuse not to talk about Brett. In all this drama—which included a detour into how revealing Kayla's clothing had become lately and what was up with that, did she want someone to get her pregnant or worse—there had been no discussion of her packing clothes for Duke.

Now, outside the Richard White Lecture Hall, our mother whipped away from us. "I told you . . ." she said. She paced up and down the length of the car, the muddy hem of her sweatpants dragging across the cement. "I told you to do it."

"You didn't," Kayla said.

"Oh-hoh, you better *think* about what you—"

"Stop!" I shouted. Then I remembered where we were, lowered my voice, and tapped at my watch. "Mom," I said, "your T-shirt is stained. Kayla, people don't wear belly shirts to college."

"I mean, they kinda do?" she said.

"Thank you for driving me to this university," I said. "I will meet you both back here at three p.m."

Our mother looked surprised and horrified. "If you think you're applying to college here—and I haven't even said yes to that, or talked about the application fees—then I get to see this place after my four-hour drive."

She started for the door. I chased after her. My hands were shaking as I caught her hand. I begged her, choking on my words. Not here. Please don't go inside. Please don't.

"We embarrass you," she said.

"No," I said, too quickly.

What I didn't say was that, on the night she ran, I wished she had kept driving. Farther north maybe, past all this. Our house was ugly and our town was homophobic and her boyfriend was unfaithful. If Brett left, I'd have no one.

Brett had never hit us. He had never yelled once, a kind of miracle to find in an adult. Brett thought my interests were legitimate; he thought *I* was legitimate. He loved space and he loved Earth, though he loved them with our people at their center. He thought people were everything in the universe and I thought they were nothing, but the more time I spent with him, the more I thought I could maybe love Earth, too. Or at least, the more I was interested in its geologic timeline and composition. If it weren't for him, there was no way I'd be thinking about taking some geology classes in college.

"You be ashamed all you want," my mother said, linking her arm in mine, dragging me toward the entrance. "But I'm always gonna be here."

The door slammed behind us. We were cut off from the light and sound of the world outside, thrown into the back of a very full, very dark room. Dr. Lars Carson was already speaking. He paused onstage, cleared his throat, and began again.

Dr. Carson lectured about the birth of a black hole. He told a story about how, recently, the Hubble Space Telescope had detected a flash of light. Within seconds, robotic telescopes around the world were redirected to face that light. Automated phone calls went out to astronomers in North and South America, alerting them to come into work. I imagined scientists waking up in the middle of the night, throwing coats on over pajamas, slipping into socks and slippers and running out into the cold. Speeding down dark, quiet streets, skipping steps up a rickety spiral staircase to their observatories, their university offices, their telescopes on a hill. Later they would share data. Giant observatories in Chile and Hawai'i would zero in on the light, would split it into different wavelengths and detect how far it had traveled. They would learn it was a high-energy gamma ray burst. The brightest light ever detected by humankind. It had traveled for 7.5 billion years to appear in our sky for thirty seconds. It was sharing the news, very late and from very far away, that a black hole had been born. Finally, and in my own way, I understood the nativity.

"An old star blows apart. A supernova forms. The collapsed core creates a neutron star. Imagine taking the mass of a mountain and collapsing it into a marble." Dr. Carson leaned into the podium. He smiled and rested his chin on his hand. He took a sip of water from a plastic bottle, looked straight into the crowd—straight at me, it felt like—and said, "It's gravity gone wild." He laughed.

I imagined myself meeting Dr. Lars Carson after his talk. Dr. Lars Carson shaking my hand. Dr. Lars Carson offering me admission to Duke on the spot, buying me a computer, asking me for help in his lab. I'd drag a step stool over to his chalkboard. I'd erase his calculations with my shirtsleeve and start from the beginning, chasing down numbers and symbols like Matt Damon in *Good Will Hunting*.

The part about the mountain crushed into a marble, though—that was the last I understood. Dr. Carson turned on the projector. He flipped between slides, waving the red dot of a laser at graphs and charts and long lists of numbers. When I blinked, bright squares were printed on the backs of my eyelids.

Dr. Carson opened the floor for questions. I raised my hand. My mother stood up and waved both hands at the front of the room. Then she pointed down at my head.

"Yes," he said, squinting. "The kid in the back."

I gasped. My mother sat, took my hand, and squeezed. A long-haired grad student in a suit appeared, holding a microphone right under my lips.

"Stephen Hawking has spoken about the possibility of time travel," I said, "provided a ship could circle a black hole at the speed of light." I hesitated; I'd never heard my voice so loud.

I took a breath and continued. "And, um, I recently read an article on the internet, in which a physicist stated that such a ship would fall apart. So, which do you think is more likely, for a ship to fly that fast or for a ship to stay intact?"

"Beautiful," my mother whispered. She pinched a loose hair off the sleeve of my blazer.

Dr. Lars Carson gave a soft laugh. "Yeah, I saw that on space dot com," he said. He took a long swig from the water bottle. "Neither is possible. It's science fiction."

The microphone was swept away from me and carried down the aisle.

My mother harumphed back in her seat. "She didn't ask which was possible," she muttered. "She said *more likely*, which means *less impossible*."

I was a dummy. I'd believed in time travel, or something like it. On *Star Trek: Voyager*, when the crew came across a wormhole and contacted a Vulcan from the past, I'd thought, *Okay. Sure.* I'd thought if it were just possible to survive spaghettification and unimaginable force—if we could live through the things we felt sure would destroy us—then *yes*. We would find something more than this. To hear Dr. Carson's laugh, how confident he was, how at ease, it was like learning definitively that there was no heaven.

I shook in my seat. My mother rubbed my back, and Dr. Carson said words that were just sounds to me, and I felt like my heart was beating way, way too fast, like any minute I would die.

Kayla opened a bag of chips, dug her hand inside, and crackled the packaging. I snapped to the side to face her, my skin hot and itchy, my lungs gasping for air.

Our mother beat me to it. "Stop that," she said.

"Calm down, Mom," Kayla said, which was not a thing we said. Our mother lifted a hand like she was set to slap her, then folded it back into her lap. I winced. Kayla smirked.

"Ma'am, please," said the man in front of us. He wore a suit. He was white-haired and scowl-faced.

Our mother ignored him. Maybe she thought he was speaking to someone else. "Kayla Anne Harper," she whispered, "you hand me that bag or there will be consequences."

Kayla fell back in her seat and tossed our mother the bag. A few potato chips fell to the floor, like confetti.

"Ma'am," the man snapped, louder this time. He twisted around and looked at her and her oversized shirt, reading ugly yellow, reading small town, reading loud tacky poor dumb. "Ma'am, I just need you to control your daughters," he said, softer now. "Some of us have been following Dr. Carson's work a long time."

Our mother breathed in and out, slowly.

The man turned back to the front.

"My *daughter*," my mother said. Stopped. Started again. "My daughter has been following Dr. Lars Carson since she was *thirteen fucking years old.*"

The man stiffened. He didn't turn around again, didn't fight back, and that was worse than anything he could have said to her. He let her words hang in the air, echoing in our ears, so that Kayla and I could hear them over and over in the silence. So we could see that she was trashy, and uncivilized, and not a person worth engaging.

Dr. Carson paced up and down the stage, waving his hands in the air to the rhythm of his own speech. He talked about the Big Bounce theory, and how we'd emerged as the kind of leftovers of a preexisting universe.

Our mother sat between us, her chest heaving forward and back, tiny sobs caught and silenced in the dark.

When we got to Kituwah it was dark. Dr. Lars Carson had gone over his allotted time. Someone had put a ticket on our mother's car, for parking in the wrong spot. She had to track down a university employee, and then she yelled at him (to no avail) over a fine that cost more than two days' work.

The ceremony was over, and there was no moon. Our mother walked toward the low mound and disappeared into shadow. I picked up a rock and put it in my pocket.

Our mother had prepared us for the ceremony at Kituwah, after she'd prepared herself. She'd asked Beth, who'd asked her mother, who told her that Kituwah was the place we came from. Where water spider carried over the first fire in a basket she'd woven on her back. When we spread out into towns across the mountains of the Southeast, Beth's mother said, we carried embers from that first fire to every town at the start of each year. So we would always be connected, and feel the pull back home.

When they tore us from the mountains, Beth's mother said to my mother who said to me, we'd hauled the embers to Oklahoma in battered tin buckets. I was still open to some things I didn't have proof of, like alien life, but the bucket story seemed far-fetched. Still, I understood that this was ours. I understood the last morning of your life in a certain place, before it's destroyed.

Sitting in the car, my sister asleep in the back seat, I realized our mother had to believe. She had to, for her life and her choices to make sense. As a young woman she had responded to every disaster—poverty, neglect, abuse—with a move one step closer to her grandmother's childhood home. In Tahlequah, before Brett, she'd been an outsider—a single mother, kinless, clinging tightly to the light blue paper of her tribal ID.

Our mother would never have Kayla's confidence, because Kayla had no memory of another self. Of another place. Of what was possible, here on Earth. Maybe what was wrong with our mother was also wrong with me.

When our mother had started talking about the ceremony at Kituwah, weeks before, I'd asked Brett to take me to the library. We'd sat together on the floor, leaning against the bookshelves. I'd learned that Kituwah was destroyed in 1776, when the Rutherford expedition razed thirty-six Cherokee villages just before harvest time. They left no homes, crops, or livestock. Survivors lived on nuts and wild game through the winter, then began to sign away land.

The Eastern Band had purchased the site back, this field and what remained of the mound, only a year ago.

Our mother walked slowly back toward us. Her knees were brown with mud, and I knew she had knelt in some kind of prayer.

Kayla groaned. She stretched out across the back with her cotton underwear showing, her short denim skirt hiked up in sleep. Her sketchbook had fallen to the floor, open, the drawing of the peacock cape ripped out and crumpled. My mother and I sat in silence awhile, headlights shining into the forest at the field's edge.

"I'm sorry I made us miss the ceremony," I said.

"Well, Duke is far," she said.

"We could stay here awhile," I said. "Maybe I could show you constellations?"

My mother laughed. She shook her head and sighed. Like I was the weight that lived on her shoulders, that crushed her sometimes.

"No, Steph," she said.

She took my head in her hands and I breathed in her smell. She kissed me at the top of my head, where she'd insisted on combing my hair that morning. Where I sometimes touched my fingers to at night before I slept.

"You're too old not to see it," she said. "The world doesn't revolve around you. You have to be a part of us. To meet us halfway, even."

The part of our lives that we spent together would be over soon, in just two more years. It seemed unfair to her, and maybe all mothers, that I'd know this and still feel so ready to run.

STEPH

HOW MANY INDIANS
DOES IT TAKE

June 1999

Brett and Beth got caught having sex. I should have known it would happen. I should have told my mother two years ago, when I saw his hand on her leg in North Carolina. But I didn't. For two extra years I'd had a father, a good one. I wasn't sure what would happen next.

Brett had been staying with his parents for three weeks. Supposedly to fix their roof, but Kayla and I were too smart for that. He and our mother needed space.

In the meantime, he'd been making moves. He was probably on the road right now, driving into town to officially announce his campaign for principal chief. I was seventeen years old, full-time employed for the summer, and saving up for my college application fees. I didn't give a shit about his run for office. My sister did.

Kayla followed me into the bathroom. She said we had to be seen standing next to Brett at his rally, because a gesture like that "matters more than you think."

"What? Where is this coming from?" I said. It was bizarre for her to care how people, or at least Cherokee people, saw her. I had to get ready for work.

"Are you coming or not?" Kayla said.

At the sink, I wrapped my head in a turban. The kind Sequoyah wore in the painting in our living room. I worked as a reenactor in a pre-Removal

Cherokee village, and my boss Will had requested the turban as a compromise. My haircut made me look like a lesbian, he said, and lesbians were historically inaccurate.

Kayla sat on the rim of the tub in an oversized T-shirt. Years before, a cheerleader had shot it at her during a baseball game Brett and Beth had taken us to together. We should have known.

"I'm serious!" Kayla said.

"You know it's weird that you're worried about his little event," I said. "Don't you have other things on your plate?"

Kayla's blog had just celebrated its six hundredth subscriber. She designed and sewed and sold (and posted about) truly beautiful powwow regalia, and I often heard her on the sewing machine late at night. What I didn't hear about, ever, was a concrete plan for her life. I worried she'd end up abused or pregnant or both, three kinds of disaster I kept top-of-mind.

Kayla leaned back, flailing a little before catching herself on the faucet.

"You'll split your head open," I said.

Kayla said it would be a huge embarrassment if I bailed. "There's gonna be a picture in the newspaper."

"Okay, and?"

"Well, that'll affect, like, how people see our family? If they don't see us up there, it'll change how they think about us!"

I made a face. "But you don't *care* what people think about you. It's, like, your one redeeming quality."

"Very funny," she said.

I'd meant it, though. If the gossip around Brett had shaken my sister, I'd never forgive him. At least with our father before Brett, my mother and I had known not to trust him. In that way Kayla had been easier to protect.

"Even Mom's going to this thing," Kayla said. "You think this is harder for *you* than for Mom?"

"Don't you have to get ready for work?" I said.

She stood up, pulled off her shirt, threw it on the floor, and shimmied a lifeguard-red bathing suit up her tanned body. "Ready," she said.

A car honked, and I looked out the bathroom window. John, this month's boyfriend, was here to pick her up. He was, as was his custom, shirtless.

Kayla pushed past me. "Three p.m.," she called behind her. "Tribal court-house. Maybe you'll think about someone besides yourself and be there."

The first tour came too soon. We weren't allowed to wear watches, which Will said "didn't exist yet." But if I kept my head down and listened, I could hear my way through the day.

The elders scraped their tools, coughed, and muttered under their breath. Theirs was quieter work, softer than the shouts coming from the stickball field. Even the carving of arrowheads was only the click of rock against rock.

I heard the shuffling of feet coming up the dirt path. Ten or so in this group, maybe more. I dipped my hand in the creek and ran a wet finger along my lips. They were dry, near to bleeding.

I registered what I could of the people around me. Sandals, strappy purple heels, and a pair of orange boots. Bright pink jelly shoes, orthopedic whites, and a dusty black cane. Rows of running shoes.

"This is my friend Saloli," said Will. "That's Cherokee for 'squirrel.' Any-one wanna try and say that?"

The girl in jelly shoes answered. "Osiyo, Saloli!"

I smiled big and waved. "Osiyo!"

That was all I had to do. Will did the talking for us all.

"Saloli is our basket weaver," he said. "Now, Cherokee basket weaving began thousands of years ago and was traditionally done by women. Saloli's baskets are made from all natural materials. Cane, white oak, honeysuckle . . . Her work is for sale in the gift shop!"

It wasn't. I had almost no experience, and there were rough-palmed and sharp-fingered women who'd been supporting their families on baskets for decades. They didn't want to sit out in the heat, though, and tourists would rather look at a barely capable young woman than a skilled one over forty. So I posed next to baskets I hadn't woven, with a hundred dollars or more going to the artist when one sold. What few pieces I finished myself, my mother displayed in our living room.

I ran my thumb against the calloused side of my index finger. As a child I'd wanted hands like this, like my mother's. I used to think the hard skin on her fingers and palms made her strong. She carried couches and fixed plumbing and bent over the hood of a car with swim goggles and a dirty cloth. She went out in the woods and chopped piles and piles of firewood, every year saying she'd take us camping so we could roast marshmallows. Every year she forgot, or got tired, or said her body was too sore from work. Her knees and back always hurt from the hours on her feet, but then off she'd go into the woods with an axe. Maybe all she'd really wanted was to cut something down.

Will shut the gate behind the fourth group of the day. The village fell back into itself. The older ladies put down their yarn and wrung out their fingers. Mr. Jack put his blowgun down and sat back on a bench with his head in his hands. Meredith, Shannon, and Brittany walked past me into the woods, carrying plastic water bottles and avoiding eye contact. Meredith still acted like I was contagious, two years after our last kiss. I dropped my basket and stepped down to the creek.

I liked to press my back against the rocks and let what water we had wash over me. If I stretched out right, I could catch it under my arms. Me, a dam. Best part, besides the smell of summertime, which was really the smell of muddy water and grass and what comes after rain, was the sound. The not-sound. The creek came up high enough to split at my feet and then skirt along the sides of my legs. High enough to fill my ears with quiet. I heard nothing and saw nothing but the blue up ahead, the occasional whishing back and forth of a tree branch. But mostly nothing. Nothing and blue. On clear days I'd look at the daytime moon.

Someone splashed water on me. I startled. Will stood on the edge of the creek bed, breathing hard. A clipboard was tucked under his arm, and his copper arm cuff clicked against the wood.

"What happened," I said.

Will's cell phone was folded open like a clamshell. He squinted at it and smashed down on the buttons.

"Will?" I said.

"Shannon got bit by a snake."

I asked if it was poisonous, and he didn't know. "I mean venomous," I said, remembering the difference. Brett had taught me that. Will didn't answer. I asked what kind of snake it was, and he said no one on staff could recognize it. He'd asked six stickball teens and two elders before deciding to drive her to the hospital. What did it look like? Long and thin. It was like a joke. *How many Indians does it take to ID a snake in the wild?* Shannon was lying in the back of his truck, a handkerchief tied around her ankle.

"You'll be me on the next tour," Will said.

I nodded.

"Starts in five minutes," he said.

I nodded. "*Wait!* I'm *you?*"

Will was walking away. He yelled behind him. "We need the others ready at their stations, but anyone can do yours. You got this!"

He was at the gate.

I said I wasn't ready.

Will said, "Break a leg!"

I swung open the gate. "OSIYOOO, NIGAD!"

Quiet.

It wasn't the crowd I'd thought it would be. Just five people, looking at me. I was still wet from the creek and embarrassed they might think it was sweat. The dust in the air had stuck to my skin, leaving patches of dirt across my arms and legs.

"Okay," I said. Then even quieter, "Okay." My voice sounded strange and far away, like when you hear a tape recording of how other people must hear you every day and you're embarrassed to be alive.

A Black woman, maybe my mother's age, stepped forward. She had red-lipsticked lips and tight curls, her nose and cheeks shiny in the sun. "This is the right place," she said, "right? The Cherokee village tour?"

I smiled. "Sure is!" I opened the gate all the way and stepped to the side. "I'd be honored to show you around my home."

I walked the group to Miss Marie. She took one look at me, leaned back against the dry mud wall of the house she pretended to live in, and said, "This oughta be good."

"Let's start here," I said, "and I'll tell you about the ancient, um, traditional art of beading."

The only child on the tour belonged to the only woman, a little boy with curls like his mother's. They swung around as he jumped up in place. He bent to rip grass from the ground. Got it. I had to pick up the pace.

"Beading has always been my favorite craft, growing up here in the mountains," I said. I gestured around me at the dry-dirt earth. "Ladies like Meli here," I said, turning to Miss Marie, "thread tiny glass seed beads onto wool, cotton, and linen. They bead beautiful designs onto things like moccasins, or bandolier bags. It demands patience. But as you can see, it's worth every hour. Besides, our people have been beading for . . . a really long time. Meli's a pro."

The little boy's mother took him by the hand. She brought him closer, for a better look at the half-beaded moccasin cuff in Miss Marie's hands. Two tall white guys—both in Tulane basketball shorts—followed suit, but an older white man in a polo shirt stayed back. He raised his hand.

I nodded.

"I read on the computer," he said, "that this exhibit is based on a Cherokee village from the early eighteenth century."

"Right! Agidoda—that means *my* edoda—well, he says the year right now is 1704." I was panicking, proving I could conjugate a word they didn't know.

"Well, you see," he said, "glass beads arrived in the area with European trade, and that started only fifty years from then. I mean . . . ago?"

I looked to Miss Marie for help. She kept beading, but did not hide her amusement.

"Sure. Right, we uh, traded to get these."

"When are we going to the tipis?" said the little boy. He tried to balance on one foot.

The tour only went downhill. I got carried away with my description of blowguns, only to be corrected by Mr. Jack when it turned out we'd never used poison in the hunting darts. "Think about it," he said. "Would you wanna eat a squirrel with poison in it?"

One of the Tulane guys said to the other, "Would you wanna eat a squirrel, like, in general?"

Mr. Jack narrowed his eyes.

Little Boy said, "May I please see a tomahawk?"

Polo-Shirt Man caught me in an error at nearly every booth we came to. He had the village brochure in hand and a heavy paperback under his arm, and he read along as I spoke. With Polo-Shirt Man, it was never "You're an idiot." He said, "Do you think maybe—" or, "Funny you should say that because—"

I said I was young. Still learning. "I usually defer to my elders." Miss Marie glared at me, because often I did not.

We stood in front of a thick-walled house. I told the group that my family lived in this one, with a firepit in the center and a hole in the roof for smoke, when it was cold. We had a less insulated version for the summer. "It's across from the stickball field," I said, pointing.

"You're telling stories," said Little Boy. "You live in a tipi. I read it in my books."

"I live here," I said. It was a lie, but it was truer than tipis and tomahawks. "No you DON'T!" he said.

We went back and forth a little, the other guests starting to quietly back away. What kind of person argues with a child?

I wanted to scream. This is not my field of expertise! I'm supposed to be an astronaut!

I wanted to show them the gold medal I got at the state science fair in May. I wanted to tell them about the Native American student recruiter with his dusty truck and his Choctaw Nation license plate, his three-piece suit and his crimson-beaded lanyard, his long black braid and the crimson hair elastic at the end of it. How he said Hollis College would be "lucky to have me." I figured that meant Harvard might, too. Harvard was even better than Hollis.

If either college really chose me—or MIT or Yale or Dartmouth or Princeton, etc.—if they chose me, even knowing the life I'd come from? It would be a sign. I could let myself believe again in me on Mars, in a way I'd struggled to since losing Exeter. I could rededicate my life to NASA.

Little Boy lay in the dirt and cried. He slapped the ground; tiny dust clouds flew up from the palms of his hands. "It's not *fair*," he moaned. "Not fair! The Indian lady's *not real*!!!"

His mother bent to meet him. She touched his shoulder and talked low, her voice suddenly deep and serious. The child quieted but stayed down, crying softly.

I kneeled. "Hey," I whispered. "What's your name?"

He let out a sob.

"Anthony," said his mother, answering for him. She looked at me carefully. Like I needed to back away, fast. This wasn't my place, and I knew it.

"Okay," I said. "Okay. Anthony, today we're gonna call you Runs-with-Thunder. That's your Indian name."

He turned his head. Sniffed. "But my Indian name is Buffalo Fire?"

"Even better," I said. "Are you having a hard day, Buffalo Fire?"

Anthony sat up. He told me about the tipis, and the tomahawks, and the bow and arrows. None of them were here. He read about Indians all the time; his bedroom wall was covered in pictures of them. Some were from the library computer and some he drew in school. I was trying to trick him.

"*Anthony*," said his mother firmly, "we don't say 'tricking.' We say, 'I'm feeling confused.'"

"Yes, ma'am," said Anthony. Then, pointing at me, "She's feeling confused."

I stood and motioned for the group to follow. "Come on," I said. "Let's go see some bow and arrows."

When we got to Mr. Andy's station, I talked about killing our enemies with arrows. About scalping them.

"I got a few good scalps I keep in a box under my—my sleeping grass," I said. "They're good medicine, for when the bad spirits come."

Mr. Andy, who hadn't talked much that whole summer, didn't look up from the flint he was carving in his lap. "And buffalos," he said.

I looked at him. "Sir?"

He smiled and turned to Anthony. "She's making us sound bad. We don't like to make enemies. We kill a lot more buffalos than people."

Mr. Andy was enjoying himself. He hadn't laughed much since his only son told him he was gay and had a boyfriend and was moving to Spain forever—at least that was the rumor Miss Marie had spread in the break room. But here he was, beaming.

"We use the whole buffalo," I said, "when we shoot it. I wash my hair with buffalo guts for the protein."

"Cool!" said Anthony. He galloped around and grabbed at his chest; he was a buffalo shot in the heart. Polo-Shirt Man nodded at me. Mr. Andy laughed, hid it in a cough, and laughed again. He put down his tools and leather mat and ambled over to our next station.

Like that, we collected people. Mr. Bobby said we didn't harvest anything from the three sisters garden, on account of it making the corn goddess mad. "It's like ripping her arms off," he said.

Mr. Andy said, "That's why we only eat buffalo."

"And squirrels," I said.

I was doing it for Anthony, because he was a child. But it wasn't only that. This job had asked too much of me. And then, looking at the elders I hadn't ever talked to enough—at Mr. Andy and Mr. Bobby and Miss Marie and Miss Diane and the others—I was surprised by what it meant to me, to see them have a good time.

At the finger-weaving station, Miss Diane said she could feel the spirits through the yarn if she wove certain patterns, like thunderbolts. "That's how my hands got like this," she said, holding up arthritic knuckles for Anthony to inspect. "I got in touch with a real bad one."

Anthony said her hands were awesome. He asked to touch them, and she said, "Sure thing, chooch."

By the time we made it to the stickball field, the whole village was with us. We didn't wrap things up after a quick explanation of the game. We broke into teams, men versus women, with visitors included. The Tulane guys had been baseball players in high school in Arkansas, and they got a kick out of what they called our "baby lacrosse sticks."

Mr. Andy hurried down the field, limping on his bad leg. Miss Marie reached to tackle him, and he hopped out of her way. Just as he caught the ball, she shouted something lewd about his little stick.

"Watch it, girl," he said, aiming for and missing the fish at the top of the pole. "I hear you'll take any damn stick you can come by."

Meredith sidled up to me.

Inside, I panicked. Meredith spent her work hours with her fellow stickball teens, who never invited me to the woods with them. In the locker room, she always waited till I was dressed and out of there before she'd take off her clothes and shower. Now, weirdly together, we squinted up at the wooden fish.

Meredith said, "Brittany said Kayla said you already wrote your college essay?"

"Just the first draft," I said. "I'm applying early."

"Me too," she said. "Applying early, I mean."

I was—stupidly—surprised. It hadn't occurred to me that my classmates would also apply to college. That they'd have plans just as I did.

"I haven't started my essay yet," she said. "How'd you decide what to write about?"

"Brett helped," I said. "We've been going to the library a lot, sending off for applications, that kind of thing? He went to OU."

"So he gave you your essay idea?" she said.

"No," I said. Quickly, defensively. "I chose that myself. But on the internet I read some advice that we could write about, like, overcoming adversity?"

"Oh," she said. Her brow furrowed.

I wondered if she thought it was morally wrong to write out my sufferings for admission to school. After all, *I* thought it was. My essay—my real essay, and not the decoy I'd shared with Brett—was pretty asinine. It was a clear manipulation, which I considered my best hope.

I couldn't think of anything normal to say to Meredith, nothing friendly or kind. Only *WHY WON'T YOU LOVE ME* on repeat in my head.

"Okay, then," she said. "Forget I asked."

She was a part of the game again, shooting across the field. I could still smell her lotion or body mist, like in a store in the mall. Like apples, lingering in the open space beside me.

No one had touched me since our school play, not like she had. In Oklahoma, I thought, no one would.

If I could figure out the money and the applications and the getting myself to college, I decided I would be gay. Or bi, maybe? At schools like Harvard, they let you figure that out.

. . .

I called everyone back to the dirt path and tried to push Meredith from my mind. My coworkers were still making up stories. I joined in.

We said we threw a virgin—"a little girl," corrected Miss Marie, suddenly concerned with little ears—to the creek spirits to keep mosquitos away. We ate a charred frog heart in the week after a baby was born. We painted with all the colors of the wind. Anthony didn't mind that we laughed. He laughed, too. When Mr. Andy said I was something like an Indian princess, Anthony lost his shit. A princess? Her?

Does your dad have his own peace pipe? Does your dad scalp his enemies? Does your dad have a war bonnet? Anthony wouldn't pause for answers. He was a stream of questions, all of them about Indians. Indians danced day and night in his head; they ran wild in the suburbs of Tulsa. ("Thank you," his mother had said to me earlier. She whispered it to me back at the creek, where Brittany had sat in my usual spot and pretended to weave baskets. "Anthony's been driving me up the wall with this stuff since his dad passed. He'll grow out of it, but for now he just needs to do the 'Indian' thing. You know little boys." I didn't.)

At the gate, Anthony ran out of words. He looked up at me, eyes wide, waiting for something.

"Yep," I said, "my dad's a chief."

Brett was a young, relatively new tribal council member, preparing for the first event of his first campaign. I suspected he'd lose.

And he wasn't my father, not officially. I sometimes wished my mother had agreed when he'd asked to adopt us. Whatever he had been, I worried it was ending.

"In fact," I said, leaning down toward Anthony and his smile, his dusty sneakers, the little burrs caught on his turned-down yellow socks, "after this I'm gonna go see him, for a ceremony in our tipi."

At the end of the tour Anthony's mother asked if we could take a group picture, all the visitors and any village staff who were willing. I hurried to stand next to Meredith and we put our arms around each other, her hand at my waist, both of us smiling forward into the camera. After the flash, we broke apart.

Polo-Shirt Man called me a smart, delightful young woman, and Anthony's mother side-hugged me goodbye. She smelled like whatever citrusy lotion my sister used, and maybe laundry detergent, and I stepped back quickly because I knew I smelled like sweat and dirt and creek water dried stiff on buckskin. I went to the locker room and stood in the shower and watched the water run brown, then clear.

I had barely left the parking lot when Will drove up beside me. He waved for me to pull over. I tried to sound relaxed. The day had been fine, I said, things were normal and good. Inside, I really felt like they could be.

I asked about Shannon, who was fine. "What a relief!" I said. "So the snake wasn't venomous?"

Will said my hijinks were unacceptable. No, it didn't matter who had told him. He said my last paycheck would be ready in a week. My behavior had been shameful. I'd played right into what they think of us.

But why did he assume they had played me, not that I had played them? Or, *with* them? Or that *we* had, all of us together?

I needed the money for my college applications. And, assuming I got in, I needed the money for a one-way ticket to a school in the Northeast. I was still out about five hundred dollars, but Will was firing me.

I said yes whenever I had to, and sorry more times than I was proud of. Will and I talked through the windows of our cars, each facing a different direction. His harsh words hit me one after another until finally I said, "Thank you," and sped down the road.

Out of his sight, I pulled over again. I parked and wrapped my head in my arms. I shook. The sun was pushing in hard. I whispered to myself that I had to keep moving, though I wasn't sure where to go.

I drove slowly down the road through many tall trees, past the museum that had fired me. I kept going.

The woods opened, and I stopped outside the memorial. Before me, in the grass, were the three last standing brick columns of the Cherokee Female Seminary. The rest of it had been destroyed in a fire.

This was where the women in my family had studied over a century before. I had come from many students and teachers, and they had come from here. The second-oldest institution of higher learning west of the Mississippi. One of the first in the country to educate women, beyond the domestic arts.

Maybe, after all the trouble I'd caused at the museum, I could try to be more like my sister. Generous with our ancestors. Curious about them. They'd been *people*, after all. I didn't have to, like, feel their spirits in the wind, to understand that they'd been people. People could be impossible. *I* could be impossible.

I touched one of the brick columns with my finger. Gently, almost afraid I'd knock it over. A family drove by in an SUV, probably leaving the museum. A hit country song blared out their open windows and faded just as fast. I pulled my hand back, embarrassed.

I tried again, pacing in a wide circle around the columns. Over the last three or four centuries, the tribe had been *nearly*, and yet not at all, destroyed. I imagined people showing up, finally, in this very spot after Removal. Building and opening a school of their own. Choosing to begin again.

I let my forehead rest against a column. It was rough, gritty with dirt. I closed my eyes.

There was more to it, I knew. Ideas my mother hadn't told me, that Brett had tried to carefully introduce. One night after dinner—after our mother had waxed on about the seminary—he'd come to talk, very quietly, to me and Kayla.

"You know, very few full-bloods could afford to go there," he said. "The ones who did probably got scholarships, and when they'd show up, most students were mixed-bloods."

He meant the people Kayla and me had come from. The lecture continued.

"Classes at the seminary were taught in English. At that point half the tribe spoke English and half spoke Cherokee, and the two halves struggled to speak to each other without interpreters."

"Ooo . . . kay?" Kayla said. She didn't look up from her sketchbook.

"The school was a real achievement for its time," Brett added. "Your mother is right to be proud of it! But it was a school for elites. I wouldn't want to be a poor kid there."

"Don't listen to him," Kayla whispered after Brett had kissed our heads and left the room. "He always talks like he's the moral authority on being Cherokee."

"And who is?" I said. "*Mom?*"

"So some Cherokees taught some Cherokees English. Christianity, whatever, stuff I bet they thought they'd need in a white world. Does he think they'd have done that if it weren't for the colonizers?"

"Well—" I wasn't sure why I had to answer for him. This was *their* fight, and I'd been pushed into it.

"I don't think Brett—I don't think *you*, actually—get what our people were up against. They assimilated to survive. People will do anything. And if the school existed in traditional times, everyone would have been equal. Also, if it were traditional times, women would have been in charge."

I was tired. I had work in the morning. This was before I'd been fired.

Kayla kept going. She said the seminary wasn't like the government boarding schools, kidnapping Indian children and cutting off their hair. It had been run by Cherokees. Its staff and students were deeply proud of being Cherokee. The hope was that they would finish their schooling and stay, to better the circumstances of their people.

I turned my back on the columns and got in the car. I slammed the door behind me. I was hot and mad, and the window wouldn't roll down.

There was more than one way to survive, I thought. People will do anything.

I could leave.

Kayla would visit me. I'd still have her. We'd sip cups of espresso, which we had never had, in cafés that lined sidewalks of cities we'd never seen. And I wouldn't be Indian. Right then, the Nation felt like a hand pressing down on my chest.

How easy it would be—or at least how *possible*, looking how I looked—to let that part of me fall away? To, absurd as it sounded even to me, *opt-out?*

To be an astronaut—to be myself—without the weight of everything that came before.

• • •

I stepped quietly into the museum gift shop, holding the door chime tight in my fist. It made a half-hearted click. Ten minutes to closing.

Each woven basket had a cream-colored, handwritten tag. Cursive. The artist's name, the little biography, the price. Just a few baskets would cover everything I needed.

I worked fast. I pulled them from the shelf, choosing only the wider ones and fitting them into a shallow stack. Slipping it under my shirt, I turned to go.

The bell jingled. Meredith came in. In the back, Brittany slumped over her grocery cart of sodas. She was refilling the fridge at the counter.

Brittany said, "Hey," to both of us. Barely interested. So she hadn't heard I was fired.

"Bathroom," I said. "I know we're closing, but I'll be fast."

I walked sideways to the back of the shop, pretending to examine items on the wall. I held my hands over my stomach.

I locked myself in a stall, frantically trying to plan my escape. I heard the wide swing of the restroom door.

A whisper. "Steph?"

Meredith stepped forward, her dusty moccasins pointing into my stall. She whispered again, even quieter this time. "Steph? It's me."

I stood up and zipped my shorts. With every shaking breath in, the rough and tight pattern of reeds pushed against my belly. I leaned against the door between us.

"Hi," I whispered.

"Put them back," Meredith said.

"What are you talking about?"

"You did a bad job rearranging things," she said. "You're gonna get caught."

I wanted to protest. But she was probably right, and she was talking to me, and wasn't that something?

"I got fired. I need the money for college."

"Well of *course* you got fired! We all thought you were trying to, like, go out with a bang?"

I was quiet.

Meredith clicked her tongue. "I'm sure you don't realize that the sales money goes to the people whose names are on the tags. Not to the gift shop."

I didn't answer. The baskets hurt now. They'd leave a mark.

"Steph, I'll cover for you. I'll make sure no one sees."

"I can't," I said.

"Prove to me I'm right; that you wouldn't want to hurt anyone. My aunt is one of the basket weavers."

I knew this already from Beth, who was distantly related to Meredith's mother and was also a huge gossip. Meredith had shown up in town the summer before ninth grade, after her family lost their apartment in Tulsa. For a while the aunt was feeding and housing all of Meredith's family, and her own family, on baskets.

"I need this, Meredith."

"There are more important things," she said carefully, "than you being an astronaut. Or you going to some Ivy League school. Or you just deciding for yourself who has to like you, and then being super weird when they don't fall in line."

I pressed the baskets closer to me, felt them stretch against themselves with the little bit of give in their weave.

"You don't get it," I said. "I *have to* leave. I don't have a choice, and you've never even asked me why. In all the years we've known each other, you still think it's just a stupid space dream."

"*Steph*," Meredith said. "We *haven't* known each other. You don't know anything about me."

I unlocked the stall door. She was beautiful, with that hard look in her eyes, with her ripped shorts and loose shirt and the dusty bag slung over her shoulder. Like she was already gone. I felt tears on the way and cleared my throat. I was humiliated.

"I'm sorry," I said. "Can you tell me about you?"

Meredith made a huffing sound, like she wanted to laugh, and she adjusted her bag on her shoulder. "I'm clocking out," she said.

I nodded.

At the restroom door, she turned. "Do what you want. I don't care enough to tell anyone, and I'll be glad when you're gone."

I stood on the courthouse steps, between my mother and sister. I didn't listen to Brett's campaign speech, not at first. I was angry with him for hurting our mother, after knowing her past with men. I felt sorry for her, but I needed her to get herself together this time. No matter how sad she got, I promised myself I wouldn't stay back.

I remembered our last night as a family, before our mother had asked him to leave. We were together in the living room. The television was set to a station with flames flickering across the screen, like we had a fireplace, and Kayla was painting Kituwah mound on a large canvas on the floor. So far it looked honest, low and grassy, unremarkable for a holy place. I was taken aback. It was like there'd been a film over her art all these years, thin and glittery, and maybe she was starting to peel it back.

I sat sideways on the couch, writing poems about space in my geo-journal, and Brett held my feet on his lap. He talked and laughed with our mother across the room; she was kneading bread in a plastic bowl.

"It's a miracle," Kayla said, still crouched over her canvas. Our mother never made bread outside of the bread factory, and she was so good at it.

"Please," our mother said. "You know, your dad's running his campaign on bread. We were working on his speech last night. Brett, did you tell them?"

He laughed and covered his face, like he was embarrassed at the attention. The next day, I would think it was because of what he knew he was doing to us, and what our mother had called him for the last time. *Your dad.*

Brett's platform was actually centered on gadugi, his favorite principle: everyone working together for the common good. Literally it meant putting together the bread, gadu, like the collective task of keeping people fed. But I didn't want to be part of the shared responsibility of my community. If I gave them nothing and they gave me nothing, that should be fair, too.

From the steps of the old courthouse, I looked out at the small crowd. They had those little paper fans stapled onto Popsicle sticks, printed with Brett's last name that wasn't ours and the words "CHEROKEE FAMILIES CHEROKEE STRONG," and they were waving them at their cheeks and nodding like there was a rhythm to what he was saying, like it was a song. The words came out one after another, flowing up and down, his voice sliding soft and deep when he talked about our struggles, climbing higher and louder when he said to forget about just surviving, because we would be *wise*, we would be *strong*, we would make our people *proud*.

Maybe Brett would really do all that. Standing there, watching him, I wasn't sure if he would. Or if he could, if he was even a good man. But right then, being part of this people didn't feel like knowing how to cure a snakebite in the woods, or how to take pride in our ancestors.

It was my mother, tall in a bright red dress and heels, staring straight ahead, doing what she could for something they must have talked about many times. Maybe on the worn couch in the house late at night, when they'd shared dreams and daughters. It was my sister, too proud to hold my hand. But her shoulder still pressed firm against mine, and her long hair tickled my arm.

Brett finished his speech with a whole thing about family, about our family. Our support and love and guidance, Kayla and me and our mother and his mother—there was a joke to be made about all the women in his life, but he was smart enough not to make it. He looked at us as he talked, and his voice reached out to us. He said we made his life good and important.

I knew, already or all at once, that I would not be like him. I believed nothing in Oklahoma, nothing in Brett's life or my mother's life or the life of anyone I knew, could make my life good or important.

"Cherokee Families! Cherokee Strong!" shouted someone in the back.

"*Yes!*" Brett said. "That's what we got. Our Cherokee families make us strong now, as a nation. Always have. And, if given the great privilege of serving as your principal chief, I plan to honor the family, once again, as the bedrock of this nation.

"That means more family reunifications, more Cherokee kids fostered or adopted by Cherokee families. Our children are the promise of our continued existence.

"That means getting working mothers and single mothers the financial support and career training that they need to build strong homes. That means subsidized housing for our young people and our elders, for hardworking people down on their luck. That means improved access to balanced, traditional diets. That means stronger, more comprehensive tribal health care starting from the moment our precious children come into this world. That means—"

Beth stood in the back of the crowd.

I hadn't seen her since I'd found her naked, beside Brett in my mother's bed. I had come home early from school that day, sick.

I didn't tell my mother. That night, he told her himself. He left out my part in it, to save me the shame of having hidden it from her. He didn't know I'd been hiding it already, for two long years.

After that, Brett and my mother worked out some kind of deal: he continued to live with us and father us, still, albeit with long and mysterious absences. And Beth disappeared from our lives. I felt sure that Brett would leave us for good, maybe soon, but I couldn't know when.

Beth looked at Brett from her place in the back, smiling, the top of her hair shining in the sun.

I would sell the baskets. I would run.

I watched Beth watch Brett.

It was how my mother would look at him, back when things were okay. Brett on the couch with us little girls on his lap and our mother standing barefoot in the doorway, watching him, unwashed hair falling into her face. The ancient green pajama pants with the splat of red paint at the knee, the way the two of them used to laugh. Smiling, smiling, like the rest of us weren't even there.

STEPH

THE COMMON APPLICATION

December 1999

FIRST-YEAR ESSAY PROMPT—QUESTION #2
The lessons we take from obstacles we encounter can be fundamental to later success. Recount a time when you faced a challenge, setback, or failure. How did it affect you, and what did you learn from the experience?

My name is Ahnawake—"Steph Harper" in English—and I am a proud Cherokee woman. I have encountered challenges, setbacks, and failures. And, someday, I will be an astronaut.

I was born far from my ancestral homelands. During the Trail of Tears, my family was forced to leave their Cherokee village in Georgia for Indian Territory. Some time later, Indian Territory was stolen by the state of Oklahoma. And some time after that, my mother grew up poor and neglected in the city of Little Rock. She ran away from home at the age of seventeen, to Dallas, where she had me and my sister and lived with our terrible, abusive biological father.

There are many challenges that come with a father who perpetrates domestic violence. Our household was chaotic, and when I started preschool I had to learn to advocate for myself in order to get there. I had to pay attention to my baby sister at home, when the adults forgot about her. I had to keep her from crying, so that our father would not hit us. I learned to read a little bit, and to make up stories in books that were too hard. I spent many evenings pretending to read for my little sister (I was only five), on the floor of our bedroom closet. I especially liked making up stories about other worlds, which would later develop into a passion for outer space.

You might wonder, why did you not leave? That would be an ungenerous question. First of all, I was a child and children have no agency—I see this as one of the great injustices facing our nation today. Second of all, my mother was a different person then. She was terrified of my biological father, so one should not blame her for the absolute hell that she dragged us through. Third of all, there is a long history of Native American children being taken away from their families and raised by white people as a method of slow cultural genocide. That means that my sister and I couldn't tell anyone about the absolute hell through which our mother was dragging us, lest we be taken away, like thousands of Native American children before us.

The worst thing about my traumatic childhood was my lack of agency. If I wanted to go to the children's science museum, but my biological father wanted to yell and throw my mother's good plates at the wall, we would not go to the children's science museum. The best thing about my traumatic childhood is that when I was almost six years old and my mother decided she was finally ready to run, she took me and my sister to our new home in the heart of the Cherokee Nation.

One thing I learned from this experience was to appreciate the beauty of life in a tribal community. Upon arrival, my sister and I were enrolled at a school with Cherokee language classes. We have been learning to speak the endangered Cherokee language ever since, and to be language warriors for our people. When other students around the country were signing up for the famous, overpriced, overhyped Space Camp in Huntsville, Alabama, I was helping my mother to establish and administer the first-ever tribally run space camp that both honored our rich, dying culture *and* exposed at-risk Native youth to a plethora of career possibilities in STEM.

I soon realized what a difference I could make in my own community. I was raised with the traditional Cherokee principle of gadugi, community self-reliance, and I understand what it is to need and be needed by my people. This is why, when I was accepted with a full merit scholarship to Phillips Exeter Academy, I made the difficult personal decision to remain in Oklahoma until college—to be in community, and to keep our traditions alive. For the last three summers, I have served as a cultural ambassador at the Cherokee Heritage Museum's living history exhibit. When my mother first saw me in my traditional clothing on the way to work, with the kind of buckskin skirt and finger-woven sash no one in our family had worn for generations, she laid down on our stained, threadbare, free-off-the-street rug and cried.

I am applying to [INSERT SCHOOL NAME] because I have lived what feels like one thousand years for someone my age, and based on the unique values of [INSERT SCHOOL NAME], I feel strongly that I would be a good fit for your institution. [INSERT SCHOOL NAME] brings together students from all over who are devoted to the betterment of the world. One day, I intend to use my degree from [INSERT SCHOOL NAME] (along with many years of training) to become an astronaut—specifically, the first Cherokee astronaut in history.

I would like to represent my people, on my journey to college and to space. It's easy to feel like we as Indigenous people have been stripped of our once-great agency, like we are all (metaphorically) living in my father's house. Still, I have made it this far. I have still further to go. I will do *whatever it takes* to get to space.

THE WELFARE OF BABY D

June 2000

This is what people know about me: *Della Owens, born 1982, adopted by Simon and Josephine Ericson of Provo, Utah.*

When journalists and legal scholars choose to be protective of the almost-adult me today, which isn't always the case, I'm referred to as "Baby D."

But Mom and Dad have fought to keep me out of the spotlight and to make sure the name from my baby blessing sticks. "You're an Ericson, sweetie."

They used to say that when I cried. I would jump in their bed during every storm, scared by the way the walls shook. I ran six blocks home from Sunday school when my teacher told our class I was a Lamanite turned "white and delightsome." When I lay in bed and light from passing cars raced across my bedroom walls, I was afraid. I saw the cameras flashing, the bright blue squares when I blinked. The guns and the screams and the fingernails pressed to my skin.

Growing up I cried more than most kids, and my parents would hold me and say, "Sweetie, you're an Ericson." Like that's all I would need to be safe in the world—the parents who won.

For the first five months of my life, in Utah, people called me Emma Ericson. Then, in Oklahoma, Della Owens. Then Emma Ericson. In the years I've lived in my parents' house, these last thirteen years of my life, I have been Emma all but twelve hours a year.

. . .

Dad woke me up at four a.m. I lay in bed and chewed on my hair and thought about not going to Oklahoma this time. It was the anniversary of Matthew's custody loss, which was also my annual visitation.

Dad's voice came out muffled from the other side of the door, and I knew he'd cupped his mouth against the painted wood. He called good moooorniiiing in this weird, high-pitched, not-Dad voice and walked away. I heard him singing "The Morning Breaks," then chopping and dropping and humming over frozen fruit shredding in the blender. I had seen the same blender in a black-and-white photo of my parents in their kitchen at the top of a *New York Times* interview. I read online that, until things got really bad, Dad tried to do every interview with a can-do attitude and a cheery disposition. Mom said he'd handled things so well because, no matter what the courts said, he had faith as a Latter-day Saint. I pulled the blanket over my face.

Dad kept coming back. His voice got lower, and louder, and he pounded on the door and said I'd miss my flight. Finally, he marched in and pulled the blanket off, which made me hate him every time, even though I loved him very much. I threw my arms over my braless T-shirt and groaned.

"I'm in the car, Emma."

Dad knew it would take me a while to get dressed, but he didn't want much to do with me on the days I visited Matthew. Neither did Mom, who was asleep and had spent the last week making sure there were no open opportunities for Matthew to parent. She took me out for highlights, made an acne follow-up appointment at the dermatologist, sent in my housing application for Hollis, restocked my purse with tampons, and washed and folded my clothes. She was methodical.

Mom had always been like this. I was the first in my class to ride a bike, the first with pierced ears, and the first to drive. I had to do everything fast, milestones mastered and checked off, just in time to disappoint my biological father. I knew she did it out of love. That's why I did it all over again.

When I was nine, I let Matthew help me get up on the purple bike he'd bought me just for that day. He ran fast, holding on to my handlebars, not letting go and not letting go till I finally said he could, and I yelled, *Look! Look!*

I'm doing it! Four years later, I asked him to take me to the mall for a second piercing. After I learned to drive, I asked him to teach me to drive stick shift.

Matthew brought flowers to the airport and dropped them when he saw me at the gate. He picked me up and spun me around and I knew he must have felt the weight I'd put on in senior year, but he didn't say I looked different. He put me down, hugged me, picked me up, spun me around the other way, put me down. We smiled at each other, me a little closer to his chin than I'd been before.

Matthew said, "Well damn, Della, it's so good to see your face."

Nobody had called me Della in a year.

I said, "Good to see you, too."

I didn't call him anything. He hadn't been Dad since *Ericson v. Cherokee Nation*, but to call him Matthew felt cruel.

"You got any bags?" he asked. "Anything I could help with?"

"No bags," I said. "I say we just do whatever fun you must got planned."

Sometimes I talked like that in Oklahoma. I'd get caught up in how much we looked alike. I talked like him, slouched like him, ate what he ate. When I was twelve, I stole some self-tanner lotion at the pharmacy so I could look more Indian in time for our visit. I ended up orange, with dark patches on my elbows and knees. Mom tried to yell at me, but her voice kept breaking.

I spent most of our visitation days on airplanes. Matthew and I had only five hours together, and there were certain things that had to get done. Seeing the family, getting my required dose of Cherokee nationalism, organized fun, and taking enough photos of said fun to fill the albums of my visits stacked on Matthew's coffee table. He took out a disposable camera and aimed it backward to capture our trip down the moving walkway.

"Say cheese," I said, laughing.

He smiled with all his teeth. "Commodity cheese!" he said. He snapped the photo.

I stared.

"It's cheese you get from the government. For being poor." He shrugged. "Indian humor."

Matthew wasn't as rich as my parents, but he wasn't poor. Was the joke funny because other Indians were poor? Was being poor part of being Indian? If I belonged here, I might have said to Matthew that I didn't like that. But then would I sound uptight, like white people?

He pulled me in for another hug, and my shoulders tensed. I felt for Matthew in waves.

Sometimes I thought about the photo from our family sealing, thirty or forty Ericsons in white dresses and three-piece suits outside the temple in Salt Lake. High above us on a spire was the Angel Moroni, golden, trumpet in hand. I was just a newborn in a long white gown, but they made sure I'd be with them for time and all eternity.

And then sometimes I saw the smallest thing in Matthew, like our matching long torsos and short legs, and I was hit with something pretty close to love, even though I didn't tell him I love you anymore. I wished I still did, that I had never stopped, so I could say it without a big proclamation. But then he'd say something with a country accent, or laugh too loud or drive too fast, and I wouldn't even know why I was there.

It was an hour to Matthew's house outside Tahlequah. I used to think it was a waste, spending all that time getting to a small town when there was more to do in Tulsa. There was a skating rink and a rock-climbing gym, and even a trampoline park.

But my old bedroom was in Matthew's town, and so was his family. He let me drive. When we got close, the road was almost empty except for the two of us. When I looked like I was coming up too close to the edge he said, "Easy there, sweet girl."

Matthew put on a George Strait tape and asked me if I'd been listening to the *Greatest Hits* album he sent me at Christmas.

"Sure have!" I said. I hated country music.

"Good," he said. "When you were little, you were crazy for him! Our whole family is. Must be in your DNA."

By that logic, I must've gotten the non–George Strait–obsessed gene from Matthew's one-night stand, the white woman who gave me away. But I didn't say that, and we didn't talk about her. All I knew was she'd grown up by a beach, which was a place I'd never been to. She might be somewhere like California, or one of countless other places, but I didn't care.

Seeing my grandma was the worst thing in my life.

She couldn't handle it so well, either, so a few years back we made it one of our rules. Family first, and family gone in an hour. It might sound harsh, but harsh is what it takes when you've got five hours once a year. There were other rules. No arguing, no talking about my parents, no talking about the Indian Child Welfare Act, and no talking about what my plans were for when I left my parents' house for college and the visitation agreement expired.

I pulled into Matthew's driveway, and his family spilled out over the porch. They held the same tattered banner they'd made thirteen years ago.

WELCOME HOME, DELLA!

They shouted and cheered and clapped, and next thing I knew there was a crowd of twenty or so standing around the truck. A neighbor sat outside his house, watching.

Della! We missed you! Look at you grown!

I jumped down from the driver's seat, and I was held. I was held and I was held and I was held. I wandered, arms out, held and let go of and held. They called my name and grabbed on to me, though I'd never learned who was who.

My grandmother was last. She was crying. Her husband had died young, and Matthew was her only child. I was her only grandchild.

I'd been told there was a time she was like my mother, that for the five years I lived here we'd slept side by side. I'd straddle her hip while she stood over the stove and warmed milk in a small pot. Most afternoons I played on the rug at her feet.

Soon after I was sent back to my parents' house, my grandmother was diagnosed with Alzheimer's. Matthew said she'd always been quiet. But now, she barely spoke.

The family gave us our space. My grandmother leaned on my arm, and I helped her up the porch steps. She gripped my elbow so hard it hurt. She muttered something I couldn't understand, kissed me on the forehead, and cried. I wished she wouldn't do that.

Matthew said she rarely knew what was happening. But when she saw me, she remembered that she was sad. I hated it. She tried to stroke my hand.

Just the feel of my grandmother's shaking fingers, the look of confusion in her eyes, the tears—any one of these things *hurt*. I wanted to run, or scream; to lie down on the floor and press my face to her slippered feet and sob. In my new, almost-adultness, I felt a heaviness, a tiredness, an awareness that I could not and did not respond to things honestly. That I was too good at pretending. The adults around me would call this maturity.

I told my grandmother I was going to college in two months. To a very famous school in Connecticut.

"I applied to a lot of places," I said. "But Hollis was the most prestigious one that let me in. After Yale. And I got into BYU, where—"

I stopped myself. My parents had wanted me to choose Yale for the slightly better name, or BYU for the (much, much) better chance at finding a husband. But mentioning my parents felt unkind.

"Did you know," I said, "Hollis has a pretty significant Native American population?

"Lots of Indians," I added, as if that would help.

My grandmother touched my cheek.

"I don't know if I'll even count as one of them, you know? Or if things might be weird," I said.

She said something.

"Well, other than that, Grandma, I don't really have much news for you. High school had plenty of drama—friend stuff, a little boy stuff—but you don't want to hear about that."

I thought about my worst secret, Ada, the girl at LDS sleepaway camp last year. She'd slipped a love letter under my pillow. For a few weeks afterward I slept with it tucked in my waistband, against my skin, until I threw it away. I didn't tell any of my three parents, who'd fought over me without knowing I'd turn out like this.

My grandmother and I were used to silence. The distance of language and memory was like we were standing on opposite sides of a canyon, shouting love that crashed down somewhere in the trench between us. I imagined it like water. Rushing, loud.

The people outside—none of them closer than a great-aunt or a first cousin once-removed—laughed together and ate sheet cake. The cake had my two-year-old face printed on the white icing, from a photo of me sitting on my grandmother's lap.

I stopped trying to talk to her. We sat side by side, holding each other, her small bones against my chest. Her white hair was pulled loosely back with a blue scrunchie, her head at rest under my chin, and she smelled like something I didn't know. We stayed that way until the people outside went home, and then she got up to take a nap. I moved to sit in the place she'd left behind.

From the passenger seat, Matthew called a cousin and asked her to make me an Indian taco. He got me one every year. Matthew's cousin—who wasn't really a full cousin, but he called her that—let us swing by to pick it up on our way to the big office supply store. Matthew took the wheel so I could eat.

The windows were down, and I balanced a Styrofoam plate on my knees. My fingers were shiny with oil, my plate streaked with bits of ground beef, shredded lettuce, diced tomatoes, and cheese. Matthew turned the dial to a country radio station, and sang along to a song. In it, a man asked his friends, in the event of his death, to prop up his corpse beside a jukebox and place an alcoholic drink in his hand.

Unconscionable.

On the other side of the car door the whole world was open. Ground, grass, trees. I considered the tiny gold cross around my neck.

"This is good," I said, holding up my messy hands as proof.

Matthew said I'd always liked fry bread. He said Indian tacos used to be too heavy for my little hands. I used to put my paper plate on the floor and dip my face into my food and then scream when it got in my eyes.

"Rule Three," I said. He wasn't supposed to talk about the old days.

Matthew tightened his grip on the steering wheel. He pressed harder on the gas. He was obviously mad at me, but I was mad right back.

Why'd he have to make all this drama in the first place? I could've been some regular-enough adopted kid with a vague idea of Native American ancestry. Instead, I had fry bread grease on my chin and parents in Provo who still cried out in their sleep, whenever they dreamed Matthew had stolen me back.

Matthew bought me a hundred and thirty dollars of school supplies to take to college. New binders, pens, and Wite-Out that came in a little pink tape dispenser, so I wouldn't have to wait for it to dry.

For everything we picked out, I'd reached first for the cheap version. Then he'd pointed to something prettier—the hardback floral planner with extra room to track weekly personal goals, the canvas backpack with a gold clasp and a pattern of tiny blue birds in flight, the rose-colored stationery set that I took as a hint I didn't write him enough.

It was an expensive trip. Then again, according to the visitation agreement, Matthew was only allowed to give me presents twice a year. Once when I visited in June, and then something "modest" mailed at Christmastime, like the stupid CD. If I'd never been adopted, I wouldn't have gone to private school and I wouldn't have had half the nice things I had in Utah, not to mention Mom and Dad. I wouldn't have had Heavenly Father, either, or at least not the way I knew Him now—but I didn't know what to do with that.

Matthew told me to turn onto the highway. He took a picture of me hunched over the steering wheel, and I rolled my eyes and laughed. I said, "What's next?"

We went to the Cherokee Heritage Museum for the thirteenth year, where we got free entry. After Matthew lost the custody case, the Cherokee Nation attorney general made it his personal mission to keep me Cherokee. He set up a fund for strangers to donate toward my future plane tickets. He drove all over Northeastern Oklahoma, getting Cherokee-owned businesses to volunteer free stuff if I visited. Most importantly, he got Mom and Dad to sign the visitation agreement, which I still can't believe they did. They had no legal requirement to go along with it, and they hated this day every year. That meant they'd done it for me.

Matthew and I looked at ancient carvings. Historical documents. Pottery. Woven baskets. Beaded moccasins. Maps of the Trail of Tears.

Outside the museum was a living history exhibit, a replica of a village, but it had been years since I'd agreed to walk through it. I hadn't liked it when one of the older workers recognized Matthew and got too excited to see me. Even worse than that had been the younger workers, kids about my age now, out in a field playing a Cherokee sport together. Their whole deal seemed to be, *We are having so much fun without you!*

Inside, the museum was like someone's basement. It was dark and cold, and smelled like the belongings of old people. I could tell which artifacts needed to be switched out by how much dust was caught in the grooves of their name plates. Glass cases smudged with layers of fingerprints lined the walls. I pressed my hands to them because sometimes I got this feeling that I wasn't in the place I was in. Like I was watching myself? It helped to touch things.

Matthew was still talking; I was getting tired, and he wanted to fill the silence. He said they've already put together the funds to build a new museum, the kind with multiple floors and some kind of modern-meets-traditional design by an up-and-coming Cherokee architect. He had gone to Hollis, too, and now he was based in Oklahoma City. "It'll be another five years or so before it's open," Matthew said, "so maybe you can come . . ."

He trailed off. When I left for college, it would be up to me to decide if and when I'd see Matthew.

He walked faster, passing several cases of stone tools. He stopped at a wall of posters detailing traditional ceremonies, the text faded nearly to gray.

I caught up to him. Matthew backed quickly away from a poster about traditional beliefs around menstrual blood. He wouldn't be as cool as Dad was about period stuff at the pharmacy.

Matthew stared at the woman pictured in the next poster. It was a black-and-white photo of a woman who had died, the last Cherokee midwife known to practice the old ways around pregnancy and birth. It was exciting, if still weird, to think how close I was to having a baby. A lot of girls I knew were moms by the end of college. That could be me in the next five years.

"Is there some kind of ceremony around babies?" I asked. "I don't know, like for the first time I ate or laughed or, I don't know, when I got my name?"

I wasn't sure why I was asking. If there was a ceremony for me to pass on—which in my imagination involved a baby dressed in eagle feathers waving an ear of corn—there was no way the Church would like it.

"Beats me!" Matthew said. "Our family isn't traditional."

That was interesting, because I would have thought they were. In my head there was some intersection between blood quantum and "being traditional," but I had no idea how or even if they overlapped. Matthew had tried to explain once that I had two official cards in my name, one that said I was Indian and one that said I was Cherokee. The attorney general had hand-delivered the cards to my parents after my transfer, but I'd never seen them. I suspected my parents had thrown them away.

"Besides," Matthew added, "you were laughing by the time I got you."

I nodded. I imagined Mom and Dad leaning over my crib. Tickling me, waving a rattle. I bet even back then Dad was doing his nose trick, where he presses the tip of his nose back like a pig and when he lets go it stays that way for a good ten seconds. It was hilarious.

"Listen, Dells," Matthew said. "If the answer to this is yes, then you can say yes, and we never have to talk about this again. But I looked into it a little, and I read that Mormon beliefs are, you know, abstinence-only, and—"

"Noooooo," I said, hands over my ears.

Matthew rolled his eyes. "I have some kind of responsibility here to ask. Do you, or do you not, understand that Hollis College offers free birth control at its student health center? They say so on the website."

I crossed my arms.

"Della, please. Can we agree I might know something about accidental pregnancies?" He smiled, just with his mouth, like we were close enough to joke with each other.

I thought about how awful this was, Matthew trying to parent me.

I thought about my parents, who had only prepared me for a temple sealing to a husband. If I did it that way, our family could be together for time and all eternity.

I thought about my first kiss, at camp last summer with my boyfriend. Ethan. It had happened right before I climbed into my tent with Ada. I woke up in the tent in the gray part of morning and her arm was around my waist, and I stayed very still like I was sleeping. *She likes me*, I thought. And also, what a terrible thing to be alive.

For six weeks after camp, Ada and I emailed every night. I'd felt like I could talk to her honestly, about all the things I was feeling. Then I thought about losing my family, in this life and the next. I blocked her email address.

"My fertility isn't your business," I said. "But I did *hear* you."

Matthew nodded. "Okay. I'm sorry. That's all I needed."

I turned sharply to the next poster. "Was I walking when I moved here?" I asked.

"Yep, already walking."

"Right."

There were things I wanted to ask him. I wanted to know what it feels like to get your daughter back. What it feels like to give her away again. What it feels like to learn that the law meant to keep kids in the tribe doesn't apply in your case, and it's maybe a tiny bit your fault, or maybe it's the power of nine non-Indians in black robes, and what you do when you're standing outside the Supreme Court with a five-year-old girl in your arms and you know she doesn't know that they're going to take her back. You don't know when they'll take her, only that they will, and the clock starts now.

More than anything, I wanted to know about the beginning. I wanted to know why he had signed me away.

I was fourteen when I'd first googled my case. I tried "Emma Ericson why dad didn't want" before being redirected to my old name. Della.

My real dad—that's how I thought of him, still—had been yelling at me for some childish infraction at Family Home Evening. My running-away fantasies led me no further than the internet. I stayed where I was—at the computer, in a nightgown, past midnight. Screen shining bright in my eyes.

I watched a lot of the old news coverage online. The footage was fuzzy, but the three people crying I knew well.

Mom and Dad say I'm "not even full-blood Indian." They count my white ancestors on many fingers. They say a number, a fraction, and one of the justices repeats it in court.

Matthew says he'd assumed my birth mother would keep me. *Assumed?*

Mom and Dad say, "This is a nightmare. This is a nightmare. This is a nightmare."

•　•　•

The county fair was another tradition. After I'd reenacted most of my firsts with Matthew, our visits came to hinge on tradition. Sometimes the visits blended together, and I could remember those afternoons at the fair with Matthew in a continuous stream of different heights and ages. As if they were many moments from our life together, and not just interruptions of the real thing. The fair was held in a field somewhere—the grass short, sharp, brown. The rides were the kind that could be taken apart and reassembled at the outskirts of many small towns, their seats flat and faded. They tie you down with thin, loose ropes and you hold on to your people and scream.

Food vendors lined up on either side of the entrance, the smell of grease thick in the air. Matthew bought me a funnel cake, and when the vendor shook the powdered sugar can, tiny flecks of white blew off like smoke in the wind. We carried the funnel cake together, each holding a side of the oil-spotted paper plate.

I told him I wanted us to do the bucket ride first. It was a knockoff of the famous Disneyland teacup ride and I was too old for it to be fun, but it was something we did together. Every year Matthew got a blurry picture of the two of us whirling in an oversized tin bucket and he had them framed and lined up on the brown-painted walls of his hallway. Twelve years of us, my eyes moving gradually from terrified to amused.

The line for the bucket ride was long, and these were the things we talked about. Food. Movies. Music. What is Happening Right Now. Basically, how I spoke with my language partner in Spanish class at school, our voices clear and earnest. *And Pablo, do you like to eat the sandwiches?*

Someone tapped Matthew on the shoulder. He turned.

It was a woman, definitely Indian—at least I thought—in short shorts and a loose tank top. I didn't recognize her, but why would I? And what made me think I knew she was Indian?

"I'm sorry, I gotta ask," she said. "You're Matthew Owens, right?"

I turned away from her and pretended to study the clouds. I slipped a lock of hair between my teeth and bit down.

"Yep," Matthew said. "Sorry, but have we met?"

The woman fiddled with her glasses and squinted over at me. "It's been a long time," she said. "But our moms wove baskets together. Wait, oh my God, is this *her*?"

"I'll tell my mom your mom said hi, okay?" Matthew pulled me behind him. His shirt was sweaty and clung to his back.

"It's really her," the woman said. "I didn't know if she'd make it back here."

If it weren't for Matthew, she wouldn't have recognized me. Mom and Dad have kept me out of the public eye, at least since the day I came home to them. I wasn't even allowed to have an AIM account anymore, because Dad found out about all the Indians sending me chat requests and invitations to play chess online. *Are you Baby Della? I used to stand in the grocery store parking lot every Sunday for you. My daughter made you a sign that said OUR CHIL-DREN ARE NOT FOR SALE.*

"We don't get much time together," Matthew whispered to her. "Let's keep this between us?"

It was too late. I heard the whispers move down the line, then right back up to us in shouts. "Baby D!" someone said. "It's her!"

Matthew held my wrist too tight, and I heard the click of a camera. I spit my hair out of my mouth.

He whispered over his shoulder. "Okay, Dells, we gotta go."

He walked fast, me almost skipping to keep up. We passed the rides. Little airplanes spinning in circles, ponies following each other in star forma-tion, swings circling higher into the sky, and I saw my world so clearly. Mom and Dad and Matthew chasing me, and me chasing them right back. A single camera flashed.

A woman pushed forward. "They took my baby niece and we never saw her again," she said. "But you found your way back, praise Jesus!" She held her camera up close to my face, and I blinked.

Grandma and I sit on the closet floor. She presses my face into her chest, and she plays with my hair and rocks me without a noise. The men bang at the door, and my father won't answer, and they bang some more until they knock it open. Grandma sucks in her breath. I hear boots on the kitchen floor, thun-dering steps kicking open doors and checking under beds. They come closer.

The closet door swings so wide it bangs the wall, and I'm taken aback by light. A man in a mask and helmet and goggles kneels to take me.

I scream. Grandma is holding me too tight, and I'm afraid to breathe. The man has a flashlight on his helmet, and a gun bigger than me under his arm. His hands pull at my feet. I cry for my father, who should be saving me but isn't. But never did.

It would be ten years before I saw the photo. It was on the cover of an old magazine. My father stands behind three men with guns. Hands behind his head, he stares toward the closet in the back room.

Matthew picked me up and carried me to the truck. I kicked and squirmed because I was a grown woman now. I didn't want to be lost in these strangers, and I didn't want to be scooped up in arms that hadn't carried me in years.

Matthew threw me into the passenger seat and slammed the door. "Duck down," he said.

I held my head between my knees, my fingers knotted in my hair.

Matthew drove fast. A cloud of dirt kicked up behind us, like cowboys on horses in old Westerns. He jerked to a stop before the highway. "Seat belt," he said, and like a dutiful daughter, I put it on.

In October 1981, the woman who was pregnant with me asked Matthew to sign away his parental rights. He did, sort of. Not in a contract but on a postcard, which would hold up five years later in court. The postcard said that if she was making him choose between paying child support or giving up his rights, then he chose option two. Matthew told me, later, that he'd thought she was keeping me. And he'd thought he could visit. When I was old enough to understand what lawyers are and why they exist, it hurt my feelings that he hadn't called one.

I would never adopt a kid or abandon one. When it was my time to be a mother, I'd need to watch my child come out of my body and never let them go. But if anything, *anything* came to complicate that, I would get that shit written in blood.

When Matthew found out I'd been adopted, he called on the Indian Child Welfare Act (ICWA). If someone eligible for membership in a tribe

(Matthew) has a child (me), and removal or adoption proceedings begin, ICWA says that the tribe (Cherokee Nation) must be notified. This allows the tribe to participate, usually to advocate for an Indian home. A reasonable effort should be made to place the child according to this order: (1) the bio-family, (2) members of the same tribe, (3) members of a different tribe, and *then* (4) non-Indians. My parents, my bio-mom, and the Utah adoption agency that had made money off me—they chose to evade that process.

But the case kept coming back to one fact, a tear in Matthew's story that made it sometimes hard to love him. He had signed me away. Before the adoption, he'd never once had custody of me. He had never wanted it.

The lawyers cared about "the critical period" when I should have been in Matthew's custody, during which he'd establish the right to fight for what would happen to me. But I didn't consider that the critical period. To me, the critical period had been my birth. When the woman who carried me called Mom and Dad, and they rushed to the hospital with a suitcase packed weeks before.

I asked my mom about it once, what the suitcase was for, and the answer reminded me who she was. Everything in it, aside from one pink crocheted outfit for me, was meant for the woman who carried me. A butter-yellow delivery gown and a matching silk robe. Many practical gifts I was afraid to think too hard about, like ice packs and special bottles and creams, to help the woman heal.

During this period, Matthew didn't know I was alive.

I once found a shoebox of photos in the attic. Mom and Dad had taken me to a few Utah powwows in the months before Matthew got custody. They'd taken photos of me there. I was a newborn in baby regalia, little dance outfits with sequined shawls and pink ribbon fringe and tiny moccasins.

Mom and Dad weren't happy to hear I'd been snooping, but they did answer my questions. The outfits had come from a mail-order catalog. The powwows had been suggested by a Mormon Navajo lady who went to BYU with someone in my uncle's ward. *Of course* the powwows stopped when I came home the second time.

"Those people don't want *you*," Mom said. "Those people want your case, so they can use it for a law that gives them the power to break up families. Just because of their *race*."

It was in the truck with Matthew, speeding away from the people who thought they knew me, that I knew I was ready.

When I went to college, I thought, I could be anyone. I could change my name back to Della. I could meet other American Indian kids and listen to them awhile to see if I should be saying Indian or Native American or whatever. I could learn how to be like them, and come back to Oklahoma a little at a time.

I didn't tell Matthew this. I knew it made him nervous, not knowing if I'd choose to see him again, but I didn't want to be pushed.

Matthew kept apologizing for the people at the fair. "I don't even remember who that lady was!" he said. "I hate that I did all those interviews. I mean, now that I know they didn't change things."

"Don't worry about it," I said. "It's fine."

Matthew sighed. He drummed the wheel lightly, with just his fingertips. "I appreciate that. I just like things to be good in the time we have."

He pulled off the road and parked outside the museum gift shop. He told me to pick out something nice. "Small, though," he said. "It's gotta fit in that teeny tiny bag."

He was teasing me. Back at the office supply store I'd turned down the sturdy black backpack I really could have used. I could tell he wanted me to choose the one that was more like a purse, beautiful but ridiculous. Dad was the same; it was one of the fun parts of having a girl.

At the gift shop, I found a small black pot with swirly etchings around the lip. There was a long paper tag with cursive writing, with the name of the artist and the price.

"For my dorm," I said. In my bedroom in Utah, it would freak out my mom.

I didn't tell Matthew that next summer I'd buy a Pendleton blanket, and one of the extra nice baskets on the top shelf, and maybe a finger-woven belt I could try to pair with a jean skirt or something. I didn't tell him that American Indian kids at school might ask me what town I was from, and I really hoped I'd have the confidence to say it outright. Totally chill, like, "Tahlequah, but I grew up in Provo."

They'd know my case, because the internet said every Indian alive felt personally invested in my fate, at least for a few months many years ago, and they'd say something like *God, you're back*. Maybe I'd move in with Matthew and my grandmother someday, just for a little while after college, or even before that on one of my school breaks if it didn't give my parents a heart attack. My grandmother would be so happy.

Matthew drove me to the airport. We kept our goodbyes short. He dropped me off in front, just like Dad had that morning. Neither one of them had wanted to walk me to my gate.

I love you, I said, just in my head. Matthew took my new tiny backpack out of the car and lifted the straps gently over each of my shoulders, like it was my first day of school.

I love you. I'm sorry. Why wouldn't you just pay child support? What if Grandma dies before I come back? What if I'm gay?

I didn't say any of these things, though I felt them harder and stronger and worse than ever before. When did Matthew stop saying I love you? When did I? Why? I hugged him hard. He patted my back, his hands a little awkward.

"Your flight, Della," Matthew said. His voice was hoarse, and it cracked under my name.

"Be safe," he said, and got back in his car.

I flew from Tulsa to Phoenix and Phoenix to Provo. It was late when I landed. Dad waved from the driver's seat and pressed the button to unlock my door.

I'd been overcome with missing him on my first flight back, suddenly, though I was only hours from seeing him again. On the layover in Phoenix, I thought about how little time we had left. I was leaving for college soon, and then I'd get married and pregnant, and then Dad and Mom would get old and die? I would never live in their house again. My childhood had raced by me. I went in a bathroom stall and sobbed until they called my name for late boarding. I was still crying when the gate agent checked my ticket. She squeezed my shoulder as I passed.

"Did you have fun today?" Dad asked.

"Yep," I said.

"Good."

That was enough. Matthew wouldn't be mentioned again, not for another year. Or maybe never, I thought, now that the visitation years were behind us. I wondered if Dad thought I was done seeing Matthew, that the part of his life he'd had to share with him was over.

Dad took the slow way home. He drove through the center of town and almost every window was lit up yellow. Students walked in pairs under streetlights, sometimes holding hands. I could be like that, I thought. In two years Ethan would be back from his mission, and he'd enroll at Brigham Young. I could transfer there from Hollis, if Hollis didn't work out. We could get married.

Dad looped past Pioneer Park, twice. Finally he was ready to talk again.

He asked about the summer calculus course, the one Mom wanted me to take at BYU to "get ahead of the game." If I passed, I'd get college credit. I might even make some new friends.

He asked how I was feeling about college, if I was nervous. "BYU would have been an easier fit for you than Hollis," he said, "in a lot of ways. But Emma, when you make up your mind about something . . ."

I waited. I wasn't ready for another lecture, but this felt different. Dad touched my shoulder, like the gate agent had only a few hours before. I remembered God was always with us.

"I believe you're up for the challenge," Dad said.

The challenge at a place like Hollis was to stay Mormon. The day I told my parents I wasn't sure about BYU, that I wanted to apply to a wider pool, Mom ordered me a sterling silver CTR ring to wear on my right hand. It was a more elegant, expensive version of the one they'd given out in Sunday school when I was six—the same green shield, the same silver letters, reminding me to Choose the Right. To live righteously.

Another stoplight. I didn't know what to say. I was surprised and moved by his faith in me.

Dad sighed. He looked at me—briefly, before the green light—and squeezed my hand. The crush of the ring between my fingers. "Your mom and I are so proud of you."

I'm afraid to leave you. It will never be like this again. Two hours ago in an airport, I thought about you dying someday and I cried so hard I threw up. What if I'm gay?

"Thanks, Dad."

I wanted to tell someone about the day I'd had. I couldn't tell Ada, or Ethan. I couldn't tell Mom or Dad or Matthew, or my grandmother. Or the woman who'd carried me, who had chosen not to know me. Every person who loved me loved me in a certain way, as a certain person I couldn't fully be.

Dad pulled into the garage and closed his car door gently. He motioned for me to do the same. He whispered, "She's probably sleeping. Your mother."

At this, he pointed toward the back of the house, as if a day in Oklahoma had made me forget who she was. *That's her, down the hall. Second bedroom on the left. Your mother.*

They did this sometimes, still.

I woke in the night to the creak of my bedroom door. I kept my eyes closed. I breathed slowly in and out, soft as sleep.

I heard them at the door. I saw the warm red on the backs of my eyelids, hallway light tumbling across my blanket. They closed the door behind them, slowly, someone's hand on the doorknob until it clicked into place. Black again.

I smelled my mother's perfume. She had bottles of designer fragrances lined up on her dresser, but now she wore the awful cheap stuff I'd once bought her as a child. The battered green tin, little red birds fluttering up to the rim. My father's scent was quiet—the kind of man you couldn't smell at all until he pulled you in, until your face was pressed against the shoulder of his sweater.

I knew they held each other now, the two of them, because I peeked once, and that image will be in my head forever.

I watched them with my eyes closed, my parents. A breeze came in from the open window, and my blanket was soft but heavy against my cheek. They were standing at the foot of my bed, fingers woven, my mother's head on my father's shoulder. I was sure of it.

PART

TWO

2000–2004

BINARY STAR

Freshman Fall
September 2000

Binary stars are two stars, orbiting a common center of mass. In a binary star system, the brighter star is classified as primary. The two are referred to as A and B. In cases of equal brightness, the discoverer will designate them and that will be honored: A and B.

I learned about binary stars in my first astronomy class, in my first semester of college. (Hollis College in rural Connecticut, a school that pledged to meet 100 percent of accepted students' demonstrated financial need. Every other school either rejected me or required student loans, so I reminded myself often that Hollis was "almost" an Ivy.)

The astronomy class was called Exploring the Universe, and before school started, I'd imagined it to be something like a biweekly field trip to a planetarium. I thought I would lie back in a dark room, look at images of planets and stars and galaxies, and have it all explained to me. Maybe from the very beginning? Like a realtor, come to walk me through a house I'd been living in all my life.

Exploring the Universe was a disappointment. It was hard. It was cold, almost brutal in its lack of poetry. Two hundred students in stadium seating. A professor with a beige-colored microphone taped to his cheek like the worst Broadway show in the world, shouting out numbers and equations related to lenses and light and color, and *so fucking much about telescopes!* We never got to look inside one.

For the second time in my life, I was beginning to doubt my career plans. I wished I'd taken something in earth sciences or biology. Animal Behavior, or Natural Disasters and Catastrophes—both real classes that might let me touch something with my hands. In Exploring the Universe, I sat in the second row and squeezed my fingers into a fist. Anchoring myself, holding on.

I spent more time than I thought I would worrying about my sister. Was she getting to school on time without my alarm clock? Was she keeping up her grades? Brett's affair, and the eyes it put on our family, had been hard on her. By the time I moved out, Kayla's paintings had gotten so, so dumb, like Plains-inspired Indian girls petting neon coyotes in the moonlight. Also, I knew she spent too much time with older boys. I worried that, without me there, she'd only become more careless.

Then, binary stars.

The professor was at a conference at UC Berkeley. He'd left a TA to teach in his place, a postdoc from India. She left the beige microphone on the long table at the front of the room and spoke in an almost-shout. I let go of my hands and listened.

Binary stars, she said, *were first observed in 1650! By Giovanni Battista Riccioli!*

The TA talked like that for an hour and a half. Her language was clear, clipped. Direct. She paced back and forth at the front of the room, moving her arms to demonstrate relative size and orbit. At one point, she even spun around. She was a planet, rotating and revolving around two stars. Star A was the podium. Star B was a heeled boot, which she had kicked off her foot mid-sentence, and she now moved around the room seriously, hobbling with great purpose.

The TA explained how binary stars form. Most often, the same pocket of dust and gas will fall into itself to form one star, and then split. But sometimes— though rarely—a massive star will capture a passing star.

How a pair evolves will depend on the space between them. Wide binaries will barely affect each other. Their orbital periods could be less than an hour, or many days, or many hundreds of thousands of years. The farther star in a wide binary may have kicked out a third star. It may even be pushed out itself.

Close binaries can change each other's futures—they can transfer mass between each other, altering their composition. If one star in a close binary explodes in a supernova, its companion may also be destroyed.

While my classmates hurried out of the auditorium, I waited in my seat for the TA. She gathered her papers into a leather folder. I wanted to know more—it had been our first lesson not on the instruments of study, but on what could be known.

The TA let me follow her all the way through the building, down the stairs into an underground tunnel, through the tunnel into another building, and into the little windowless office in a basement that she shared with a German man on an astrophysics fellowship. She didn't have a chair for visitors, so I leaned against the wall, which was gray-painted cinder block, and knocked my knuckles against it behind my back. I tried to get my head around this dark and pitiful office as a part of the greater universe. And me, right now, a part of it, too.

I asked the TA if life could exist in a binary system, and she looked like she could hug me. She sat the wrong way around, holding the back of her chair to her chest. "I am *literally* trying to answer that question," she said. "For seven years I've been working on it."

On just that? I thought. I did not understand the slow march of research. I asked for her best guess.

"I don't think life can exist in most binary systems," she said. "And of course long-term planetary orbits are unlikely to be stable over the millions and billions of years that are needed for life to form. A lot of people would agree with that, so all my work is in the word 'most.' Trying to get the data to point toward something conclusive."

"Unstable like, it's too hot?" I said. "Like, double suns?"

She nodded, and I felt something fall open inside me. I had a much firmer idea now, than I'd had as a kid, of what this feeling was. How it pointed to what *I* was. But now I was old enough to know I had no chance with her.

"Yes," she said. "But you could also have a habitable zone. A position with two orbiting stars where the conditions *are* compatible with life, and then *oops*, now they've zoomed out of the habitable zone and everything freezes!"

I laughed. My face felt hot. Did she think I could belong here, with a prestigious posting in a terrible basement office someday, like her? If she showed me her research, could I skim my eyes down the third or fourth page of numbers and lines and *boom*, figure it all out? And now she's so grateful I did that for her, she's running with me through the tunnels under the school and she's holding me against a heavy oak door, her palm pressed flat under my collarbone, and she's whispering in my neck about how smart I am?

In real life, the TA leaned over a stack of books on her desk between us, like a little wall.

She talked about a hypothetical star at either face of a hypothetical planet, killing nighttime.

"It's total instability," I said, echoing the point she'd just made.

She smiled patiently and nodded.

My crush on the TA was short-lived. But I promised myself I would remember that half hour with her, always. I would look out for news on binary stars, for any discoveries that might change the way we see and understand them. A small part of it would be for her, because I'd wonder where her life would take her after the postdoc in Connecticut.

Mostly, it was because I was sentimental. A life in science might be hard and slow and lonely—much like the promise of my time in Exploring the Universe. I wanted to stay loyal to binary stars, to stay aware at least, a kind of thank-you for how they had pulled me back in.

The TA, of course, did not hit on me that afternoon. By the next class, she'd forgotten my name.

Almost immediately I found someone else. A door opened, and I ran through it.

STEPH

DATE A LESBIAN,
I'M BEGGING YOU

On the day we met, at the welcome barbecue for Native American students at Hollis, Della Ericson was wearing the wrong moccasins. (They were Chicka-maugas, a cheesy Native-inspired brand famously started by a mostly white cult in Oregon.) No one said anything about them, but they did all stare at her feet, which gave me time to guess who she was. Non-Cherokees might remember her as "Baby D," but where I was from, people still talked about her case. People knew her full names, both of them, from her two lives. It seemed like now she'd mushed them together.

I pulled her over to a picnic table to eat with me and Sam Sherman, a Prairie Band Potawatomi boy I'd met minutes before. He seemed awkward but innocuous. Della said very little and looked down often at her plate. But she made us laugh at one point, just once, and Sam drew a map of Connecti-cut for her on a napkin. He was from a small town and had never left Kansas till that morning; he just felt it was important to know all the states.

Two months later, Della and I had still never been alone together. But we were often in the same big gatherings, as members of the Native community. (I, truthfully, had tried hard to make friends in what the school's president called *the greater Hollis community*, but had recently given up. The greater Hollis community shared things with one another that I did not, like wearing identical black Patagonia fleece pullovers and being better than me at writing long but coherent essays with two nights' notice.)

When Sandra invited all the girls to her dorm room before a party, Della arrived a little after I had.

Sandra took one look at her and said, "You are *so* wearing the wrong underwear."

I would have died. But this was how girls were, it seemed, in girl groups. I'd never been part of a girl group before and now I was, with no effort on my part, just by showing up to Hollis and being Indian and a girl. By being a nassie. (Nassies were members of NASA, the Native American Student Association. When I called home in September, I'd told my mother about that and she'd laughed and laughed before saying, "Well, Steph, you've made it. You can come home now.")

Part of being in a girl group was that sometimes someone would tell you to take off your underwear and you'd laugh like it was the most normal thing in the world. That's what Della did.

Sandra tossed Della's underwear—cotton, high-waisted from a pack, like mine—into her own laundry hamper and replaced it with a thong from a drawer bursting with lace. Sandra was Ojibwe from Minneapolis. Her accent was weirdly rez-adjacent, and she said she'd be the first in her family to earn a doctorate. Sam thought her dad might own every Subway in Minnesota. She had a black Patagonia pullover that she often announced as thrifted, and she'd taken a gap year during her reign as Miss Indian World.

"Much better," Sandra said. "Now they won't see the line of your seam through the fabric of that skirt. Trust me on this." She nodded approvingly at Della's butt.

"They" meant the boys. For as long as I had been in a girl group at Hollis, "they" always meant the boys. Or "white people," sometimes, but that was complicated, so no one talked about it.

Sandra caught the cross at Della's neck in her hand, and the two launched into a talk about Jesus and their personal relationship with him. Sandra said she was "nondenominational," which just meant Christian. What I thought of as the regular kind, and what my family had sort-of been (if only because our mother had thought church could help get us friends).

I stood against the wall, observing the culture of girl group. The conversation turned back to boys, with whom I had even less of a personal relationship than I did with Jesus Christ. Della finished her own eye makeup and pulled me in to face her while she did mine.

I tolerated it, the bristles of brushes along my cheekbones and eyelids, because I wanted to be a good citizen of girl group and I wanted Della to touch my face. I'd wanted that since we'd first met in September, even before I'd realized who she was. Della put her hand on my waist for a moment, as if to steady me, but I wasn't falling. I leaned, slightly, into her touch.

"Ethan's on mission," Della said, in answer to a question I hadn't heard. "So we write."

Sandra laughed. "He's in Japan the entire year, and you're like, what? Pen pals?"

"I think it's cute," April said. "Email or regular?" April was Lakota, from Standing Rock.

"I think it's cute, too," Jess said. She was Inupiaq, from Alaska, and already a unit—platonically, of course—with April. I wished I'd gotten in on that. They were always leaning into each other and following each other across campus; they laughed at jokes with hidden doors and windows, and passed notes in our first-year writing seminar without me.

"I've got a heck of a lot of stationery," Della said.

"*Even cuter*," April said.

I said, "What do your parents think?" I just wanted to know who Della considered to be her parents.

I'd been trying to ignore that Della was Indian-famous, that as a child I'd seen her on TV. I mean, the almost-end of the Indian Child Welfare Act! The National Guard! The photo of that night, Della crying in a dress with purple roses embroidered along the hem. Della's grandmother holding her in her arms—one fist of roses, one wrinkled hand over dark-haired head. Behind them, steady, the barrel of a gun.

The photo was printed everywhere after Della's transfer, even in newspapers overseas. My sister had used it recently in a mixed-media piece to raise awareness on violence against Native women and girls. I'd seen it on her blog. How she embroidered tiny purple roses onto the delicate black magazine paper. How she dipped the bottom edge of the photo in cow's blood, procured from the butcher father of a grass dancer she had slept with. (Did Kayla have to be so dramatic?) I told myself, again, to stop worrying about my sister. To let myself be where I was.

Della looked at me, mascara wand balanced in the air, like she was deciding where it was supposed to go. *On my eyelashes!* I wanted to say. I felt like a child, like I wanted to impress her however I could.

"My parents love Ethan," Della said. "I got to know him at camp, but we met before that. He's from our ward."

"*Both* your parents love him?" I asked, hoping she'd mention her bio-dad. That was as far as I could push it. All I really wanted was to *know* this girl who smelled like the limoncello in the bottle Sandra had held to her lips at the door, whose breath was hot on my neck when she leaned in closer to line my eyes in black. Her palm was sweaty but firm on my chin. I'd known the ghost of her at the sidelines of my life. On televisions, once or twice on magazine covers in the check-out line. Now she had a body.

Della didn't pause, or step back, or betray uncertainty in her voice. She said, "Yes. They're both excited. It's like a *thing* for us. Us Mormons? We write letters on mission, and then we date, and then if that's working out— obviously if we *want* to, like with anyone—we get married.

"But I'm not there yet. I mean, like, I'm literally *here*." She waved her hands around Sandra's room, indicating her college experience.

"I mean, I bet *he's* there already," Sandra said. "The abstinence thing is *so* much harder for boys."

April and Jess laughed behind me. They pretended to read erotic love letters from invisible scrolls they held out at arm's length. They poured shots and spritzed perfume and dabbed lipstick on tissues. Three other girls crowded around Sandra's bathroom mirror.

Della finished my makeup and crossed the room. She clinked a "Proud Hollis Parent" shot glass with a senior girl I didn't know. Before the first frat party of the semester, Della had proudly announced to the girl group that she didn't drink alcohol and never would.

Was she done with *all* the Mormon rules now, or just some of them? And why tonight? Did the boyfriend know? Ethan? If Ethan found out, somehow, would he break up with her?

Della made a terrible face when she swallowed. She coughed and laughed and glanced across the room at me. I'd been staring. She looked away.

I leaned against the wall and watched her, and kept watching her, even after she caught me again. Each time this happened she would blush, look away, pretend to be engaged in something as simple as twisting on and off her green-and-silver ring.

How to translate a hand on my waist? How to recognize the kind of girl I stood a chance with, when I wasn't sure I'd ever met one? People like me didn't live in Oklahoma.

I knew I wasn't straight. I told myself that was half the equation. Della was something to be puzzled out. I had the upper hand in a game unspoken, and I wanted to win. I stared, daring her to do something or to have something done to her, to let herself be seen.

On my September call home, I had talked to Kayla the longest. I said I had friends now, easily ten, and that most of us lived together in a house for Native students. Sam had driven all the girls to a secondhand store, and sometimes we shared clothes. Once a week we held Indigenous Women Activists meetings, where we watched documentaries about things like the Kanehsatà:ke Resistance and planned fundraisers for the Hollis powwow. We beaded peyote-stitch earrings in a circle on the floor.

Kayla wasn't impressed. She accused me of something I was desperate not to admit. That I liked these Indians because I thought they were better than me. That I thought the others, all the people back home, were worse.

I should have known she wouldn't get it. I missed how Kayla had been just a year ago, before she'd become so defensive. Now everything she did, even the stupid, rebellious things, were backed up by something she called "praxis" that made her better than me. I didn't know who she thought was looking at her all the time, but she seemed to believe someone was.

From Sandra's, the girl group went to the pre-game together. We stomped the snow off our boots outside Jason Palakiko's dorm room, like a heavily made-up stampede in the hall.

Jason was a nontraditional student, with no interest in living in the nassie house. He was Native Hawaiian and pre-law and served as most of the girl group's most unattainable crush. He was also a veteran, having returned from the NATO operation in Kosovo just before starting college at twenty-one.

All the boys had warrior syndrome. They wanted to hear battle stories, to sit beside him and walk too close to him and pester him to come out with them at night. Jason was good to them, though. He never let them feel too hard their own moments of unkindness. It was common knowledge that when a certain sophomore boy asked Jason if he'd ever killed a man, Jason took the drink from the boy's hand and gently set it down. He spoke slowly, carefully. Jason told him it was a conversation they could have someday, maybe, but it wouldn't happen a week after meeting, and it wouldn't happen drunk.

We poured into the room, where the nassie boys waited for us. They passed out drinks and I held mine close to my chest. I breathed slowly through the turning of the walls.

I sat next to Della on Jason's desk, knowing it wasn't quite big enough. Our arms and legs touched.

"You've got like, the *most* intense stare," Della said.

We'd never been alone together until now, if this could count as alone. Sam was, annoyingly, almost always next to her.

This was my own fault. I'd walked Della over to Sam's big, pitiful, just-him picnic table, because I felt bad for him. For both of them. The possibility that they'd like each other *this* much—that Della would like him more than she liked me!—hadn't crossed my mind.

It should have. Sam was easy to like. He had been nice to me early on, when I failed my first test in Exploring the Universe. "Assholes," he'd said, after catching me crying in the nassie house basement. Even though I was the one who'd thought I shouldn't need to study. "They oughta call it Exploring My Ass." Della, watching this, had snorted at the word "ass," then blushed like a child caught.

Another thing about Sam was that I suspected he was gay. I hoped, at least, this said something promising about Della. If she didn't like me the way

I wanted her to, maybe she'd at least be kinder about it than Meredith had been.

"What changed for you tonight?" I asked. "To make you try drinking?"

Della laughed and shook her head. "Steph Harper," she said. "Master of deflection."

"How so?" I raised my eyebrows and sat up straight, so I'd be taller than her. I was aware of the look I was going for. I'd seen it in boys when they flirted with my sister.

"Deflection," Della said. "Like, you want to be in charge of the conversation, and you'll rearrange things to make it that way."

"I know the *definition*," I said. "And that's exactly what *you* did when I asked about drinking."

"Fine. But I can't talk about alcohol yet," she said.

Della looked down, either shy or pretending to be. "It's only been like two hours of alcohol. Who knows if I'll hate it."

"But I'm curious," I said. "Why tonight? Why'd you suddenly decide not to keep—"

Della held up a hand. She shook her head, her face mock-serious even as she held back a laugh. "No, no," she sang. "Can't ask that. Too soon to tell."

"So are you done with other stuff, then?" I said. "Other Mormon stuff?"

"Like what?" Della said. "What kind of Mormon stuff do you think you know about?"

"You know," I said. I wanted to ask if she was done thinking marriage was an eternal covenant between a man, a woman, and God. Or, at least, if she was done with True Love Waits?

Instead I asked, "Are you going to bear false witness now? Or covet thy neighbor's wife?"

"Too soon to tell," she said. But she was laughing, and she leaned toward me and uncrossed her legs. She let her hand fall on my thigh, and then took it away.

I slumped down and held a hand to my forehead. "Ohhh, but I *wish* you *wouldn't*," I said. "Everyone at this institution is always coveting my wife. It's exhausting."

I was not out of the closet, in the sense that there had been no declaration. The joke, which left me scared and exhilarated, was like my hand reaching out to her.

"There, there," Della said. Touching my thigh again; little pats. "It's only exhausting if you wait up for her."

"Ha ha." *Relief.* "Where do you stand on adultery?"

"Depends who's offering," she said.

"Can we be serious a minute?"

Della snorted. She turned toward the room and lowered her voice, as if making a statement to the press. "For the record, I'm neither offering nor accepting any services of that kind."

I nodded at her little joke. "Listen, Della," I said. "It feels weird not to tell you this? Since it's been like two months? But I've known about you for *years.* You were on the news all the time when I was in first grade."

I was trying to tear her secrets out. (Better hers than mine.) I wanted to break something down maybe, so we'd have no choice but to be close.

Della looked at me, surprise and anger there and then gone, hidden so fast I nearly missed it. There were so many other people in the room, I realized, even on the bed just beside us, shouting and cheering as two boys did shots in some kind of contest. Amid all the noise and the shuffling of bodies and the heat, I wondered: Had I ruined it?

"*Everyone* freaking knows that, Steph," Della said. The looseness in her was gone, and none of her body was touching mine. "You think you're the first person here to recognize me? They just don't bring up my contested adoption at parties—because they're nice to me."

"Oh," I said. "Sorry."

A silence. I knew I should leave her alone.

"That's why you're Mormon, right?" I said. "That came from your adoptive parents?"

"It's rude to make fun of other people's religions."

"I wasn't making fun."

"You think it's weird, though. Obviously. Like my cross necklace. You keep looking at it. You obviously hate my necklace."

"No!" I said, too fast. Part of my early success in girl group, I thought, was that I hadn't been noticed. I could stand toward the back of the group and even make faces sometimes at things I thought were dumb, and no one would notice me. Here Della was, noticing me, and I wasn't prepared.

She didn't look away. I was starting to think she didn't hide from things, not like I did. She pushed right through them to take something she wanted, something for herself.

Della said, "Tell me about the Nation."

"Where I'm from?"

Della nodded. "Where *we're* from, technically."

"So you're interested?"

Della looked at me like I was clueless. She nodded at the room of Indians. As if to say, *I am here on purpose.*

"Right," I said. "Sorry. I didn't used to get asked that. And then here it's like we're all asking and answering where we're from all the time, describing something we've never had to describe before? It makes me wonder if the rest of our lives will be like that, talking about where we left."

I was talking too much, and too honestly. I worried about my pitch and my accent—I often worried about my accent. Sandra took Sam's fist and waved it in the air. He swayed in his seat. Everyone cheered.

"Maybe?" Della said. "But that's just if we never go back."

"That's the plan!" I said. "What about you?"

"Why is that the plan?" Della said.

"Wait, are *you* going back?"

"I want to," Della said simply. "To Tahlequah, not Provo."

"And your adoptive parents are cool with that?"

"I call them my parents. And stop it, Steph. You still haven't told me why you hate Oklahoma."

"I don't exactly *hate* it," I said. "And anyway, I just left. Too soon to tell."

Della stared up at the ceiling, at the neat lines of warm yellow lights. Like this was a garden party in the English countryside, and not what it was. The windows were open and it was snowing outside, hard, but still far too hot in the room. She looked faraway in her eyes, despite her small hand firm on my arm, then my shoulder, then my neck.

I had seen her father on television a few times, crying on a bench in a courthouse or swaying Della back and forth in his arms. I'd pretended my own father, my real one, had been like that. That he'd wanted us *that* bad, more than he'd wanted to escape the end times.

He had something in him he couldn't change. My mother had told me that, but still she'd abandoned him. I'd look at photos in the newspaper of Della's dad being an absolute wreck, sitting at a kitchen table with his head in his hands all devastated, and I'd let myself think, *My dad, too.*

Della was taken from her father. We had left ours for somebody else to bury.

"Can I ask a lighter question?" I said, when I needed to stop remembering. "If you're comfortable with it . . . I've just always wondered. What has it *been* like with your parents, after what they did?"

"Fuck you," Della said, with the shaky softness of a pretty girl who'd never cursed. "That's not a lighter question."

"I'm sorry."

"You say sorry a lot, for someone who never means it," Della said. But she didn't leave.

A thought occurred to me. If I could be like *that*, meaning an asshole, and Della stayed close to me—even just literally, physically close to me on this desk—maybe she was a lesbian?

Run, an upperclassman in my stats class had said, only days before. She wore a flannel button-down every day and held some kind of executive position in the Gay Straight Alliance. Somehow, she'd already clocked me. And she knew just enough about Della, and about me, about who ate lunch with whom at our small school. She turned and whispered a warning to me, as our professor handed back papers. *Date a lesbian*, she'd said. *I'm begging you. It hurts to watch.* She swiveled her chair back to face the front.

I didn't run. I walked with Della, and with basically every Native American at Hollis, to the frats after the pre-game. She swayed and leaned into me in the back of the group. I knew this was her way of pushing through something that might have scared her, as it scared me.

It was the way she got closer to me with each streetlight, how her breath was warm on my neck as she moved, falling into me over and over in a way that could still look like an accident, maybe. I glanced down at the thin fabric over her chest—she had left her coat unzipped in this storm, maybe for this, for me? I looked there, then up to her eyes, a smile, down to her breasts, staring, shameless, undressing her in my head on the snow-covered path, all but fucking her there with the confidence I hoped I'd have if this were real. If she were really in my bed, under me, and I had any idea what to do with her.

Each time I broke away from her, from the rise in her chest and the dip in her bare collarbone, how it caught the glare of the streetlight and swallowed it, I looked up at Della and she held my gaze. Firm, unshaking, daring me back.

We took off our coats at the door of Alpha Omega and tied them together by the arms. When it was time to go it would be easier to find them in the dark, in the massive pile accumulated on a stranger's bed. And it was safer, Sandra said, because the number one rule of going out together was going home together. In our first week of school, Sandra had stood in the kitchen and demonstrated the arm-tying trick with her coat and April's coat, saying, "So now if I'm super drunk, like, black-out drunk, and some guy's trying to take me back to his dorm, I can't leave without going through the whole rope of coats. And while I'm standing there wrestling with the arm-knots, you people can save me."

In the basement I danced with Della, who seemed like she'd never danced before. She jumped up and down and jerked from side to side. She moved in a way that was exaggerated and silly, shielding her from the embarrassment of trying. I did my best to lead.

What had gone wrong with Meredith, I told myself, was my openness. A willingness to be led, her lifting my hand with her hand and putting it where she wanted it. Me falling into something I couldn't control. If I were in charge this time, things would be better.

I knotted the back of Della's shirt in my fist, pulling her closer against me. She breathed hard in the hot air, avoiding my eyes. My other hand was low on her hip, and when I stretched my fingers down I felt the absence of fabric under her skirt. I remembered the change of underwear.

Sandra cut in. I stumbled back into the circle of the girl group, all of them shrieking and laughing. There was so much space between Della and Sandra. They spun around and held hands and swayed from side to side.

In the line for the bathroom I saw the upperclassman from my stats class. She was wearing yet another flannel button-down. We smiled and nodded at each other with our mouths closed; I couldn't remember her name.

"You brought your girlfriend?" she asked, nodding at Della across the room.

"*What?* No!" Immediately my reaction felt unsophisticated and small-town. Things were different here.

"*Geeze.* Homophobic much?"

"Sorry," I said.

"Whatever. If she were gay, I'd know."

"And if *I* were?" I asked. "Seeing as how you manage the registry?"

The girl from stats leaned back against the wall. She made a long show of looking at me. The hair I'd sprayed into place like Shawn from *Boy Meets World*, the pegged jeans and heavy boots, the blue satin Goodwill button-down buttoned all the way up.

She laughed. "You are"—she looked me over again—"*obviously* already registered."

I was taken aback. Could Della see what the girl from stats saw? Could I be recognized, somehow, even by someone from a church with no gay people? When we'd first met, Della had stared at me from across the picnic table with her head cocked to the side. Like she couldn't place me but believed we had met. It made me wish we had.

Della appeared, out of breath. The girl from stats gave me a knowing look like, *ah yes, your girlfriend*, and stepped into the bathroom.

I felt uneasy. Like I needed to take charge of the situation, or the situation would spin out.

Della stood close to me, silent. Was she waiting for me? Some guy bent over a trash can by the basement steps, and Sam rubbed his back, the gentleness jarring between two men. I felt the beat of the music pounding through the wall behind my shoulders.

"I'm sorry for teasing you and, I don't know, things being weird tonight?" I said. "We've never really talked alone, so I had questions—probably too many? I wanted to know you better. I like you."

It was a stupid risk. In the girl group, we shared every one of our friends. I felt how reckless I was being, in the long and painful silence that followed.

Then, an almost whisper: "What do you mean by *like?*"

I slipped my hand around her waist. She didn't turn her head to look at me. Behind her back, hidden in the space between Della and the wall, I slipped my fingers under the hem of her shirt. I ran them slow up her spine.

The bathroom door opened and the girl from stats walked out. She nodded so subtly as she passed, like we were both in the cartel and the cartel was gay.

I took Della's hand and led her into the bathroom. She locked the door behind us. A click. Her expression was serious, determined, and in it I saw everything she believed I could do to her. I must have looked this way to Meredith—helpless and wanting, waiting to be taught—the last time I'd been kissed. Now I steeled myself for what was coming. Della couldn't know I was nervous.

There were things I knew to be true, some before they even happened:

I knew I could depend on the intimacy of women. Two girls together in a bathroom are presumed innocent.

I knew that the things that scared me would stay with me, as they always had, but that when Della touched my cheek and kissed me, I'd be pulled out of my father's house in Dallas and back into the world, into a little bathroom. There's the soap dispenser, and the paper towel holder, and there's her heartbeat, warm in her chest, there's my hand pulling her softly back by the hair, there's the place between my neck and shoulder, there's my tongue.

But how could I have known how we would talk, our best and longest and truest talk, in my bed? Hours. Was there anything she didn't tell me? In the early hours of the day she came quietly into my hand, and collapsed in tears. Deep, heavy sobs. I scooped her up under the blue quilt I'd stolen from my mother's house. I rocked her in my arms till she laughed.

How could I have known about the morning? How little time we had. My alarm clock. Della moaning for water, oh my head, what happened, oh no. Della calling it a kiss, a mistake, "so crazy!" How many shots?

Here is what I knew, even then:

The precision of her fingers against me, the focus in her eyes, the perfectly straight line of crescent moons down my shoulder. How carefully she'd marked me with her teeth.

DELLA

PRESERVATION

After I broke the law of chastity, I could not bear the thought of going home. I skulked from Steph's bed to a long shower, then to the hallway outside the office of the LDS Student Association, where I sat in a chair for an hour till the student adviser showed up for work.

I begged for a spot on the winter break mission trip to Mexico, which I stupidly thought might be in Cancún. I'd finally see the beach, at least, on my way to hell. The trip was to Mexico City, though, land-locked, and it was full.

"But I'm having a *faith crisis*?" I said, and a spot materialized. I also received an offer of weekly coffee meetings with the LDS student adviser, an email from the bishop of the ward I'd grown up in, and a phone call from my parents, who had been alerted by said bishop.

"I'm so sorry," my mother said, and at the sound of her voice I cried into the phone. We were supposed to be together for all eternity, as a family. Having that, a family and an afterlife with them, was a gift I had received through God's grace, for being my parents' daughter. I hadn't had to go searching for it, and then find it, and then likely be separated from my parents after death. That's how it was for converts, if their parents wouldn't join them in the church. All I had to do was be worthy of what I already had. Wasn't that more important than the kind of trick my body could do now, than the mechanics I'd realized overnight?

Over the phone Mom told me, for the first time, about her own faith crisis. She'd been almost thirty, childless, and starting to question God.

"In all the years I waited for you," she said. "I felt like I'd been put on this earth to be your mother. Like you already existed, somewhere, and I just needed to find you. And when that didn't happen? And I had to go, not pregnant, to those freaking baby showers for every woman I'd ever met?"

The word "freaking" was unlike her. She laughed and breathed out. I could picture her, how she'd lean against the kitchen counter with the phone cord wrapped in rows across her arm.

"*Honey*. When I didn't have you? It made me doubt the whole world."

Our bishop thought I should come straight home, and Dad agreed with him. He missed me. Hollis had been a mistake. But Mom was the only one of the three of them who had ever experienced a faith crisis. She said that when people pushed too hard, like how her parents and, frankly, her husband had with her, it only made things worse. She said the mission trip might be just what I needed. It would do me good to see how other people lived, and to learn how I could serve them in God's name. Sometimes we get stuck in our own earthly problems, which are only temporary after all. She said she'd talk Dad into it, and they would pay. If it didn't work out, I could always come home.

When she hung up, I thought about Steph's hands as "earthly problems," both of them, and made myself walk three miles to J.Crew to keep from touching myself. I put a long pink peasant skirt on my parents' card.

I brought in the new year in an orphanage in Mexico City. A small earthquake sent us scrambling to carry the children outside. I stood on the street—a street I had been warned to avoid for its poverty and violence. There was a baby in my arms, somebody's baby, and despite a full week at the orphanage I felt newly panicked by the anonymity of his parents. Were they even dead? Where had he come from? In a crowd of neighbors I'd been warned against, I stood still. Together we watched buildings sway back and forth without falling. What if I died? What would happen to me?

I lived. When we were given the all clear, I went back inside and pulled a rose-colored card and matching envelope from the outside pocket of my duffel. I wrote a letter to Ethan, breaking up with him. I couldn't get engaged, let alone married, when I was like this. I sang "How Great Thou Art" at midnight on a cold tile floor that smelled strongly of bleach, two small children asleep against my chest.

• • •

In the spring, I repented. I ignored the open question of a major and took only the courses I'd have to take anyway, like rhetoric and math. I devoted myself to becoming a godly woman and a good friend to all. Even to Steph as a fellow member of the Native community—though I'd never spend time with her alone.

Steph didn't seem to mind. I'd assumed she was obsessed with me, but I was wrong. She was actually obsessed with, unbelievably, *becoming an astronaut.* It was one of those dream jobs like "fireman" or "president" that little kids grow out of, but she apparently hadn't. When I tore out of Steph's room, the morning after what we'd done, she didn't chase me. She probably just went to the library.

Summer break was a problem to get ahead of. I was still afraid to visit my parents. They would look at me and they would know.

Another work-around. I'd spend two months traveling through small towns in Poland, as part of a free interfaith trip to restore Jewish graveyards. The graveyards had been established long before the Holocaust, holding deaths by natural causes or illness or childbirth—but it was the Holocaust that ended the generations of community upkeep. No one had been left to care for them.

The trip was free mostly due to a grant and partly due to fundraisers like bake sales, which we had to commit to helping out with once a week for a semester. The free part mattered because my parents wanted me to visit them, and if they couldn't have that, they'd rather I travel with our church. When Dad heard about the trip to Poland, he was frustrated with himself for not seeing earlier that I had a heart for service. "We should have encouraged you to serve a full-time mission—given you a year or two before all that pressure to choose a college."

Steph was going to Poland, too, surprisingly. There weren't any free summer programs that were space-themed. And the Poland trip seemed to be half Jewish people and half non-Jews avoiding their families? I didn't ask Steph what was wrong with hers.

I didn't *have to* go to Poland. Sam put his mother on the phone so she could invite me to spend the whole summer with their family in Kansas. "Stay as long as you want," she said. "We'd get a real kick out of meeting Sammy's best friend!"

Sam looked embarrassed.

I brought him a hot chocolate later that afternoon, with a little bag of marshmallows to share, and said no thank you. I'd been required to take a weekly extracurricular Holocaust class as part of the grant, and to read memoirs of survivors between sessions. I said Poland was starting to feel bigger than avoiding my parents.

Sam asked if I was just excited to be with Steph.

"Why would you say that?"

"Come on, Della," he said, but his tone was cautious. He was the only person, besides Steph, who knew what I had done with her. He had guessed the morning it happened, and I'd been too shocked and upset to correct him. I had my own guesses about Sam, but it didn't feel right to bring that up.

"Fine. It's kind of exciting being near her," I said. "Even though, like, *nothing* would ever happen."

"Duh?" he said. "It's called sexual tension?"

I threw a marshmallow at him. He caught it in his mouth.

In June I went to Poland. I asked to switch seats with the rabbi who was our chaperone, so I could sit next to Steph on the plane. Steph gave me a weird look as I buckled my seat belt, probably because even in Holocaust class I'd stayed on the other side of the room from her. She put on a giant set of headphones and watched movies from takeoff to landing.

For weeks we worked beside each other in mostly silence, scrubbing moss and dirt and once even spray-painted swastikas from Hebrew-lettered tombstones. Sometimes we had the help of local Polish teenagers who had never met Jewish people before, recruited by their high school teachers as part of a cultural exchange program.

Aaron, a junior theater major I'd first met at a frat party, would follow behind the rest of us and squint at the faded letters before transcribing them in a notebook. His writing looked like a different language than the Hebrew letters on the stones, but Aaron said it was just cursive. And then Aaron's tattoo-covered girlfriend Helen would sit under a tree and type them back into print letters, which did look like the letters on the tombstones, and she'd upload the names and dates to an international online database. This would help survivors, and the people who had and would come from survivors, to find their ancestors.

Every day I thought about these descendants, logging on to computers scattered across the world to learn the names of the towns they were maybe supposed to have lived in. According to Helen, who was majoring in genocide, before the war there'd been Jews in Poland for over a thousand years. Matthew's family—my family—had only lived in Oklahoma since the Trail of Tears. But where had they been before that—back East? It was a feeling I turned over daily that summer—a life I was maybe supposed to have lived.

Over the course of this work, I backslid. I started talking to Steph, alone, in a conversation that stretched across six small Polish towns. On the last week of the trip, we went on a walk. We heard people drinking and shouting just down the road, in the market square where, decades ago, they had rounded up the Jews. In a field, in the shadow of a barn, I reached my hands out and pulled Steph into my face.

She gasped. She put her hand on my forehead and pushed me, gently, away. "*Jesus! Ericson!* Are you out of your mind?"

I shifted on my feet like a child.

"We're in Poland!"

I nodded, not understanding.

"Della. I wanted that to happen *all year.* Didn't you realize?"

"I—"

"Oh my God, I thought you'd decided you were straight. But no, you were just waiting till *Poland*? This is like, one of the worst places in Europe for you to stage your gay awakening."

"Oops?" I said.

Steph laughed and shook her head. She looked past the barn at three men walking in the middle of the road. She took a step back. "I am begging you. *Begging you,*" she said. "Try that again at a small liberal arts college."

• • •

At the end of the trip we went to Auschwitz. I made the whole thing about me in my head.

I held Steph's hand outside the visitors' center restrooms and cried because I missed my parents, and I loved them, and I knew they wouldn't want me the way I had turned out. I was so afraid of losing them. I didn't want to die, ever, for anyone ever to die, or for the world to end as Steph said it someday had to, and I didn't want to think about all the Holocaust victims suffering in hell because they hadn't accepted Jesus.

Aaron stepped out of the men's restroom just then, looking appropriately somber, and I threw my hand to my face, faking a coughing fit while Steph patted me hard on the back. I wiped my tears on my sleeve and kept my shit together the rest of the tour, only crying a little bit and for the right reasons, in the right places, when other people around me cried, too. But in the privacy of my own body, standing before a pile of the shoes of children, I left my faith.

DELLA

VISITATION

Freshman Summer
August 2001

My grandmother died. Matthew didn't tell me till I visited him in Oklahoma, on my secret stupidly-out-of-the-way layover between New York and Connecticut. I'd told my parents I was going straight to Hollis from Poland, and on principle they never looked at my debit card statements. They trusted me to choose the right.

Matthew emailed me the name of a diner outside the Tulsa airport. No tattered welcome home sign, no porch overflowing with relatives. I had missed the funeral. Would I see them again?

At the counter where we met and placed our orders, Matthew gave me a light hug—like I was a stranger he was scared to touch. He looked off into the distance when it was time to pay for my coffee, an insult my entire body was screaming to tell Steph about.

At the table, Matthew looked down at his hands. "Well, what can I say. She suffered."

There was a moment there when I could have learned more. I'd thought her cause of death was old age, or the complications of Alzheimer's, and I still thought it most likely was. But I had just spent two months in death, in different stories of different ways to die. I didn't want to know how she had hurt.

"Why didn't you tell me?" I said.

"You were in Europe."

Was he looking past me, over my shoulder? I turned around. There was a window behind me, and an endless parking lot. Past that, an airport budget hotel.

I turned back to him. "But . . . you thought I was in Utah! Until I emailed you to set this up last week, you *never* would have guessed I was in *Poland*!" The word "Poland" felt important. A gray palette of former communism, the non-chicness of the place. My parents had more money than Matthew did—what if he thought I'd been in Paris?

"You could've told me," I added. "I would've come back—"

"—home?" Matthew said. "You mean, *my* home? You don't have to do that anymore. You're busy."

His face was blank. Was he angry I hadn't come in June, for our first non-mandated summer visit?

I'd long assumed this layover would count in its place. The extra day of flying. The long wait outside baggage claim. The apparently pay-your-own-way coffee. The coffee was cold in this thin mug, on this wobbly table—he had chosen somewhere cheap.

"I'm so sorry for . . . the loss," I said quietly. I was afraid to say "your," equally afraid to say "our."

"You still don't call me anything," he said. His voice was hoarse, pained.

I pretended to sip from my stupid cup, pretended to swallow.

"Not 'Dad,' which, whatever—but not even 'Matthew'? You thought I'd never catch that?" He pretended to read his watch, tucked too far up his stained sleeve. "But hey, I gotta get you back for your next flight."

He looked out the window again, paused, sighed. He held his palms flat against his eyes.

"I'm sorry," he said finally. "I'm being an asshole. I miss her. I wish you'd . . . It was an absolute *disgrace*—"

He stopped.

He choked back a sob, but it came out anyway, a short wail. A waitress holding a coffee pot took two steps backward and turned on her heel.

Then Matthew said, almost in a whisper, "I didn't want you to see it. It was a disgrace, how she suffered."

DELLA

KIN SELECTION

Sophomore Fall
September 2001

The night before the first day of sophomore year, the nassies had a guest speaker flown in. He was an elder. So far it was always an elder, except for the couple who'd taught themselves and their baby Ojibwe, and the Osage business jock with his all-Indian investment company. This time the speaker was from Montana. He had long, black-streaked gray hair tied back in a worn elastic. It slid down a little when he bent over sweetgrass. Or maybe sage? His cigarette lighter was beaded.

I felt jittery, and anxious for the talk to end. It would be a long wait after this before people went to sleep and I could sneak to Steph's room down the hall. When it was my turn in the circle, I cupped my hands and waved the air over the burning something, still unsure how to do it right. I brushed my palms across my face and felt the oil forever on my skin.

The elder had us say how we'd use our degrees to strengthen our nations. Beside me, Steph gripped the bottom of her chair and let go and gripped again.

Lawyer for Indian child welfare cases.

IHS doctor for urban Indian youth.

Director of a literacy program for Alaska Native youth.

Founder of a theater troupe to promote positive representations of the sovereign Indigenous female body, for youth.

Astronaut.

I escaped to the bathroom.

The mirror was foggy from a recent shower. I couldn't see myself in it. Someone had taped the periodic table to the door.

It was unclear how I planned on changing the world, or even what I'd major in. I felt my most noteworthy days were behind me. I wasn't sure I had what it took to be important on my own.

There had been a period of my life when I was fought over and famous. After that I was wrapped up in family, and community, and God's love. What was I supposed to be now?

I missed my grandmother.

The cemeteries in Poland had changed how I thought about my ancestors, and with my grandmother's death I felt like branches had been snapped off a tree and burned. The church valued genealogy, so I knew everything about my adoptive ancestors. I'd assumed Matthew could teach me about the Cherokee side of his family, but he couldn't. He said whatever people knew about the history of families like my grandmother's came from stories and memories you could hold in your head. No one had bothered to document them, except their names and ages and assumed blood quantum during allotment. I didn't know if people "like Grandma" meant poor people or something else, since I still didn't understand when Cherokees said "traditional" or "full-blood," or what other categories there were. I'd been too embarrassed to ask.

Alone in the bathroom, my back against the mirror, I tried to hold her in my head. I remembered the bed we'd shared. Grandma on the right and me on the left. Sometimes, the hooting of owls on the other side of the wall.

As had become our custom, I left Steph's room at six a.m. with a giant telescope in my arms. If anyone caught me in the hallway, I could tell them I'd just gone to borrow it from her. At night, we'd reverse this—I'd carry it back, so Steph could borrow it from me. The telescope was heavy and awkward, but she'd cleared a large space for it on a tripod under her window.

After breakfast, Sandra walked me and Steph to our first class, Animal Behavior. There was something belittling about being escorted there, considering we weren't freshmen anymore and Sandra was in our same grade, but she was a premed bio major and had helped us select the class. I'd needed something with a lab component for my science requirement. Steph said it just sounded fun to take a class with me. She had room in her schedule to consider what sounded "fun," because she'd declared her major in freshman fall. Her remaining required classes were plotted out perfectly through graduation.

Sandra left us on either side of the wide glass door. I needed space to keep from kissing Steph in public, and I was embarrassed by all the ways we'd touched the night before. A year ago, we'd moved fast. Now we had time, hours each night, and I'd spent the last few days burning in both shame and surprise. I'd been raised to expect a feeling like angels with trumpets in the heavens over my marital bed. Instead, I was just a body. I wanted someone to want to touch me.

Professor Andrews let everyone call her Lucy, but I couldn't do it. I thought allowing that was a bad call on her part, considering how young she looked already. I calculated how quickly a person could get out of grad school and secure a teaching position—was she even thirty years old?—before finding myself again distracted by the fact that she was Black. (I had never had a Black teacher before, not once in fourteen years of school, and had never noticed until then.)

Professor Andrews told stories about animals. She used these stories as a jumping-off point for terms I couldn't place. Dollo's law, warning coloration, the Bruce effect. I knew I was missing a whole layer that mattered, that bio-majors nodded to all around me. But the stories shook me awake.

I learned things about animals that were dark and upsetting, but also funny. I felt myself relaxing into biology each time I laughed, easing into it, even if I only understood things on the surface. Professor Andrews talked about a study on tadpoles. Related tadpoles in one pond, unrelated tadpoles in the other. The finding? Related tadpoles didn't mate as much. Why not?

"Incest!" I said.

Professor Andrews looked at me. A beat too long, but not unkindly. "Yes," she said. "But in the biology department, we like to call that inbreeding."

On Tuesday we had lab.

The lab had tables like the classroom, only they were riddled with microscopes and Bunsen burners, scales and chunky protective goggles. There was a showerhead for chemicals on your body, and two fountains for chemicals in your eyes. Everywhere warnings, everywhere signs.

I approached my new lab group, which Steph had already taken over. "I bet we could ask Lucy for more males," she said. Lizard males, she meant. "And then we could test how a male reacts to being in a tank with a female, versus with two or three competing males?"

Sam nodded at Steph. He was taking the class as, what he'd called, "an easy A." Beside him was a white Styrofoam cup of coffee with my name written on it in Sharpie. It was a sweet gesture, if against lab rules in case we poisoned ourselves.

"Della, hey!" he said. "I'm glad you came."

"Me too," Steph said. When she said it, it was kind of a joke. Like she hadn't woken up that morning with her arms around my waist.

I hadn't spent as much time with Sam lately, not since I'd become a sodomite. I could tell Sam knew things had changed for me in Poland. He'd want to sit down together and ask if I'd told my parents about Steph yet and say supportive things like, *They'd be crazy not to love you!*

But I wasn't ready to tell my parents, and Steph hadn't asked me to. Maybe she thought they knew already?

Neither of us talked about our parents. Steph talked about her sister sometimes, but only out of concern because her sister sounded like a mess. She was supposed to graduate high school in the spring, and Steph worried she wouldn't. Steph said her sister had no shame, which was lovely for her, but she was also hostile to "Eurocentric" models of success. It was the second part that Steph had no patience for.

When I went to the supply closet to select our first male lizard, Steph followed me in. The Carolina anole was browner than the lime green I'd expected from television, firm where Matthew's lizard-shaped fish bait had been fantastically gooey. I wanted to name it, but Steph said no.

"Things happen in labs," she said. As far as I knew, this was Steph's first time in one. That could have been obnoxious, but I liked the idea that she knew things.

She was like that in bed, too, guiding me along. It was easy to forget she was as inexperienced as I was.

In the supply closet, I sat on the floor and filled out the labels for each terrarium. I told Steph I'd never had a pet. She nodded and leaned against the shelves. It was dark and peaceful.

"Hey, Della?" she said. "Do you wanna be official?"

"Seriously?" I laughed. "We're *literally* in a closet."

"Ha ha," she said. She pretended to return to work. She looked so young and uncertain to me, cross-legged on the floor.

"I'm playing the long game here," Steph hummed, as if to the lizard before her. "If one were to want to officially come out and also have a girlfriend, then one might be glad to have been given the opportunity."

I laughed and leaned back on my hands. "Tell me one thing about me," I said, "that isn't, like, part of a game you're trying to win."

"What do you mean?"

"One thing." I looked down at my hands, at the empty white label I'd stuck to my palm. "If you really think we could be something—and like, I'm not even promising that because *some* people should just be happy they're getting what I wouldn't give them for a year, and getting it all the darn time now, in whatever way they like—"

"Hey!" she said. "You like, too!"

I paused. Nodded once. "If you really think we could be something, I need you to say something about me that's not to get you to some finish line."

Steph was quiet longer than I expected, and I didn't look up from my hands. I wondered if she'd gone back to her inventory sheet.

"I'm sorry I made you feel like this was a game. I told you I'm not as experienced as I seem, and . . ." She turned back to a whisper. "Well, I think I could get better? Like if I were a girlfriend, officially, I think I could be a good one?"

"*One thing*, Steph," I said. She was still talking about herself. It was hard to be firm with her, and I almost never tried.

"Okay. Sorry. Here's something—You left home a little after I got there."

Home and *there* meant Oklahoma.

Steph continued. "But the thing is, I remember you. We'd *just* moved; it was a crazy time for my family—" She stopped herself, took a breath. "And anyway, the tribe had a fundraiser for your family. A cookout? I was shy, but I saw you. You ran around in the grass with my little sister and a bunch of other kids, till my mother took us home."

I smiled. I ran my finger along the edge of the terrarium between us.

I didn't have that memory, but I wanted to. If I went back to Oklahoma and Matthew didn't care, Steph would still be happy to see me.

I felt the warmth of her body in the dim light beside me. She was a window, a way back to a place I had lost.

A female cuckoo bird will lay eggs in the nest of some other mother, so some other mother will care for her young. After the female cuckoo is gone, the cuckoo hatchlings drop the other mother's eggs from her nest. The cuckoo hatchlings, as the survivors, are the sole focus of the surrogate's parental energy.

My own adoption was desperately wanted, with medical bills and paperwork and lawyers. And if my biological mother *did* let me go and move on, if she didn't think I was worth any great investment in parental energy, did it matter? With all the many pulls on my heart, I told myself it could not.

On the couch in the basement of the nassie house, Steph sat beside me. The plane flew into the second tower.

They played it over and over again. We fought about changing the channel. We changed the channel, but it was everywhere.

The day passed. Our friends joined us. Sam put his arm around my shoulder. Steph stared at him, unhappy over the wrong thing, and then the news zoomed in on the face of a firefighter. His eyes tracked downward as a person fell to the ground. Steph left to call her sister.

On ABC, Peter Jennings looked like he'd been crying. He said he'd just checked in with his children, and that they were very stressed. "If you're a parent and you've got a kid in some other part of the country, call 'em up."

Dad called me long-distance from Utah. I left the basement and took my cell phone outside. I sat in the grass, in the sunlight, while he told me that everything would be okay. He said he had missed me like crazy over the summer, and hoped I'd come home for Christmas. He told me not to be scared. He said I was the light of his life.

Kin selection means doing what it takes for your genetic material to survive. Survival means being passed on.

According to kin selection, tadpoles are more likely to eat each other when they're third or fourth cousins than when they're siblings or first cousins. Red squirrel mothers will adopt related, but not unrelated, orphaned pups. Matthew has a biological need to take care of me and see me be safe in this world.

And yet, in the brief hours I thought the world would end, I wanted nothing more than to bury my face in Dad's thick-sweatered shoulder. I knew no safer place.

Many hours after the second tower fell, Sandra said, "Sorry if this is weird. But I ordered pizza? We still have to eat?"

The pizza was late, and cold. But in a fit of generosity, Sandra had ordered enough for everyone. It was delivered by an old man in a gray sport coat. He owned the restaurant. "Oh, I sent them home," he said, when Sandra asked about the high school kids who did deliveries. "Just in case," he added. He looked up at the sky, for what couldn't have been his first time that day.

Back on the couch, Steph slid closer to me. I felt her arm against my arm, the warmth, the weight. I didn't move.

After dark, Jason came over from his dorm. He was the only nassie who hadn't spent the day in the basement. He turned off the television and told us to go to bed.

"What about war?" said a freshman boy. "They could draft all the guys here."

Sam made a sound I couldn't interpret. Annoyance? Exhaustion? He stood up and stomped up the stairs.

"It doesn't work like that," said Jason. "Go to bed."

Later I went to Steph's room, without the telescope. I didn't knock. She sat alone on her bed, doing nothing, looking for something outside her window. I'd rarely seen her without a textbook within reach, or a binder. She looked scared.

"We're together now," I said. "Officially, publicly, all of it."

"Oh," she said. "Okay."

"I'm going to tell my mom and dad."

Steph nodded. I didn't think she understood what a big deal that was, because she didn't have any follow-up questions. She didn't even seem surprised. But that was okay. People were dying in the rubble, buried, and would be for days. We did not need to talk about my parents.

"If that happens again," I said, "you can put your arm around me. People will deal."

Steph looked terrified.

I shouldn't have said it could happen again. I didn't mean that. We'd seen images on TV that we shouldn't have seen, that we would never forget. No one had been there to stop us, to protect us.

I ached for my parents.

"Come here," I said.

I got into Steph's bed and pulled her in beside me. I took off my shirt and put her head on my chest. I wrapped her in my arms. We slept like that, my hands in her hair.

SEXUAL REPRODUCTION

October 2001

A month later, the war started. American flags were everywhere. Sam's sister, who'd been working on her GED after getting sober, was deployed straight from basic training to Afghanistan. He was furious about that, and wasted days trying to contact the recruiter who'd presented a Go Army slideshow for the residents at her halfway house. Jason told Sam it was pointless. "Then tell me," Sam said, "who the fuck else can I yell at?"

The rest of us, slowly coming to understand that there would be more death, and it would happen to people far from here, stopped watching the news at night. We turned our attention to other things.

My coming-out was not as dramatic as I'd expected. People were mostly nice about it when Steph kissed me on the cheek in hallways and library study rooms, way nicer than they would have been at BYU. I had already lost my friends from the LDS Student Association, during my faith crisis. The worst part about coming out would be coming out to my parents, but I planned to tell them in person. Winter break was still two months away.

Sam came out, too, but only to me. He said it was the war that had changed things. He was buzzing with anxiety and needed one person to know. What was the point of telling everyone—"throwing myself a parade," was how Sam said it—when he was determined to stay single? He worried about his sister all the time, and whatever energy he had leftover went toward his classes. "I can date when I'm a doctor," he said.

I felt accidentally chided, for letting Steph become the focus of my life when space travel was the focus of hers. For waiting alone in her room at night, to see her the moment she came home.

After that, I started joining Sam in the library. I even stayed late, which Steph did, too. But I made it a point to stay away from the basement level, where she liked to study alone.

The lizards wouldn't mate with our faces against the glass.

Steph had the idea to set up a video camera in front of the terrarium. We sat under the table, huddled around a television that was attached to the camera. We watched the male lizard flare up and approach the female. I squinted at its toes, its back, its tail, the way its feet raced forward and then froze.

We replaced the lizards and began again. I'd come to like that, how everything we thought we knew still had to be tested. I moved to prep the next trial, something the bio-majors in the group always raced to do themselves.

Sam jumped to his feet. "I can take care of that. These guys can be hard to get a good hold of."

"I got it," I said, tired of being useless. I already had a corner of the mesh terrarium top open. My hand slid down the warm glass walls, hovering above the lizard.

It stopped. Waited. Ran.

I swung my arm to the side, sweeping across the terrarium. I slapped forward, catching it by the tail.

"*Got it!*" I said. But the others were reaching out and throwing themselves on the floor, cupping their hands and cursing when they missed. There was the lizard, a little gray blur speeding across the floor. Steph caught it. I looked down. I was still holding the tail.

Sam walked slowly back over to me. "It happens," he said.

"They can give up their own tails?"

"Yep," Sam said. "But it's never something we want to happen. Growing a new one takes a shit-ton of metabolic energy. And it won't grow back as bone. Just cartilage."

The next day I came home to a terrarium on my dresser. There was the lizard, tailless still, with a palm-sized Hollis College diploma taped to the glass. He had graduated with high honors and a major in biology. The diploma had a gold gel-pen border and a background of red colored pencil. It was in Steph's handwriting.

Beside it was another terrarium, plastic and much smaller. Inside it, many live crickets.

Once a year, gray whales migrate from the coastal waters of Mexico to their Arctic feeding grounds. The mothers cannot head north until their calves are strong enough. The older whales and male whales leave. The mothers stay behind for weeks, nursing their calves until they're ready to make the journey.

Sometimes, this is when the orcas come in. A pack of orcas will coordinate an attack, each taking part in an hours-long battle to separate calf from mother. Sometimes the mother fights. She swings her tail and beats away the danger. Sometimes the calf is separated from the mother and killed. The mother swims on alone.

The footage would come to haunt me. I found it online after class one day, and returned to it when I was being unkind to myself. Sometimes I'd think, dramatically, what would it be like to be loved like that? To be protected?

If I thought too carefully about kin selection, and the careful order of the world of living things, I knew I was an outlier. Biology had taught me I didn't belong. I was made of traits and behaviors inherited from people who did not know me well. Who might not ever want to know me at all. What did it say if I knew the evolutionary history of greenish warblers but couldn't give a doctor my own family medical history?

I asked myself where I felt known and wanted—it had to be both. The answer, louder each time, was Steph.

I didn't know where my biological mother was. After she'd been made to testify in court, the newspapers had called her a bad mom. The case ended, and for the second and maybe last time in my life, I was taken out of the room she was in. She had since made herself impossible to find. I sometimes woke in tears over this, *still* sometimes, after all these years.

Steph turned over in bed. Every time, instantly. She pulled me into her arms and held my face to her chest. *Shh, shh.*

The night before our midterm I fell asleep in Steph's room with a textbook under my arm, waiting for her. She was in the library. She often stayed late there, much later than I did—because I was becoming someone who needed people, and she was becoming someone who didn't. We'd had to move sex to the early mornings, which I didn't like as much as at night, because it better fit Steph's tyrannical study schedule.

"Sure, I could chill out," she said, when I gently hinted that she was killing herself. "But if *I* chill out, and my ten thousand competitors don't, one of them will go to the moon."

"Wait, what?"

"Did you know," Steph said, "statistically, I have a better shot at having triplets than becoming an astronaut?"

"I thought you didn't want to be the, um, carrying partner?"

"Exactly."

We walked together to the exam, holding hands. I bought us both caramel macchiatos on the way and wrote xoxo good luck! on the sleeve of her cup. She did great. I got an F.

Professor Andrews summoned me to office hours. She said, "Your midterm."

I said, "Yes?"

"Before we delve into it," she said. "On the day you took this exam—was there a death in the family?"

There would be no writing off her class. Before this semester, she had never opened the course to nonmajors. "It would be a shame," she said, "if you made me regret my change of heart."

Professor Andrews went through my midterm with me. I remembered studying, how I'd memorized each animal study she'd told us about in class. My head was full of them. The midterm had been nothing like that. It was all graphs and charts and math problems. Analysis. Like there was a second, murky layer to everything, like groundwater. It flowed under my feet, unde-tected.

Professor Andrews said I had to turn in a first draft of every lab report and short essay, giving the TA enough time to make comments and return it to me for edits before the deadline. I had to record her lectures on a tape recorder and listen to them with headphones, which I did during group bead-ing sessions at the house. I still sat in a circle with the other girls, but I was somewhere else. Whatever they talked about I missed, for all the biology pulsing through my ears. Ring species. Food caching. Concealed ovulation.

Once a week, Professor Andrews had me come to office hours. Always the same day and time. I'd give her a summary of each unit. In the beginning, I made the same mistake I'd made on my midterm. I stayed on the surface, airy and full of human bias.

"When a male lion joins a pride," I said, "the first thing it does is kill off all the defenseless cubs. And when a baboon—"

She stopped me and set her hand down firmly on the desk. Her nails were short, neat, and manicured with see-through nail polish. She wore her hair in braids, swept into a loose ponytail at the nape of her neck.

"Hold up," she said. "Why are you telling me this? What's the point?"

"The lion . . ." I started. Stopped.

I tried again. "Well, we were talking about kin selection, which is about helping your genetic material get passed on. This new lion is the head of the pride, and he has no shared genes with the cubs hanging around."

"Take it further," she said. "What does that mean?"

"Survival is difficult. The burden of feeding and defending the pride will fall on him. The lion doesn't want—the lion *won't*—spend his energy fighting for genes inherited elsewhere."

Professor Andrews leaned back in her chair. She looked out the window, then back at me.

"He'll need to invest in his own offspring, when they come." I was careful not to say "children." I knew better.

"And there you go," she said, looking back at me. There was a change in her tone, a finality, and I knew we were done for the day.

"I realize you could recite back every story of the semester," Professor

Andrews said. "And that's a good thing. A sense of story is important in a scientist, and not everyone realizes that.

"But you need to focus on analysis now. On data, on patterns. When you're reviewing your notes, try to clarify what lies behind the story. I want you to ask why things are the way they are."

THE MINIMUM INVESTMENT

December 2001

On the last Sunday night before reading period, NASA had another guest. He was a Navajo poet—a young, attractive one, which was obvious from the event poster taped to the house refrigerator.

"*What* a hottie," said Sandra. She looked at me. "Oh. Oops, sorry!"

Sandra was uncomfortable with me being gay. Maybe especially with me being gay in the room above hers, though we weren't nearly as loud as some other people. Still, Sandra was a good friend. Because she'd grown up in a religious world with some overlap to mine, I knew exactly what she was doing. "Love the sinner hate the sin," "in the world but not of it," etc. Which was fine. I'd done that, too, before Poland.

I forgave Sandra, solemnly. Behind her back, I made a face at Steph. She was smiling at me, trying not to laugh.

I liked her so much. My girlfriend! I would never be sad again.

Steph and I went to lectures together at least once a week, and to almost every event sponsored by the astronomy or biology departments. She had cleared out several drawers for me, more than she'd left for herself. I'd even moved my lizard into her room so I could spend time with him and she could select the poor crickets for death. I'd named him Walela, off a list of Cherokee words I'd found on the tribe's website.

When Steph came home from the library, no matter how late, I would wake up and reach for her. I was happy, happy enough that when Steph pulled me close, I could set aside my parents and Matthew and my grandmother and God. I'd finally taken off my CTR ring, and eventually even my gold cross necklace, because it felt disrespectful to watch it bounce on my chest when I was on top. Lately, all I could think about was animal behavior, and how much I depended on Steph.

The female poison dart frog lays eggs on the rainforest floor. The male fertilizes them. He stands guard until they hatch. Tiny tadpoles wiggle up onto the mother's back, and she starts a days-long journey up one-hundred-foot trees. She carries them to a safe haven, to collected pools of rainwater in thick, green leaves.

As a child I demanded to be carried. The Cherokee Nation social worker and then the Provo child psychologist said it was a perfectly normal reaction to early childhood trauma. It would fade with the baby talk and the whining and the hiding my face in my father's pant legs.

I had sat on wooden benches in my shiniest shoes, through waves of court decisions and microphones in my face. When it was over, someone would pick me up and carry me away. Mom or Dad or Matthew. Always, I was chosen.

The poet read aloud for half an hour, which was too long. His poems were boring and had too many sheep in them. His hands gripped his chapbook so hard his veins stood out, green, and as I followed them down his wrists and up his arms, I thought about how risky I'd been with my life—earthly and celestial—since my decision to come out. What if I liked men, too, like this one, who really was so handsome? Sandra was right. What would it be like to have sex with him? Would he hold my arms above my head and smile approvingly, like Steph had done the night before? Was that what was wrong with poor Ethan, that he wouldn't have done that? And if I liked that, if I liked maybe any gender of person who might make me feel good doing things I felt bad about, could I still get sealed to a man in the temple? Did I want to? Or would I rather call Mom (like I'd told Steph I planned to, but that she had never checked in on) and make an official announcement, something about being GLBT? The poet shut the book; I snapped back into the world.

The poet answered questions. He talked about his inspirations and his writing process, the rough time he'd had growing up and how much his grandmother had meant to him. When he was put in foster care she tracked him down, then raised him herself with just the earnings from her weaving. Every time he wrote a poem, his grandmother had taped it to her bedroom wall, even though she'd never learned to read. His grandmother gave him a lamb, a real one, for him to help care for, and when his first poem was accepted by a literary magazine, she cooked the lamb for dinner. It was a bit much. Or I was jealous and missed my grandmother.

We went around and said what jobs we wanted, again. This time I stayed in the room, but lied. I said something about getting involved in social work back home, which was a phrase I'd started experimenting with to mean Oklahoma. As in, "there are harmful effects of colonization *back home.*"

Afterward, Steph followed me upstairs. She closed her door behind us, a little too hard. "Come on," she said. "Over my dead body will you major in *psychology.*"

I fell back on the bed, exhausted. "You might not realize, but I spent a lot of time with social workers when I was a kid. A few of them were Cherokee Nation employees. Who even knows where I'd be today, if it weren't for—"

"You'd be *here,* Della. You got into Hollis 'cause you got good grades. Not through the collective struggle of the Cherokee people."

I stared her down. Steph never went to the gym, but her body was sturdy in a way that looked grown-up. She looked ready to push her way through anyone, even me.

"I'm gonna ignore how weirdly hostile you are about being Cherokee," I said. "Because what matters—"

"Della—"

"No. What matters is that I don't want to be a scientist."

"Respectfully, you do. An animal behaviorist. I don't know, maybe you'll specialize in some ecosystem or species. But all signs point to you being a bio major."

Immediately, I thought of frilled sharks. They were my latest obsession, though I'd shared them with no one. It embarrassed me that I was so into them, and that I'd still never been to the beach.

Frilled sharks lived deeper than humans could reach underwater, some of them even in the Mariana Trench, and only once so far had one been seen alive. Their family lineage dated back to the Paleozoic Era, and they'd survived a mass extinction event that killed 80 percent of marine species.

"I'm not even good at science," I said.

"*No one* is good at science!" Steph was almost shouting. "It's just the scientists who stick with it. Sandra says the highest average in Chem II right now is a C-plus."

Two floors below us, the drum circle started up. A few of the boys practiced on Sunday nights. On the other side of the wall, Sam played a song on a CD player about a man whose girlfriend had left him. At night the man left every light in his house on, in case she changed her mind. Once a month Sam bought a new country album, listened to it, then mailed it to Afghanistan. He told me he felt guilty every day for leaving for Hollis when his sister had asked him for help.

I told Steph I needed to do something for our tribe, something crucial to the story of our survival. "Think about it. The last thing Cherokee Nation needs is a marine biologist."

I realized, as I said it, that this specificity had come from me. Steph had said animal behaviorist, which was close. But now that I had been asked, I knew. I wanted to be a marine biologist.

Steph let out a long sigh. "You know what my old science teacher said to me once, back in high school?"

"Wait, Steph, you mean your dad?"

There was a blink of pain on her forehead, the smallest of creases smoothed out. "Yeah, sure," she said. "Brett."

I didn't get where this was going. Steph's dad was really a stepdad, and she was almost as weird about him as she was about her bio-dad. That said something, coming from me! She'd told me her bio-dad died in a car accident, but she refused to answer questions or ever discuss him again. With her stepdad, she brought him up casually maybe twice a semester and kept his telescope pointed at the sky out her window. I didn't *think* he was dead, so maybe the telescope had been a gift.

"What'd Brett say?" I asked.

"He said to stop thinking of our tribe as its history."

"Huh . . . what does this have to do with you bullying me into being a bio major?"

Steph leaned back on the bed and closed her eyes. "Della, I know you think I'm selfish."

"What?"

"For wanting to be an astronaut. My sister thinks so, too. And my mom. It's fine. It's all fine. You don't *have to* be a scientist."

"You're giving up on my science career? Already?" I laughed, but Steph didn't join me.

"I don't think it's about being *crucial to the story of Cherokee survival* or whatever," she said, her voice too close to mocking me. "You do something, you're Cherokee—cool. Brett would say that's part of the Cherokee story. I just think you should be allowed, like any person without your, um, *your past*, to do what you want?"

Steph lifted her arm over her head, an invitation, and I laid my head down on her shoulder. She kissed me on the head. We both looked up at the ceiling, quiet, and listened to the music on the other side of the wall. The man with the glowing house sang that if he ever got over his ex, she'd know it when he turned the lights out one by one.

"What if I want something different from what you want?" I said.

"You definitely *do!*" Steph said. "If you ask me, the ocean is overrated. Earth, too."

"I mean something that could get between us. Like, what if I decide to stick with science, and then we get into two different grad schools?"

When Steph answered, there was less warmth in her voice than before. The difference was so slight, I wondered if I'd imagined it. "Della, we're sophomores," she said.

Something fell inside me. She could have made some vague gesture of compromise, knowing it wasn't a promise. Something like, *We'll figure it out together.*

She didn't really think it was too early to plan. I'd seen her color-coded lists of every active astronaut, their bios, and what degrees they had from which schools.

But maybe I was being unfair about commitment. Was this the natural order of things, for gay, godless college sophomores who hadn't said I love you yet? Was I still too afraid of losing people? Or of people choosing to leave me behind?

Sam turned off the CD player and banged his fists on our shared wall. He shouted about going to the cafeteria.

I slapped my hands fast against the wall, a little drumroll, and told him to wait for us.

Steph followed me to the door, swinging her winter boots by the laces. "Just think about what I said?" She kissed me hard.

"Do whatever I want?" I said.

"Yes. Whatever *I* want." She kissed me again, stepped back, and held open the door.

Parental investment is not equal across the board. Human males invest years of energy into providing for the extended childhood of feeding, protection, and education we have recently come to ask of them. Human females, too, though it's considered less heroic.

Then there's the minimum. The minimum investment required of a human male is the fertilization of an egg. Without medical support, the minimum investment required of a human female is about thirty-seven-weeks' development in utero.

I started to think about having a baby. Not that night, of course. That night I thought about the ocean and everything in it—how much I wanted to see it for myself.

But the more I learned about animal reproduction, the more I imagined what that might be like. I could be the start, sort of, of someone's family tree. One person on earth who would know me, need me, and share my genetic history.

The minimum investment, I realized, wasn't minimal at all. I started to imagine that I would, someday, be pregnant. I imagined that, when no one was around, I'd call the fetus inside me "baby" and "love." I'd spend two thousand hours lying in bed with my arms wrapped around myself, wrapped around my child, and I'd know that the woman who carried me had felt this once. Somewhere in Oklahoma, somewhere in two thousand hours already decades gone—maybe—I had been loved like that.

・ ・ ・

A week after the poet's visit, the Christmas lights came out. Everywhere on campus, still, were oversized American flags, faded in the rough weather we'd had since September.

I passed easily twenty of them on my walk to Professor Andrews's office to pick up the take-home final. She gave me her home phone number and told me to call if I had any questions. She said she'd stay near her phone for the next eight hours while our class was working through the test.

I got a B- on the exam, and a C+ for the semester. I went out with the nassie girls on the night the grades came in. We were all one step closer to something, whether or not we knew what it was. For that night, anyway, we stood close in a circle and danced in high heels through the throbbing in our feet and the sticking-unsticking of years of spilled beer on the frat basement floor.

We left the frat together, laughing at the mess of our knotted coats. Sandra and I had matching black Patagonias, and when she realized she was wearing mine, she spent the rest of the walk home pretending to be me. She hung on Steph's elbow and shouted horrific fake facts about the reproductive lives of pandas, scaring a freshman on the street. There were other jokes that followed, poking fun at every part of me, until Sandra fell screaming into a snowbank. But none were about my case, or about lesbians, or even about Mormons. Laughing, one in a chain of girls who said, "One-Two-Three, HEAVE!" to pull Sandra from the snow, I felt known.

We went to sleep around four, spread across the living room. We were wrapped in comforters and throw blankets and Pendletons dragged down the stairs from our beds.

I showered and jumped into sweatpants and snow boots. I nearly tripped over April and Jess, who touched foreheads in sleep but were not gay. I ran to the biological sciences building and made my way to the fourth floor, then down a hallway painted brown. It was so different from the carved wood and woven rugs of the English building, and the glass walls and metal beams of the chemistry building.

I entered a room with a large, cluttered table. Two empty coffee pots. On the bookcase perched a brown taxidermied owl. Beside it was the casting of a small species of freshwater shark. Everything smelled weird. I loved it.

Professor Andrews sat on the edge of the chair beside me, looking anxious to return to her own office. She reviewed a printed list of major requirements, which I would have two and a half years to complete. "For the next six months," she said, "you can still change your major."

Part of me wanted to reassure her, to reassure myself, of how sure I was. How biology had built a frame around me, a scaffolding. I could put the pieces of my life on it, because this was the study of life. There was space even for one like mine.

I could be happy with other things, I now knew. Other majors, other careers. In allowing myself to love *this*—to not become a social worker or a teacher or a nurse—I had filled in yet more of the details of that shadow-life we carry alongside us, the choices we could have made. Every year of my new adulthood, I thought, I would choose something, and I would un-choose something else, and the outline of that other woman I hadn't chosen to become would stand close to me, breathing softly at my shoulder, her hand gentle on the small of my back.

I had choices. This was the part of my life that I got to choose—so much of it is, I realized, when you are finished being a child—and I chose this.

I didn't need to explain that to Professor Andrews. She would have her own reasons for being a scientist, like Steph had hers. Like Sam, too, and Sandra.

Professor Andrews recommended I register for the bio intro class in the spring, Exploring the Cell. I wanted to make Steph laugh at that, how it was basically the opposite of her old class Exploring the Universe.

Professor Andrews signed my major card and wished me luck.

As I walked across the quad, I bent to pull my wool socks higher. Cold morning air blew straight against my skin through my shirt and unzipped coat. My cheeks stung from the slap of the wind, a winter storm on the way. I was ready to go home.

STEPH

WINTER CARNIVAL

Sophomore Spring
January 2002

In January, four months into us being official, I took Della to Dominic's Pizza
Kitchen. I told her I loved her. She told me she loved me back, and even
kissed me on the mouth inside the restaurant where anyone could see. My
neck burned over the tea light candle between us, and I pulled back. Della
held my hand across the table.

All was going according to plan. Della was officially a bio major now,
which would be good for her long-term happiness. I had waited an appropri-
ate amount of time to declare my love. While I'd assumed Della wouldn't tell
her parents about me quite yet, not till we graduated and she came along with
me to grad school, it turned out she'd already told them. This had happened
over winter break, her first visit home since she'd left for college, and she said
it had gone well.

"That's so cool of them," I said.

Della nodded, ordered dessert, and changed the subject to me and my
sister. How much fun had it been, the two of us reunited?

As an only child, Della loved the idea of sisters. She and Kayla sometimes instant messaged each other, despite never having met in person. They
seemed to really like talking to each other, behind my back.

"I barely saw her," I said.

"Don't you two still share a bunk bed?"

"When I *visit*," I said. I wished I hadn't shared that detail with Della, now that I knew she'd been one of those girls with a princess canopy over her bed.

"Kayla's busy," I added. "She spent a lot of nights out at parties. Plus, she's got a boyfriend and a job, and her blog has been picking up."

"I know, I saw her post about hitting fifteen hundred subscribers! I bet colleges will like that."

The dessert arrived, a chocolate mousse, and I stabbed my fork through it with a loud clack. I hadn't had a mousse before. I hadn't expected it to be soft, like lukewarm ice cream. Della was better than me at knowing what to do in nice restaurants, which she always paid for with her parents' debit card. Her money came from her parents' seemingly unshakable belief that whatever she spent money on must be important, and the trust that Della had built with her frugality.

I patted the corners of my mouth with the heavy napkin, like I'd seen Della do. "I'm sure they will," I said brightly. "She's just ironing out where to apply."

This wasn't true. Kayla had dropped out of high school almost one year ago, which she hadn't told Della. (And which, frankly, never would have happened on my watch. Our mother was asleep at the wheel.)

But in Della's world, everybody went to college. And Kayla still could. It was better to give it time. That's what my mother had said over the break, when I'd complained about Kayla not being parented. Why was Kayla posting photos of custom-order jingle dresses on her blog at four a.m.? My mother said, "You've gotta let your sister forge her own path."

Whatever happened to our mother's rules—the old ban on boyfriends, all the ways she'd once tried to protect us? It felt like as long as Kayla stayed geographically close to our mother, and maybe spiritually close to our tribe, she could run wild. I deserved a prize for being the good child, the one with an actual plan, but no such recognition was in sight.

Della didn't need to know any of this. I asked for the check, and Della signed her full birth name in loopy cursive on the bottom of it. I thought about asking if it bothered her to have to do that, to write *Emma*. Did her parents use money, maybe, to remind her where she belonged?

I didn't ask. Her trip home had gone well, and I had enough on my plate. All I could do was read Kayla's blog posts each day, watch her subscriber count steadily climb, and write dumb but encouraging things in the comments section like "wowza" and "great art!" I sent her brochures for community colleges and tribal colleges with visual art programs, and even for a four-year school (Haskell, in Kansas), hoping Kayla would perk up at the *Indian Nations University* in its name. She was a bad student but a good Indian. Where would that get her?

Then in February she fought with our mother, quit her job at the diner, and moved in with her least-mature friend, Brittany. Two days later, the friendship forever ruined, Kayla took forty-six hours of Greyhound buses to Hollis for winter carnival. She picked the lock on the door to my room, asked to join Della on her way to swim laps, talked poor Della's ear off about the Indian Child Welfare Act, sat next to Jason Palakiko at the weekly nassie meeting, had unprotected sex with him three hours later, and got pregnant with his baby.

Then she walked herself to the bus station, let herself into our mother's house, reenrolled at her old high school, got her old job back, and didn't say anything to anyone for months.

When Kayla told me about the pregnancy in May, I was in the library googling Jupiter's moons. She sent me an email that came out with both things right away—about the baby, and about the keeping of the baby—and I cried into my hands. Kayla wasn't going to Haskell Indian Nations University. Incredibly, for someone with just three remaining credits, she refused—again—to finish high school. I hated that part most of all, how her pride felt like spite.

Her life, I figured, was over. I put my head down in my arms on the gray metal table. A librarian brought me a thin plastic cup of warm water, which collapsed in my grip.

I walked, still crying, to the phone booth on the first floor and called Della's cell. She already knew. My sister, seeking advice and confidentiality back in her first trimester, had told Della first.

STEPH

JOYRIDE

Sophomore Summer
July 2002

Toward the end of the semester, Della asked to come home with me for the summer before junior year. Her parents were on a two-year mission in Lebanon, leaving Della with nowhere to go. Her bio-dad, literally famous for having wanted to parent her, had apparently said they should "get a bite to eat" over the break if she stayed with my family. Clearly something was going on there.

I thought all three of them were being weird. My own mother had only one more summer after this one when I would *have to* come home to her (meaning, when I'd be a student kicked out of housing on breaks), and she would never agree to losing one. I'd skipped out on her once, for Poland, and had never heard the end of it.

Della tried to defend her parents, if not Matthew. She said they really did miss her *so much*, but the Lebanon mission was coveted and nearly impossible to get. Middle Eastern countries were less permissive of missionaries, so her parents had been waiting for years to get their mission call letter. It was an honor, and I would understand that if my own short-lived religious life had gone beyond what Della called "Sometimes Church."

In June, my mother and Kayla picked us up from the Tulsa airport. They carried signs and a heart-shaped balloon, greeting us in the parking lot like returning soldiers. My mother looked so happy. She didn't know about the baby.

Every Thursday night, Della used her parents' debit card to take us all out for a thank-you dinner. She said her dad said it was the least he could do, but my mother was still careful to choose somewhere inexpensive. She told Della she'd be delighted to take the Ericsons out for dinner, whenever they finally got to meet. Maybe at graduation? Della smiled. Eyes wide, mouth full of potatoes.

After dinner one of those Thursday nights, I got in the driver's seat. My mother sat beside me. In my rearview mirror, Kayla and Della whispered, hands cupped over each other's ears like children.

I'd been furious with Kayla, back in May, for telling me after Della about the baby. Della could have told me, but I tried not to let myself be mad at her. Whenever I felt myself getting jealous of the trust Della seemed to place in my sister, or Sam, or even her adviser Lucy over me, I made myself think about her terrible childhood. It was my job to be gentle with her, to let her decide to let me in.

"Mom, can I tell you something?" Kayla said.

I stopped the car at an intersection, red light swinging lightly from a wire.

"Hm?" our mother said. Her hand was hanging out the window; she wore her favorite floral cotton shirt.

Now? I thought. *On the drive home from Burger King?* Still, I turned down the radio.

"I'm having a baby!"

A car screeched alongside us and came to a stop, both of us waiting for the light. It was a red truck, huge, sparkling clean. Two men sat in the front seat.

Kayla had silenced us. On the radio, a man and a woman bantered quietly about home insurance.

I leaned back and stared up through the windshield. Starless. I turned off the radio and my mother turned it back on.

"Ma?" Kayla said.

"I won't allow it," our mother said. "Absolutely not."

This was almost funny, considering how far along Kayla was. Five months! She was showing, even in the loose and flowy dresses she'd sewn for herself. It was weird of our mother to have wished away any notice of this.

In my peripheral view of the truck idling beside us, the passenger-side window lowered. I tightened my grip on the wheel.

"Mom, that's insane," Kayla said. "And there's nothing to worry about? I'm going to be a *good* mom."

"Oh? And I wasn't?"

Huh, I thought. It sure said something, her asking that.

The man in the passenger seat folded his arm over the edge of his car door. He rested his head on his palm. I knew he was close enough to reach out and touch me.

"Jason and I are keeping the baby," Kayla said.

"Who in God's name is *Jason*?"

To meet the man's eyes was to lose. To lock the car door was to lose. I was scared. He revved his engine, louder each time. From the seat behind me, Della put a soft hand on my shoulder, steady.

The light turned green.

"*Dyke*," the man said. He turned his head toward me and spit. He sped away.

I stayed there, foot on the brake. I felt the wet on my cheek. I couldn't bear to touch it. Della wiped my cheek, too roughly, with a crumpled napkin.

I made a right turn from the left-most lane, then a U-turn. Where was I going? Another U-turn. The radio was only noise. It took so much not to cry.

"It's the haircut," my mother snapped.

"The fuck?" I said.

Della passed me a tiny packet of tissues from her beaded purse, and I tore them all from the plastic in a fist. I bunched them together and pressed them to my cheek, though Della had already taken care of that. They—the man in the truck? My mother?—would *not* make me cry.

"*We do not talk like that!*" My mother punched a finger at the radio knob and the music stopped. "You girls are out of control."

She stopped herself. "Not you, Della. I only meant my daughters. You're doing fine, considering."

"Considering *what*?" Della said. "Ma'am," she added.

In the rearview mirror, Kayla raised a tentative hand. No one called on her.

"Respectfully," Kayla said, "Steph only meant that her lesbian haircut shouldn't make her to blame for her hate crime."

"I wouldn't call it *my hate crime*," I said.

Della rubbed my shoulders like I needed comfort, which was embarrassing. "But isn't it a bi haircut?" she whispered too loudly. "Do they know you're bi?"

I banged my head against the back of my seat. I hadn't thought I was bi since freshman fall! Della and I never talked about our sexual orientations with each other, which felt like something clinical or administrative. I wanted everyone around me to forget my gayness immediately upon learning it, to avoid situations like this.

"Oh, honey, I'm not blaming you," my mother said. "Haircuts like that are sacred to the lesbian people."

"Jesus take the wheel," I muttered. My mother said *the lesbian people* the same way she might say *the Seminole people* or *the Muskogee people*. I missed another turn.

"I'm only looking out for your safety. You were so beautiful. You used to have such long, dark hair. And it might have kept you a little safer from . . . people like that."

"Mom, her hair's light brown?" Kayla said. "Like, that hasn't changed?" She must have been relieved. We were supposed to be talking about her pregnancy, and her vendetta against public education as a colonizing force, and her lack of plans for the rest of her life.

I did not want to be beautiful. I wanted to stop the car on the side of the road and leave them there, together.

I wanted to spread a towel on the grass below a short and leafless tree, to wait for the space station to fly by. It always did, if you knew what to look for. It was a constant in my life, arriving where and when it was scheduled, pointing me to where I belonged. I'd find it, white speck falling slow across the sky—and I'd picture an astronaut watching me back. Some astronaut would call his daughter through mission control and she'd say tell me what you see and he'd say oh, the Northern Hemisphere, North America, and that would be true, but also true was Oklahoma, a field, a tree. A girl alone, looking up.

Kayla's announcement ruined July, as well as the first half of August. One night, while Kayla and my mother were once again yelling at each other across the room, I said to Della, "Don't you wish you were converting the Lebanese?!" She looked confused, then laughed, then left the house to get some air.

It was after midnight. I was making my bed in the living room (with Della staying with us, Kayla and I switched off weeks on the couch).

Della came back inside, her face expressionless. "The LDS mission in Lebanon is non-proselytizing. It's strictly humanitarian," she said, and then left the room again.

When our mother was at work, Kayla would follow me and Della around and talk shit about her. Kayla said she couldn't stand our mother's disappointment and practical mindedness. She hated how our mother brought home help-wanted flyers and little ripped-off phone numbers for house cleaners and babysitters. How she picked up brochures for community colleges and left them under Kayla's pillow like the tooth fairy. How she nagged Kayla to be ready to "provide" for her baby, which meant less time making art and regalia and posting photos of it on her blog. (This was, I thought, fair.)

I thought Jason could be helpful here—unlike Kayla, he had plans. In the car before my hate crime, Kayla had said "Jason and I" when it came to keeping the baby. But I had no reason to think he even knew Kayla was pregnant. Weirdly, our mother hadn't asked about him once.

In the last week of summer, when Kayla still claimed to be "figuring stuff out," our mother summoned us all into the living room. Very delicately, she brought up the matter of adoption. Kayla stormed out the front door, Della close behind. Our mother stormed out the back door.

At eight o'clock, still alone in the living room and waiting to see how far they'd take this, I made myself a peanut butter sandwich. I sat at the computer and read the bios, again, of the seven astronauts chosen for the upcoming *Columbia* mission to space. Then I climbed out on the roof and squinted up at the sky, but there was more light pollution in our area than there'd been in my childhood. I missed my telescope, in storage in Connecticut, or maybe I just missed Brett.

The night before I graduated high school, Brett had driven over to my mother's house to give me his telescope. It wasn't supposed to be like that. The summer before senior year, Brett and my mother had promised he'd keep parenting us. They'd put a weekly family dinner on the calendar. But between our mother's crying and Kayla's sudden rise in acting out that year and my constant anxiety around college application season, it was canceled more often than not. By the time I got into Hollis—*off the waitlist*, a secret I'd take to my grave—I hadn't seen Brett in a couple of months. He'd had to hear about Hollis at work, off a bulletin board list of student achievements.

The telescope had been repaired and cleaned. It had a velvet bow around it, elaborately tied—maybe Beth's doing. Brett gave me a heartfelt greeting card with his phone number and new address on the back, and said he'd always be there for me and Kayla. He couldn't wait to see where our lives would take us.

I was cold to him that night, and never wrote back to the letters he mailed to me at Hollis. It took a year for him to stop writing, and for me to move his telescope from my dorm closet to the window. If he were with us now—even just with me, here on the roof—I wasn't sure he'd like where our lives had taken us.

Della brought my mother and Kayla home at ten o'clock and asked to speak to me in private.

"The three of us figured it out. It's handled now." Della said *the three of us* with some attitude, like I should have been the one to facilitate this treaty.

But no one wanted that. My best advice would have been an abortion—followed by a GED, a Pell Grant, a free associate's degree, and the grades to transfer to a four-year school. The abortion part of this plan would have only been relevant if Kayla had told me earlier. When she'd told Della.

With Della as mediator at a waffle restaurant nearby, this was where they landed:

Our mother would not provide free housing to Kayla and the baby, not unless Kayla had a job. She also had to have a savings account (I was horrified to learn that Kayla kept her money in cash, in a clay pot under her bed, in solidarity with reservation Indians living in bank deserts. I was pretty sure this was something she'd decided on her own, and not part of a movement any reservation Indians had asked for).

Kayla would not get "stuck in a job" that was not the right fit, "like Mom," an addendum that did not go over well with Mom.

Kayla would tell Jason about the baby, and Jason would decide for himself on his contribution to the cause.

My contribution was, apparently, financial—and not for me to decide for myself, though they knew I had almost nothing. I would pay to fly Kayla, now fully six months pregnant, back with Della and me to Hollis.

I SPENT A STAR
AGE IN FLAMES

Junior Fall
October 2002

Homecoming brought the Native Alumni Association to campus. We called them Big NASA and they called us Little NASA. They were there to make us spaghetti and to network and advise. None of them were astronauts.

My sister, dressed in all-black, sat at the head of the table. She leaned back on a pillow in her chair, at the only angle she said let her breathe while pregnant. Jason was in the kitchen, piling food for her on a plate. Della and Sam and Sandra sat on either side of her, also dressed in all-black. Had I been left off an email?

When I asked about it, Sandra laughed like I was joking and said, obviously, it was in protest of the op-ed. Kayla had stolen all my friends.

I'd fought hard to get to Hollis. I still had to fight to distinguish myself for my eventual application to be an astronaut. Meanwhile, I saved money for grad school. I let grad students do experiments on me. I ate ten almonds a day for six months with weekly urine samples, listened to classical music while people looked at my brain, and even sold plasma on what I'd come to call Plasma Mondays. I got very close to becoming a rich person when I was approved to sell my eggs, but Kayla tattled. Our mother said it would kill her, knowing her grandchildren wandered the earth in anonymity. When I tried to complain to Della, she was disappointed in me. "Steph, they would be your genetic offspring," she said. "It's a biological imperative that you care for them, which I hope is worth more to you than five thousand dollars."

In great contrast to my willingness to succeed in college by doing *whatever it takes*, Kayla had just shown up. Free. She was squatting in Jason's dorm room, except when they revisited the fight about how she hadn't told him about the baby until August, or the one about how she still didn't have a job. When that happened, she slept in Della's room, since Della slept in mine.

Over a paper plate of spaghetti, Sandra told Big NASA about the op-ed. She got louder as she talked, excited, her beaded headband slipping back from her hair. The op-ed referred to the latest ruder-than-it-had-to-be article in the *Hollis Examiner*, a conservative student publication on campus.

In the op-ed, the editor wrote that the nassies' recent event for Indigenous Peoples' Day—in opposition to Columbus Day—was an attack on America when America was still in mourning. *In this historic moment of collective American pain, the Native American Student Association must stand either with our country and its fallen patriots, soil still fresh on their graves—or with al-Qaeda.*

"And y'all voted not to retaliate?" asked one of the alumni. "You won't even publish a rebuttal?" He had shoulder-length, graying hair in thin braids that ended in tiny wet curls.

"*Some* people were strongly against it," Della said. She glared at me, but I knew it was only half-real. Della and I had voted on opposite sides of the issue the night before, even raising our voices during open debate. But afterward she stomped to my room, pouting; took her clothes off, forcefully; threw them at my head, laughing; and fell asleep in my arms.

The alumni made fun of us. "Ohhh, you might wanna rethink that vote," one of them said.

These were people who had known real trouble on campus, far beyond the op-ed. They were some of the first Native students to enroll back in the seventies, and the first thing they'd done was fight to have the school's Indian mascot banned. They spent years burning its effigy in the lot behind the football stadium on game days, even chaining themselves once to the president's gate. They made local headlines with a hunger strike, though it ended quickly for final exams.

Now they said, darkly, "It's never over."

They said, "You have to fight back when these people give you trouble, or they'll never stop coming for you."

One of them put his hand on my knee, and my stomach dropped straight down to the basement, but he didn't squeeze. "You're a part of this now," he said, staring straight into my eyes. "And it's never gonna stop. If you don't want to let it take over your lives here, you have to act."

"We come from warriors," said a man at the end of the table. He wore a ripped, faded American Indian Movement shirt, which looked older than he was.

"We *are* warriors," he added, nodding at Jason and Sam.

Jason, a literal veteran, nodded back. He stood behind my sister and held her shoulders in his giant hands—not romantically, but protectively.

Sam gave me a (rare) knowing look, like, *oh cool, straight guys.* It was the kind of thing he would have normally shared with Della, but Della was culturally straight and fully taken in by this display.

I didn't feel like I was a warrior, not that the men at the table thought I should. I didn't feel like I came from warriors, either. I felt like I came from exhausted women.

Every year, on homecoming weekend, the seniors built a bonfire and made the rest of us run circles around it. The event had been canceled the year before. This year it was back on, in order to "not let the terrorists win."

Some students at the bonfire wore red, white, and blue in support of the troops in Afghanistan. Some wore all-black, in protest of the coming war in Iraq. And some wore Hollis-crimson, like it was any other year. The nassies had voted to skip it, in protest of the op-ed, but I went on my own out the back door.

It was always when I felt the least secure in something that I was the most defensive of it. I wouldn't admit it to Della, and especially not to Kayla, but the op-ed had left me feeling shaky about my place in *the greater Hollis community*. Skipping the bonfire felt like surrendering to the idea that they didn't want me. I wanted to be part of a Hollis tradition, like everyone else was. I wanted to paint red streaks under my eyes and run in circles like I belonged, until I believed it.

I started my one hundred laps, my neck weighed down in plastic necklaces that slapped my chest. One side of my body froze in the chill night air. The other side, the fire side, dripped sweat down to my socks. I was one of *hundreds*! Hundreds of the smartest kids in the country! I was also, immediately, out of breath.

A line of boys ran into the circle, all in red Speedos. Maybe thirty of them? Maybe a frat? They melted into one another.

They were shouting, singing—it was the school's old, banned fight song. "HOO WA HEY! HOO WA HEY! UGA WUGGA UGA WUGGA HOO WA HEY!"

A girl I'd been following for many laps, her hair pulled back in a gold-and-red scrunchie, was picked up and thrown over a boy's shoulder. She laughed and cheered and beat her fists against his back in mock-resistance. "Ha," I said, trying it out. Look at me, being chill.

Rough fingers pinched my waist. I screamed. I jerked away, and a hand scratched my hip. I ducked under the police tape that separated the runners from the crowd.

I shivered on the lawn outside the library. There was a little dip in the grass outside the building, with a grate I thought of as my own.

That was something my mother had taught me: find a place to be yours. "It could be a sewer, for all I care," she'd said. "Just so long as no one can find you there."

Since my first month at college, the grate had been mine. Even a year later, when I'd started dating Della, she'd never had to know about it. I could finish up in the library and sit directly over it, warm air venting up from the ground. I could look at the sky and be with myself for a while.

I was tired of being with myself.

I sat on the grate and picked the red paint off my cheeks with my fingernails. I thought about Della sipping cocktails at the bar in town right then, the fizzy sweetness, laughing with our friends and the alumni.

I thought about my sister's baby in the room with them all, in a way—the baby was supposed to have working ears now, and was so close to being born. What kind of world would they meet? I worried about the war in Iraq, though we'd already invaded Afghanistan. I worried about weapons of mass destruction, though I didn't know if they were in Iraq. They were already here, meaning everywhere, twenty thousand of them positioned around the Earth. I worried about nuclear war, and how little we'd done to save ourselves on Mars or the moon. When the time came, there'd be nowhere to run.

The next morning, the president of the college sent an email to campus. "The Incident at Homecoming," though not strictly in violation of the Hollis College code of conduct (and therefore not strictly meriting any disciplinary action), had indeed not been in the spirit of the Hollis College value of community respect.

Sandra decided we should steal the frat's beer pong table. The pong table had been a focal point in the basement of Alpha Omega since the seventies, disposable cups knocked over the face and chest of a painted Indian girl.

This time, there wasn't a vote. Sandra waited till midnight, started out the door, and assumed (rightly) that we would follow her.

With a thick knit scarf wrapped around her arm and elbow, she broke the window in the basement door of the frat. As the heir to all of Minnesota's Subways, which Sandra had finally admitted to after Jess googled the cost of her snow boots, she agreed she could afford to risk getting in trouble.

Sandra reached through the jagged opening and turned the lock from the inside.

I volunteered to be lookout. Nick did, too. He was a freshman, a Black Cherokee from California. When we'd met, we'd tried to play the what-Cherokees-do-you-know game. (I had waited till Della left the room, as she was sensitive about being terrible at it.)

Nick knew Brett from an event in Bakersfield. Apparently, Brett had taken a political interest in Cherokees who lived outside of the tribe's jurisdiction, and made up the majority of tribal citizens. He traveled around the country, to places like Bakersfield, to try to better engage them. I'd told Nick that Brett had been my teacher, just my teacher, with enough unnecessary hostility in my voice to kill the conversation. Now the two of us stood in awkward silence in the dark, waiting for the pong table to be carried past us.

Later, on the edge of the riverbank, Sandra and Della flipped the table onto its side. The ice cracked sharp and fast, too thin to hold any more than itself. The table disappeared downstream, face down.

That night in bed, I thought of my father. I remembered his voice, his judgment, how fearful I had been. I remembered him saying that Kayla and I weren't Indian. Or we might be, a little bit, but it didn't matter. Our mother would tell us stories, and he'd untell them later. "Don't get mixed up in that stuff," he'd say. "When we're fighting for space in a fallout shelter, no one's gonna care what my grandpa was, before American."

Now I realized this implied my great-grandfather was from somewhere else, and my mother had not told me where.

At Hollis, my father's message had merged with other things. Things I had read, or seen on the news, or heard people argue in class—until I felt like I could imagine his view on the world, the one I would have known if we'd stayed with him.

My father would say our mascot war was trivial. A real war was coming, between survivors of the Earth. He would look at us on the riverbank in the dead of night, the table sinking through cracked ice. He'd scrunch his eyes together. He'd say half of us were racially white—unplaceable Indians. He'd say that if we didn't live together and walk everywhere in a group together, and minor in Native American Studies, and sign our emails with some version of "thanks!" in our respective indigenous languages—none of this would have happened to us.

I should have just kept my head down. I'd let myself lose sight of too much.

Two days later I walked home from the library. It was early, still dark. I'd spent most of the night working on a presentation in Russian, a class I was taking in hopes of cooperating better with cosmonauts on the International Space Station. I hadn't spoken a word of Cherokee in more than two years.

"Gavareetye pazhalooysta pomyedleeney," I whispered to myself, practicing my accent.

I was tired, but proud of my progress. I imagined myself in microgravity beside a Russian crew member, both of us in jumpsuits and fuzzy socks, both of us sipping from packets of Capri-Sun.

I liked the wind around the coat my mother had bought me before the school year started, especially how it had come folded between tissue paper in a box with a ribbon. The coat was cerulean blue like a NASA flight jacket, but long and fitted and silver-buttoned. It wasn't practical, which my mother knew I too often was, and—though late—it felt like permission to be happy.

She might have just been glad I wasn't pregnant. Kayla hadn't been presented with a back-to-school coat. Not that Kayla was in school. She was just *at* school, hanging out. Kayla was like a stowaway on a boat, her baby like a stowaway within a stowaway, only nobody cared! Jason fed them (at least, he fed Kayla) three times a day from his tray in the cafeteria. Kayla was really, really big now, yet apparently invisible to the Campus Dining staff.

I turned onto Maple Street and walked across the quad. I passed the registrar's office and the admissions center, first in the line of old brick buildings. They were covered in white flyers. I stepped closer.

My own face was on a flyer, and next to it was a copy of the same flyer, and next to that were dozens more, in straight rows across the walls. On the flyer was a collage, photos pasted over the background of our school's only censored mural.

The mural could only be uncovered by the special collections librarians, by appointment, usually for Native American Studies or Gender Studies classes. It was a mural of naked Indian women, live-painted from white women attending Smith in the 1950s. Under them, the song about the missionary and founder of the school. *Old Sir Ishmael taught them deep in the pines / With the Good Lord's Word and a barrel of wine.*

Pasted over the faces in the painting, for whatever point these flyers wished to make, were our faces.

There was my face, the grainy black-and-white version from the freshman face book. And Della's and Sandra's, and several others. The twelve of us leaned against trees in the forest, giggling into our hands or holding sprigs of pine over our privates. A painted, delicate version of my right hand cupped a rounded version of my left breast, in offering.

Back at the house, I stayed downstairs. I was too tired to deal with Della, and how she'd react if I told her. She'd cry or get angry. She'd want to hold hands and process a conflict that was irrelevant to the life I wanted.

Even in the best-case scenario, I'd go upstairs and Della would sleepily roll over to meet me. She'd lift her shirt, eyes still closed. There was a hum she did in the mornings sometimes, a kind of helpless sound that killed me. There was a good chance she'd lift my hand and drag it down her naked body, after my all-nighter, which had come after an exam, and after another protest against the Iraq War that she'd dragged me to.

When I woke on the couch a couple of hours later, I was already late for my own presentation. I threw my coat on over the clothes I had worn all night and the day before, and ran across campus, cringing under the feel of my own oily skin. The sky was a gray blue, and the coffee shop across from the admissions building had a line that snaked out the door.

I turned onto the quad, students racing across it between classes, and stopped.

All along the buildings that circled us, professors lined the walls. Their backs were to us, and they swayed from foot to foot as they worked. Oxford shoes wet in the morning dew and narrow heels sinking in the ground. All the khaki, brown, and black in Connecticut. Facing the theater department and the biology building and the registrar and all the walls in between. So many of them, their jacketed shoulders touched. Our teachers, together, tearing flyers from the walls.

Sam called a meeting that night.

I spoke quickly, urging everyone to let the college disciplinary committee deal with the flyers. The flyers were gone now. There was a process in place.

Sam interrupted me to say that, over a private phone call with a dean earlier that day, he'd been told that the frat would not be placed on probation. Sam had insisted to the dean that the flyers were the frat's second strike—a second strike that pre-law Jason had declared a Title IX violation—and that either way, a second strike always meant probation. The dean had said that the flyers fell under free speech, though like the Incident at Homecoming, they were not in line with the values of Hollis College.

I tried again, from another angle. Didn't we want to graduate? Wasn't that—wasn't graduating—the most important thing that we could do? *For our people?*

Della didn't bother raising her hand. She stood up. "I think some of us"—she meant me—"are under a lot of pressure to keep up with the other students here on an academic level. I know that can be very hard."

Was Della telling everyone I was an idiot? Della, my closest friend, my *girlfriend*, who had cried in my arms that afternoon at having seen her image, once again, in public—Della was telling everyone I didn't deserve to be here?

"But honestly," Della said, "we have a responsibility to future Native students, and to their sense of personal safety at Hollis. The administration—the president of the college, specifically—has been very clear that he won't protect us."

"Unless we make him," Kayla muttered.

We? She wasn't even supposed to be here! Yet here she was, absurdly pregnant, sitting stone-faced on a fucking birthing ball in the corner of the room. She was still planning on an unmedicated dorm birth, which was insane, even after I'd filled out and mailed in her application for Medicaid.

Frozen rain tapped against the window. Nick typed fast on a laptop, heavy-fingered. He was the new nassie secretary. I hated that this would be written down.

"It was nice of the teachers to take down the flyers," Sam said. "But to change the culture here, we need the attention of the administration. Della's right. We should demand a statement from the president of the college."

"We should protest outside his house," Della said.

Kayla nodded at Della across the room, her head in rhythm with her bounces on the ball. I wanted to throw something at her.

"And we should do it tonight," Della said, and she sat down.

"Are you *out* of your *mind*?" I said, standing.

In the back of the room, Jason snorted.

Sam banged his gavel. He'd bought it himself at a thrift shop, crazy with power since being elected nassie president. "Sit down, Steph," he said. He dropped the gavel dramatically beside his dinner plate.

When I didn't move, Sam gestured at my seat with a slice of pizza.

I sat down.

I could get arrested. Or expelled. Or photographed in a newspaper article that would still be on the internet when my NASA app was being considered. Any of these options would ruin my career. The only reason I joined Della at her Iraq War protests was because they'd been pre-authorized by the college.

I stood back up. "What if we wait one day," I said. "Give it one day, and I volunteer to submit the paperwork with campus security to officially—"

"Steph," Kayla said, before an overly long pause. The pause involved huffing and puffing. "Should you go outside and cool down?"

If we were children, and if she weren't constantly out of breath, I would have crossed the room and tackled her. As it was, she did wide, weird hip circles on her birthing ball while Jason pushed on her lower back. Whatever was happening over there felt a little too animalistic.

"I'm sorry," I said. "I just worry. We have our whole lives to regret this."

"All right, Steph, you've said your piece," Sandra said. She looked bored.

"Is this what the world needs from us right now? Us kids in our ivory tower? What about the war in Iraq?"

Sam laughed. "That is literally the *first* thing you've ever said about Iraq."

Della looked disgusted. "Seriously, you have no sense of moral—"

"Della, please!" I said. "You were raised *white*."

Nick stopped typing. Della took one long, heavy breath.

I lowered my voice. "I mean, we all appreciate your situation." I gestured around the room. No one would meet my eye.

I tried again. "I get where you're coming from. But you don't have to prove yourself by getting pissed at some shit that's brand-new to you."

"And there it is," Sam said, his voice low. Like he'd been waiting for something to make Della break up with me. He leaned back in his chair, crossed his arms, and stared me down.

Sandra laced her fingers with Della's. Jess wrapped an arm around her shoulders.

Della looked at me like she was years older than I was, like there were hundreds of moments of hurt in her eyes and now I was one of them. Like no matter what happened next, I would always be one of them.

Della told me once what she was most afraid of. It was the night that I'd first told her I loved her. She said she worried she'd never get back what was taken from her. That she'd never feel known and wanted as all that she was.

She had trusted me to see her.

I sat back, low in my seat, and slowly the air shifted.

People talked about the timing for the protest that night, and who had cardboard for signs. I traced the pattern of the wood grain on the dining table, the stains and scratches, and I wished I were somewhere else. But where could I go?

The meeting ended. I tried to talk to Della. She nodded, silently, encircled (*protected*, I worried) by her friends. She didn't get a real apology. Sam reached across Jess to squeeze Della's shoulder, and he rolled his eyes when I finished. Della looked at me and hesitated. She was on the edge of something. Maybe giving in?

She stood and took a step toward me, shrugging off the many hands that held her. She lifted her own hands to the space between us—maybe in forgiveness, maybe habit. Then she brought them down, clasped them together behind her back, shook her head, and left the room.

I spent most of that night in the library, avoiding my friends (*if they're even still my friends*, I thought, hunkered down in self-pity). I sat at a long table reading in Russian, not understanding, my finger moving slowly across the page.

I tried not to think about what I had done. I thought about my sister, only two weeks from her due date. If she drew attention to herself with this protest, surely the school would notice she was squatting.

Mostly I thought about Della.

Della had flicked on a light switch inside me. When I met her, there were suddenly all these *things* to be aware of that I didn't want to look at, shirts and pants I had at some point folded into the darkest closet of myself. The powerlessness I'd felt as a child. The pain. The striving of my family and nation.

The way other people saw me, and the way other people left me, and the way I left other people. The fear of who I was and the fear of who I was becoming.

All of these, Della saw. She pulled them out, unfolded them, and asked me to help her understand. She hung them on a clothesline in the front yard. She talked about her own life, and mine, openly.

I was ashamed. Della was not. Where I found weakness in my past, she found strength in hers. She found defiance, persistence, absolute confidence in the full story of her life. Even the parts that had been written for her—she felt sure she would write them again.

From my table in the library, I heard faraway shouts. I opened the window to the freezing cold. I heard the banging of sticks on a gate.

Then, around midnight, sirens.

THE SKY BEYOND
THE SKY BEYOND THE SKY

Later I learned what had happened to my sister. Where she was when I was in the library, and how she got there. Like everyone, I saw the photo.

After that night we would always call it that—The Photo. First printed in the *Hollis Daily News*, and then the *Naugatuck Crier*, and then *The New York Times*. It was everywhere.

In the photo, my sister stands defiant, under a low, old-fashioned gas street lamp, one arm in a fist above her head. The other is handcuffed to the president's gate. Della kneels in the corner of the frame, shielding her face from the camera. The first time I saw the photo, I wanted to pick up her crouching body from the newsprint and hold her safe in my palm.

In the photo, my sister wears something between regalia and performance art. A long, high-necked, fitted white dress. The cut is feminine but severe, silver-buttoned, like shirtwaists in the boarding-school era. In a wide curve under her belly, where my sister carries her baby, the first row of perfect, silver-colored jingle cones. Each tin cone hangs from a tiny, knotted satin ribbon. Red, perfectly placed. Glinting. As the rows of cones repeat down the dress, the length and placement of the ribbons become uneven. The cones collapse into themselves, as if crushed in many fists. They're muddied, cut into sharp and jagged shapes, missing altogether. She has dipped the full hem of her dress in something red.

In the photo, the other protesters wear jeans, coats, and hats. They did not bring handcuffs. My sister's handcuffs are beaded, neon pink and blue and purple. Like she has been waiting for a night like this. They are glow-in-the-dark, spotless, shining.

In the photo, campus police surround her. There are thirteen of them, the crimson Hollis crest sewn to their black collared shirts like my sister has crossed into a new nation. On the other side of the gate, in the far back corner of the photo, spilling out of the president's house: a yellow light. The shadow of someone—someone small, a child?—stands in a window, holds back a curtain, looks down.

In the photo, my sister is having contractions.

In the photo, Jason stands in front of her. His arms are wide, his body is between my sister and the officers. He is chest to chest with one, his eyes terrified but his posture tall. I can see the past version of him, the soldier, part of the peacekeeping patrol on the Kosovo border. He is shouting something. There's a bend to his knees. If you look carefully, you can see the sweat on his face. The muscles tight in his jaw.

In the photo, Kayla looks up and the camera flashes white against her skin. Her mouth is wide, screaming. Her face is angled toward the lens and her eyes scrunch into flattened stars. There is a flicker of strength at the corner of her lips. She looks determined, happy almost, even in this wave of pain.

STEPH

SURPRISE

Two Months Earlier
September 2002

In September, before homecoming and what I said to Della and the birth of my niece Felicia Palakiko, I turned twenty-one years old. I had never had a happier birthday. When I was lonely, later on, I would torture myself with memories of it.

Della threw me a surprise party. The theme she chose was *Columbia*, because the shuttle's upcoming mission would be in January and I'd been counting down to it for months. I had memorized the names of the seven astronauts, where they were from, and what they had done to make it this far. I knew where they'd gone to college and grad school. I knew the names of their children, and how old they were. That last part was what Della called "going too far."

I sat beside her on our bed, textbooks still in my arms, and looked around.

Planets hastily drawn on notebook paper, taped to the walls. Rockets made of toilet paper rolls, swinging from the ceiling at the ends of mint-green floss. Captioned images of the Crab Nebula and the recently discovered black hole MACHO-96-BLG-5, printed in black and white, hanging from the posts at the foot of our bed. There were posters of the *Columbia* shuttle— hand-drawn by my sister. My desk was littered with candy. Milky Ways and Mars Bars and Galaxy Bars and gum—Eclipse and Orbit.

I could picture Della standing on a chair, ripping tape from the roll with her front teeth. Cursing at the printer for turning colorful star systems into gray-and-black squares.

Della, like most people, didn't care about *Columbia*. What set her apart was, at best, her extraordinary thoughtfulness. At worst, how she could quietly fold her life into the envelope of another person.

Della cleared her throat. Everyone jumped out of their hiding places and sang. We did shots.

Della held a bite of cake in her hand for me, and when Sam turned around to pour more shots, I sucked the icing off her fingers. She looked at me like I was in trouble and then laughed.

Nobody but me knew anything about *Columbia*, but they were kind and drunk and happy to play along. They appreciated a weird party theme, like when the Sigma Chis filled their basement with foam or the Sigma Nus filled their basement with sand. Della put the names of five experiments planned for the mission in a hat, and made everyone guess them through charades. If they got them wrong, everyone had to drink. Della asked me trivia questions about the shuttle's previous missions, and if I got them right, everyone had to drink. Della taped the names of the seven astronauts on our foreheads and had us walk around and ask questions to figure out which one we were. Everybody lost. I won! Della put a blindfold on me in front of a map of the US, spun me around, kissed the back of my neck, and said to pin the shuttle on the launchpad.

On our fifth round of shots, Sandra announced her candidacy as Della's maid of honor when we eventually got married, and Sam said no way, she'd be having a best man, and the two of them fought over this even though gay marriage was illegal and also, it was my birthday not hers.

But I wasn't jealous. Finally, I really wasn't. Everyone loved Della, and why wouldn't they? I couldn't believe she loved me back.

That night, when everyone had left, we had sex in a way we hadn't before. I didn't know what to say, how to let her know what I was feeling. I was only myself, which was something very small and uncertain. I didn't want to pretend I was more experienced than her, like I was in any position to tell her what to do. Did she know how desperately I now needed her? How terrible it was to realize that, to be both weak and lucky in that way.

In my quiet, Della heard me. She rolled over and moved over me, slowly, cradling my face. Shushing me in comfort when I had said nothing, when I stayed very still and looked up at her in awe. When I spoke, finally, I said I wanted only to be close. She nodded and told me she loved me. She held me and asked me no questions, and together we fell asleep.

On the night Felicia was born, Della was at the president's gate. Then she was at the hospital with Jason and Kayla, holding her hand through rushed stages of labor. My mother was in her car, driving through the night from Oklahoma. I was in the library, trying to read in Russian.

In the early morning Sandra found me there and berated me all the way to the hospital. I walked into the postpartum recovery room and Della was there, her eyes red, holding the smallest baby in a striped blanket. She moved to pass the baby back to Kayla, twisting at the waist, the two women meeting each other in the middle to support the baby's head and neck. Then she hurried past me, into the hallway.

The email Della sent later that day said she was breaking up with me. It wasn't because of what I'd said at the meeting, though that had been unkind.

Della said she'd seen my niece be born into the world, and she wanted that. She wanted that someday, with a person she could trust. She loved me, but she didn't trust me. It was over.

AFTERMATH

December 2002

Kayla had become a little bit famous—though not the kind that makes money—in the six weeks since the photo of her handcuffed to the president's gate. Twelve thousand people subscribed to her blog.

She threw herself, harder than ever, into long posts that referenced "decolonial ways of being" and "food sovereignty." She posted photos of her art, but also an increasing number of herself, gathering roots and berries while being beautiful. The baby napped in a cradleboard strapped to her back. In one of the photos, Kayla—topless in December—breastfed a fur-wrapped Felicia in the woods behind the dining hall.

Our mother had spent four days on the road round-trip, with two days in the middle to see the baby before she had to return to work. In those two days Kayla had taken many, many black-and-white film photographs of our mother and herself and Felicia in traditional clothing, the three generations together. The series was popular on the internet. I wasn't asked to be in it, maybe because my haircut wasn't old-world or maybe because I had no descendants.

Kayla worked long shifts with the townies at Dominic's Pizza Kitchen, and every three hours I had to carry the baby to the back alley for her to nurse. It was hard, on both of us, but Kayla and Jason were struggling to make rent after the administration had evicted her from Jason's dorm room. They'd had to move into a small, dark bedroom in a shared house off-campus. There was one window, looking out on an aging yellow billboard across the street. The billboard said *Teeth in Six Hours!*—which Kayla and I thought was funny, but that Jason said depressed him. He'd hoped to provide nicer things for his daughter. He'd been raised rich, it turned out, by parents too focused on having grown up poor. They said they intended to help, though not anytime soon, lest he not learn to hustle. (Now that I could trace his service back to that, not to the GI Bill but to his once-poor parents' belief in the hustle, I was appalled.)

Jason was never with Kayla, always studying, always coming home late night from whichever part of the library I wasn't in. Sandra told me there was no way he was studying that much, that she was *actually really concerned*, and I told her to quit spreading rumors that would only hurt my sister and niece. Sandra seemed to feel genuinely bad about this, and in the morning I found a set of silk pajamas, new with the tags on, in a wrapped gift box outside my door. I gave them as a hint to Kayla, who had been boobs-out full-time since late October.

Jason was learning to hustle. He was doing his best to graduate early so he could move his surprise new family to law school and earn a salary within three years. He'd devoted his fall semester to the LSATs, which left one semester to get in somewhere and finish college. He seemed dazed whenever I talked to him, like he'd turned around and a woman and child were just, *there*. None of this made it into Kayla's blog.

When Della broke up with me, I didn't want to talk about it. I spent all my free time taking care of the baby, burying my heart in the miracle of my niece. Kayla and I were *obsessed*. We could sit side by side in her horrible firetrap of a bedroom for hours, silent, watching Felicia sleep on a towel on the floor.

I tried to support my sister. I stayed on campus for winter break and watched Felicia while Kayla was at work and Jason fulfilled credits at the community college that could be transferred over. I heard from other people that Della spent Christmas with Sam. I didn't know why and I didn't ask.

Life with my niece was slow in a way I had never experienced. I had time to sit around looking at her, and to think. I thought less about being good enough for Della, and more about going to space.

I stared at Felicia and thought about her smallness—our smallness—in the larger universe. How that idea had once taken me aback, across from my TA in her basement office. But now it was okay. Felicia had come to us from a single weekend trip to Connecticut, from one of hundreds of arguments between my mother and sister. Before Connecticut, there had been Oklahoma. There had been Texas. My mother would reach back to loss, to the Trail of Tears, as a kind of origin to hold on to. My sister would reach still further, to the orderliness of families connected by the traditional clan system. Everyone in their place, accounted for.

It was Brett who first explained the Big Bang theory to me when I was very young. Not just what it was, but the evidence that had led us there. Many people and many years of work, reaching for a story in the dark.

MISSION DAYS

Junior Spring
January 2003

On the eighth day of the space shuttle *Columbia*'s flight, the astronauts tested the ability of bacteria to attach to surfaces in microgravity. The results could lend support to the panspermia theory, the idea that life had begun somewhere else. That the earliest, simplest living organisms had been thrown against our planet on the backs of asteroids.

I was in shambles, still, in my constant missing of Della. It had been eighty-nine days since we last kissed. She turned twenty-one without me. I sometimes forgot meals. When I went to visit the baby, and my sister forced me to shower and eat something before I was allowed to hold her, too much hair would collect at the drain. Several times a week I'd stay up late and read about the Big Bang theory on the internet. Or the panspermia theory. Or I'd check in on the *Columbia* shuttle as it orbited the Earth. I'd see what experiments had been done that day.

I reminded myself that eventually I could be part of that, too. Maybe in space I'd discover something important about the origin of life, or the universe, and Della would understand what I'd been working toward? I didn't think I'd ever loved anyone so much, or ever would.

On the fifth day of the space shuttle *Columbia*'s flight, the astronauts studied microbial physiology. There was concern that bacteria, in space, might become resistant to antibiotics. The results would be relevant for astronauts on long-duration missions.

When I had told Della about this, back in October when she was still in love with me, I'd said the data would be of use on the first manned mission to Mars.

We didn't have the science, or the funding, or the public support. To the mission specialists on board *Columbia*, such a mission must have felt far away. I told myself they were like the old man planting carob trees, who was asked if he'd live to see them bear fruit. The carob trees came from a story from the Talmud, which my apparently religious thesis adviser passed on to me. He'd tell it at least once a semester, when I was impatient and dismissive of the scientists who'd come before me. "When I was born into this world, I found carob trees planted by my father and grandfather." You plant the tree and you wait, quietly, as long as you can.

I had told Della I couldn't wait to follow the *Columbia* mission, for January, when it would finally launch. "I hope they're proud of their work coming with us to the next planet," I said, "should we need to abandon this one."

Della looked horrified. She said she was late to office hours with Lucy.

On the fourteenth day of the space shuttle *Columbia*'s flight, everything stopped. It was 11:38 a.m. on the anniversary of the *Challenger* disaster. Orbiting the planet, experiments were paused and put away, the crew fell silent. They hooked socked feet into grips on the floor and pulled their hair back with elastic bands. They pushed their hands into their pockets, as still as is possible in space, as respectful. A moment of silence.

When I was a teenager and had heard of enough witnesses to the live coverage of the *Challenger* disaster to be some terrible version of jealous, I begged my mother to tell me if I had been one of them. Had I seen it, maybe on one of the satellite stations set up for schools? My mother, after years of questioning, finally told me.

In 1986 I was four years old and we lived in Dallas with my father. My father wanted to be at the shuttle launch, at the Kennedy Space Center in Florida. He thought I'd like it, too. He was a person of extremes, my mother said, and would do anything to be loved after whatever he did to ruin things.

My father woke up very early and put me in his car. My mother and sister were sleeping. He drove seventeen hours straight. (This was my mother's guess, after the fact, because he'd put me in a diaper. I had graduated from them at that point, and on this trip wet myself many times over.) I got a rash on my neck from the seat belt, from sitting in the front when I wasn't supposed to. So he unbuckled me.

My mother described this whole event to me as "a horrible lapse in judgment," and said she was certain we wouldn't have been let into the Kennedy Space Center. She said we probably parked in a field somewhere; maybe we'd pulled off on the side of the highway. When the *Challenger* exploded in the sky, there was no way of knowing if I had seen it. She hoped not. If I couldn't remember this, she said, or other things, hard things, from that time, then wasn't that for the best?

When my father and I returned to Texas, my mother was sitting on the front stoop with my baby sister in her arms. Waiting. Eyes bloodshot, face white, half-convinced I was dead.

I looked up the driving time when I was in college, once there were websites for questions like that. Our trip—my kidnapping, however short-lived— would have taken at least three days. *How dare she*, I thought, *not have called the police.*

STEPH

8:59

February 1, 2003
8:59 a.m. EST

On the morning of *Columbia*'s return to Earth, I woke early. We all did. The fire alarm went off for no reason, and we had to wait outside, freezing, for the fire department. When we were allowed back in the house, I went immediately to the basement and switched on NASA TV. I wished I could share this with Brett. I missed him, and only lately had started to regret not answering his letters all freshman year. Now it was too late. Della was through with me, and my thesis adviser found me annoying. I had no one to share the shuttle's return with. But I felt sure that somewhere Brett was watching it, too.

The station broadcast two hours of mission footage taken in space over the last fourteen days. I had seen much of it before. Then the countdown to reentry. Live coverage. Mission control.

Nothing happened. The camera had been placed on a tripod in the corner of the room, looking out at rows of screens and chairs and the backs of workers in collared shirts. The workers were still. I held my own hands tight in my lap. The landing had been scheduled for three seconds before. The runway was clear.

I moved to the floor and sat on my knees, just under the television. I waited.

Why hadn't I asked someone to be with me? I'd seen flyers for a community watch party with free bagels, put on by the student union, and felt like a dummy for staying home. I changed the channel to the regular news, hoping someone might talk directly to the camera.

On the screen was a bright white ball with a long white tail, falling from the sky. It looked like a shooting star. A man in a windbreaker talked over the recording, pointing out small white dots as they fell. It was the shuttle, breaking apart.

No one would say it, but *Columbia* was lost. Seven astronauts were dead or dying. I closed my eyes and said a prayer, my first in many years. I prayed that they were dead. That they had died instantly. Their families waited for them in a van, parked beside the runway at the Kennedy Space Center.

The recording of the streak in the sky played on a loop, repeated every two minutes. Over the zoomed-in and slowed-down breaking apart, a voice repeated that we could not confirm what had happened. We could only hope.

The white van sped away. I let out a cry and covered my face. The density of grief held in one van of people—and where could they possibly be taken? Who was behind the wheel, responsible for the spouses and children, given the order to drive on?

There must be a room for this. Somewhere set aside, decided on months or years ago. It would be comfortable and quiet. There would be long hours of waiting together in that room. This was all part of the contingency plan.

I touched the television with my hand and switched it back to NASA TV. I knew the protocol. No one could leave the control room until the flight data had been retrieved, stored, and analyzed. There would be a black binder at each desk, with a checklist for everything that would follow. The flight director would make the call.

On-screen, the flight director paced back and forth. In one hand, a binder. His other hand moved between his waist, his shoulders, his head, his face. He shifted his weight like a man who had trained his whole life not to cry in this moment.

The flight director said, "FCOH contingency plan procedure; FCOH checklist page two point eight dash five."

Around the room, the sound of the turning of pages.

The flight director said, "Lock the doors."

I watched. The neat, straight lines of screens and numbers and maps and flight paths. Ordinary-looking people in ordinary-looking clothes, not a glance at the television camera stationed behind them. Whispers and leaning over desks and fast-typing fingers and coughing and throat-clearing and sniffling. Palms pressed soft against the eyes, only for a moment. The gestures of not-crying so loud I felt a future aching in me, a new knowledge, something I would carry.

STEPH

RETURN

Della lay in bed beside me.

She ran her hand up and down my shoulder, under the wide sleeve of my T-shirt, and across my chest. But not *on* my chest, not like there was anything she wanted that I could give her.

I did not deserve this, or her.

Della whispered again. "Do you want to talk about it?"

"I don't."

It had been like this for hours. Della holding me, rubbing my back, bringing me water while I cried and slept and woke and cried again. I shivered under my blankets and hers. She took my temperature. She left once, briefly, and I thought she had come to her senses. I thought she'd remembered how impossible I was. She came back with Tylenol, a mug of tea for herself, and a study guide for her next exam.

Della had found me minutes after the explosion, alone on the basement floor. She led me up the stairs to my room. She had been at the free-bagels community watch party with all our friends, and I told her I was surprised they'd been interested in the shuttle return. "You don't own space!" she snapped. Then she pushed me gently into bed and wiped my forehead with a cool washcloth.

Beside me now, her voice was fading. It was late. "Okay," she said. "Fine. But if you do want to talk about it, wake me up."

I tried not to think about why she had left me, or how I had handled myself in the three months without her. Like a person out of control.

Della pulled her knees up against the backs of my knees; she tucked my back into her chest. She kissed my shoulder. I felt my body waking into her. Then I saw the explosion, bright light falling through blue sky.

I was terrified of dying in space. I was ashamed to think, again, of myself. Twelve children that morning had lost a mother or father.

It was obvious to me now. I couldn't be a parent on a shuttle to space. I couldn't be a spouse.

Della fell asleep with the full weight of her arm across my chest, and I stared up at the green-blue glow-in-the-dark stars, at the nonsense patterns she'd once placed them in. I thought of Brett's constellations on the ceiling of my childhood, as perfectly charted as a map. I thought about people in Texas and Arkansas, flashlights in hand, walking slowly through their fields: a search party for fallen astronauts.

STEPH

I HAVE LOVED THE
STARS TOO FONDLY

On the day after the *Columbia* shuttle disaster, I left the house in the dark. I moved slowly, careful not to wake Della.

In the library, a custodian waxed the floors. I emailed my thesis adviser about the Fulbright research grant application cycle. I said I appreciated how he had said, many times, that a relatively isolated year in Russia seemed "unwise" for my mental health. And that he didn't believe I was ready for it, scholastically speaking.

But, I said, heads-up! I'd be doing it anyway. I would apply in the fall of senior year, and hope to leave the country after graduation. If Della hadn't left me by then, maybe she'd come along.

Through the window beside my row of computers, I stole glances at the sunrise. I registered for scuba diving lessons held in the pool of the campus rec center. I signed up for a weight-lifting PE class three afternoons a week, and another class (daily, at five a.m.) called Kardio Konditioning. I read one article titled "Alcohol's Effects on Physical Fitness" and decided I'd never drink again. I emailed a nearby flight school and asked about pricing for the fall.

I would get my scuba license. My pilot license. My skydiving license. I would get a Fulbright research grant. I would get abs. All this I could manage before or during grad school, ten or more years from when I'd need it in astronaut training. All this would terrify me, would push me, would tie me more tightly to the life I'd chosen.

I should have stayed in bed with Della. Or, if not, I should have returned from the library with coffee. Two croissants in a box tied with a string. Hadn't she given herself back to me when I most needed her? Hadn't she asked for nothing in return?

But when I came home—three hours later, croissant-less—Della would only smile, and say she had missed me.

I thought often about death. Shuttles exploding, asteroids crashing, astronauts with broken tethers running slowly out of air. Astronauts, floating alone through space.

I told myself, *Della is back. A miracle. Della loves me.*

In bed, we stopped pretending I knew anything. Della took care of us both. Her voice and hands were careful, like I'd break.

But when I slept, after, I saw astronauts. The seven of them, waving and smiling at the crowd. Stepping into the shuttle and closing the door.

I saw my mother one day, alone. Standing at the kitchen window in that small house, in that small town. My mother, who'd lost her parents, her husband, Brett, and maybe someday me? I had to act under the knowledge that this could happen.

I knew what could have been. I imagined myself a high school science teacher, like Brett; Brett who'd made a difference in my life and in that of many others. I imagined Della as a scientist, or a teacher at my same school. Tahlequah. Babies who looked like Della. Holiday-themed sugar cookies. Summer camp programs in music or theater or something else, whatever pulled at our children like the stars had once pulled at me.

After *Columbia* I realized: It was a tugging that would never stop. I was forever at the end of a rope, tied to a world too far from my own, and I could cry and scream and mourn the shuttle loss, the loss of good people and good science, and I could be afraid of it, too, so afraid I'd wake up sweating and shaking in the middle of the night from dreams of sirens and fire and rocketing toward the Earth—Della above me, shaking my shoulders, telling me it's fine, you're here, you're only here.

But I wouldn't take comfort in that. I worried I would never take comfort in my belonging—finally—to and with another person. Over the next year of loving Della, I came to know how fiercely she held on to people. She was willing to wait for me, anywhere, even on a runway in a van full of terrified children. And I was willing to die.

DELLA

TO BE FEARFUL OF THE NIGHT

Senior Spring

April 29, 2004
From: della.ericson@hollis.edu
To: lucy.andrews@hollis.edu

Dear Lucy,

I owe you an email and this isn't it. I'm not going to send this, but I'm writing it, maybe to psych myself up for the real one. (The *professional* one, probably short, where I won't shake out the sheet of my soul and show it to you.)

It was very kind of you to write me those recommendation letters for PhD programs, and I meant what I said in my thank-you card. You believed in me and put time into preparing me for a life in the biological sciences. You guided me from animal behavior to marine biology to the Mariana Trench to the frilled shark, to the oceanography professor down the hall. And even then, when you could have just handed me off to Prof. Hardiman—you stayed.

Whenever I think about rejecting the offer from UC Santa Barbara, rejecting the PhD adviser *you* convinced to take me on, I feel sick. I'm too ashamed to tell you what I've decided, so I haven't yet.

I remember you telling me about your own PhD program, all the freedom and independence, the years you got to study the visual patterns of wolf spiders. I realized you were the only person in the world studying that tiny bit of knowledge for the rest of us—that it didn't have to be big, but it was *yours*. No one could take that away. You have a whole world that's completely mysterious to me (read: Are you gay?), but you're a professional, so you've never told me anything by mistake.

I decided a long time ago not to share any of this. At least, not with you. Definitely not with my girlfriend. But I thought it might help to write it down?

I came out to my parents in my sophomore year, on the last day of winter break. They said I wasn't their daughter anymore. (My dad said this to me. My mom sat next to him on the couch and held his hand while he said it.) I didn't tell anyone, because then I'd have to hear someone say something asinine like, "Didn't they make a whole fucking thing out of wanting to be your parents?" I didn't want people to think they were any *less* my parents than other parents, even when that was exactly what they were saying.

In one of our thesis advising meetings a few weeks later, I cried in your office about children. How I wanted them someday and couldn't have them, now that I'd become a lesbian. I thought you would understand that, because you're the one who taught me about the importance of genetic kinship in the animal kingdom. (And because I think you're gay?) What I couldn't tell you was that I wanted children, and my parents didn't want *me*.

You said that my impressions of GLBT family-building were "obviously incorrect," and you gave me half the chocolate bar you kept in a drawer in your desk. It was horrible, bitter, no milk or sugar at all. Twenty percent of the proceeds went toward saving the rainforest. You said you believed there were *many* things you'd taught me about in the animal kingdom, like Christmas Island red crabs cannibalizing their young, that I did not seem to have taken as instruction for my life.

You told me about a class being offered on assisted reproductive technologies, which I registered for. The professor was a man with one earring, and two classes in he said (casually, and to the whole room) that he was gay. (Are you?)

I told everyone my parents were missionaries abroad and I had nowhere to go till they came home. I spent two summers with my girlfriend in Oklahoma, which my parents would never have allowed if they were still trying to parent me. I spent one Christmas with my friend Sam's family in Kansas. (Sam didn't believe the missionary story for a minute, and his giant family treated me like the second coming of Jesus, even though they had real hardships of their own. They brought me tea and cookies and tissues while I lay sobbing under their Christmas tree for a week. It pisses me off a little, still, that my girlfriend has never suspected a thing.)

The first summer in Oklahoma, I emailed my bio-dad Matthew and asked to see him. I wore a sleeveless shirt with a detached buckskin collar I'd learned to fully bead myself, and a silk skirt. My girlfriend's sister had embellished it with ribbons woven into each other like a basket. Matthew picked me up with his new wife in the car, and they took me to Burger King. I sat in my plastic chair in my best clothes, because I thought he was taking me to . . . *not* Burger King? And Matthew let his new/pregnant wife go on about "the good parts" of the Iraq War.

The second year, Matthew left his new/postpartum wife at home with his new whole-ass child, whom I haven't made myself meet despite having always wanted a sibling. Matthew wore a flannel shirt and unstained jeans and took me to a Mexican restaurant. He ordered us main courses but also appetizers and a dessert, flan that we shared while a Mariachi soloist sang over a CD player on a small stage in the corner. I was so relieved that the wife and the baby weren't there. I wanted to tell Matthew everything, all the things I'm pretending to tell you now, but I didn't. I was scared I'd lose him, too.

For the two years and three months that my Utah parents weren't speaking to me, they only communicated in two ways: (1) They paid my tuition and kept me on their debit card in my old name, which felt both manipulative and miraculous, and (2) They sent books to my campus PO Box:

- *Born That Way?*
- *My Battle with Same-Sex Attraction*
- *Understanding and Helping Individuals with Homosexual Problems*

I waited them out. I don't know if you would have had a braver solution for that, or if you've ever had to deal with something like this (Are you gay?). For two years and three months, I didn't engage. I threw their books away. They tracked down an old friend of mine from LDS summer camp, Ada, a twenty-one-year-old, formerly gay girl who went to a retreat (read: conversion therapy) and now has a husband and a baby. She's a blogger and a public speaker. She wrote me a long letter about the retreat and how, even though she'd been scared to go, it had helped her. She said my parents had told her to tell me that, if I went, they would pay for it.

I set the letter on fire in the bathroom sink. The smoke alarm went off. It was six in the morning, and we all had to stand on the street with coats over our pajamas until the fire department gave the all clear. No one knew it was me.

(I've mentioned my girlfriend to you a few times, in a professional way, when it seemed casual and relevant. But I never told you I broke up with her just before the Christmas I spent crying in Kansas. I got back together with her, too. I got back together with her after the *Columbia* shuttle disaster, which was when I read that letter from Ada.)

Last month, my parents called me. They'd suddenly realized I was almost done with school and starting a whole life after that, and I guess they didn't want to miss it. My dad cried into the phone, and I remembered that someday they'd be dead. I said they could come to graduation. I told them a few things I thought they should know, like my plans for next year, which they were careful not to react to.

My girlfriend won a Fulbright for a year in Russia. I'm supposed to go with her and work as one of many assistants in a lab in Moscow—nine hours from the Baltic Sea, where there are no frilled sharks. I haven't told you about the lab yet, because I know you'll ask whose lab it is and I'll say Dr. Dmitri Fedorov, and you'll sigh and look out your office window—like I am just another disappointment, like it is exhausting to try to build anything for young people—and you'll turn back to face me and say, "Who?"

All my life, things have been taken from me. Decided for me. I've had to fight for so much, even my own name. I hold my girlfriend's niece in my arms and I know *exactly* what I want. A child, the kind of family I could love and depend on. Someone who sees me, exactly as much as I choose to let them. Someone who stays.

Lately I've been thinking back on my life. (Please don't laugh at me for doing that. I know I must seem young to you, but I have had a life.) It's like the volume on other people's voices has been turned up from the start, and they have only gotten louder. When I do have a chance to think, it's often because someone else has asked me questions. They've sat quietly enough, for long enough, to listen to me, and they have turned down the dial on everything else. Does that make sense to you?

You have done that for me. So has my girlfriend, in her own way. She writes out a possible world for us, a path to a life where I am not left behind. She says we can have a baby someday, together. That I can choose how and when.

For all her faults, for all the ways she can't see past herself? My girlfriend has never left me, and I feel sure she never would.

Declining the PhD programs, going to Russia—I understand what it means to make that sacrifice. If I choose to take what she's offering, I will give something over of myself. Something I worked for—that *you* worked for, when I couldn't imagine it yet.

You would say this is a terrible choice. The wrong one. Short-sighted and naïve, irresponsible, reckless. You will say all that, I'm sure, when I get up the nerve to really tell you. But if it is, let's say, a terrible choice—it's still mine.

NAUGATUCK OYSTER BAR

May 2004

The day before graduation, Della's parents flew in from Utah. Kayla and Felicia took the bus to Hollis from Boston, where they lived with Jason in graduate family housing at Harvard Law. I had told my mother not to come, knowing both the expense and the rumors that the factory where she worked might be closing. Still, she came. She insisted on a big, celebratory family dinner. And family, she said, "of course" included the Ericsons.

Naugatuck Oyster Bar was a restaurant, not a bar, with white cloth napkins and a real pianist in a black turtleneck in the corner. Vintage canoes hung upside down on thin wires from the ceiling. I worried one of them would fall on our heads.

My mother complimented the visible grain of the wood at her place-setting, covering her disappointment with the lack of tablecloths, and the waiter told her it was reclaimed pine from the White Mountains. "White indeed," she whispered to Della in the leather-backed chair beside her, and Della laughed. When Della had stayed with us in Oklahoma, the two of them spent slow, early mornings together. They sat together on the front stoop, even in December, under the blue quilt my mother had noticed was missing and made me give back to her. They'd never told me what they talked about.

"I'm so darn proud of our girls," my mother said, raising a glass of wine.

Heavy pour, I thought. Since dedicating my body to a more serious pursuit of NASA, I had stopped drinking not only alcohol, but also soda and (for the most part) coffee. Now I was healthier and also more judgmental.

"To the graduates!" Mrs. Ericson said.

Kayla, Della, and Della's parents knocked cups of Sprite against my water. My mother's delicate wineglass looked out of place, her grip too tight, her hands calloused and heavy and scarred. This was my default, judging her. Hadn't she said "darn" instead of "damn"? Couldn't I just chill out?

My mother talked. When other people talked, she responded with laughter, exclamations, theatrical gasps. She talked constantly and stopped to excessively thank the waiter every time he approached ("We couldn't be happier," or "No, we're more than fine here, honey"). It was me who had changed. I'd lived in New England for four years, where the waiters were thin, quick, and sharply dressed. They were thanked discreetly, and in moderation.

But my mother was a hit. It took me shamefully long to realize that. To see how they smiled at her, how even baby Felicia delighted as her grandmother bounced her in her lap. Della's dad laughed, too, between long gulps of Sprite.

Mr. Ericson folded his arms, smiling, and leaned back in his chair. The waiter, passing behind him, had to flatten himself against the wall.

"*Steph,*" Mr. Ericson said. His tone was weird, and I thought of dads cleaning shotguns before prom. "What are your plans for a year from now?"

Kayla shook her head at me. Everyone at the table knew I had plans. I had a prioritized list of advisers and schools I was already talking to. The Fulbright year in Russia was just a stop on my way to probably-Berkeley (where my thesis adviser thought his old colleague might be "hostile yet open" to me studying both astronomy and geology). Then I'd do a postdoc and then a fellowship or two, maybe even an actual job, while I waited for NASA's next call for astronauts.

"I'm strongly considering a PhD, sir," I said.

"That's wonderful," he said. "Ambitious!"

Della had warned me that "ambitious" wasn't a compliment. Especially for a girl. Growing up it had been shorthand for caring about the wrong things.

I thought there might be more to it. I was too ambitious for a regular girl, but Della thought her dad would still expect me to take care of her. I figured that meant paying for things, and doing our taxes, and being strong enough to save her in an Earth-ending event. I wanted, just as much as he did, for Della to be safe.

"Those programs sure are hard to get into," my mother said.

She was trying to be kind; I'd told her privately about Della's many rejections from PhD programs. This recent failure—along with Della's interest in getting immediately pregnant despite no serious engagement with the problem of sperm—had prepared me for the idea that I'd be the primary earner.

"Well, apparently not *that* hard," Mr. Ericson said.

I bristled. "As a matter of fact, sir, some of the smartest people in our class were rejected. Getting in can be *very* hard, *especially* if you're applying for one of the fully funded programs, in which case—"

"Are we ready to order?" Della said. Her hand was on my leg, but not in a sexy way. Like I was an animal to pin down.

The waiter stood at Della's side, holding a pen and a black leather pad.

I made a little show of ordering coq au vin for Della, though I should have ordered oysters. For myself, I panicked and pointed somewhere on the menu.

Della's parents, she'd said, needed me to "be the boy." Kayla would hate that. She'd call it benevolent homophobia, and tell me to rebel against the gender binary. But Kayla would've made a better lesbian than me. I liked taking care of Della.

When this was over, I could take her home. I'd pull the fabric flowers from her braids and put them carefully into the etched clay pot by our bed. I'd hang her dress on the hook by the door, promise to take it to the dry cleaner, and ask her what she'd thought about our evening.

Felicia stood on Kayla's knees and stared, open-mouthed, at Della's mother. She gave a series of little claps, her latest party trick.

Mrs. Ericson smiled tightly and reached for her husband's hand. There was the soft curve of her silk collar, and the necklace that matched her daughter's. Only hours ago I had closed the clasp on Della's, the gold cross dangling over the ridge of her collarbone. I'd kissed her like I'd seen men do in movies—rough fingers buttoning, fastening, zipping things up the narrow backs of girls.

"Speaking of next year," said Mrs. Ericson. "Hannah, I assume you've already heard? Della says she'll be investigating how salty the water is in Russia."

She looked at me, not at Della, for the answer to a question she hadn't directly asked. Della's research would be more sophisticated than *that*! But barely.

Felicia whined. Kayla shushed her and leaned in closer to hear.

"She'll have the opportunity to work under the esteemed Dr. Dmitri Fedorov," I said. "I'm very proud of her."

Was that patronizing? I *was* proud of her, persevering through two straight months of rejections. I pictured her standing alone in the campus mail center, ripping up each letter before coming home to me with a brave face. Her parents should know I'd been there for her.

"Well, thank God he's *esteemed*," Kayla said.

So what if Dr. Fedorov wasn't esteemed? Since when was it Kayla's job to rank marine biologists?

I thought of Jason's email to me that morning, how he'd said he was too "stressed-out" with law school to make it to my graduation. This was different from what Kayla had told me and her blog readers, which was that she'd insisted on a "girls' trip." Reframing the truth was apparently fine, but only when Kayla did it.

"The things we do . . ." Mrs. Ericson started, the words sharp in her mouth.

For love, I wanted to say. But that felt incriminating, like I knew Della's how-salty-is-the-sea assistantship was kind of dumb.

The problem with going to college somewhere like Hollis is that you spend the rest of your life categorizing people's choices as adequately or inadequately prestigious. When Sam was announced as one of thirty-two Rhodes Scholars, *nationwide*, Della baked him a pan of brownies. I went to the gym to work out my rage. I spent an hour deadlifting above my training regimen, even though I'd never even applied for a Rhodes. Two years at Oxford was not part of my pre-NASA strategy.

There was a long silence. I didn't know what kind of meat I'd ordered, only that it was new to me and I didn't like it. The pianist started playing a new piece, and my mother said, "I love this song!"

Della would be no help; she was making faces at the baby.

Della's dress was new, and surprisingly short for a meal with her parents; under the table it rode up her thighs. In the candlelight, its shades of blue glitter shifted, like waves at night. I wanted to stand up already. I wanted to take her back to our room, lie underneath her, and drown.

Mrs. Ericson said to Della, unprovoked, "We get it now, honey. You know that."

"You get *what* now?" I said.

Mrs. Ericson took a slow, careful breath.

Kayla leaned forward again. Felicia raised a steak knife over her little head. Della gently took it from her.

"We just—It's important that you two are on the same page," Mrs. Ericson said, "what with Della's sudden change in plans."

"What change in plans?" I said.

"Oh, no," my mother said. "Della, you *didn't*."

"Mom, Hannah," Della said, "everything is okay." She smiled between the two women, pleadingly. My mother had begged Della to call her Hannah, forever ago it seemed.

"Emma doesn't need a big-shot career," Mr. Ericson said. "She's wanted kids since she was a kid herself!"

"No. Her name is *Della*," Kayla said. She unbuttoned her shirt, cupped a whole boob like a grapefruit in her hand, and put it in Felicia's mouth. Mr. Ericson threw his neck to the side, averting his eyes.

"Jeez, Dad," Della said, ignoring the matter of her name. "Thanks for the vote of confidence."

"What your dad *means* is that we want you to have some stability," Mrs. Ericson said. "Someone with your best interests—always—at top of mind."

"Guys?" Della said. "Wherever you're going with this . . . it's my graduation dinner."

"Your mother has a point, though," Mr. Ericson said. "We're proud as heck. We just hope you've got a plan for what comes after Russia."

"That would be a year from now, sir," I said. "Applications for the 2005–2006 academic year haven't opened yet."

"*Dad*," Della said. "What did you do to celebrate, the night before your graduation?"

Under the table she reached for my hand. She ran my fingers under the hem of her dress—almost to remind me she was mine? Or—and this thought worried me—to keep me calm? She really seemed to think I'd fight her father.

When she shifted away from me, just as fast as she'd come, her dress left dark blue glitter on my fingertips.

Mr. Ericson sighed and put down his Sprite. "In ancient times, you mean? Back when I was at the Y?"

"BYU," Della translated.

My mother nodded, her eyes blank.

Della tried again. "Mormon college. It's actually a really good school."

"I'm sorry," Mrs. Ericson said, "did you just say *actually*?"

Kayla passed me a note over Felicia's head. I opened it. whos paying? it said.

"I think the night before graduation would've been just a regular night for us," Mr. Ericson said. "Your mom and I were married by then, keeping up our own apartment and hoping for a baby. We thought you'd be there any minute."

He reached across the table and touched Della on the cheek. He looked at her with so much tenderness, like all had turned out as it should have. The years of waiting were nothing now. I liked that.

"Oh, the good old days," said Mrs. Ericson, teasing. She reached for Della and rubbed her arm. Della looked embarrassed by this, maybe, but also more relaxed than usual? She was different with her family. It made me wish she'd invited me to Provo, even once.

I turned over Kayla's paper and wrote on the back. idk i can cover bill for della + mom + you but just assume everyone for themselves ok?

I'd been saving. Though I'd had to stop Plasma Mondays when I started lifting weights, I was now in the non-Parkinson's group for a clinical trial. I'd earned almost four hundred dollars over the semester, mostly for not having Parkinson's.

My mother nodded at Mrs. Ericson. "So you went there, too? The Y?"

I wondered if she was doing the math, which I'd done the moment we'd sat down—everyone at the table had gone to college, except her and her daughter and the baby her daughter had had too soon.

"For a time," Mrs. Ericson said.

"Whoa, a fellow dropout?" Kayla said. She held out a hand for a high five. I could've slapped her. Felicia stopped nursing and swatted her own hand in the air, copying Kayla.

Mrs. Ericson stiffened. Slowly, daintily almost—she touched her hand to Kayla's. Then to the baby's.

My mother laughed uncomfortably. The waiter took our plates. Kayla buttoned her shirt and the pianist returned from his break.

"*God* I love this song," my mother said. "You know, education has always been really important in our family. Sacred, even. It's why this weekend is so moving for us. My great-grandmother and *both* my grandparents, on my mom's side—all of them were teachers."

"Until the US government shut down Cherokee schools," said Kayla.

I wanted to remind Kayla that there wasn't a camera here, no mostly white blog subscribers eager for the Indian point-of-view. This dinner was for our family and the Ericsons, who had not controlled Congress in the early 1900s.

Mrs. Ericson cleared her throat. "When I made the personal choice not to finish my degree—" Her tone was careful, practiced. Like she was giving a speech. "I had to prioritize what felt right for me and my family."

She reached across the table and took Della's hand. Her face was set with a certain solemnity, like she was sharing a secret of womanhood. "I *knew* I had someone I could trust to take care of me," she said. "And he married me. That made all the difference."

"We . . . literally can't get married," I said. "It's against the law."

"Get a grip," Della said, not even looking at me. She and her mother still held hands, their arms a little barricade between me and the salt and pepper shakers.

The pianist started another song, which my mother loved. "This is *such* a good song," she said. "I love it."

Kayla dropped another note into my lap. srsly can we trust these fuckers to pay for their own meals? Plz help. & omg stop saying awk stuff ur embarrassing ur gf

"It was a different time," Mr. Ericson said. "Back then at the Y, people—um, heterosexual persons, which was all they had at the Y in those days—they wouldn't go on dating more than a month or two without that solid commitment to the marriage covenant.

"And now we've got *you two*, doing *your* thing, without the traditional blueprint for who makes sacrifices for who. I've gotta say I'm impressed with how mature you two are, figuring things out together."

Our thing, I supposed, was homosexuality. Still, he was trying.

"Excuse me," my mother said, "but what-all are you talking about?"

Mrs. Ericson's face scrunched in confusion. "What do you mean?"

"That word," my mother said. "*Sacrifice.* It's a heavy one. Did I miss something? Is everything all right?"

"Everything is great, Hannah," Della said. "It's a beautiful evening." She stared up at the canoe over our table.

"Of course," my mother said. "You're right. It's a beautiful evening. We're very proud of you both.

"But if we've offended you, or your parents? I mean . . . it just seems like you-all are maybe trying to say something, but—in code?—and I'm not quite smart enough to get it?"

"Nothing's wrong, Mom," I said. "And you're very smart."

"How do *you* know nothing is wrong, Steph?" Kayla said. Felicia pointed her chubby little finger at me, like I was being accused in court.

"Della," Kayla said, "you said you'd tell her."

"Back off, Kayla." Della lifted her glass to her mouth, tipped it back, and even pretended to gulp. It had been empty half an hour.

"Of course she told her," said Mrs. Ericson.

"Well, shit," my mother said, leaving me the last one out of the loop. She winced at Mr. Ericson. "Sorry."

Felicia reached for Mrs. Ericson's napkin. She dropped it onto Kayla's dirty plate and banged her fist against the table. "Ma!" she said. "Ma! Ma! Ma!"

"Shh," Kayla said to the baby. She turned to Della. "You have three seconds to tell my sister, or I'll tell her myself."

"Why must you always be so dramatic?" I said.

"*One,*" Kayla said.

Mr. Ericson raised his chin. Instantly a waiter appeared.

"How will you be taking care of the check, sir?" the waiter said.

I took out my wallet. Inside was the Parkinson's money, all of it, in fifties I'd deemed crisp enough to accept from the bank teller.

My mother heaved a giant handbag onto the table. "I've got it!" She pulled out bills, tens and twenties, and stacked them by her plate. Felicia clapped.

"Mom, do *not*," Kayla said.

"Don't worry about it," Mr. Ericson said. He handed his credit card to the waiter.

"Thanks, Simon," Kayla said. "You too, Josephine." Kayla stuffed the bills back into our mother's bag. "Della, that's *two*. Aaand—"

"Della, do we need to discuss something in private?" I said. "Maybe after dinner?"

"—*three*," Kayla said.

"If you tell her," Della said, her gaze steady on my sister, "I'll hate you forever."

"Emma!" Mrs. Ericson said. "*Kindness.*"

A flash of pain on Della's face.

"She got into grad school," Kayla said.

"Go to hell," Della said.

"*Emma!*" Mrs. Ericson touched a hand to her chest like she'd been shot. "Language!"

"What?" I said.

"Don't even go there, Steph," Kayla said. "It was obvious and you know it."

"But Della told me—" I started.

"She got into *all* the grad schools, you mean," Mr. Ericson said. "Every place she applied. Honey, you didn't tell your friend that?"

Della put her elbows on the table, her face in her hands. She began to cry. Was I allowed to touch her? Her shoulders shook, lines of candlelight jumping across the glitter of her dress. I sat still.

Felicia followed suit, not in stillness but in crying, and slammed her face against her mother's chest. Kayla unbuttoned her shirt to her navel and took out both breasts, the second one completely uncalled for, and Mr. Ericson turned his whole chair to face sideways. A waiter returned the card and check to him.

"I wanted to contribute," my mother said. She took the bills from her bag once again and waved them in her hand, like playing cards in Vegas. "It's *gradu-ation*. In our family, that means something really spe—"

"Simon, Josephine," Kayla said, left boob hanging useless, "it was a pleasure."

Felicia turned to smile at us, fully exposing her mother. Breast milk spilled out of the corner of her open mouth. At the table in front of ours, over the shoulder of his date, a man stared at Kayla. She must have seen him—she was facing him, as I was—but she made no move to clean or cover herself.

I remembered her as a kid in the woods with Daniel, how I'd known from her bikini strings that Daniel had touched her chest. I'd seen her body as a place for people to hurt her. She seemed to see it as a weapon.

"Our treat," Mr. Ericson said, still looking away. "I'm sure your airfare was pricey."

Our mother stood. Her chair scraped against the floor, loud.

"Not worth it, Ma," Kayla said.

"Was my airfare pricier than yours?" our mother said.

"I'm sorry?" Mr. Ericson said.

Poor Della was still crying. It was crazy that no one was comforting her. Sure, I'd suspected she'd maybe gotten into *one* graduate program, and maybe decided not to tell me. But I'd decided not to push her on it or demand the truth. I'd let myself believe no one wanted her.

But, *every* school? Who got into every school? I'd been rejected by seven.

"We aren't poor people," our mother said. She clutched her terrible, faux-snakeskin bag to her stomach. "We're a good family."

A woman in a long, low-cut, velvet dress—the date of the man still ogling my sister—whispered something to our waiter as he passed. He nodded.

"I'm sure you are," Mrs. Ericson said. "Truly, we only wanted to help." Her back was to my mother. She was undoing Della's braid, her fingers like a comb, tearing the fabric flowers from her hair. I wanted to get on my knees and collect them from the floor, to put them carefully by our bed where they belonged.

"I want to apologize for all of us Harpers," our mother said. "Anything rude from my daughters, after you came all the way here and—I mean, apparently—*sponsored* this beautiful family meal. I know they're adults now. But, as a mother, you know how it is! They make mistakes."

"We came here for Emma," Mrs. Ericson said. "Not for anyone else. We've tried our best to be supportive, but—seeing her hitch her wagon like this, to someone who doesn't care about her?"

"Um, Mrs. Ericson, I love her," I said. My voice was shaky like a little girl's, humiliating. Della groaned, apparently annoyed by my big announcement, and continued to cry into her hands.

The waiter approached Kayla. "Ma'am," he said, "may we assist you and your baby on your way out?"

"You may not," Kayla said, "but thank you for offering."

Abruptly, Mr. Ericson left the restaurant.

Slowly, almost seductively, Kayla buttoned her shirt up to the collar. She gave a little wave to the couple at the other table.

"Steph made a mistake," our mother said. "Della told her something crazy, and Steph apparently decided to believe it. Let's let the kids work this out on their own?"

"Hannah, please," Mrs. Ericson said. She gestured at the messy table, the crumpled napkins, Della wet-cheeked and slumped over the table. "This is not the treatment that Emma—that *Della*—deserves. I won't just watch while your kid ruins my kid's life."

"*Two years and three months,*" my mother said, her voice low. "You let that girl wander around like an orphan."

Della gave a long, slow breath out. She folded her dirty napkin three times, like she'd found it. She walked, jacketless and glittering, out to the street.

Mrs. Ericson approached the end of the table. Gently, her face expressionless, she took several bills out of my mother's hand. She didn't pause to count them. She left the restaurant, money crumpled in each fist like trash.

My mother fell back in her seat. She looked up at the canoes as if dazed, as if finally realizing they didn't belong.

"Mom," I said. "Did Della's parents stop talking to her or something?"

"Jesus Christ, kid." She was still, warily, looking up. "Do you two even talk?"

STEPH

WHERE HAS THE TREE GONE, THAT LOCKED EARTH TO THE SKY?

Della waited for me outside the restaurant, shivering in her short dress and heels. It was softly raining, still cold in May. Had she dressed like this, sleeveless even, to prove something to her parents? Had she chosen me for the same reason? And if so, why the silver-and-green ring back on her finger? Why the gold cross?

At the stoplight on the corner of the brick-paved street, a barbershop quartet sang the Hollis fight song. It was the updated version from the 1980s, with the old Indian war whoop erased. I laid my sport coat over Della's shoulders.

I took her hand. She let me. A tiny burst of hope.

Della wrapped her arms around my waist. I kissed the back of her head, where her hair fell in waves from the undone braids. We walked down the street and across the quad. Della recited her plans for us, as she had on many nights before.

"We'll have four or five," Della said, speaking into my shirt. "Stick 'em all in a room at first, bunk beds, since we'll be starving scientists for a while. You take me on a date every week—no, *twice* a week—so we don't kill each other."

Her voice was muffled. I pressed my palm against her cheek to warm it, but she kept talking. "If we work in Tulsa I could drive the kids to Tahlequah for the Cherokee language preschool they're opening—is that crazy? Or allowed? I know you'd have to be in Houston, eventually, but—"

"Come here, Dells," I said.

She giggled, stumbling a little. She'd had no alcohol at dinner. It was a childlike mode she sometimes liked to step into: in bed at the end of a long day, or when she was desperately sad. I held her by the shoulders and pulled her to the side, out of the grass, positioning her feet over the grate outside the library.

Della started to say something, but I shook my head. I held her hands and pressed my forehead to hers. "Can we be quiet? Is that okay? Give it a minute."

I hadn't told anyone about the grate in the nearly four years since I'd found it. I had needed it to be mine; a private warmth in a cold place where, in those moments, no one could track me down. I stood with Della and felt the warmth of her breath in the space between us, the heat from the library blowing softly up our legs. She smiled with her eyes closed.

"Della," I said, and then lost my nerve.

"Baby," I whispered, though I had never called her that. I'd been scared she'd laugh at me.

Della gave a soft hum.

"Did your parents stop talking to you?"

She nodded, eyes still closed, forehead bumping against my nose. "But then they started again," she said matter-of-factly.

"I wish you'd told me."

"No," she said, her voice calm. She opened her eyes and took a step back. "It was my private business to figure out with them, which I did. You wouldn't get it, and you had other things going on."

"Other things like what, my senior thesis? You think I was too busy like, *being interested in space* to talk about your parents disowning you?"

"Oh my God, Steph, they didn't *disown* me! They came all the way here to watch me graduate."

"*Oh*," I said, taken aback. I had forgotten how she loved. She held on for dear life.

I tried again. "I'm sorry you felt like you couldn't tell me. All that time you must've felt—"

What was I trying to say? That she was lonely, lonelier than I had understood?

And yet—she had told my mother she was banned from home. She had told my sister, and even her parents, about her acceptance to PhD programs. What had I done—who had I become—for her to keep the worst and the best of her life from me?

"You don't have to come to Russia," I said. "I wouldn't have even suggested it if I'd known you had a better offer! We can do long-distance, or—I don't know. I want you to do what's best for you."

"You think you know what's best for me?"

"I think we're at an age where we can't compromise on our lives. Not yet."

She glared at me.

I reached for something she could hold. "I mean, my mom? Her life turned out, like, the opposite of your mom's, even though they both went all-in on a man when they were young. They both made sacrifices, like I guess you're trying to do here, but . . . for *my* mom it didn't work out."

"You're not gonna hit me, are you?"

Fuck.

I had never told her, or anyone. Had my mother? Had Kayla?

I swung my body away from her and sucked in the cold air. Of course I didn't want to hit her. I wanted to run.

It occurred to me that the bar, for Della, was so low.

I turned back to face her.

"I didn't want this," Della said, gesturing at the grate between us. "This whole conversation! It's not your life. I knew if I shared stuff, you'd try to tell me what to do."

"I hope you can learn the difference," I said evenly, "between the National Guard at gunpoint and like, talking through decisions with people who love you."

"That's so unkind. And anyway, I told them no."

"Told who?"

"The PhD programs," she said. "Last month."

"You did *what*?"

"We have Moscow."

Not exactly, I thought. *I* had Moscow.

Della had told me at the end of March, after all the rejections had supposedly come in, that she wanted a gap year. She wanted it with me. How easily I'd let myself believe in her failure.

"And *then* what, Della? We should figure out whatever *you* need, to get *your* career set up. We can talk to Lucy; maybe she'd use her network to help you find something last-minute, and then we could—"

Della pulled away from me. I felt the cold air at the edge of the grate cut through the sleeve of my oxford shirt. Della was still wearing my sport coat, still glittering blue waves in the space between the lapels. I wanted to go back to earlier that evening and who I'd been then—willfully ignorant, and excited to unzip a dress.

"I can't believe this." Her eyes narrowed. "You're going to leave me."

I held my palms open. "I won't. I wouldn't—"

"Don't tell me what to do, and don't act like you've got any clue what's best for me, and don't try to decide—"

"Okay, okay," I said. I stepped off the grate and into the cold. Spikes of wet grass scratched my ankles. "Della, I know, it's your choice. I love you. I'm sorry."

"I'm going with you to Russia. I get to choose."

"I know," I said. I pulled her close. I thought of Matthew and her mother and her father, my mother and my sister and myself, everyone who'd broken her trust. All she had asked for, over and over, was to choose her life. Couldn't I understand that?

"I know," I said into her neck. "You're okay."

I loved her. I thought I had before, but only then did I know it completely. When I clearly saw myself, and what I was capable of. I wanted so much for her.

I touched my lips to her forehead. I squeezed my eyes shut and quieted an aching part of me. A knowing part. We could have children, and breakfast. A small apartment. A kitchen with a window.

I struggled with the key to the nassie house, while Della laughed and tried to loosen my collar and kiss me down my shoulder. Somewhere in the last half hour, it was like dinner had never happened. Her parents had sent her a text message. They were at their hotel. They were sorry. They couldn't wait to see her in her cap and gown.

The kitchen was brightly lit and warm, crowded with people I felt a part of. Della shot her hands up over her head and screamed, like she hadn't seen our friends in many years. "SAM!" she said, jumping into his arms. "You *can't* go to Oxford! The Brits are trying to tear us *apart*!"

I stepped back, hands out in surrender. "She's been stuck on this most of the walk home. Apparently, we're all supposed to stay here, in undergraduate housing, forever?"

Sam swung her around once and gently put her down. "Della! No! That's the daftest bloody thing you've ever said!"

Jess rolled her eyes. "Sam is practicing what he believes is British. Because he was awarded a *Rhodes Scholarship* and he's going to *Oxford*. Did you know he's a Rhodes Scholar, one of maybe forty in the country?"

"No, I hadn't heard. Has he ever mentioned it?" April said.

"One of *thirty-two*," Sam corrected, smiling.

"What? Oh my God!" Sandra said. "If only you'd been on, like, the local news."

He had been. Della laughed. Somewhere between the grate and the house, she had decided to be happy.

"All right, people, lay off," I said. "The Rhodes is, you know, very cool."

Sam patted me on the back, harder than needed. "Good on you, mate."

Jess thrust a stovetop-roasted marshmallow in my face. "Eat this!"

We would never see each other again, or never again all at once. I wanted to stay in this moment. A dozen friends in the kitchen finding any excuse to stand close, making both pancakes and fry bread, April spraying whipped cream into open mouths while her visiting little cousins sat quietly suffering in the corner on the floor. Sandra and Nick dancing with a potato balanced between their foreheads, Della riding piggy-back on Jess, then the two of them roasting anything they could find on chopsticks over the electric burner. This version of Della that was all weirdness and joy and still pausing to smile across the room at me. Still radiantly, undeservedly mine.

• • •

Something I tried not to think about:

When the space shuttle *Columbia* fell to pieces in the sky, and Della's footsteps pounded down the basement stairs—to find me, to comfort me and choose me—I already knew I would hurt her.

Not yet, but someday. One moment I had wanted a life with her. Then reentry, a penetrated heat shield, the breaking of a shuttle over Texas and Louisiana. Della and I were beginning again, and also we were ending, in the last minutes before she would choose me at all.

Part of it was that I could die in space. I could leave her so suddenly, and our children. I could change the shape of her life in an instant. She had lost people before.

But also, I could hurt her. I *had* hurt her. Surely I would again. I would never deserve what Della was willing to give me, because Della was willing to give me herself.

I had a clear idea now, after Naugatuck Oyster Bar, of what it would cost her to stay with me. Unexpectedly, I thought about the Cherokee language. I'd forgotten so much.

I remembered the phrase, gvgeyui, how to love her meant to be stingy with her. To love her so much I wouldn't let anyone use her up. That meant not even me. I had to take care of Della, if Della wouldn't take care of herself.

I was the first to head upstairs. "Keep having fun," I told Della. "I should feed Walela."

I paused in the hall outside the kitchen. I kissed her on the cheek—serious, lingering. "I love you," I said.

Della took a beer from the fridge. Sam gave me a funny look and led her back to the kitchen table.

Walela waited in a terrarium on our dresser. My dresser. Over time his home had grown crowded with Kayla's art projects, mini habitats made of clay and Popsicle sticks. She still mailed them to us from Boston sometimes, and asked us to send back photos for her blog. A lizard tipi, a lizard hogan, a lizard longhouse made of tiny sticks hot-glued together. His tail had grown back, but Della said it was only cartilage.

I dropped a live cricket a few inches from Walela. He peeked out of his white felt tipi. He froze, waiting.

He pounced.

I began to gather Della's things, to fold them and stack them in better order than I'd found them. I carried everything across the hall, to the room the college had considered to be hers. I put clean sheets on her bed and a pillow in a pillowcase, and laid out her red Pendleton blanket. I turned it down at the corner. Della hadn't slept there in at least a year.

I filled her steamer with water and placed it, unplugged, on a wooden stool by the outlet. I hung her garment bag with her graduation clothes over the closet door, everything she'd been so proud and excited to wear. The cream-colored trade shirt. The wool wrap skirt she'd sewn from a pattern online. The moccasins she'd carried in her backpack for months, beading just one or two rows a day. A woven belt she had ordered over the phone, from the gift shop at the museum back home.

I would not cry. I hurried back across the hall and closed my door. I sat straight-backed on the edge of my mattress and waited for Della to see what I had done.

PART

THREE

2005–2015

Facebook Group

GLBT Singles Looking to Mingle at UC Berkeley

Steph Harper

September 28, 2005 / 7:35 p.m.

[Photo: A stack of hardcover books on a heavy wooden table. Steph folds her arms over them and looks down toward the camera, unsmiling. She wears a ribbed white undershirt, no bra, a ripped denim jacket, and four silver rings. Around her upper arm is a wide, bronze cuff, etched with waves and repeated angles; it is a gift made by her sister. People blur in the background, clustered below a wide, gold-colored chandelier.]

Age: 24
Undergrad or Grad: Grad (PhD candidate)
Dept: Astronomy and Geology
Orientation: lesbian
Looking for: casual

Yes this photo was taken in the library. Send me a private message if you're here too and want a quick study break. Not looking to waste time texting. Not looking for a relationship. Just scoping things out after a god-awful year in Russia.

I'm available M/W/Th 8-9pm (ONLY) and I know a spot.

October 1, 2007

Steph, PhD student, UC Berkeley

[First photo: A red-checkered picnic blanket, a wicker basket, and a tray of cheese and crackers beside tiny flowered plates. A bottle of rosé and two plastic champagne flutes. Second photo: Steph, in overalls, a sports bra, and no shirt. Big glasses, short hair middle-parted and falling in her eyes. She holds a flute of sparkling water out to the camera.]

Age: 26
Seeking: I am a <u>woman</u> looking for a <u>woman</u> for <u>casual fun</u> or <u>a relationship</u>

Selected reviews from people I've met on this godforsaken website:

"Bad date, good snacks." —Abbie.

"A true gentleman." —Molly.

"idk, I came like 3 times?" —Sarah.

"Berkeley ladies! If you're looking for a low-drama gateway experience to lesbianism, look no further." —Alice.

"You srsly want me to text you a review? So you can put it on your weird internet dating profile? Wtf is wrong with you?" —Lucía.

STEPH

SUPERNOVA

January 2008–March 2010

A supernova lets out more energy than our sun ever has, or will, in its lifetime. It's a large explosion in the universe, a sudden burst of light.

In a Type II supernova, my favorite, a star runs out of fuel. Heavier elements accumulate inside of it—the heaviest at its core, with gradually lighter elements layering toward the surface. There's a certain mass that the core will reach, which we call the Chandrasekhar limit.

When a star's core reaches and surpasses the Chandrasekhar limit, it will implode.

The first recorded observation of a supernova came almost two thousand years ago, in 185 CE. It was visible to the naked eye for eight months, and described by Chinese astronomers as a "guest star."

In 1054 CE, Chinese and Korean astronomers recorded another remnant of a supernova—the Crab Nebula. A star's explosion so bright that, for a full month, they could see it during the day. I was taught in college that Native people recorded it, too, that there were cave paintings of the supernova found in the American Southwest. It was a popular story, based on a paper, which was based on two photos of one cave wall taken in 1955.

When the story was disproven, I was twenty-seven years old. I was at a conference in Maryland, chosen partly for its proximity to my girlfriend's childhood home. I would meet her parents that night, in a window I had open now that both my college and my grad school advisers had bailed on me. I imagined them getting drinks together anyway, commiserating over what a pain I was to work with.

At the conference, the man seated next to me raised his hand and called the whole thing depressing. How disappointing to tell his students that the cave paintings were just a head with a horn, or a knife, or a Hopi kachina.

Native people would have seen it, though, even if they hadn't painted it. They were still here, in the world. There was a strange new object in the sky. And then there wasn't. No explanation, no data, just the mystery of it. I think of my ancestors, wary eyes on a foreign light. I would have been terrified.

I dated the physicist from Maryland longer than anyone since Della. I hadn't meant for it to happen. A real relationship, someone with the power to hold me down. She was a postdoc at Berkeley. An intended one-night stand with the same need for time alone as me, the same acquaintances as me (to her they were friends), and the same devotion to her work. She was like me in many ways, but with the gift of flexibility. "Just two years on the job market," she always said, "and if no one hires me, I'll teach high school." She refused to fall into what she called "the hell of sunk-costs academia," which to her meant moving constantly for a job few people could get.

The physicist pursued me so slowly, and so diligently, months passed before I knew I'd been caught. By then, she had adjusted to my schedule. We spent our days in our respective labs, before reuniting in the library. We'd type into the evening, across from each other at a long glossy table till our fingers were sore and cold. Then we'd jog the six blocks back to my apartment and reward ourselves with dinner and sex.

Once, in the loose and extravagant way I sometimes talked in bed, I told her that I had changed. That she had changed me. "I used to think I was incapable of love," I said like an idiot.

The physicist selected a ring with an emerald, lab-grown, and I bought it with my stipend. For months I carried it in the large white pocket of my lab coat and touched it throughout the day. When Prop 8 passed, and I'd missed the brief window in which our wedding would have been real, the physicist said it hadn't been my fault. We'd get a domestic partnership, she said, and no one could stop her from calling it a marriage.

While I was pacing alone in the lab one evening—late to meet the physi-cist for our second anniversary, ring box sweaty in my palm as I practiced my speech—my colleagues Alicia Soderberg and Edo Berger made an important scientific discovery.

They caught a supernova in the act of exploding, using data from NASA's Swift Gamma-Ray Burst Mission X-ray space telescope. No one had ever done that before.

I, too, had access to data from NASA's Gamma-Ray Burst Mission X-ray space telescope, data that I ignored, data that was making its way across the fucking monitor four feet behind my fucking back as I practiced (practiced!) getting in a half-kneel and pulling out the ring box in one smooth fucking gesture.

Alicia and Edo alerted teams around the world. The Hubble Space Tele-scope in low Earth orbit, the Gemini South telescope in Chile, the Lick Ob-servatory in California, the Keck I telescope in Hawai'i—all of them moved to record the event. Because of Alicia and Edo—who were in love, by the way, and engaged to be straight-people real-married, and watching the supernova together over dinner—we would forever know what X-ray pattern to look for. Now, because of Alicia and Edo, hundreds of supernovae would be discovered annually, exactly at the moment of their explosion.

I didn't know that yet. I only knew I was late. I ran several blocks to the res-taurant in a wrinkled and sweaty blazer, my lab coat stuffed into the bottom of my backpack. The physicist stood up to kiss me. She wore a new black dress with dozens of tiny pleats at the waist, the neckline plunging to meet it. I wanted so badly to run my finger along the hem, to follow it down from the neck to its end. I wanted to skip dinner, take her home, and hold up her breasts in my hands. Her wineglass, mostly empty by the time I'd arrived, glowed yellow under rows of string lights. Like she'd caught the stars in the bowl of her glass.

The physicist didn't say I'd made her wait, though I had. She had a small *Star Trek* paperback with her, clearly secondhand, which she tucked carefully into a soft leather clutch.

She said she'd been offered a job at Yale. She was leaving. I did not ask her to marry me. I found out about the supernova four hours after it hap-pened, on space.com.

・　・　・

The physicist moved out. I spent two months of that winter in bed.

I let my phone die and didn't charge it. I ate crackers and peanut butter, only crackers and peanut butter, alone in a room with towels duct-taped over the windows. I put the engagement ring on my tongue and spit it out and threw it in the air and caught it. I slept.

My PhD adviser found my sister's Facebook account online. She left a comment on a recent selfie Kayla had posted. My adviser meant well—she always meant well—but we frustrated each other. The selfie she chose to comment under had six hundred likes.

The comment said she hadn't seen me in seven weeks, that no one in the department had, and that she was concerned. It said (for the world and theoretically NASA to see) that I could be "erratic." A word Kayla would needlessly repeat to me, and which I would never forget.

Kayla wrote down my adviser's phone number, and swiftly deleted the comment.

Within six hours she was on a plane from Boston to California, leaving Jason—a third-year-associate—to scramble for twelve-hour days of child-care. Kayla found me where the physicist had left me, back in January—in bed, dark-eyed and dangerously underweight.

"Oh, Steph."

I didn't move.

"Steph, oh my God, what happened." She stood at the door, near tears.

"Alicia Soderberg saw the birth of a supernova," I croaked.

I realized this was a ridiculous thing to say, that the whole situation was ridiculous. I started to laugh.

My sister did, too, lightly, humoring me—but then she stepped carefully into the room. She looked around at it, at me. She sniffed and made a new sound like *oh*, then a crack in her voice.

"It's okay," she said, running her eyes slowly from ceiling to floor. "Wait. Wait. I'll be right there."

My sister dropped her duffel bag outside the door. She tore the towels from the windows and opened them. A shock of cold air.

She turned on every light she could find, plugged in the electric kettle, and proceeded to clean my entire apartment while I watched. Two months of laundry and two months of dishes. I heard the vacuum and then the swish of the mop in its bucket. From the bathroom came the sharp smell of bleach.

Finally, Kayla took off her shoes. She crossed the room to my bed.

My sheets were still dirty. *I* was dirty. Kayla fell onto the mattress and held the mess of me against her body. She cried so quietly I only knew it from the wet on my shoulder.

In the shower she scrubbed my skin. She was businesslike somehow, even though she was wearing my swim trunks and sports bra. I was naked. I held my face to the tile wall. I couldn't look at myself, at my body and what I had done to it.

Kayla filled my kitchen with groceries. Pre-cooked meals. Vegetables, washed and cut and put away in new glass containers. From a chair she had placed by the window I made the faintest of jokes about my hard-won abs, how easily they'd disappeared, and she sucked in a breath. "Steph, *no*," she said.

I understood I'd again disappointed her. "The abs were a project for space," I said.

"You need another project," she said. "A fresh start."

"Huh?"

"Think about it. Space has never been good to you."

I sat up in my chair, ready to fight her on this, but I was so tired. I lay my head on the windowsill. Outside, on the sidewalk, a man in a big fleece jacket carried a toddler in a little fleece jacket uphill in some kind of structured hiking backpack. They disappeared into the fog.

In the morning we sat on the roof of my building under freshly laundered blankets, our faces angled up toward the sun. My sister took the blue knit hat from her head and put it on mine. She folded it over my ears. We drank coffee she'd made with the new French press she'd bought me—ceramic, bright yellow, what small joy—and I decided to try again.

Holding me gently at the elbow, Kayla walked me to a salon. I got a buzzcut for the first time, and wished I had gay friends (or friends in general) to make a big deal out of it. Kayla said, "Looks good." Then she took me to a bakery, where a warm croissant in wax paper was pressed into my hand. Then to the low gray building of a psychologist. Outside it, on a bench, Kayla and I screamed at each other.

"Oh my God, Steph, you *have to go!*" she said.

"I literally *cannot,*" I said.

"I'll pay for it! I'll pay for all of it! However many sessions this lady says it fucking takes!"

"Stop trying to fix me with Jason's money!"

"How many times must I explain shared assets to you? Domestic labor is *labor!* Motherhood is *work!*"

"I don't fucking *care* that you don't have a *job!*"

Kayla looked ready to throw me to the ground.

I held up a hand and lowered my voice. "No one's asked you to pay for this, and I'm not going. Spend it on Felicia."

"It's better for me to buy you help"—Kayla took a long, labored breath—"than to fly cross-country the next time you want to kill yourself."

"I didn't want to kill myself!"

An elderly couple passed us with a dog. Kayla turned away from me to wipe at her cheek. I'd made her cry. "You know who Mom said wouldn't get help?"

When I, someday, applied to NASA, as one of maybe twelve thousand applicants, there would be a psychosocial evaluation. I knew this. I was in the habit, after each annual physical, of checking my body and mind against the pdf of disqualifying illnesses for astronauts. One of them, on page forty-four: "a presence or history of depressive disorders." On the bench outside the psychologist's office, carefully, I explained this to Kayla.

She groaned. She closed her eyes, leaned back, and stayed that way for several seconds.

"Twelve thousand applicants?" she said.

I nodded.

"And when is the next, like, hiring round for astronauts?"

"The last one was in 2004. No one knows when the next one will be."

"Huh."

Kayla clearly didn't think I'd make it. Still, she dropped the issue of therapy.

"At least tell me why you broke up," she said. Kayla had met the physicist—once, on a layover—and declared her "good" for me. She and my mother had been visibly relieved at the very idea of the physicist, with her willingness to take me in and deal with me. I'd felt like the troubled family dog, finally rehomed.

"She didn't want to marry me," I said.

"Bullshit," Kayla said. "She picked out the ring she wanted. You told me that."

Kayla was right about the physicist. In the end, she'd been the one to propose that night. Not with a romantic speech or a ring, but with a just and thoughtful compromise. After graduation, she said, I would follow her to Yale. Gay marriage was newly legal in Connecticut. If I were actually accepted as an astronaut candidate someday (and it killed me, the truth in that word—*actually*), she promised to leave her position. No matter what, even if she were only a year out from tenure. Even if she *had* tenure, or a zillion-dollar lab in her name. She promised to move to Houston, even if she'd never work again.

She had offered to put all this in writing. In a legal contract, even. A pre-nup! This last part she added in tears later that night, in a perfect half-kneel in our apartment. She was shirtless, though we'd already had sex the last time without knowing it. She was just comfortable like that. She had felt at home with me.

"Kayla," I said, "not everyone wants your life! I can't be in a relationship, and I can't go to therapy. I can't even turn around for five minutes without missing the discovery of a lifetime."

My sister stood. She looked exhausted. She was realizing, maybe, what I couldn't say.

This was not about the physicist. For nine weeks now, since I'd left the physicist sobbing on the floor, I had imagined myself heartbroken. The kind of person who could be heartbroken.

But I wasn't. After brushing my teeth that night, on my way to bed for weeks, I'd stepped over her body as she sobbed on the floor. I was the kind of person who destroyed herself over missed data from an X-ray space telescope. Over a supernova, the death of a star.

UCB LGBT Singles GRADUATE SCHOOL [no undergrads!]
Steph Harper
April 25, 2010 / 2:05 a.m.

[Photo: Hastily taken selfie, bad lighting. Steph is in bed, no shirt, flannel red-and-black sheet pulled up and tucked under her arms. In her left hand is a mug of coffee with plain black writing: WORLD'S BEST DAD. There are gray circles under her eyes. She squints at the camera and smiles, with only her lips.]

Age: 28
Sex: F
Orientation: gay
Looking for: friendship, if even that?

Recently out of a long-term relationship. Trying to finish the dissertation and get out of here. I want to spend more time outdoors, and to get back into a gym routine that I miss and think is fun but that my ex once called "a ridiculous and vain time-suck" and "not going to impress anyone in academia." I don't drink or smoke. Not interested in marijuana culture. Not looking for anything with long-term potential, now or ever again.

Would you like to join me for something active and outdoors, like a strenuous hike or rock-climbing?

New Profile, Tinder

August 4, 2013

Steph, 31, scientist

[Photo: Steph sits in a parking lot alone, under a highway sign written in Japanese. Behind her is a forest. Looming over the forest is Mount Sakurajima, an active stratovolcano in the midst of an eruption. Gray plumes burst into the sky, spilling ash onto the forest below. Steph sits cross-legged on the pavement. She wears hiking boots, bunched socks, high-waisted jean shorts, and a brown belt. A loose black tank top, dusted with gray ash, is tucked in at her waist. Her arms and legs are specked with green Band-Aids, her skin tan, her cheeks and nose sunburned. She wears a blue surgical mask. Steph holds out her arms and looks up at the sky, her eyes wide and jokingly desperate, like Why Me?]

SOS. I am in Tsukuba for my second year of a TWO-YEAR fellowship and NOBODY IS GAY.

Looking for literally anything. Friends, lovers, people in Tsukuba (not Tokyo) I can talk to as I slowly lose my mind. All I do is work (alone), go to the gym (alone), and take the train to Tokyo once a month for an "Expats Brunch!" with some of the worst straight people you will ever meet. If you are gay then it's *likely* I'm a two-hour train ride from where you live. But at least I'm sexually adventurous?

August 21, 2014

Steph, 32, scientist

[Photo: Steph leans against the yellow-painted cement wall of a gelateria, waffle cone in hand. She wears sunglasses. Double-pierced ears with plain gold studs. A faded, once-orange Space-Culture Camp T-shirt with the sleeves cut off. Beside her are blue wooden shutters. A cobblestone road, shiny after a summer shower. Rows of little houses, a flower shop, a bakery. Towering over this, in the distance, is Mount Vesuvius.]

Here for the (academic) year and open to anything (except moving here, compromising on career stuff, or getting same-sex-civil-unioned). Even if you're about to swipe left (and I celebrate that; You Do You) I personally would LOVE IT if you could cooperate with the municipality's planned evacuation drill in a few months (SAVE THE DATE! DECEMBER 21, 2014). If you're reading this you're almost definitely living in the evacuation zone and from what I have seen so far you are all too beautiful to die.

Edit: The people of Italy have been DMing me in terror—the December thing I want you to participate in is a planned DRILL, not a planned ERUPTION. I do not have the power to plan an eruption!

I promise you would know if Vesuvius was gonna blow. When the day comes there will be signs. It will be on the news! Scientists like me will stand in the streets in orange vests, screaming for you to comply with evac orders. Because you participated in our drill, you will know which way to run.

This will happen someday. Maybe in decades and maybe in centuries, when you have already died peacefully in the arms of your true love (which could be me, assuming you aren't too attached to this place?).

WE SEE WE ARE
WALKING ON BONES

December 2014

Christmas in Italy was Kayla's idea. She wanted to pick up the whole family, our mother included, and drop them outside my lab on a volcano. "It'll be fun!" she said. But Christmas in Italy was still six days away, and my sister already hated it.

I blamed the internet. Ever since Kayla's first #indigenouswomentravel post, the photo of her fluffy socks peeking out of moccasins as she boarded Alitalia Airways, the comments had been flying in. *#RICHindigenouswomentravel, must be nice to spend Christmas in Italy, have you ever even taken your kid to the rez*, etc.

Another possibility was that Jason—I suspected, but also it was obvious—thought Kayla's whole platform was lame. So what if it was lame, I thought. You married her! You have to click "heart" under all her little posts!

I did. Our mother did. Even Felicia did, and she had to do chores to earn coupons for time online.

After the family photo in Pompeii, when our mother was struggling to catch her breath from the steep walk while also asking Kayla if something seemed "a little off with Felicia lately," Jason asked Kayla—weirdly calm, his hand in her hair—not to post the photo on Facebook. Why? In case a client saw it. His clients, every one of them mid-divorce, got sad and needy over the holidays. They texted him more than usual, and what was usual was already too much.

Not posting a family vacation photo was a big ask for a mommy blogger (my term, not hers). But also, Kayla had migrated from Facebook to Instagram in 2012! I said, "Mom, what are you talking about? Felicia is fine!" and Kayla said, "Hold up, babe, do you even *follow* me?"

Kayla and Jason fought, gripping each other's hands as they stomped through the halls of the archaeological museum. They fought with hushed voices and long, respectful bouts of listening. It looked exhausting. Jason had gone into divorce litigation for the money and the interesting drama, but now he was terrified of conflict.

My mother took me and Felicia down the street for gelato. On our return to the museum, they were still fighting. (Jason called it "hearing each other.")

My mother looked at me, worry clear on her face. I put my arm around Felicia and guided her to the outdoor section of the museum, the aftermath of the eruption. Felicia loved it—even the bodies of two people embracing as they burned alive—until she saw the dog. I had forgotten about the dog. Like the people it was dead, kind of mummified by the casting of the ash. It was in the position it had died in two thousand years ago, on its back with its mouth wide open.

Felicia screamed. My mother held Felicia's face to her belly and rocked back and forth, a babying move which made Felicia scream louder. Kayla and Jason came running out of the museum, still holding hands.

"Steph, what the hell, you took her to see the *dog*?" Kayla said.

"How do you even know about the dog?" I said.

"I read about every place I take her before we go! We skipped the dog *intentionally*!"

In what world, I thought, had Kayla led the family on some preplanned tour of the museum? We had gotten gelato without her.

"Mom, I'm too old for you to be screening stuff for me," Felicia said, suddenly composed. "I can choose for myself."

Kayla smiled, one eyebrow raised. There was no way, I thought, she'd give her twelve-year-old choices. She let go of Jason, took Felicia by the hand, and dragged her to the exit.

．　．　．

The restaurant walls were a faded yellow, the tables a scratched, honey-colored wood. My mother laid her napkin out flat and put her plate and silverware on top of it—a weird, makeshift tablecloth.

Crowded around tables in mismatched chairs were mostly older men— drinking and laughing, and bent over large plates of ham and shellfish. The whole room seemed to be served by one woman. I realized, as she pulled out her notepad to take our orders, that we had had sex.

The woman had long brown hair and wore a short, black apron tight around her waist. She stood with one hip jutted to the side and looked at me, unfazed.

"My daughter will have spaghetti, please," Kayla said. "No sauce."

The server nodded, still looking at me. Was she remembering it, too? Months ago. A dating app, a bar, a cramped apartment with roommates over a restaurant. This restaurant? Her hand on my cheek, too intimate. She was in school for something, maybe nursing.

"I can order for myself," Felicia said. "Spaghetti, please! But no sauce."

Dinner had been Jason's idea. Diffusing tension was always Jason's idea.

Kayla had told our mother and me, in a weirdly braggy way on the first night of the trip, that every January Jason scheduled them quarterly sessions with a marriage counselor. "Just to check in." When they argued, Kayla said, they had this elaborate process of listening to each other's feelings, stating them back to each other, asking questions "from a place of curiosity," and holding hands. One of the questions was, "When I did _____, and you felt _____, did that remind you of anything from your childhood?"

When I heard that, I said that for some people remembering childhood must be better in theory than in practice. Our mother laughed and laughed, choosing to be part of the joke and not the butt of it.

Earlier, in line for a taxi outside the airport when they'd arrived, Kayla had pulled me aside. She said she'd started searching for information about our father.

I tensed. Had she found something? Did our mother know she was looking?

"Nothing yet," she whispered.

Relief.

"That's insane, and I want no part in it," I'd said. "You should give up. He died before people put stuff on the internet."

"Don't you want to know his whole deal? We're missing *basic* facts about who he was. Mom won't even talk about the accident that killed him!"

"If you find anything," I said, "don't tell me."

Kayla glared at me, and the taxi arrived.

At the restaurant, our mother asked, "Do they have gelato here?" She was smiling, resting her elbow on top of Felicia's head.

"Elisi, we had gelato before dinner!" Felicia said, batting her arm away and laughing. Felicia was the first Harper in who knows how long to use the Cherokee word for grandma, though she didn't know to conjugate its possessive. She called Jason's mother "Tutu," in Hawaiian.

"Steph," Kayla said, "how's the rest of your night looking? Think you'll be free after this?"

I turned to the server. She yelled good-naturedly at an old man in the corner. He was calling her over in Italian: girl girl girl girl.

"Una bottiglia di acqua, insalata e pesce," I said.

"You've sure been practicing," our mother said. She meant, I thought, something like *you've sure stopped caring about indigenous language revitalization*; or, *I bet all your Cherokee is gone!*

It mostly was. I ignored her. She ordered fettuccine alfredo.

The server nodded slowly at the touristy request, and I suspected she'd bring my mother noodles with a pat of butter. She turned to me. "I'll be back to take care of you." She moved her eyes slowly down my body. When she left, Jason was watching me, smiling and shaking his head.

"*Well, Auntie Steph,*" he said, leaning back in his chair. "I sure hope you're enjoying yourself in Italy."

"I do all right." I gave my shoulder a little brush.

"Steph," Kayla said again, "let's go for a drink tonight. After Jason gets everyone settled at the hotel?"

"I can get myself settled," our mother said. "Don't mind me!"

"Me too," Felicia said, not looking up. "I've been working my way up to brushing my own teeth." The server had clocked her as much younger than twelve, handing her a pack of crayons and a coloring sheet when we'd sat down. Instead of taking offense, Felicia quietly shaded in a small elephant.

"It's a bad night for me," I said. "I'll be up at four a.m. I've gotta get my workout in before I help prep for the volcano drill, and then make it down to your hotel for breakfast."

"Steph, please," Kayla said.

"Plus, I haven't had a drink since like, 2003?"

Kayla sighed. "I haven't been *invited* to come visit you since you-know-when. I'm sorry if I'm not up to date."

"Wait, since when?" Felicia asked. "I *don't* know when!"

The adults ignored her. After recovering back in grad school from what I called "a bad breakup," I was embarrassed at how weak I'd been. Many things worse than a bad breakup could happen in the world, and I had not proven myself ready for them.

Also, I had a reputation to save. I went full force on the PhD. (The *two* PhDs, in astronomy and geology, which had been *almost* impossible to convince my adviser to let me do. She'd tried very hard to mentor me, but said I was stubborn and impatient.) I had no real relationships and saw no family or friends. I had my work, my physical fitness, and sometimes sex. After graduation I won a fellowship in Japan and then this, a fellowship in Italy. It was only this fall, when NASA finally put out a new call for astronaut candidate applications and I finally clicked "submit," that I'd told Kayla she could come see me.

I would have jumped at the chance to spend time alone with her. Just the two of us, like old times. A bar would've been fine. I went to bars all the time, for cranberry juice and little bowls of peanuts. But tonight I felt sure I knew what Kayla was really after: winning my vote against the thirty-meter telescope.

NASA wanted to build it on Mauna Kea, a volcano sacred to Native Hawaiians. Kayla wanted me to help her—and the group of Native Hawaiians leading the cause—to *stop* them.

My involvement was a dumb idea. In half a year, NASA would come to a decision on my candidacy. Until then, I wasn't allowed to update my CV, or even add references. I had to stay out of trouble. If all went well, and I were chosen, I still wouldn't be at Kayla's protest. I'd be at Johnson Space Center in Houston, or maybe off training in some extreme location. I'd read about missions in the wilderness, the ocean, and the Arctic Circle.

"Come on, Steph," our mother said. "You can skip the workout to make time for your sister, can't you? You know, a sibling is the one person in the world who knows you from childhood to death."

Felicia looked up from her coloring page. "I don't have any siblings. And I don't want anyone to die. Elisi, how old are you?"

"Young. She had a baby in high school," Jason said.

"Jason!" Kayla said. He shrugged. They'd had a baby in college.

"It's not a secret," our mother said. "And it's not just me who will die. By the time *you* die, Felicia, we hope your parents will have been dead a long time."

Jason looked wearily across the table. "Felicia, this is all a long way off. You'll be very old, even older than your Elisi and your Tutu. And you don't need a sibling; you'll have your husband and kids."

"Will she, now?" I said.

"I haven't seen my brothers," our mother said, "in . . . oh . . . maybe thirty-three years? Or my parents. Or my grandparents." She spoke slowly, as if realizing it now. "Well. I've just got y'all."

Kayla and I looked at each other, worried. Since when did our mother talk like this? Sure, she loved telling stories about our distant ancestors and the legacy they'd left behind. But the recent past was off-limits and always had been.

"What was your grandma like?" Felicia said.

Our mother looked surprised at the question. "Well . . ." she started. "My grandparents on my mother's side were very poor. It was the Depression—"

"That's when the stock market crashed," Jason said to Felicia, who nodded seriously like she had been there.

"Yes. Like I said, they were poor. They took my mother to some distant cousins in Arkansas and left her in a barn. Then they went back to Oklahoma."

"*What?*" said Felicia.

"Now that I think about it, she was around your age."

"Jesus Christ," Jason said under his breath.

Kayla nudged him to be quiet. "Say more, Ma."

"My mother grew up and she married a soybean farmer, not Cherokee, and she spent our whole childhood talking about how our life was beneath her. *We knew Greek and Latin*, that kind of thing. While she herself had a sixth-grade education! She meant her ancestors, whenever she said *we*."

"You mean she talked about the seminary," I said. *Like you did.*

There was a small accusation in my voice, which she didn't pick up on. I couldn't believe how her story had shifted. She had been just like her mother, so prideful. What had changed for her, in the time since I'd left home?

"Yes, the seminary," she said. "But the Greek and Latin part came up a lot. Usually when our dad would hit her and leave the house to cool down. Then she'd—"

"When your dad would *what?*" Kayla said. This was new information to both of us, but it wasn't a shock to me. Unlike Kayla, I remembered Texas.

"Hit her," she repeated, "and leave the house to calm down. And then—"

Jason waved a hand across the table. "Hannah, I'm so sorry—but should Felicia be hearing about domestic—"

Kayla shushed him, hard. She stared at our mother across the table, waiting.

"Okay. So." Our mother cleared her throat. "When that happened, she'd sit us kids down and tell us who we came from. Indians in ball gowns, Indians with pianos, that sort of thing."

"But why'd your dad hit your mom?" Felicia said.

"All this, when all you'd asked was what my granny was like!" Our mother laughed at herself. The sound was forced, her smile tense. Her old impulse to smooth things over. "I'll tell you. There was one time when my father kicked us out, and my mother drove us kids to Oklahoma. *That's* when I met my granny."

Kayla looked at me. Maybe for help? I shrugged.

"I remember the storytelling kicked up that summer, from both of them. They made sure we learned our history. My mother seemed very forgiving about having been left in a barn, or maybe just glad to have somewhere to go. I read. I ate well. It was lovely."

"Huh. Then what?" Felicia said.

Kayla shook her head, guessing at what might come. She put an arm around her daughter.

"My father found us. My mother swung the door open all the way, like he was an old friend. I think my granny knew she wouldn't see us again. She went straight to bed that afternoon and wouldn't come out to say goodbye."

Then, like an afterthought, she added, "That was in the 1970s. She'll be dead by now."

Felicia's mouth hung open.

Our mother waited, maybe for something specific, but none of us knew what to say. She excused herself for the restroom. Kayla and I exchanged glances, a question. Neither of us followed her.

I wasn't surprised by what I had learned. It made sense to me that our messed-up family came from messed-up family. Children could be left to raise themselves in barns; fathers could be left half-dead in cars. All this to say nothing of the ground under their feet, the Earth alone and vulnerable in space.

Kayla looked confused, turning over pieces that didn't fit. I realized, with annoyance, that this new information would only reinforce her interest in googling our father. She would want to know more than she should.

"Mom?" Felicia said. She sounded a little scared.

"Auntie Steph!" Jason said. He did a little drumroll on his daughter's shoulders, and she relaxed back into his hands. "Tell me about this volcano drill."

Jason had a stabilizing presence, a talent for subtle redirection. I thought of how he'd talk softly to the younger guys in college, calming them. This was probably most relevant to his time in Kosovo, where diffusing conflict had been life-or-death. But strangely, now it made me think of Brett.

"At this point," I said, "Felicia knows more about the drill than I do."

Felicia smiled faintly. She needed a distraction.

"Take it away?"

Felicia explained the drill I'd help run in the morning. The service part of my research fellowship was in zone 1—an area where the highest number of people would be killed in an eruption.

No town in the region had ever successfully planned an evacuation. It was like moving mountains, my supervisor said, ha ha ha, to get the government to authorize and fund a drill.

"So," Felicia said, "helping people run away before Vesuvius explodes—"

"Erupts," I said.

"—erupts, is like the same as Auntie Steph's *future* job, which is getting a few humans onto Mars. That's so *they* stay alive, when everybody else in the world gets burned up by an asteroid."

"Oh, honey," Kayla said. "Have you been having bad dreams?"

"That is not my job!" I said. "Even if I were an astronaut, even if I were chosen, that would not be my job!"

"Maika'i, e ku'u kaikamahine," Jason said, beaming at Felicia. Recently he'd been learning short phrases in Hawaiian, especially praise. Kayla smiled at this, though I knew it made her jealous. She hadn't been good enough at Cherokee to pass it on. In the background of photos on Kayla's Instagram page, there were small Hawaiian flashcards on the walls that I had never commented on.

"Osda," our mother said in Cherokee, belatedly. She was back from the restroom with her lipstick reapplied, having collected herself. But her voice sounded tired, like sharing so much truth had taken something from her.

Felicia didn't respond. She knew only a handful of basic Cherokee words, and I wasn't sure that was one of them. She leaned on my arm. "Auntie, they're gonna hire you. I know it. That's gonna be your job."

The night before, or rather very early that morning, a taxi driver had asked me what my job was. After dropping off my family at their hotel I'd gone to La Grotta, a club in Ercolano where I sometimes went to pretend I wasn't myself. At La Grotta, I often lied about my life and let Italian women explain volcanoes to me. Twice I'd had sex in the restroom, the painted wooden door clicking rhythmically against the lock. I'd learned to do that in my twenties, to periodically have sex with rootless girls who couldn't plan past next week. Now, at thirty-three, it was starting to get old.

Sometimes, I'd see them again. It was a small town. Someone who'd asked me to hit them in bed would later sell me socks in the open market or pass a cup of espresso across a counter. Once I recognized a woman in an alley in the early morning, a baby strapped to her chest and two small children holding her hands. Most of the time, they didn't recognize me.

I told the taxi driver I was an astronomer and a geologist. Yes, yes, it's extremely rare to be both. Yes, I went to school for a long time.

"So you'll be here for the drill," said the taxi driver, and I said yes, and he laughed.

"You are going to be disappointed," he said.

"Disappointed?"

"People here . . ." he said. "You have to understand me. We live on the ruins of people who lived where we live, who died where we live. So, we laugh."

"But if you'd cooperate—I mean, the evacuation plan could save thousands of lives in the long-term, if people would just—"

The driver stopped on the side of the road.

"Listen, bella," he said, the meter ticking out its little paper behind him. "You know what happens if we try what you say? We let you do your drill, we think about it, we prepare. Then we wake up, we look around. We see we are walking on bones."

In the restaurant, the server returned to our table. Food! Finally! We tore into it. The server stood behind my chair. Looking down at me, she traced the back of my neck with the tip of a finger.

"What else can I do for you?" she asked in Italian. It was coming back to me—the tight jeans, the high heels, the way she'd pushed me off her as she came.

Jason ordered a piece of cake, even as Kayla and I looked at him like, *Why are you extending this nightmare?* I shouldn't have been surprised. Jason liked to tell his clients to "get comfortable with discomfort."

"YOLO," Felicia sang and ordered a triple sundae.

I smiled sheepishly at the server and shrugged my shoulders like, *Wow, Americans, am I right?* She looked at me for a moment, ripped half a page from her notepad, and handed it to me. A phone number.

She went back to the kitchen. The double doors swung closed.

Jason said, "All right, *all right!*" We high-fived. My mother adjusted her napkin-tablecloth at the corner with two fingers. Kayla snorted, and Felicia said, "What's it say?"

"That's not for Steph to share with us," our mother said. She straightened her fork in its place.

"*It's a phone number,*" I said in a stage-whisper. "*It means she thinks I'm cute.*" I gave Felicia a little bow.

"*Cool*," Felicia whispered. All she seemed to want, increasingly it seemed, was for people to tell her things.

"That's enough, Steph," our mother said, still looking down.

There was an edge in her voice, but I knew her well enough to know it wasn't (at least, it wasn't only) that the server was a woman. It was that the server seemed fun and unserious, a reminder of the kinds of partnership I'd given up on. If it weren't for outer space, my mother was convinced I'd be happy by now. Maybe even married. If it weren't for outer space, I wanted to say, there'd be no context for me.

Jason argued quietly with Kayla about the use of her phone during family dinner. Kayla said it was for her job. Jason said he didn't bring couples in arbitration to family dinner, and I didn't bring moon rocks. "Well, sure. But Steph *isn't* an astronaut!" Kayla said.

"Cheap shot," I said.

Kayla put her phone down, sighed, and stared across the room.

I followed her gaze. The server seemed to be flirting with half the restaurant. She was good at what she did—a chair pushed in for a little girl, a laughing toss of her hair beside an old man seated at the head of a table. Her hips were always moving, her chest pressed forward. Her skirt, shorter than her apron, grazed her thighs. She seemed, in my imagined idea of her, at ease—in this body in this job in this town crouched under a volcano.

It hit me then that the strangeness of her world wasn't the sexiness of it. Or her country, language, family, or job. It was the acceptance. I imagined her growing up here, staying here, dying here—what Tahlequah could have been for me—and I imagined her content. As if I knew anything about her life.

I wondered if I could do it. Any day now, or at least any month, I'd get an answer from NASA. A door opened or closed. Could I feel at home if this were all there was? Not just in Oklahoma, but on Earth itself?

It was absurd, I realized, that I didn't have a backup plan.

I came home late that night (after, admittedly, La Grotta) to many voice messages. They were all from my sister.

Kayla said Felicia had run away. She'd been sharing a hotel room with her grandmother, who was asleep and didn't notice her absence till almost midnight.

Jason left immediately for the police station. Kayla waited in the hotel lobby, filling up the voicemail on my cell. "I have a feeling she went up there," she said. "Don't come here. Stay there. Call me if you see her on your fucking volcano, and for God's sake, charge your phone."

I found Felicia at the summit, standing over the crater. It was the first place I looked for her, near the observatory where I lived with six other geologists. I'd told her, maybe unwisely, that this was where I went to think.

A plume of steam blew silently up from the side, concealing her slightly. She looked like a person from another world, small but still. The shape of her flickered behind the steam, so she was there and not there and there. I ran to her.

"You could die out here!"

"Don't be dramatic, Auntie," Felicia said.

"You could get very, very cold out here."

"Better. I couldn't sleep, so I hailed a taxi. It took me halfway, and then I walked."

"In the dark?"

"I'm fine." Felicia leaned over the metal barrier. She wore hiking boots and a puffy winter coat, unzipped. The edge of her bathrobe blew over her knees in the wind, exposing cartoon-stamped pajama pants.

There were no stadium lights over the volcano, no streetlights or taillights. The sky was lit with stars, in a way that once might have shocked me. My niece's face was bright in moonlight, her shoulders dusted in snow. I pulled her into me.

"I said I'm fine, Auntie," Felicia said. Her voice was muffled against my coat. "Seriously, let me outta here!"

I stepped back, still holding her by the shoulders. "You're standing over a volcano in the middle of the night. What am I supposed to think?"

She looked at me like she was ancient, like she couldn't believe she had to deal with this. "You're supposed to think I wanted some time alone?" she said. "There doesn't have to be something wrong with me for me to want some time alone."

I watched her, shivering over the edge of the volcano's rim, her arms crossed tight over her chest. Where had she heard there was something wrong with her?

Felicia was twelve and I was thirty-three, and I hadn't seen her in far too long. I had let myself miss years, and only remembered her as shy. Now, though, she seemed almost comfortable. Like she was on her way there. I was impressed.

Every four hours of every day, a timer dinged on my phone and I checked for an email from NASA. With every sound of the timer I was a child again, waiting for Exeter, watching my mother carry water to the mailman.

"It's not gonna blow, is it?" Felicia pointed down into the crater, a drop of steep rock without the rolling pool of lava she'd been expecting. Everyone expects it. As geologists, we're in the business of letting them down.

"You see that?" I pointed to a fissure in the rock, a hundred meters below us. Steam rose from it.

"That's it?"

"That's the part for us, yes. Everything else is hidden underneath, like magma."

She didn't ask what type of magma, though I'd hoped she would. We were quiet. It was cold. Who knew how long she'd been out there?

I ran my arm up and down her shoulder, pulling her against my side. "We've gotta go call your mom," I said. "She'll have a heart attack."

I put my gloves on her hands and picked gently at the fleece material, guiding her fingers through. I put my hat on her head, the blue knit one her mother had given me in San Francisco, in a story Felicia didn't need to know.

She looked up at the sky. "I wanna come with you tomorrow," she said, "for the evacuation drill."

I imagined Felicia getting sick, getting frostbite, getting the tip of her nose amputated in the little hospital at the base of the volcano. Kayla saying, *Why didn't you call me, why'd you let your phone die, why'd you let her stand out there in the snow? What is wrong with you?*

How unwomanly I'd built myself, uncaring maybe, shaping myself to slip unobtrusively through the men in my field. Some of it was overkill—the wide cargo pants and orange fleece vests, the decision to laugh at a colleague's crass joke. I knew there were women who fought for the right to avoid what I'd done. I wasn't the first or the only. Sally Ride had passed two years before, the first American woman in space. Only in her obituary did we learn she was gay.

I was out at work, but quietly. I knew the way I dressed and acted confused some people, in a way that didn't bother me. I wasn't hiding. I just wasn't sharing, either.

Felicia pulled on the sleeve of my coat. "You should come live with us," she said.

"Ha! I live *here*!" I pointed down the path, toward the observatory.

"You have a fellowship here. Before that you were in Japan, and before that California, and before that you were at college when I was being born. Also—no offense?—my mom says it's one in a million you'll be an astronaut."

"Whoa, there! Kid!" I put on an exaggerated Russian accent, like she and her mother hadn't just hurt my feelings. "How do you forget my time in Russia?"

"You're crazy," Felicia said. "I never wanna have to move again."

Felicia had been eight when her family moved to Hawai'i. Kayla wrote many long Instagram captions, linked to even longer blog posts, about how they'd wanted to center their indigenous values over the big money Jason was up for as a future partner in Boston. (The move happened very suddenly, and at the time I worried it meant trouble in their marriage. Like how people will buy a house or have a baby, as a Hail Mary after things take a turn? But Kayla never told me anything was amiss, and five years passed. I decided I was wrong. I needed more examples, better examples, than my father and Brett.)

After the move, Kayla had rebranded from urban Indian to homelands Indian—not her homelands, but Jason's. Felicia had, by all accounts, slipped seamlessly into the Hawaiian language school. It was a perfect fit until, recently, it wasn't. She'd suddenly lost her large group of friends and replaced them with two girls with nose rings.

That was how Kayla had described it over the phone, just a week before coming to Italy. "I think she's gay," she'd said. "Maybe you could talk to her?"

"I'm not going to *ask her* if she's *gay*," I'd said. "Also, what's the evidence?"

"The nose-ring girls! They're pretty young to have nose rings. I think they're gay, too."

Beside me, Felicia crossed her arms. She seemed cold, but wasn't ready to admit it.

"You sure you want to stay where you are?" I said. "No moving, ever again?"

"Yeah," she said, suspicion in her voice. "That's what I said."

"There's a chance you'll change your mind someday." I laughed, then regretted it.

She looked at me stone-faced, tight-lipped, like she was too old and too tired to be laughed at.

"I'm sorry," I said.

Felicia shook her head. "We've got volcanoes, and universities, and three huge telescopes already on Mauna Kea, even if I don't really think they should be there . . . I bet there's more jobs for you in Hawai'i than most other places. And there's us."

"I'll visit more," I said.

"I think my mom needs you?"

"Your mom is superhuman."

"No." She sounded so much older now. "Mom's having a hard time. She won't talk about it, and she tries to look like she's fine. You should come help her."

"What kind of hard time?"

Maybe this was about Jason, or her inexplicable curiosity around our father. Maybe her internet job was as unbearable as it seemed? She'd done a full one-eighty from her childhood self, a girl I remembered as almost *too* confident. I thought her online platform, despite its calls for radical self-love in Indigenous girls and women, had made her kind of insecure.

"I just said she won't talk about it!" Felicia said. "Nobody tells me shit-all about jack-shit."

I didn't laugh. Felicia had a whole world in her, even if she hadn't learned how to be careful with it. She had taxied herself up a volcano in the night.

"I wish we could rappel down," Felicia said. She stared into the crater, which was only black.

"We can't."

"I *know*. I'm not dumb."

I needed to take Felicia inside. To call her mother and say she was safe.

I never told my mother I was gay. Not explicitly. I told my sister over winter break of sophomore year that I was dating Della, and asked her to pass the message along. "I don't want to talk about it as long as I live," I said, "but Mom should probably be aware."

Kayla threw her arms around me. She pulled a few yards of rainbow chevron fabric out of a drawer—she'd apparently been *waiting* for this announcement—and explained her plans for a jingle dress-turned-jumpsuit piece of "wearable art" that I could already see getting me gay-bashed on a powwow online forum. She wanted me to wear it in a special coming-out post on her blog. I said I'd rather kill myself, and she said what kind of message would that send to Two-Spirit youth?

Our mother stayed in bed all weekend. I stomped around the house, mad, while Kayla did the cooking and laundry and dishes. On Sunday night, our mother came downstairs and boiled three hot dogs over the stove. Like nothing was different. Or if it was, if there was now something a little bit wrong with me, that was okay.

I wanted to tell Felicia she would be okay, there was nothing wrong with her, these days things didn't have to be so hard. I hoped it was true. I could make no promises.

I gestured for her to be careful. I leaned over the safety railing and toward the rocky darkness, plumes of steam rising slowly to the sky.

Beside her, bare hands holding tight to the cold railing, I screamed down into the crater.

I turned back to Felicia, expecting her to laugh or to worry, to not understand. But she looked ready. She stepped closer to the edge. We threw our voices down together, and waited for their return.

Instagram Post

May 2, 2015

thatindigenousmama

[Photo: A small backyard with a wooden swing set, overlooking a sandy path to the beach. Steph is on her knees, her hands crossed over her chest, her head pressed to the ground. A cell phone lies several feet away, thrown across the frame. Felicia is barefoot, smiling, in a backward orange baseball cap over chin-length hair. She stands tall, and looks directly at the camera.]

My sister @stephharperscientist happened to be visiting us in HI today on her way home from a year in Italy when she got the call we've been waiting for since she was, idk, seven years old? FOLX I GIVE YOU THE FIRST NATIVE AMERICAN WOMAN TO EVER BE SELECTED AS AN ASTRONAUT CANDIDATE, AS PART OF NASA'S INCOMING ASTRONAUT CLASS!

Six minutes later
when @stephharperscientist stopped crying into the dirt, she made me write the official position title like that. Because apparentlyyy you aren't an astronaut until you're *chosen for* and *assigned to* and *embark on* . . . a mission? There's no guarantee of a mission assignment, so until that happens Steph insists on being called an "ascan" (an astronaut candidate). But, just like I tried to tell her, *no one* in the comments knows what I'm talking about, so, MY SISTER IS GOING TO BE AN ASTRONAUT, OKAY????

Four minutes later
follow @stephharperscientist please. I'm aware her only post is a headshot from work, but she has me so we are going to work on her online presence lol

Twenty-six minutes later
I'm privileged to have a large following and with it comes the constant and unreasonable nitpicking of people who think they know my life (#hatersgonnahate). Also, with it comes responsibility.

Yes, I absolutely denounce @NASAofficial's flagrant attack on sacred land in the illegally occupied Kingdom of Hawai'i. @NASAofficial has not backed down on plans to build the thirty-meter telescope on Mauna Kea, and my family supports the land protectors on the front lines.

My husband and daughter are Native Hawaiian, and this is the land that has graciously hosted me for the last five years. During the Trail of Tears, my own

Cherokee family lost our home village of Dalonige'i in what is now known by settlers as the State of Georgia. Today it's a white town, a tourist destination featured in *Southern Living*. They have wineries and resorts and luxury retirement communities. They have an annual festival to celebrate that one time a black bear wandered onto the town square. On stolen land, that's about all the history they've got. My husband and I want better for our daughter.

I am here to fight, every day, for our #collective #indigenous #sovereignty. Toward our collective liberation. And against further desecration of our homelands.

ALSO, I #support #nativewomen—today and every day. In my sister's time with NASA, I trust she will do great things for our people. Instead of tearing each other down and engaging in #lateralviolence, why don't we take a minute today to lift each other up? Today's #gratitudechallenge is to send a quick message to any #indigenouswoman who has been a positive example for you of everything we're capable of.

When even one #indigenouswoman is given a seat at the table—or in this case, maybe a spot on a space shuttle—there's really no stopping us. #nativeexcellence #proudsister #resist

Two hours later
Post deleted.

PART

FOUR

2016

THE EARTH OF EARTH, THE EARTH OF MARS

March 28, 2016

In a small, white dome, on a volcano, we practiced the protocol of Mars.

Before I climbed into my hazmat suit, my crewmate Adisu took my temperature. On Mars, if this were Mars, I'd have a suit with built-in heaters, protection from a cold more than a hundred degrees below zero. Here, in Hawai'i, I wore a tiny fan on a string around my neck. Our comm system was a walkie-talkie, clipped to a fanny pack at my belt.

Adisu gave me a thumbs-up. He noted my trip in the log and motioned me through the air lock. What we called the air lock was a hanging clear tarp, before a gap, before another clear tarp. I stood in the gap for five minutes, simulating the time needed to adjust the air pressure. It was the honor system; Adisu had already returned to his research. An egg timer dinged, and I stepped outside.

The slopes of Mauna Loa looked similar, somewhat, to the Tharsis region on Mars. The volcano was as close as we could get, and for now we focused on research—on morale, stress management, and best practices for group cohesion. Together with my crewmates, I was part of that. One year of total isolation, of logbooks and rations and constant surveys measuring factors and trends in conflicts across crew relationships.

I looked behind me at the hab. It was a geodesic habitation dome, white with a frame of metal supports. To our crew of six, it was home for the year. ("It looks like Epcot," my mother had said, clicking through photos before I'd left. "Appropriating marginalized cultures on stolen land," Kayla said, "*just like Epcot.*")

Kayla hated that I was here. She didn't care how promising it was that I'd been asked, just one month into my life as an astronaut candidate. (In our entire, newly sworn-in ascan class of twelve, this honor had gone only to three of us: me, Aziz, and Nadia. Our peers would spend the year in Houston, in some combination of training and desk jobs.) If I answered the call to serve, if I was uncomplaining and never rushed my way through the air lock even though it wasn't real? A likely recommendation from my commander. A necessary step toward a *mission*, the real kind.

When I reached the day's collection site, I paused to rest. I sipped water through the tube that hung at my shoulder. Exercise in the hab was limited— we took turns on a treadmill in the kitchen. It would be boring if not for Nadia, who averaged out her personal best each week and posted it on a whiteboard. We were always neck and neck.

I'd met her the night before our swearing in. It was mid-December, at a house party in the Houston suburbs by and for the new ascans. Three Apollo Era astronauts and a young woman in a bikini showed up together, uninvited, and made a beeline for the hot tub. Nadia picked an ill-advised fight with one of them about 1960s gender norms before being chewed out by the woman herself, a petite but fully adult astrophysicist. By the hydrangeas I held Nadia's hair, small curls pouring out over my fists, when she thought she might (but thankfully, did not) throw up out of embarrassment. Over brunch the next day, where I'd planned to ask if she was gay so we could become colleagues with benefits, Nadia said that she deeply regretted her outburst. Ascans were colleagues, she said, not friends, and in the future she'd behave more professionally. For the last two months, nearly all of our mission so far, I had unprofessionally thought of her many times.

Within the hour, I'd bagged six samples at the collection site: mugearite, alkali basalt, and tholeiitic basalt. I labeled them in awkward, uppercase writing, and snapped them shut in the case I carried.

My walkie-talkie beeped. Allison's voice was garbled and staticky, like she was drowning. "Allison to Steph. Do you copy?"

"Copy that."

"I got an alert from mission control, level orange. We're looking at an unauthorized group, upwards of thirty civilians, approaching the hab on foot. All crew members return to base; we're on lockdown till they're ID'd."

"We thinking extraterrestrial beings?"

"Cute. Hurry back. Over and out."

The sun was overhead. I was hungry and tired, walking quickly, a fast drumming in my heart. I felt caged in my suit, though they'd trained us not to feel that way.

Static again. Allison. "Well, come on," she said. "You gotta move faster."

I saw them, close behind.

Protesters. Native Hawaiians. "Kānaka Maoli," as Kayla always said. For almost a year, she'd been tweeting and posting and blogging and protesting, all in opposition to the thirty-meter telescope planned on nearby Mauna Kea.

But we weren't even there! We were in a temporary structure, on Mauna Loa, which as I understood from my pre-mission googling was *also* sacred but maybe—at least from what I could tell—not *quite* as big a deal? When I'd told Kayla this, she'd said it wasn't my place to rank how sacred other people's volcanoes were.

"What I'm hearing," I'd told Kayla, "is that the Mauna Kea protesters will leave us alone on Mauna Loa."

Kayla groaned into the phone. I was in Houston, packing for the mission. I heard the sliding of the screen door, imagined Felicia coming home from the beach. The drag of her surfboard laid out on the deck. Sand everywhere. Kayla said, "That's not at all what I'm saying?"

The protesters, now coming up the slope behind me, wore shorts and T-shirts, jeans and sneakers. They wore lauhala hats and aloha shirts, and held flags with green, red, and yellow stripes. There was a boy in a loincloth, holding an umbrella over the head of an older woman in a long, loose dress. People carried signs. I couldn't read them through the fog on my face shield; I was running too fast and breathing too hard, afraid to know if my sister was among them. When we were younger, and she'd started going to protests, I'd always come along. I'd had this idea that I was there to protect her.

A shirtless Hawaiian man with black tattoos on his legs bent to carry a long-haired little girl. A Black woman with bright purple glasses ran past them, waving something in her hands. She was holding a flyer, jogging, trying to slip it between my gloved fingers. "Wait," she said. "We just want to talk?"

I gasped, ran straight through the air lock, and slammed the real door behind me.

I leaned against it and tried to catch my breath.

Adisu was waiting for me with his clipboard. He didn't say anything about the rushed protocol. He unzipped my suit and helped me out of it. My hair stuck to my neck and shoulders; I was sweaty and worn out and hoped Allison would authorize a second shower.

There was a single porthole by the door, and the crew crowded around it. Jed put his hand on my shoulder. Jed who was always trying, always doing too much. The concern in his eyes was like I'd narrowly survived.

Nadia stood apart from us—back straight, hair pulled into a high bun. Silent, interested, she studied the protesters from afar.

"Mission control just confirmed an offshoot of protests against the thirty-meter telescope," said Allison. "The hab is now a secondary target."

I moved closer to Nadia and looked out. A banner stretched across the crowd and bunched at the top, held in many hands. Its message was painted in red, dripping at the feet of each letter, a message repeated till the cloth ran out.

YOU ARE ON SACRED LAND.
YOU ARE ON SACRED LAND.
YOU ARE ON SACRED LAND.

Instagram Post

April 13, 2016

thatindigenousmama

Video Title: "Get Ready with Me as a Stay-at-Home Mom Defending Sacred Hawaiian Land."

[Video: a montage of clips follow Kayla throughout the morning, starting as she waves up at the camera from a sleeping bag in a tent.]

Audio: "Welcome to week two of 'Walking the Walk,' AKA asking myself what I'm *really* doing to protect my Indigenous daughter's future and then going and *doing* just that. For you, climate justice might mean composting, or (please, for the love of God) limiting your fast-fashion purchases. For our family, it means protecting Indigenous land rights for future generations.

"Here's me and my daughter waking up in our tent, here on Mauna Loa. Very, *very* slowly, because fifty percent of us are teenagers. If you're new here, here's my constant little disclaimer that I'm a Cherokee Nation citizen and my husband is Kanaka Maoli and, crucially, I am a *guest* here on Hawaiian lands. I never speak for our Indigenous brothers and sisters of Hawai'i, but I do try my best to amplify their voices while I parent my own very sleepy, very cool Kanaka Maoli and Cherokee daughter.

"Here we are brushing our teeth with water bottles, freshening up, but *not* with disposable wipes like I would have done in my dark, dark past. We are learning, every day! Here are our wet little washcloths doing the best they can.

"Then we did our makeup.

"JK, JK, we live outside! My makeup tutorials are on hiatus, until NASA agrees to cease its Mars simulation project on sacred land. But here's me putting on lip balm from a Kanaka—owned small business. Affiliate link in the caption for 10% off!

"Then we went to the community kitchen for our breakfast shifts. Nothing formal— we all pitch in when we can. Here I am peeling garlic. And here's my 13-year-old peeling potatoes, all woebegone, looking like a prisoner of war.

"We ate!

"Here's me waving to my daughter while she walks across the base of the volcano, where the camp school is set up. Does anyone else think School on a Volcano is just a very cool concept?

"While Felicia's at school today, I'm gonna attend a training on nonviolent protesting led by some of our kūpuna—that means our elders. After that I might go sort supplies in the medic tent, help the All-Nations Indigenous Youth Council plan their social media strategy, and maybe read up on the history of Native Hawaiian protest movements while I wait for instructions on the next direct action.

"And that's a wrap on our morning! If you want to learn more, today's follow rec is one of my new friends here, @kanakakween!"

Steph Harper's Hab Log

May 1, 2016

Hello, anonymous team of researchers! Please enjoy this snapshot of current crew dynamics.

As you know, the focus of this mission is honesty—reporting the good and the bad of this experience, through both quantitative and qualitative data. (As part of my ongoing assessment of your assessment, let me just say that I appreciate NASA's choice to go out-of-house in selecting your research team. I've been humiliatingly vulnerable in this hab log for the sake of science, but I might present myself differently for the astronaut selection committee.)

Some updates:

Despite mission control's hysterics, the protesters have not caused problems for us. They stay at their own camp a couple of miles out. Sometimes they sing. Usually it's corny. I *almost* wish they'd come around more, stir some shit up. Or keep singing, but better. That's how bored we all are.

Things have gotten harder in the hab since we passed the four-month mark. Nearly once a week in our recorded group sharing session, one of us (but never me) will say something like, "this really might be my breaking point," despite knowing full well it can't be! If this were real life, we'd be only one-third of the way to Mars. Do they not get that?

Last week, Jed was the one to say it. He's said it three weeks in a row now, because his wife asked over email for a divorce. We all feel bad. He told Allison he was ready for his Emergency Breakdown Box, which is what I've taken to calling the one care package we get over the course of the year. (I personally believe you should be falling apart to ask for it, which I won't be doing, so I'll be opening mine at the end of the mission.)

Jed's Emergency Breakdown Box was packed by his mom (not his wife—foreshadowing!), and here's what was in it. A rosary. *The Catholic All Year Prayer Companion.* Holy water in an Aquafina bottle! This made him feel even worse. He told Adisu he'd been hoping for a nice bottle of whiskey.

Nadia said she asked for her box on Day 1, so she could just enjoy it at a leisurely pace. Oh, to be a person with such chill. Her mom packed hers, too. It had three pages of compliments and twenty-five pounds of candy. My eyes got big at that so she said, "Maybe I'll have you over sometime, if I can find it in my heart to share." (!!! WHAT do you think? I know you can't answer. But like, flirty, yes???)

I don't actually think she wants to sleep with me, which is a shame because uncomplicated sex in the hab could be a real game changer for my mental health. (Maybe hers, too!) It could also be good for science, and help NASA (finally) take a stance on sexual relationships during long-term missions. (For the record, my stance is pro.)

That being said, I don't even know if she's gay? The weird thing about Nadia is how private (and how professional) she is with her crewmates in the hab, versus how vulnerable I've seen her be with strangers on the internet. Before we came here and they blocked all our apps, I watched a decent number of the videos she'd posted. Her Instagram page was partly about her being a terraforming fangirl, where she'd rate different ideas for making other planets and moons habitable. And it was partly about her journey to space. The day she learned she'd be an ascan, she propped a video camera up against a coffee mug and filmed her end of The Call. A tiny, messy, Brooklyn apartment. Stained workout clothes, hair tied under an old silk scarf. She was sitting on her kitchen floor. She was crying!

I've learned, not from talking to my sister but from watching her, that nothing is real on the internet. Everything we see is something Kayla wants us to see, the way Kayla wants to be known. She would never in a million years risk letting someone see her fail.

I didn't tell Nadia I'd watched *everything*, going back to videos like "I'm the only woman at this Engineering Major Happy Hour," and later, "HELP! Should I go to grad school or get a real job?"

But I did ask her about the choice to film The Call. I said she could have easily been rejected.

"Rude, but yes," Nadia said. "That was the most likely outcome." We were sitting on the floor in her quarters. Alone for the first time, eating candy—just like she'd said.

"And then would you have posted it? Years and years of videos about wanting this, and then failing?"

Nadia smirked. "You've watched years and years of my videos, huh?"

"No! I just assume most ascans ruin their lives to be here."

"Ha." She looked down at a packet of M&M's, rummaging around, picking out the red ones and setting them to the side. I had mentioned that I like them, even if they all taste the same.

Finally, she looked at me. "I got lucky. We all did. It's completely insane that we're here."

I nodded. Over the last couple of weeks, I had let myself forget that.

Nadia continued. "Most people who want to be astronauts won't be astronauts. Who knows if even you or I will ever be assigned a mission? The kids who watch my terraforming videos probably aren't going to space, but they'll go somewhere else. Us, too."

I nodded, though I had no interest in making peace with *going somewhere else*.

We finished the M&M's, and I waited around to see if we'd have sex. Instead I think I overstayed my welcome. Nadia sat at least two feet away from me the whole time, buttoned up to the neck in her uniform. Then she said it was almost her turn in the shower, even though it wasn't. The schedule is laminated and posted on the door.

05/18/2016 sent at 14:02 from feliciaaaaaa1019@gmail.com

Hi Auntie—

Mom said that this whole time (since JANUARY) you've been easily contactable, which is crazy because nobody told me! She said I just had to send it to the special NASA portal or whatever. She also said that the portal waits twenty minutes to send messages to you after they come in, because apparently when humans are on MARS it's so far there'll be a 12 to 25-minute communications delay? I think acting out that part is too much! They should let you text! It's going to be like two hundred years before we go to mars (if you ask me! sorryyy), and by then the whole email delay thing will probably be fixed (or we'll have telepathy).

Anyway no thanks to Mom for being the *real* communications delay . . . FOUR MONTHS!

I have an emergency. I haven't been in school since before winter break. Not real school, anyway. But I'm still able to text my friends, if I stand at the highest point of camp and hold my phone up in the air. I've been doing a lot of that, and there's this girl, and we message every day? Maybe like, two months now?

The emergency is that I don't know if she likes me. I almost got into this whole thing with Mom the other day but she was like, *TELL HER HOW YOU FEEL!* Because Mom is obsessed with me and thinks anyone would be delighted to find out I like them. But I don't know if this girl is gay, or just really into texting ppl? I don't want to get into it but I had to switch up all my friends at school last year. I can't make things weird with this girl because she's in the *new*, smaller friend group and if things went south I'd have to do a THIRD switcheroo.

Spring Fling is extremely soon. If I'm gonna tell her (should I?) then Spring Fling is like a good deadline or reason or whatever to bring it up lol. But I also don't know if I'll be home for Spring Fling, which is like a week from now????

Please advise. Also, if you ever talk to my mom and you get an idea of what's going on with my immediate family, please let me know. I miss my dad, and I thought he'd be at camp with us on weekends but he's only visited two times since we got here. I have to know if Mom's telling him not to come, or if he just doesn't miss me?

Mom is really, really happy even though we never see Dad. And that's rude because I never see the girl I text with and that doesn't make me happy, it makes me want to like die for her?

In conclusion, please forward any intel along to your favorite niece. The older I get the more I think all the adults are lying to me, or at least keeping me out of the loop, and I hate it. I'd like to avoid being surprised by any future developments. Even little logistical ones, like when tf I'm going home?

Love,
F

DRESS REHEARSAL FOR MARS

May 20, 2016

There was no one to enter my trip into the log; no one to check my hazmat suit. I knew I shouldn't be doing this. Upstairs in their quarters, my crewmates slept.

I looked up at the bare, metal staircase. I still had a clean record. I could go back to bed. I'd come so far to get here, and I had so far to go. Was I willing to risk a mission to space?

I was. I now knew—though I'd suspected it before—that Kayla and Felicia were at the camp. Felicia had emailed to ask for dating advice, but it seemed to me bigger things had gone wrong. I finally believed what she'd tried to tell me in Italy. Kayla needed help.

I lifted my suit from its hook on the wall and quietly zipped myself into it. For as far as the hab's outdoor cameras could reach, in case anyone thought to monitor them, I needed to follow protocol. I slipped on my boots and gloves and turned on and off the electric lantern at my side. I would have to feel my way to the perimeter. In the air lock, whether out of loyalty or fear, I waited the full five minutes.

I listened closely to my own footsteps, scared. Was I really doing this? What if I got caught? What would I tell them I was doing here?

Twenty minutes later, I made it to the perimeter. The end of NASA territory and the start of something else. I closed my eyes, breathing in the chill air that slipped through the stiff fibers of my suit. I remembered the night sky. Our authorized Mars walks, always scheduled for daylight hours, had kept me away from it since January. I looked up.

Stars, nebulae, and planets, the deep black of outer space. I sat down on the ground and felt the steadiness of the Earth below me, and the possibility of everything above. *You are on sacred land.*

Behind me, someone ran. I stood and jumped back, nearly tripping on my lantern. I switched it on and held up my hands.

"Don't shoot!" I said.

Two people stepped into my light. It was the tattooed man, with his little girl beside him. They looked at me and laughed.

"Calm down," said the man. He reached for the girl and swung her up on his hip. "Look at that, Mahina. We found you an astronaut."

The little girl, Mahina, hid her face in the man's neck, giggling. She whispered something. Inside my suit, I felt farther from them than I was.

He kept his gaze steady on me. "What brought you out here?"

"I want to talk to my sister. Kayla Palakiko. If she's still at the camp? One of the protesters?"

"The protectors," he corrected. The man squinted, trying to see me through my face shield and hood. "I know about you. Weird you waited all these months to come see her. Weird you people are living in that dome."

"Are you Kanaka?" Mahina said.

This was when most Native people would clarify that they weren't from *this* nation but they were from *a* nation, when they'd roll out the name of their people. That way you were like them, even when you weren't.

"No," I said.

"Stay here," the man said. He turned partly away, keeping an eye on me as he murmured into a walkie-talkie. He spoke and listened and spoke, and then held it to his daughter's mouth and let her pretend to transmit a message. Several minutes later, my sister came running at me.

She was frazzled and out of breath, almost shaking. "STEPH! Holy shit! I'm *so* glad to see you. I mean, I didn't tell you to come to camp 'cause, like, I didn't think you'd even consider it, you know? Did they let you out of there? I would've asked to see you, but I knew you couldn't—"

She hugged me. My suit crumpled around me, like an animal crushed in its shell. I looked at her feet. They were dusty, tied up in worn sandals over high, knit socks. That was unlike her.

The man's name was Mark. He told me this, gruffly, and from many feet away, before leading me and Kayla toward the camp. At the entrance (*KAPU— You are entering Kingdom Land*), I all but tore off my hazmat suit. I left it in a plastic crate, where it looked like a discarded tarp. I didn't trust these people. Any one of them could take a picture and post it, alerting NASA to their ascan visitor.

Kayla and I sat across from each other, on camping chairs facing a bonfire. I asked where Felicia was.

"Asleep. Or maybe wandering around?" Kayla said. "Lately she's into that. And this place is safer than home. I can let her have her space and not worry about murder, since there's community accountability and mutual aid and all these traditional teachings that have gotten lost in the postcolonial world. We've built an intentional community here. Steph, I'm really glad you get to see it."

"You know people say that when they mean a cult, right? An *intentional community*?"

Kayla laughed. "Steph, we aren't twelve! You can't get my goat."

I looked across the circle, past the black air turned gold around the flames. The tents were quiet, most people asleep. In the center of the camp was a kitchen built of poles, ropes, and frayed blue tarps; kerosene sat at the entrance, four huge metal barrels. I counted sixteen tents, one wickiup, and one tipi before giving up. The last two were weirdly out of place, and told me there was mainland interest in the protest. Then I wondered what I was assessing, and who I was doing it for.

Kayla grabbed my shoulder and pointed up. "Shooting star!"

"Cool!" I said. "You know, they're not really stars."

"Got it," she said.

"They're meteors. Tiny dust particles falling through our atmosphere."

"'Kay."

"Where they vaporize, due to the heat of friction with atmospheric gases."

"Stop ruining the sky."

"Where's Jason?" I said.

"*Okay* then," she said. "Why'd you come out here in a fucking *hazmat suit*?"

"I was just asking?"

"You weren't," Kayla said. "But I've got more important things I want to talk through with you."

She started braiding her hair like she had as a child, absently, not bothering to untangle the knots. She said we should be able to discuss what was happening without fighting.

"Please don't make us do Jason's 'hearing each other' exercise."

Kayla didn't laugh, which made me worry. "You can't ignore what's happening here at camp," she said.

I looked at her. Looking at Kayla, when she was so young she wouldn't remember it, used to be like looking at myself. I took care of her, and made her my place in the world.

"You know I have respect for the movement as a whole," I said, "right?"

"*Here* we go."

"I'm a *scientist*. Thinking carefully about where we are and where we need to be, analyzing which actions will get us there faster and safer and with the most gained—you can't ask me not to do that."

"You assume we're bumbling around out here," she said. "You barely know what we're fighting for, but when you hear 'Indigenous-led,' it's like, *Oh wait, that can't include scientists!* Must be a bunch of impulsive, woo-woo activists who don't really know what—"

"This isn't the first or last Indigenous-led protest," I said. "It's just the only one I can't be at. I heard there's an encampment in North Dakota, at Standing Rock? If they're still protesting that oil pipeline after my mission, I'm there. Go home, wait for me to finish out my mission, and we'll make a family trip out of it. Mom would die of happiness."

"You think everything's about you!"

"You came to my place of work!" I said. "What if you had a real job for once in your life—in, like, an office—and I showed up at your cubicle with twenty people and a fucking banner?"

Kayla's voice was perfectly, scarily even. "I have a real job."

"Being a mom, I know, *hardest job in the world*."

An old look passed between us, like she was ready to tackle me.

"But if you out me as your sister?" I said. "If I get caught—even just this once, for visiting you, once!—it would ruin me."

"I appreciate the sacrifice no one asked for," Kayla said. "But I have a moral obligation to be here."

"There are other people here, actual Hawaiians, who are leading this. They'd be fine without you. Besides, Felicia wants to go home."

Kayla picked up a handful of dirt and passed it between her hands. I could tell I'd hurt her feelings, bringing her daughter into this.

I shouldn't have come.

"Felicia is Kanaka," Kayla said. "Cherokee, Kanaka, and getting to the age where she won't tell me what's going on with her."

Felicia had said almost the same thing to me in Italy, that her mother kept too much of herself hidden. I wanted to line up the world's mothers and daughters, shake them, and tell them to talk to each other.

"But I can tell this place is good for her," Kayla said. "She's going to elder talks, hearing these old stories about the volcano and the islands and the ceremonies—all this stuff she comes from. It's the kind of traditional stuff Mom doesn't know, that our family could easily never get back. You know how *little* Felicia knows about our side?"

I shrugged. I could guess at the stories my sister had chosen to pass on. She'd been right there beside me, our mother giving us heroes and Brett cutting them down. I'd let it go; there was more freedom in being a person alone.

But Kayla still looked to our ancestors as fighters, people whose every complexity could be forgiven in their fight to survive. She had always refused to talk to me about Brett's caveats to our history, because they didn't fit into the kind of Indian she wanted to be. Or—I thought, especially in recent years—the kind she needed to be seen as.

Only once had our mother told a story without a lesson. Without a good ancestor to guide us.

It was the story of her father finding them in Oklahoma, following their car the whole drive back to Arkansas. The grandmother she'd never see again. I still wondered why our mother had allowed herself to tell it to us.

Kayla shook her head. "The stuff Felicia is learning, at least about her dad's side, it's giving her a context for who she is. When you have kids—when a person has kids, I mean—*nothing* matters more than giving them that sense of self."

"You're lecturing," I said.

"I'm staying," Kayla said.

"Kayla."

"Think about it. How many millions of dollars are they putting into this, your little dress rehearsal for Mars? As for the real thing, you know the space station is the most expensive building ever made? Just hanging around up there, in orbit! It can't even go places."

"Kayla," I said again.

"The government or whatever, they're putting *so much* into you. I read it costs like fifty million to send one person to space. You know how insulting that is to, like, refugees? Repairing one woman's fistula costs six hundred dollars. Half the world lives on seven dollars a day!"

"I'm not allowed to have goals? Until when, I've eradicated malaria? You wouldn't be on my butt about this protest, if it weren't for our Indian side."

Kayla rolled her eyes hard at that, *our Indian side*, a phrase I'd never said in my life. But we were sisters and I was mad. To question who I was let me question her, too.

"You're *allowed* to have whatever goals you want, Steph. I just think the ones you have are selfish, and they disregard the work of everyone who came before you. And I think you're old enough for people to say that to your face."

I wasn't sure what to say to that. We watched the fire die down, despite the chopped wood ready at our feet. The sky turned from black to blue. Little bursts of flashlight through tent walls revealed shadows of huddled bodies. In the distance I saw the hab, its white domed walls almost ghostly in the dark.

Walking back, alone in my rumpled hazmat suit, I thought about what Mahina had asked me. "Are you Kanaka?"

She was a kid. How easy it would have been to say, "Nope, Cherokee." To let us have that.

Why did I set myself apart, always? Our family and where we'd come from—it was my sister's first answer for who she was and where she was, what she was doing and why. It was my last answer, or my quietest, like something that dragged behind me on a rope.

Steph Harper's Hab Log

May 25, 2016

It took five months on this mission before Allison paired me and Nadia on a Mars walk. I'd gone with everyone else at least once. (With Aziz four times! Though it did cement our friendship.) For a minute there, I was worried Nadia might have put in a request to not spend time with me. You spend maybe thirty minutes too long in someone's quarters after being invited in for candy, once, like a month ago, and suddenly you're dead to them.

Nadia's kept her distance. She'd call it, I'm sure, "professional conduct." She gets fully dressed in the closet-sized bathroom after each shower, while the rest of us run up the stairs to our quarters in a towel. We never even see her in pajamas. She's the only one who stays up as late as I do, working at her station behind mine most nights. When she finishes her work she says, "goodnight!" cheerily, and leaves.

On our walk, a full five hours outside together—enough time for Aziz to tell me the life story of every woman he'd ever dated—Nadia focused on the samples we had and hadn't yet collected. She was hot (even in her hazmat suit she was hot), but I'd finally convinced myself she was boring. Work-obsessed, task-oriented, guarded, definitely straight—it was like bumbling along in the dirt beside the Mars Rover.

Then we passed the protest camp, which all my previous companions had pretended not to see. Like the protesters weren't supposed to be there, so they weren't? A group of maybe twenty children marched behind a teacher. They were too far away for me to spot Felicia, but I squinted at them anyway.

Nadia hopped to attention. She waved her arms wide over her head. She shouted, "WE COME IN PEACE!"

The kids and the teacher laughed. They waved hello, she waved hello, and this went on a weirdly long while before the children scattered. I checked the watch that dangled from my fanny pack. The end of the school day, probably.

When I looked up, Nadia was staring at me. "You hate kids?"

"Um, no. I just hadn't decided how to interpret them, for the purpose of our simulation. Aliens? Cosmonauts? Colleagues we'd believed were dead? It affects how we should receive them."

I was serious, mostly, but I could tell she was trying not to laugh.

Then she said she liked that. She said it was crazy, sure—but out of everyone on crew, the two of us were clearly the most Willing to Die for NASA.

"I agree," I said. "In fact, we should just murder-suicide right here, save ourselves the drama of waiting for a mission assignment."

Nadia laughed for real then, her cheeks unprofessionally pink behind her face shield, and I think that's when we became friends.

Now we talk to each other, even about things we haven't figured out yet. I guess not about being gay (like, if she is or isn't), but about plenty of other things.

Nadia told me she likes people "way, way" more than science, which I think no one would guess since she's so unfriendly. But she called engineering, AND I QUOTE, "a snooze fest"?

The reason she lit up with the kids out there wasn't because she wants to have babies, but because—and she said this completely genuinely—"they're kind of the whole point of this." She said they're why she cares about terraforming. Science is, to her, a means to an end. And the end is, I guess, there not being an end.

I agree with that, though her version is pretty far from my dad's. She said she doesn't lie awake at night thinking about asteroids and how to escape them, which some of us do. She wants a future, here. I like that. And, gay as she may or may not be, I like her.

SHE Profiles

[Photo: Nadia in the hab, smiling at her workstation in a white lab coat. Under that, her blue collared uniform shirt is buttoned all the way up. Behind her, in the narrow light of a porthole, is a wall of plants grown tall since the start of the mission. Nadia wears large sunglasses, stolen from Adisu. Her hair is pulled into a high bun, held by Allison's black scrunchie. On her lapel is a gold pin of two crisscrossed Russian and American flags. It has been missing from Steph's workstation for two days.]

Nadia, 36, Super-Accomplished Engineer / Astronaut on Training Wheels.

About Me: Are there lesbians on mars?

[Photo: Steph's face, zoomed-in, through the shining plastic shield of her yellow hazmat suit. Her mouth is open. Her eyes are wide, laughing.]

Steph, 34, Geologist / Astronomer / Professor / Researcher / Ascan / Pretend Crew member on Pretend Mission to Mars / Gay.

About Me: wtf we have *SHE*? They blocked every dating app except *SHE*? Lmaooooooooo I never thought to check till today. It's the worst one! To my literal only match: how long have you been on here??? give me back my stupid little flag pin!!! It has sentimental value to one of the worst years of my life!

also—YOU COULDN'T HAVE MENTIONED THAT YOU'RE GAY???

Updated SHE Profiles

[Photo: Nadia, lying over a blanket on a twin bed. The camera looks straight down at her face from hands raised over her head, and she smiles up at the lens from two stacked pillows. The photo is cropped high, just under the chin. On her head is an orange baseball hat with white embroidered writing in Cherokee.]

Nadia, 36, 1 of 2 (confirmed) lesbians on Mars.

About Me: To my literal only match: come to my quarters after lights-out? I have M&M's.

[Photo: Steph, lying under the covers in her own bed. Like Nadia, she holds the camera from above. She wears a large Hollis sweatshirt over her uniform and an orange baseball hat with white embroidered writing in Cherokee.]

Steph, 34, The Sleepiest Pretend Astronaut in the World.

About Me: To my literal only match: thank you for sharing your M&M's, on a planet with so few M&M's.

Steph Harper's Hab Log

May 29, 2016

We aren't the generation that goes to Mars. I know that. Maybe we're the people who go back to the moon? And, obviously, we're the people who learn things for the people who go to Mars.

Allison says the psych team (you guys—hi) wants us to focus on just one relationship in our hab logs tonight. (Because in space, one mishandled relationship could kill us all! But that's not what we talk about here. We talk about best practices for group cohesion.)

Here's what I've learned, so far, from five months living with Nadia.

I wanted to sleep with her immediately. We're peers, she seemed kinda gay, and as you know it's allowed (at least on this mission, which would make a decent setup for a reality TV show?). I don't mean to imply that on a future Mars crew, all gay astronauts will fall in love if you recommend that NASA allow it. But some of us aren't looking to be tied down for life with our most-compatible match. And if we aren't, and you put us on a three-year mission to space? A mature, casual, physical relationship might not be bad for morale!

In her quarters last night, Nadia said that when we first met she thought I was hypercompetitive and "a little annoying." I said, "Okay, cool, but could you tell I was gay?" and she made a face like she thought I was joking.

To be clear, she didn't invite me in last night so we could kiss. In fact, she literally said that she was "looking for a friend," which I found surprising and disappointing. But I get why now, because one of the things I learned last night is that she refuses to do short-term relationships. Of *any* kind, even friendship. Like, she didn't date for two years before this mission because she hadn't met anyone she'd consider marrying— which is, I think, a ridiculously high bar. And it took her five months to consider being friends with me!

When she'd finished hitting me over the head with her high standards, I asked her, "Why space?"

Nadia went straight into the story. She didn't try to play it down, or make jokes at the expense of her old self.

When she was a ten-year-old New York City kid, unaccompanied on the subway, a man was shot and killed in front of her. She doesn't know why. The shooter panicked and blocked the door to the train car, trapping her and eight others. An older man tried to rush at him. The shooter killed him, then fled.

Nadia and the other witnesses were taken to the station to give statements, strangers held together in a room. The process took seven hours and she was the only child, traumatized but doted on. The shooter was never found.

This began a period of needed answers. She became a devout Catholic, which her ex-Catholic father hated. Then she became a devout Muslim, which her ex-Muslim mother hated. She refused to ride the subway and begged her parents to move out of the city and googled things like "why do people do bad things" and "what's the meaning of life." She joined her school's astronomy club after school, because the teacher who led it had a car and agreed to drive her home.

"So you joined the astronomy club," I said, "and space saved you?"

Nadia rolled her eyes. "Nothing saved me. And space introduces more questions than answers. But people helped."

"People" meant the people she met at her grandmother's church. When their answers felt too rigid for her, too sure of their certainty despite a lack of evidence, it came to mean the people she met at her other grandmother's mosque. By then she had taught herself to let answers flow over and around her, like she was one of many objects in a current. Things got picked up and carried like sediment, prophets and stories appearing in these last two thousand years of the Holocene.

(That was really how she said it! It's fun for me to have a friend who has a favorite geological epoch, even if it's lame of her to choose the one with humans that started like a millisecond ago.)

Mostly, people to Nadia meant her fellow witnesses. When she was sixteen, one of the witnesses put them all together in a Facebook group. Now they write messages on each other's birthdays and try to meet annually on the anniversary of what happened. They order pizza and ride the train together, to the end of the line and back.

Nadia said, "What about you?"

"Huh?"

"Why space?"

I've been asked that before. Before I flew to Houston for my final ascan interview, Kayla had me practice over the phone every night for a week. She wanted me to answer in a way that would make it sound, she said, "like you have an inner life." So I talked about Brett's story with the frog and the eclipse. And Space-Culture Camp, and how it had changed me.

I didn't want to tell Nadia what I'd told NASA, which was not what I'd practiced over the phone. I told NASA about my dad and the accident and the moon. Kayla can't know, either. It's my last way left to look out for her.

"I was really good at science as a kid," I said.

Nadia didn't say anything at first. Then she said, "I can't tell if you're being serious."

"Yeah. I was really good at science, and specifically astronomy, and that turned into . . . you know, wanting to go to space."

She looked almost mad at that, which made no sense. She said, "Tell me where you were when marriage equality passed."

The question came out of nowhere, and I didn't have an answer.

I still don't. I know it happened maybe a year ago—after I was chosen as an ascan but before I was sworn in. I was happy about it, even if I can't remember the day itself. I didn't take to the streets or anything.

Nadia asked again. Her tone was off, like she was testing me? I still don't know what she wanted to hear, or why. How it had anything to do with space.

"It's late," she said. She crumpled up the sleeve of M&M's and put it in the little trash can. She stretched her arms over her head and shook her hair out between her fingers, and I knew she was ready for me to leave.

Instagram Post

June 12, 2016

thatindigenousmama

[Photo: Diana Watts stands at the front of a large tent, a cracked green chalkboard staked into the dirt behind her. There are no walls to the tent, and the sandaled feet of adults are seen passing outside. Diana wears a bright yellow turban, patterned with tiny white flowers. She has purple glasses, red lipstick, and a red shirt over high-waisted jean shorts. In front of Diana are many children of many ages. She faces them, her expression wide and dramatic, smiling and holding a small rock. The children sit close together on a blue tarp, pouring out into the bottom of the frame. On the board, in large white letters: CRYSTALS! Highly ordered microscopic structures in a chaotic world!]

Meet Dr. Diana Watts, my #1 since Day 1 (we both showed up at camp at the end of March). Diana is a Chickasaw Freedmen descendant originally from Tishomingo, Oklahoma, about three hours from where I grew up. She's also a teacher at the prestigious Phillips Exeter Academy, and she decided to spend her well-deserved sabbatical year serving others. Diana has been teaching *all* the children here at camp, for *months*, and with a sudden influx of land protectors we want to make sure she gets the funds and supplies she needs to educate and empower the next generation.

The link to donate is over on her profile, @dianasaurusrex. Once you're there, give her a follow. Lately our (Kānaka-centered) camp has become surprisingly pan-Indigenous with the gracious support of visiting allies to our mainland from the continent, especially as the movement at Standing Rock has raised global awareness on Native issues (#NoDAPL #waterislife). We've been getting almost daily class visits from artists and activists around the Indigenous world. Diana posts about them all!

BEST PRACTICES FOR GROUP COHESION

June 21, 2016

It was Adisu's turn to pull a block from the tower, and he was taking his time. He had long fingers, surgeon's hands, his nails always trimmed. There was no rule to keep them like that on the mission, with hardly any latex gloves to rip, but he said it was a habit. A comfort, even. Like his wedding ring, which he still pinned to the inside of his scrub pocket each morning.

Jed said, "*Today*, Adisu."

Adisu paused, centimeters from the wooden blocks, and held his hand perfectly still. It was like a magic trick. He wiggled an eyebrow at Jed.

The five of us sat in a circle on the gray rug in the hab living room. With the exception of the bathroom and the storeroom, the entire downstairs was one open round area. The bottom of the dome.

We called this the living room for normalcy, but it was just a couch, a rug, and a television. A clear plastic box of ten DVDs, which we hated and knew by heart. Behind the couch was the cooking area. Behind that were six portholes with a small desk and chair below each one. Beside the tarp-covered door, six hooks held six yellow hazmat suits. Then a small washing machine, a drying rack, one more porthole, and a treadmill. A whiteboard listed names and running times, with "NADIA!!!!!!!" circled several times over. On top of the *N* in her name, Aziz had drawn a small yellow crown.

The month of Ramadan, soon coming to a close, was the reason for the new Jenga routine. After a later and nicer-than-usual dinner, we now played it most nights. Aligning our meal schedule with the end of Aziz's fast each night, and being more generous with the rations, had been Allison's idea. She'd gone full force on Operation Make Ramadan Meaningful, not because it was a religious crew—Aziz called himself a "Ramadan-only Muslim" and Nadia called herself "raised atheist, with Irish-Catholic and Moroccan-Muslim grandparents who hated each other." Rather, Allison said celebrating our diverse cultures would allow us to recognize the collaborative nature of our mission, which was in fact a best practice for group cohesion. In space, she said, this could mean the difference between life and death.

I hated Jenga, but liked the extra time with Nadia. Even in a group.

Adisu pulled a block out of the tower and placed it on the top. He danced the tips of three fingers across the side without making it shake, just to make us crazy.

"Honestly," said Allison, "we oughta put Jenga in the same category as Operation! Can y'all really put up with this showboat six more months?"

Jed dragged a hand through his hair. He leaned back against the foot of the couch. "*Six months*," he said. "Fuck." He was struggling. The divorce was final now, his house sold without him and his stuff moved into a storage unit. The hab, in the meantime, was a hard place to start over.

"Jed, would you find that comment helpful to group morale?" Allison said.

Aziz perked right up. He, like me and Nadia, needed that letter of rec.

Outside, the protesters started to sing. None of us moved to look.

"Sorry. I'm just tired of this shit," Jed said.

He could say that. He wasn't an ascan. For Jed and Adisu and Allison, two non-ascans and a NASA commander, the hab was part of a prestigious fellowship to fund and complete a year of research and writing. They didn't have to impress NASA.

"I think it's pretty cool," Nadia said. She was trying, by impressing Allison, to impress NASA. "So long as they don't interfere with our hab, which they haven't? If this were Mars, we'd be lucky to have such interesting human neighbors."

"You think they'll be a security threat?" Adisu said. Almost hopefully.

He was ready for disaster, desperate to be helpful even if he had to dream up the trouble himself. Only days ago he'd taught us how to tie tourniquets at the dinner table. I understood wanting to be useful. I carried my new tourniquet with me everywhere, purple and rolled up very small in my pocket, and had already resolved to continue this practice after the mission.

"At ease, soldier," Allison said. She left the circle and came back quickly from the storeroom with a chocolate bar. She threw it at us, dangerously close to the Jenga tower. "I'm not telling y'all where I'm hiding these," she said, "but I think we could use a treat."

The protesters outside quieted. Inside, we looked at one another.

Then they started to chant. *Focus on Earth! This planet has worth!*

A new one. Nadia snorted. Across the circle, she smiled at me.

"Hey, hey, it's not so bad," Adisu said. "Don't you remember? *This isn't even Mars! We can still put you behind bars!*"

We laughed. Adisu beamed. He seemed to care the most about genuinely being liked, to invest the most into group cohesion even when he didn't have to. When we blew through our alcohol rations in February, which had been just two cases of beer to begin with, Adisu figured out how to sub in commercial yeast for a plant found in Ethiopian grocery stores but not on Mars. Then he fermented a kind of honey-based wine that only Jed and Allison liked, but that everyone found impressive. Allison reminded us that the real mission would be sober, but looked the other way because we were "celebrating our diverse cultures." This was true, but Nadia thought it had more to do with Allison being raised in her family's distillery in Kentucky.

Nadia passed out the chocolate. Her fingers lingered on mine, maybe, just for a second?

It was my turn. I bent over the tower.

I was thinking carefully about which block to move and what to do about Nadia. Almost every night now, I went to her quarters at lights-out. We whispered, shared stored-away snacks, laughed quietly with our hands over our mouths. I'd somehow graduated from my old place on the floor, and we sat facing each other on the two ends of her bed. Matching, stupidly, always in our crew-mandated collared pajamas. At some point Nadia stopped wearing a bra under hers. I couldn't decide if that meant she was, or was not, keeping things professional. Within half an hour or so, without fail, she'd send me back to my quarters.

We were real friends. I already knew that would be one of my biggest takeaways from the experiment. I was ready to tell the psych team that Nadia had made a big difference in my morale, and that it went deeper than my initial hope of having someone to sleep with. To be clear, I still wanted that. But Nadia operated differently than me. I felt totally out of practice with people like her—people like the physicist and Della—who believed in the long-term.

I reached for a block at the bottom of the tower. The chanting had died down, replaced with a round dance song. This was new for the camp and not Hawaiian, likely brought in by visitors from the mainland now that Standing Rock had people all riled up. I could picture it, dark-haired boys and hand drums, the words of a love song changed to meet the moment. *Baby I'm getting called to the front lines / in my heart I'll be seein' you / don't you leave me / please believe me / I'll come home to you / heya heya hey.*

"Steph?" said Jed.

"Hmm?"

"I can't believe I've never asked you—as a Native American, what do *you* think about the protest?"

"I don't think about it much." There was a slight tremble in my voice. What if my sister did something? After I'd come this far?

Jed gestured at the door. "Really? The rest of us think about it all the time."

"Best practices," Allison said, the words singsongy and stretched out. A warning.

Jed lowered his voice. "Sorry. I know they're not Native Americans. I didn't mean to assume a connection between, um . . . different varieties of aboriginal peoples."

"This is fun!" Aziz said. He and Nadia smiled at each other, holding back laughter.

"I'm calling it," Allison said. "Bedtime." She gave Jed a look, the one she gave us when we'd have to have a talk with her later in the storeroom.

Jed opened his mouth, like he had more to say. I tapped my finger against the tower and watched it fall.

Text Messages

July 25, 2016

Hannah Harper:
You're still out there, right?

Kayla Palakiko:
Yes. Said I'd update when there's new info?

Kayla Palakiko:
But we're doing great! Here's a pic of your granddaughter
with my friend Sandra I met when I was living at Hollis
(she did 1 week at Standing Rock and then 1 week here,
then 1 week at a resort in Maui lol.) Remember her?

Hannah Harper:
I don't! how is Felicia's school going?

Kayla Palakiko:
good! Here's a pic w/ her teacher at the camp, who
just got an AISES educational resources grant.

Hannah Harper:
AISES?

Kayla Palakiko:
American Indians in science and engineering

Hannah Harper:
[thumbs-up emoji] [eagle feather emoji]
[scientist with a test tube emoji]

Hannah Harper:
any thoughts on her schooling for next
year? Maybe somewhere bigger?

Hannah Harper:
maybe indoors?

Kayla Palakiko:
lmao

Hannah Harper:
forgot to ask also how is Jason doing?
Has he visited you two? Lately?

Kayla Palakiko:
have you heard from Steph? Some bigger direct
actions being planned now, with all the new summer
ppl here. Good time for her to leave HI.

Kayla Palakiko:
maybe she could make a statement?

Kayla Palakiko:
I've been thinking. Could you write down for me (and
email me the doc for me to keep safe for Felicia
someday) some stories about our ancestors? Especially
ones where they were dealing with idk displacement,
survival? Environmental stewardship? Activism? That
would be really encouraging for Steph. You could talk
to her and help her decide to do the right thing

Hannah Harper:
happy to write some family stories down. Especially for
Felicia. But as for talking to Steph about what you think
she should do, you know I can't insert myself like that

Kayla Palakiko:
lol mom you JUST asked me how Jason is

Hannah Harper:
Wait is that bad? Am I not allowed to ask that?

Hannah Harper:
Is he okay? Should I be worried?

Hannah Harper:
[hospital emoji] [question mark emoji]
[boy and girl with a heart in between them emoji]

STEPH

BY THE LIGHT OF JUPITER

July 31, 2016

Nadia sat on her bed, waiting for me. Most of her candy was gone. She had said, several times now, that I should ask Allison for my box already. Maybe my mother had filled it with candy? Or wine we wouldn't have to ferment ourselves? I was sure she hadn't.

Nadia talked me through practical solutions for planet-ending catastrophes. Between us, in the vast open area of green duvet, was an open plastic packet of peanut butter crackers. (My contribution, from lunch.)

"You're not listening," Nadia said.

"I am! You want our great-great-great-great-grandchildren to take on this massive space engineering project so that in one million years their descendants have somewhere to live." I recited this quickly, hoping for praise.

"I'm serious, though. We'll still be here in a *hundred* million years. Way past a million."

"Nadia," I said, "we'll be dead."

She didn't laugh. She was a pure and hopeful person disguised in sharp edges. Too smart for me. Too tender. I wanted to tuck her into her blankets and say goodnight, even knowing she was stronger than I was. I knew her better than I'd known anyone new in a long time. Maybe since the physicist, who had mostly shared what I wanted to hear.

Nadia, unlike me, had been a city kid. Her parents had met as teenagers during a protest against the Vietnam War, after a police officer chained them together and threw them in the back of a van. All four immigrant grandparents were horrified, both by the interfaith relationship and by jail. The young couple held a listening session for their parents' concerns, eloped in an atheist ceremony at a friend's apartment, got arrested for disturbing the peace three more times, and had Nadia by accident ten years later. By age four, Nadia was infamous at preschool for yelling things like "Believe nothing!" and "Question everything!" on the playground.

Nadia took another cracker from the plate between us on the bed. She talked about terraforming Jupiter's moons. It was her favorite (impossible) project, a preempt to any (possible, if not inevitable) mass extinction event. Our species had to be multi-planetary.

I told Nadia that when I'd explained this concept to my mother, she'd laughed and said, "Guess you can't put all your eggs in one basket!"

In response to this, Nadia did an impression of her own mother, who'd been furious with her as a newly religious teen. "Human life is insignificant and inconsequential!"

"Are you still that?" I said.

"What, religious?" She looked surprised that I'd asked.

I nodded.

"Ohh," she said, "this is about last night."

The night before, we'd talked about our lives and friendships outside the mission. Nadia had framed the question as being about "our communities," a phrase I might have judged as somewhat meaningless if my sister had used it. But I understood what Nadia meant. She was part of a mostly New York–based group of queer Muslims and had been since college. Even after her move to Houston, she still planned to fly "pretty often" to see them.

"I'm not part of that group because I feel super religious," she said now. "We have an experience in common, and we look out for each other. I don't feel like we have to be fully aligned in our every belief, when like, who is?"

I nodded and tried to sit with this. Nadia went, very suddenly, back to terraforming.

Nadia said if it were up to her—*it definitely wouldn't be*, is something I didn't say—the people of the future would invest in black hole seeding.

Why not have two homes to rely on—two star-warmed, terraformed, livable homes—rather than one?

A hundred million years, I thought, *is a long time for earthlings to hope for the best*. But I didn't say that. Nadia looked too revved up and happy, and maybe inclined to kiss me? This was solely based on her position on the bed, about a foot closer to me than usual.

The best candidate for stellification in our solar system—for *us! creating a star! out of a planet!*—was, "obviously," Jupiter. Jupiter was already a gas giant. If we could make Jupiter a star, we'd be free to live on its moons.

To do this, Nadia explained, the future-people would need to locate a black hole in our solar system. "A microscopic one." I shook my head at that, at how confident Nadia was in our future competence. And then they'd "drag it on over" to Jupiter (*apparently, we'd know how to do this*) and "push it" into orbit. This process, just the orbit stuff, would take about a century. Our president had just sealed a deal with Iran to curb its nuclear arms program, and in just three months we'd elect or not elect the candidate who'd called this the "worst deal ever." I had my doubts about our world in consensus for one hundred years.

I smiled and said something like "hmm." I was tired and a little anxious, still trying to read her.

Nadia talked about the Eddington limit. Gas from Jupiter would be pulled into the black hole. The heat and energy pushing outward would become equal and opposite to the gravitational pull inward. Somehow, the black hole would not swallow the body of Jupiter. Instead, over a few million years (*lol!* I did not say), it would raise Jupiter's average temperature to over 1,000 kelvins—creating a dull, red star.

"Cool," I whispered.

"Tell me what's next." She was teasing me. She knew my attention was not on Jupiter.

"The moons," I said, too fast. "Then they'll be hot enough. Habitable. People on moons."

"People on Jupiter's moons, in fewer than a hundred million years," Nadia whispered. "And whoever's still on Earth? They could read books at night. Outside by the light of Jupiter, which would be red."

"I don't know, Nadia."

"What don't you know?"

"A hundred million years is too long," I said. "I'm less interested in making stars. We have no control over what people will do in the time it takes to make that happen. Better to plop some people down on Mars, stat."

Something flared up in her. She moved quickly to my side of the bed. Warmth came off her *like my own star*, I thought, like a dummy.

"We need both," she said. "We need everything we can possibly manage for survival. Even if it isn't here, or on Mars—you're telling me you don't agree with that?"

"Uh, yeah I agree," I said. "I'm trying to be an astronaut."

"Don't you care about the world?"

"Yes?"

"This one," she said. "Not the Mars colony we'll be dead for."

"I know that," I said. Defensively. It was strange to argue with her about something so abstract, so impossible for either of us to have a say in. It was strange to argue with anyone, to be challenged by someone who wasn't my sister. There was a buzzing in me.

"Steph, be real with me. We eat snacks, I talk, and you sit here giving me nothing, like you're in the witness protection program."

She wasn't whispering anymore. It was well after midnight. "What's the point in being alive," she said, "if you're just trying to prove yourself? If you can't even, I don't know"—she swung her arm out—"open your stupid care package from your mom?"

I took her hand.

In the air between us I held it tight, and Nadia didn't fight me. My hand shook, but she didn't laugh.

She watched me. Slowly, and so afraid, I moved her arm gently down to her lap. I kissed her, like a question, on the cheek.

When had I ever been so soft, so careful with another person? The kiss was light, a brush of my lips, like at any moment she could say no and I could say I'm sorry, I'd only fallen into her. But I fell again, and again; finally I pressed my mouth to hers. With the tips of my fingers I touched her neck.

Nadia was in my lap, straddling me, taking my hand from her face. She kissed me, harder than I had. Her fingers moved fast under my neck, the undoing of many buttons and then cool air on my chest. She pulled my shirt off over my shoulders, scratching my arm with her nails by mistake. No apology.

Her hands were gentle on my breasts with the soft part of her fingers, like she intended to coax me open. I gasped.

Nadia lowered me onto the bed, carefully, her hand behind my head. A finger to her lips. I was under her, trapped between her legs, at her mercy in a way that was unfamiliar. She took my breast into her mouth. The flick of her tongue. A small sound fell out of me.

I swung out from under her. Her neck was bright under the lamp, exposed. I kissed it, sucked it, bit it—the bite came from shame at the sound I'd made.

"Keep going," Nadia said, her voice lower than before. "While I talk."

I came up for air, and the start of a laugh. "No more terraforming," I said. "Nothing farther than five minutes from the present mo—"

Abruptly, she opened her eyes. She looked almost angry, though I couldn't think why.

"I wanted to tell you I checked the handbook," she said. "It's pretty clear. 'NASA expects its astronauts to maintain a high level of professionalism while on duty . . .'"

"Oh my God, Nadia, *please*," I said. My wrists hung uselessly from her waistband. I'd been waiting for permission to take off her pants.

"'. . . Astronauts are highly trained professionals who must focus on the mission at hand, and any romantic relationships should not interfere with their ability to perform their duties.'"

"Are we role-playing HR Rep versus Bad Ascan?" I asked. "Is that what this is?"

"I'm setting expectations."

"We aren't astronauts," I said. "And relationships, if they don't interfere with duties, are allowed."

"Is that what you're saying, Steph? That this is a relationship?"

I laughed. Never, in all my sexually active life, had I been asked before orgasm to define the relationship.

"And there's my answer," she said.

"Wait, Nadia," I said. What was happening?

Nadia sat up and carefully buttoned her shirt. She tied the drawstring on her pajama pants into a perfect bow. There was more control in her, even just in her gestures, than I felt I'd ever be capable of.

"Please," I said. "Can we talk this through?"

"No," she said. "And I'm not mad. But with where I'm at in my life, with these stakes?" She moved her arm in a long arc, maybe like a spaceship or the hab we lived in. "I'm not interested in something casual."

August 3, 2016
From: hannahharper@gmail.com
To: kaylapalakiko@gmail.com

Dear Kayla,

I have what you asked me for last week. No, I won't send activist-themed stories to your sister, because these people didn't live for you to use them for whatever point you're out to make.

But lately I've been thinking I should be more open with some of these family stories. Just for the sake of your knowing. And what you said about Felicia knowing them, too, which was a good point. So here's just one story, to start.

Your great-great-grandfather, Walter, I think qualifies as what we'd want to call an activist. I'm sending you a PDF of what-all he said in court in the late 1800s. This was before they ignored what he was asking for, stole what land they'd promised would stay Indian Territory, and turned it into Oklahoma.

Before statehood, Cherokee land was shared by Cherokee people. You only owned improvements you made on top of it, like a house. After statehood, every Cherokee man was assigned a private allotment of land—with the rest going to settlers. The federal government took possession of all Cherokee property. They closed our schools. They closed our jails, courts, and legislature.

Cherokees names were listed on the rolls beside their age, sex, and blood quantum, with the blood part meant to "get rid of the Indian problem." I know you know this, probably better than I do. But I think it's important that the government thought Indian children at one-half or one-quarter and so on would mean we'd no longer exist. I'm proud of you and your sister and your daughter, who exist so much.

But back to Walter. He was one of many people who fought to stop all that and couldn't. As for the next generation after him? When the schools closed and the money ran out, Walter's daughter and son-in-law left their kid (my mom) in a barn. You know that part.

I don't mean to be bitter. I made a new friend at the Cherokee Heritage Museum who sent me to the archives. Reading about these things, only recently and for the first time, has gotten under my skin.

I'll just say—the more I get to know the people we come from, the less I think you should rely on them for inspiration. There are things about our family that I haven't told you about, that I won't get into over email.

Maybe I'll show you when you come home . . . *if* you and Felicia are ready to come home? I think you two have done your part.

I know you'll make all the right choices at that camp. Your sister will, too, where she is. I haven't heard from her since she first left for her mission, which I'm not telling you like I'm mad about it. I'm telling you only to encourage you to join me, in giving her whatever space she seems to need right now. She knows we're here for her, and she knows we always will be.

Please don't share any of this unless she asks for it. Try and trust her?

Love,
Mom

TRANSMISSION *from Kayla Palakiko to Stephanie Harper*

08/4/2016 sent at 1:13 from kaylapalakiko@gmail.com

Hey Steph –

Emailing to share something Mom emailed me yesterday. I'd asked her to start telling us more family stories, and she sent me one.

I'm sure she'd be happy to tell you this story in more detail, if you were to stop your mission early and go home to see her. But I'll share one little part of it for my own purposes, about an activist in our family.

Apparently, our great-great-grandfather was a Cherokee nationalist. He argued against the US government when it wanted to swallow us up. Meaning—and this is the part that stuck out to me—it wasn't like people imagine, where the tribe lay back and died after the Trail of Tears. We fought!

Mom said that in the late 1800s, our ancestor (Walter Adair Duncan) took a train from Indian Territory to DC. He had ten minutes to try to protect communal Cherokee lands from being terminated. There was a stenographer in the room— Mom sent me the transcript from that day in court. I copied and pasted an excerpt, so you can't say you don't have access.

> ". . . if we are to be abruptly forced, as advised by the commissioners who had no business to come here and endeavor to urge a bill through Congress—if we are thus abruptly to be forced into a territorial form of government, those very men now clamoring for our country would combine to run the government and courts to the great detriment of the Indians, as was done in the State of Georgia when my father resided there.
>   I beg you, gentlemen, to let us stand; I beg you in the name of your own humanity, and in the name of your own Christianity, and in the name of your own God to whom we must all bow—I beg you to give us time, not that we are cowards, not that we are afraid; but we plead for justice at your hands."

It was a different time, obviously, re: Christianity / assimilation. Walter could have taken up arms . . . maybe he would have in traditional times? But he used what he had. He suited up. He begged in the name of the Christian God for the end to come more slowly.

Whoever he called on, whatever he wore—it was still a fight. I'm not that interested in *how* people step up (boycotts, encampments, admittedly cringe videos on the internet). But it's the people who fight who stop that end from coming.

I'm sending this to you because you don't have a poetic or romantic bone in your body but you do have (I think) a strong sense of justice, in your own self-centered and roundabout way—though maybe so roundabout it's basically lost. Or a sense of continuation, for your future Mars people if no one else?

Things are changing where I am, in ways I know won't be good for you. I want you to resign from your mission and leave, and to trust me that this is a good and just thing to do. I feel crazy using the example of an ancestor to try to convince you of something when you've never seemed interested in our people before. But don't you see it's the same? Walter (your own great-great-grandfather) fighting to keep our home and government, to protect it and maintain it for *you*.

You could protect this land for your niece. For her, and everyone who comes after. You could pick up where he left off.

FLASH FROM
THE FAR FUTURE

August 6, 2016

I thought about Nadia nonstop, in the context of my own mess of a life. My niece and my mother and my sister. And my sister's message! Why on earth, I thought, was she sending PDF transcripts, typewritten one hundred years ago, to my work email portal? Like it was some kind of Ancestry.com archive? What about my camp visits, which I had (unwisely) kept up once a month? Was that not enough of a sacrifice for her? And what if I got caught sneaking out, and then mission control assumed Nadia knew about it or was part of it or something, and one way or another I ruined her life?

Nadia could find someone better than me in just five months, when the mission ended. She wanted someone who could commit to her, and I wanted to be okay with that. We avoided each other, as much as was possible in a geodesic dome, for nearly a week. Just get yourself to space, I told myself. That was all that mattered.

I threw open the door to her quarters.

"Nadia?" I whispered. Her bedside light was on. She was sitting up, reading, fully dressed in her uniform pajamas.

"Hm?"

I sat on the edge of her bed, facing her. "Forget the far future."

"Terraforming?" she said. "Why would I? Terraforming is cool."

"Sure. I don't mean *that* far in the future. I meant like, how you said you don't want anything short-term? I thought about it. I'm thirty-four. I'm an ascan! At this point, there's literally nothing stopping me from having a girl-friend."

Nadia scrunched up her face.

"I mean, *you* could stop me, obviously. But—" I reached over the blanket for her hand.

"This is wildly unromantic," she said.

"I know. I'm sorry. I had this speech in mind. It had to do with short-term commitment and long-term commitment. And there was a terraform-ing metaphor I thought you'd like about Jupiter? But I thought of it like two seconds ago, so—"

"Oh, good, an impulsive decision!"

I covered my face and groaned. "Can I have a do-over?"

"No," she said, but she was smiling. She turned off her e-reader and put it on the table beside her. She folded her arms. "You know what makes you lucky?" she said.

I shook my head.

"You're funny. At least, I've decided you are. You're cute. You *mean* well, I think."

"I do!"

"And, if we're on Mars, you're my only option for an average of . . . 140 million miles."

I laughed. What a relief to hear her laugh, too.

"If you can commit to a relationship in the near future—which basically means not wasting my time," she said, "I'll have sex with you."

It felt too easy, like I'd dreamed myself through a locked door. I said yes.

I took her hands in mine, gently, and put them down beside her. I touched a finger to her cheek and chin and lips, and she took it into her mouth and sucked. I let out a soft sound, and she pulled me in deeper.

With my other hand, I hesitated at the drawstring of her pants. Afraid to ask and afraid to take. She nodded up at me, and whimpered when I slipped my finger from her mouth. Another sound, almost angry, when I pushed into her.

I lost all sense of fear and carefulness, many months of holding back. We moved fast, like we'd be caught. Or, despite what I'd just promised, like this was our only chance. Nadia shook under me. She reached up, gasping, and touched my stomach as I worked.

"It's . . ." she said, before a gasp. She squeezed her eyes closed and lifted her hips. "It's ridiculous that you have abs."

I laughed, all-breath, careful in the quiet. I pulled out.

Nadia groaned. "Steph, what the hell."

"Do you think we should slow down?"

She groaned, exasperated, and caught my wrist in her hand. Swift like a slap. She tried to pull it back down to her, but I smiled and shook my head. I freed my hand and leaned over her body, holding her by the wrists. *There.* There was a certain look in her eyes. Like she'd fallen out of herself.

I moved my fingers down. Lightly, little circles on her thighs. Her lower belly. Nadia bit her arm. Her eyes watered and I stopped to watch her. I could do this forever. A goal of no end.

"*Please.*" There was a new urgency in her voice. She shook under me, breathing hard. She reached for herself with her own hand, and I pulled it away.

"You *can't* tease me like this," she whispered. "I'll scream."

"Hang in there," I said.

Another moan; her hand a small fist over her mouth. "We'll wake them up."

I moved my fingers inside her.

A cry from Nadia.

"I'm not worried about it." I started to move hard and fast. "You need that rec letter just as much as I do. Right?"

She closed her eyes, braced herself, and nodded.

Nadia tensed so completely, every muscle, the scratch of her toes on my leg as she pointed them. A lurch in her hips. My free hand hot and wet over her mouth. A low sound from the back of her throat, almost silent, but strange and strong. I pushed myself to keep going, to hold on to her even as I'd taken on too much, like I couldn't hold all of this in my hands. Like I'd tipped over a glass too full, and Nadia was spilling over.

•   •   •

In the early morning, we lay still. I would have to leave soon, to appear to wake in my own quarters. Nadia was tucked behind me in this small bed, holding me, making plans for the near future. In two months, we agreed, if we were still together, we'd tell HR. We were required to disclose formal relationships, but it was wise to make sure we were sure.

While Nadia talked about two months from now, I found myself thinking about the far future. The very far—what she'd said about the moons of Jupiter. Hadn't she told me we'd be able to read outside at night? Not "we," but our descendants. She'd said the new star would shine red.

I pulled Nadia's arms tighter around me. I recognized something. If not the image, the urge behind it to believe in survival. The comfort of filling in those edges with a story. I could see a girl—not really see, but sense a girl— reading a book on a front stoop, under a blanket. The world red, like a sunset. The feel of the page in her hand. The girl, I knew, came from Felicia. From my sister's descendants, and not from mine.

I realized then, in that flash from the far future, that I would not have children. And that it was okay, and also sad, but okay. I would do other things, I would be—I would cry, I knew, later in my own bed. I would feel a powerful relief, a letting out of breath, my hands against my body like an old friend.

In bed with Nadia, now, I wanted to be in space. Not because something was chasing me, or telling me to leave. Only because it was a place I'd like to know.

The promise of a place to go, beyond a place to run away from. I felt a kinship with my mother, who had found her place, who was maybe right then awake in her bed, in the house she brought me to, built on the memory of one peaceful summer.

Nadia's breath was even against my neck. "Steph?" she said. "You still awake?"

She moved her hand gently over my face, then the hair I buzzed back every other Sunday. The heel of her palm came to rest at the top of my forehead, where I'd parted my hair as a child.

We began to speak about things we hadn't. Her eyes closed, her voice soft. I asked her about her mother. I told her about mine.

TRANSMISSION from Felicia Palakiko to Stephanie Harper

August 7, 2016
From: feliciaaaaaa1019@gmail.com

Hi Auntie

Did you get my email? Are you going to talk to my mom or not? fyi I missed Spring Fling.

Felicia

FOR THE DURATION
OF THE MISSION

August 8, 2016

On any given night that I snuck out to the camp, I invalidated the results of our study. If I were caught, I'd be fired. I understood that, and I continued to go.

I noticed everything when I was there—who was in charge, what the camp's objectives were for that week or month, and how they carried them out. The more I visited, the more people told me things.

Whatever I learned—names and plans, potential threats to my own mission—I wrote down immediately upon returning to the hab. I was a scientist, in the habit of collecting information. Data, even data entered in a camp log in a notebook under my mattress, helped me feel in control. (Control had been lacking since the start of the simulation, and my feelings for Nadia hadn't helped.)

On my first day of having a girlfriend, I decided to stop visiting the camp. I'd repaired things with my sister well enough, at great personal risk over several months of visits. I'd done my part. It was time to turn over a new leaf. Maybe I could build something stable with Nadia, at least for the duration of the mission.

But on my third day of having a girlfriend, she sneezed four times after lunch. Adisu promptly quarantined her, grasping desperately for a medical emergency. Late that night, with Nadia medicated and isolated in her quarters, I pulled my suit from its hook by the air lock. I worried over its color, how it seemed to be a little darker than the others. Was I imagining that it was dirtier now, or more worn down? I zipped myself into it and stood in the air lock, making a mental note to wipe down my suit the next chance I got. Maybe I could volunteer to wash them all.

I felt my way to the perimeter in near-total darkness. I had not yet been caught.

On my walk to the camp, I felt a longing for it. Not just for my sister but the world she was a part of. I had spent nights at bonfires with Native Hawaiian people, and with people indigenous to all parts of the Earth. A Sakha poet had visited from a city in Siberia—the coldest major city in the world, Kayla said—and recited eight thousand verses about the disintegration of nomadic society. Four Sardinian separatists had sung field songs in harmony in a tight circle at night, mimicking the voices of a cow, a sheep, a shepherd, and the wind. Ten Maori doctors doing a short residency in Honolulu had flown down to film a haka at the base of the volcano.

There'd been songs, drums, and little girls practicing hula. Teenage boys with ripped and faded red armbands muttered into walkie-talkies. They'd wanted to be the camp's security team, to feel strong and protective, and the elders let them. I had hummed along to every protest song. I'd sipped Navajo tea gathered from the side of a highway in Arizona. My hazmat suit was always hidden in a crate. When the space station flew over us, I had gathered people close to me and pointed up. I had traced it across the sky.

I felt myself getting closer to something. As a child I'd sit outside the circle in a camp chair—with Brett, a paperback, a flashlight. I'd watch him watch my mother and sister move slow in a round dance, their arms wrapped in blankets, their feet pressing flat to the grass with dozens of others in step. Sometimes I thought about flipping the switch on my flashlight. Setting my book face down on the chair, stepping into the circle and taking their hands. But I never had.

I sat across from Kayla, working up the courage to ask if Felicia could leave. She wanted to see her father, to get some reassurance that he wasn't dropping out of her life. She also wanted to go back to her old school. There was no way these asks would go over well, because they implied Kayla had been seen as a bad mom. That was something she couldn't tolerate.

"I'm not happy," she said. The bottoms of her shoes had melted down smooth, after too many nights held up too close to fire.

"I know. I got your email asking me to leave. But if I drop out, they won't assign me a mission to space."

Kayla looked at me, tired. She and her new friend Diana had cut each other's hair short, and I pictured them matching, like sisters. Kayla had once done entire YouTube videos of her beach waves wash day routine, with sponsored product recommendations for every step. She flattened it down now, with dusty hats and bandanas.

"Ha," she said. "I wasn't talking about you. I meant I have feelings for Mark."

"The tattoo guy?"

"The *traditional* tattoo guy. One of the few people alive who's achieved the right to pass on kākau uhi. And before you judge me, no, we haven't done anything."

She would have judged me, I thought, if our roles had been reversed.

"Diana thinks it's just a crush," Kayla said. "She says it's a sign I'm not happy with my life. She says when people have affairs—*not that I've had one*—when people do that, it's never about the new guy."

I prickled at the thought of Diana and her advice, though I agreed with it completely. When my sister had lived at Hollis, she'd often chosen Della over me for help.

"What's it about then," I said, too harshly.

I softened and tried again. "What do you think it might be about?"

"If you say *I told you so*, I'll scream," said Kayla. "But I wish I'd carved out more time for myself when I was younger. Figured out my job, what I'm trying to do, and what I want to say with my art?"

"Yeah. Do you think you should have gone to college?"

"Steph, I swear to God. I'm trying to talk to you."

"Sorry! It was an honest question! I'll just listen."

"Things have obviously worked out," Kayla said. "I'm smart, I work hard, I built everything I have. And Felicia! Felicia is perfect."

Jason had brought in some wealth, I thought, and a beachside home inherited from his late grandparents—impossible to afford in Hawai'i today. Felicia was not perfect, she was *good*, which was different from perfect. Which I loved.

I nodded, vigorously. I could be supportive, like Diana.

"It's not about what I did with what I had," Kayla said. "I did fine."

I said nothing, and she spoke again. "It's about this period of life when you have like a zillion options—so many different lives you could live because you're young and undecided. And then you make a choice, even a great one, like Felicia—and overnight they're all gone. All but a few, with a guy who's good enough but he's—"

"Felicia's *father*," I said.

I was trying to stop this, to block her from saying something she'd regret. What if this was all just a reaction to her months at camp?

It was a failure to see outside myself. Felicia didn't need two parents in love. All she'd ever asked for was information.

I was pushing my sister back toward Jason, because no one had tried to push me. Della had come up the stairs. She'd seen her bed made, her drawers filled, the lizard in the terrarium moved onto her dresser. I'd heard the swing and click of her door. My mother and sister never spoke of it. Not even after the ceremony when I met them in the crowd, alone, diploma in a crimson folder clutched to my chest. When I fell short in love, no one was surprised.

Kayla looked behind her at the hab in the distance, circled in lights for security. She was disappointed. I wanted to put my arm around her, but I didn't. My crewmates weren't touching, seeing, or even talking to people outside the hab.

"It's a crush," she said. "Diana was right."

Updated SHE Profile

Nadia, 36, Perplexed.

About Me: Where were you last night?

Notes, passed under doors on August 10

Steph, what the fuck. Adisu let me out of quarantine when my fever broke. If you weren't in your quarters at two a.m., where were you?

Nadia

N,

I'm so sorry. Please please delete your SHE account. That is the *only* rule you've broken this mission, and I don't want you to get in trouble.

I took a walk. It wasn't authorized. I'm telling you where I was because I don't want you to think I was in the hab. (I wasn't cheating. I hope that's a given. But I'm scared of you thinking that, asking our crewmates if I was with them, and accidentally alerting them to my absence.)

It was stupid. I shouldn't have gone. I can't talk to you because I'm worried that if we stay close then people will think you know things that you don't know, or that you were involved in any way in some bad decisions I've made. I'm scared I'll hurt your career.

Again, please, delete the app. And when you're done reading this note, rip it up. I don't want you to be traced back to me.

Steph—

"traced back to me" wtf?????? This is not Spy Kids. *You're being insane.*

Your note is like "I promise Nadia, I took a walk," but with the tone someone would use for "I've been running a drug trafficking ring out of the hab." I'm not trying to be funny. I'm just pointing out how stupid this is, that you "took a walk," demanded my silence, and announced via passed notes that we can't "stay close." Very middle school–coded.

When adults experience conflict, they talk to each other. I'm too old to care if someone *likes me* but I do expect to be treated like I exist.

—Nadia

SHE, Direct Messages

August 15, 2016

Nadia: *I know you're seeing this. Your stupid profile is still posted.*
    Nadia: *Srsly you're 30+ yrs old and ghosting me?*
    Nadia: *WE LIVE IN A GEODESIC DOME.*

SHE, Direct Messages

August 22, 2016

Nadia: *This is beneath me.*

Updated SHE Profiles

August 22, 2016

Nadia, 36. [Account Deactivated]

Steph, 34. [Account Deactivated]

TRANSMISSION from Felicia Palakiko to Stephanie Harper

09/01/2016 sent at 16:32 from feliciaaaaaa1019@gmail.com

Whatsup Auntie

Happy bday! I hope you're having a better time than me!!!!!! Mom says all I do is complain and maybe I should go complain to you instead of her for once and I was like you know what WHY NOT? Here goes.

1. The girl I was talking to broke up with me yesterday and it's because I haven't been home to see her once in our entire relationship including Spring Fling. And 'cause I could only talk to her when I stood on the volcano to get cell service but like, doesn't that show COMMITMENT?? And maybe a cool-person sense of adventure? Also the only reason I couldn't go home to see her once in our entire relationship including Spring Fling is because I CAN'T DRIVE. Shouldn't that matter? Young ppl have no agency it freaking sucks.

2. Now that summer is over the camp is starting to get tiny again and it's probably (I think) gonna fall apart soon. Not like we're here on Mauna Loa for nothing, but I think the thirty-meter telescope issue is a bigger deal so they're saying people should go to Mauna Kea instead. (Or even—for people who can afford to get to North Dakota, duh—to Standing Rock? They're still going strong out there.)

3. I think I was more on board with the goals of The Mission last year when I was a kid, but now I'm older and have new / different opinions that Mom calls "giving up."

4. Mom is set on staying here basically forever and doesn't care that it's bad for my education and bad for my relationship with my long-lost dad / with my elisi in Oklahoma / with my tutu in Honolulu who says "protests are for the young." And also btw it *was* bad for my [now-dead] relationship with the only lesbian in my grade.

5. lmao my new joke is that I say to Mom what, is this your hill to die on?!

6. Do you think things are weird between my mom and dad?

7. Mom acts like everything is okay, and you're her sister but like I don't know who else to talk to about this! I think things might secretly be terrible? Related to this (under category of Mom is Fake as Hell), she's always taking pictures of me when I'm doing something outdoorsy and Hawaiian while smiling, and then putting them on the internet with overly long captions. This is embarrassing because

   a. I'm doing puberty rn and all my photos are awk

   b. The only lesbian in my grade probably thinks I'm over her because I'm cheesing all the time! When really it's just that Mom won't take any *actually* cool pictures of me standing over the volcano with my fists clenched, looking out into the distance, thinking of my lost love, etc.

Okay that's all my complaints. Really I'm emailing to see if you can just talk to my mom (don't tell her I sent you) and see if you can get her to TAKE ME HOME ALREADY? I told her it's like I'm imprisoned in the stockades before the Trail of Tears. (She didn't think that was funny, either.)

Srsly I think this whole protest is gonna end soon anyway. And if I don't go home by Sept then my chances of getting back together with the only lesbian in my grade are probably going to be zero (they're already going down like every day. And anyway I started talking to a new girl from the All-Nations Indigenous Youth Council?).

SOS

Love,
Felicia

STEPH

ATTACK!

September 12, 2016

I reached out in panic for the space beside me. I'd given up Nadia a month ago.

There was a sound, the beating of drums, and the thin white walls of the hab lit up. I threw off my blanket.

"Headlights," called Allison through the wall.

Then, louder, "All crew, awake and downstairs! ALL CREW!"

Two quick steps to the door. I crossed my arms over my chest and looked over the railing from the half-moon landing, the doors of all six crew quarters shut behind me. Adisu was already downstairs. He was fully dressed in his uniform, green scrubs and white sneakers, looking out the porthole above his desk. I hurried to join him.

"It's bad," he said.

"What happened?"

"Nothing and something. We're surrounded by these cars, seven that I can see, and they have their brights on. It doesn't feel safe."

Allison, Jed, Aziz, and Nadia stomped down the stairs. We crowded around a porthole and looked out.

These people weren't dangerous. I recognized them, and their numbers were down dramatically. There was the camp medic from Honolulu, and a woman from Hilo who taught hula. There was Diana, Felicia's teacher and Kayla's new best friend. Felicia said Diana was constantly interrupted at the school by people giving spontaneous lessons on the history of Hawaiian re-sistance and sustainable gardening and—once, weirdly, by a visiting academic from the mainland—the Navajo language. On my walks I sometimes saw Diana with a parade of children, pointing at birds and squatting before vol-canic rocks. I often left crystals for them. I laid them at the edge of camp, in places I knew they'd be found.

The protesters circled our hab, the women holding children on their hips and the children holding tiny, closed fists in the air. They should have let them sleep, I thought. The adults wore jean jackets and scarves, bandanas knotted in upside-down triangles over noses and mouths. Did they really think we'd gas them? Their banner, faded now, flapped in the wind, folding and concealing the words painted across it.

My crewmates looked like they were caged in, surrounded by predators.

Nadia was so practiced at avoiding me at this point, with barely a glance in my direction. Now, my heart beat a little faster at her proximity. She wore a long black linen robe over her pajamas, and a black silk scarf knotted over her hair. She wore a single gold bracelet, even to sleep.

When Nadia had caught my absence from the hab, I'd panicked. The stakes were too high. I imagined her reporting it. I imagined an investigation into me, which would lead to the relationship with Nadia that I'd documented in my hab log for the good of science, which would lead to the suspicion that she had been part of the camp. That she had at least known about my role in it? I imagined the impossible, me losing space. I imagined Nadia losing it, too.

"We need to send a message to mission control," Nadia said, not to me. "They should have been monitoring this for us."

"We've been around these people for nine months," I said. "Their protest is on its last legs. If they were interested in harming some research subjects, they would have."

We heard a noise then, a rhythmic scraping.

"Well, shit," said Allison.

"What," said Jed.

"Jed, check the faucet."

Outside, they were singing. They were always singing.

"Ten-four. What am I looking for?"

Allison pushed past him. The flip of the faucet, a spit of water, a drip, and then nothing. "The mother*fuckers!*"

The scraping sound had been a saw on PVC pipe. They'd cut off our water. We were still a week off from the scheduled resupply, and our remaining allotment poured out into the ground. The motherfuckers.

"Look," said Jed. "I say we go out there. Confront them ourselves. I know you're thinking we should alert mission control about the water, and we will. But if we were in trouble on Mars, we couldn't expect police. If we really want to test group cohesion under the stresses of Mars life, we need to respond in a way that would be feasible for that crew."

"So in this scenario," I said, "the future Mars crew is encircled by aliens?"

Adisu shook his head. "I oversee the health and safety of *this* crew, not the future Mars crew. *This* crew cannot leave the hab. We have one doctor for the five of you, and mobs have a history of targeting medics."

"Wait," I said. "Now they're a mob?"

"*Steph*," Nadia said. She gave me a meaningful look, her first in weeks. A warning?

"We have to assume that they're armed," Aziz said.

"Be serious," I said.

Allison threw up a hand. "I haven't come to a decision yet." She glared at Adisu, then Aziz, then me. "As your commander, *I* will be the one to decide."

Outside the hab, a woman stepped toward the porthole. She was backlit by a headlight, her features eclipsed in her silhouette.

She lifted a megaphone to her mouth. "Steph," she said. "It's me. Kayla."

A pull in my stomach. She was outing me. She had made herself their spokesperson.

"I stand on Hawaiian lands," Kayla said, "with representatives of many Indigenous nations. All we ask is that you listen."

"Did she say *Steph*?" Adisu said.

Kayla said, again, "Steph."

Allison looked up at the ceiling, gathering herself.

"How do you know her?" Nadia said. She leaned against the wall, arms crossed tightly over her chest.

"I understand more than anyone," Kayla said, "what kind of pressure you're under. But our movement is about protecting this planet and ensuring a sustained Indigenous presence on Earth. Yours is about giving up on this planet, and colonizing somewhere we can't even breathe."

Aziz groaned. "Whoever this woman is to you," he said, "you've done a shit job explaining our work to her."

Kayla continued. "Who do you think will make it to your new world? We understand settler colonialism better than anyone. First, it'll be the necessary people, the scientists and engineers. Then the adventurers, the millionaires, the one percent. If you turn your back on Earth, and you let it burn—you understand our people will be abandoned in its ashes."

"What is even happening right now?" said Jed.

Kayla said, "As you cower in your hab, we stand here as witnesses to your inaction."

Kayla handed the megaphone off to a Hawaiian woman, a cook I'd once met named Anna, who shouted out orders to the small crowd. Slowly, singing a song I strained to recognize, they started back toward their cars.

I turned around. My crewmates stared at me.

"Right," I said, "I do know her."

Silence.

"The woman with the megaphone is my little sister," I said. "Kayla Palakiko."

Silence. The fluorescent lights buzzed at the top of the dome. Outside the door, the plastic sheet of the air lock snapped against itself in the wind.

Nadia said, "Thatindigenousmama?"

"Yes?" I swayed a little, squeezing my hands together behind my back.

"Your *sister* is *thatindigenousmama*?"

I nodded. Nadia made a face, like she didn't believe me or couldn't believe I hadn't told her. I had known that Nadia followed Kayla before the mission. Once, assuming I'd be interested because Kayla was Cherokee, Nadia had talked about her as a content creator who was doing some cool things. I'd pretended to be unfamiliar.

But I'd only been following Kayla's lead! When I was accepted into NASA and Kayla was nearly canceled for congratulating me, she'd deleted every trace of me from her Instagram account. Years of photos with captions about #sisters #family #gratitude—gone.

Jed paced full circles around the hab, trapped in its thirty-six square feet of diameter. He'd disappear behind the bathroom and the staircase before reappearing, hands folded over his forehead. "No fucking way," he muttered, "no *fucking* way."

In the kitchen he stopped. Briefly, he closed his eyes.

"So she's your sister?" he said. "You mean to say that our entire year, the outcome of this scientists-in-prison experiment is riding on whether your *sister* convinces you to sabotage the mission?"

"I'm afraid that maybe she already has," said Adisu.

I felt sick. I wanted to run for my quarters, or better yet, the air lock.

"I think that, for some time now, Steph has been—" said Adisu.

"Adisu," said Nadia. She looked at him hard, hard like, *Stop*. Like, *Who do you think this would help?*

It occurred to me that Nadia had been guarding my secret. Why hadn't I been normal about it when she'd asked? I could have said I'd been sick in the bathroom that night, even sick just outside the walls of the hab. If I'd stayed cool I could have brushed it away. It was in my not telling, my sudden and total destruction of what we'd had, that Nadia must have guessed where I'd gone.

Adisu sat on the foot of the stairs. He pressed his hands to his forehead. Allison sat beside him.

"Steph," Adisu said, "tell them."

I shrugged, like I didn't know what he meant. I thought immediately of Jess from college, how she'd lost her dream job with the FBI by answering truthfully that she'd shared a joint in the last year. I wanted more than a high-security clearance. I wanted *space*. I shook my head at Adisu, pleadingly.

He sighed. "I think Steph goes on walks at night, maybe to visit the camp. I didn't say anything because I wasn't sure. A false accusation would be bad for group cohesion. For the last few weeks I've done nightly checks for her suit on its hook, with the plan to report it if my theory was confirmed."

He pulled a folded piece of paper from his breast pocket and waved it in the air before putting it back. What was even on it? Tallies of each time he *hadn't* caught me?

"Her contact with people outside the crew," Adisu said. "It invalidates the study."

Allison opened her mouth and closed it. I moved to speak, and she glared at me.

"*Not a word of this,*" she hissed. "Not a fucking word to anybody. Go to bed, all of you, and for God's sakes, don't write about this in your hab logs."

No one moved.

"Dismissed!"

We stared at her. She remembered her position and lowered her voice. "We'll do a late breakfast, at eight hundred hours. Go. Get some sleep, people."

Jed walked heavy-footed up the stairs. The others followed.

I ran up the stairs behind Nadia, last in line. I touched her wrist. She looked pointedly at my hand on her body like she couldn't believe it was there again, that I'd even dare.

I let go. "You're an engineer," I whispered. "A scientist! You have to hold tonight's findings against months of observed behavior, to acknowledge that those camp visits are an outlier."

"No," she snapped. She stepped back and steadied her hand on the railing. "Scientists are just *people*, Steph. That's all we are."

I backed against the wall, and Nadia rushed up the stairs. One by one, my crewmates closed their doors.

I wondered how close my sister was now. Had the protesters made it back to camp yet? If Kayla turned back from the crowd, could she see any part of me in the pinprick light of the porthole? We hadn't hugged in months—only the one time she'd crushed my suit around me. I'd held back since then, my own compromise toward the isolation I owed to the crew.

Alone, halfway up the thin metal staircase, I felt so far from the wind just outside. From the sharp smell of the woods behind my mother's house, of trees and fire and wild onions in mud. The world was getting away from me.

Text Messages

September 13, 2016

Hannah Harper:
!!!!!!!!!!!!!!!!!!!!!!!!

Hannah Harper:
!!!!!!!!!!!!!!!!!!!!!!

Hannah Harper:
WHY DIDN'T YOU TELL ME THEY DID A STORY ON YOU
IN THE NEW YORK TIMES???????????????????????

Hannah Harper:
You there?

Hannah Harper:
I should start with wow! Congrats!

Kayla Palakiko:
hi mom. lol it was not a story on *me* it was a story on
the movement, via interviews with me and three other
land protectors. Two were from Standing Rock, where
they just got attacked with pepper spray and dogs. And
it was v cool that the other two of us were from here!!
Very exciting. Sorry I've been on phone less lately!

Hannah Harper:
haha you are on your phone every damn day.

Hannah Harper:
But yes, proud of you! GREAT photo of you + lava.
very cool + spooky! *[volcano emoji] [ghost emoji]*

Kayla Palakiko:
ha

Kayla Palakiko:
thx. How's home?

Hannah Harper:
Good.

Hannah Harper:
How's school going for Felicia?

Kayla Palakiko:
Mom come onnnn

Hannah Harper:
?????? just asking about my only granddaughter????

Kayla Palakiko:
She's getting a great education learning lots of impt teachings at a critical moment in history i.e. indig ways of knowing, herstory, survivance, etc

Hannah Harper:
wow cool

Hannah Harper:
Is herstory like history but for girls?

Hannah Harper:
what's survivance?

Hannah Harper:
School indoor or outdoor?

Hannah Harper:
???????

Hannah Harper:
Felicia could come stay with me

Hannah Harper:
You both could come live here if you ever wanted or needed to, for any reason okay?

Hannah Harper:
You know that, right?

Hannah Harper:
Kayla????????

Kayla Harper:
thx I know + I'm married with a house?

Hannah Harper:
with a tent ha ha ha

Hannah Harper:
just a little joke

Hannah Harper:
[smiley face in a cowboy hat emoji]

Hannah Harper:
?

Hannah Harper:
okay congratulations on the newspaper I love you

Kayla Harper:
same

Recent Blog Posts:

1. *Five Products I Can't Live Without as an Indigenous Mother in a Protest Encampment*
2. *Ask a Kanaka Friend: What's the Difference Between the Mauna Kea Protests and the Mauna Loa Protests?*
3. *Three Things I Hate About Settler Tourism in the Kingdom of Hawai'i*
4. *Here's Everything I Eat in a Day as an Indigenous Mother on Month #7 in a Protest Encampment*
5. *Hear from the Youth Councils at Mauna Loa and Standing Rock: What Is Indigenous Solidarity + Why Does It Matter Now, More Than Ever?*
6. *Teacher Tuesdays with @dianasaurusrex: What Makes a Volcano Erupt?*
7. *Instagram vs. Reality: Trying to Complete a Book Proposal on that Glamorous Indian Activist Life, But I'm Balancing My Laptop on a Rock at a Protest Encampment*
8. *My Husband Came to Visit! Here's What I Planned for Our Rugged/Outdoorsy 14th Anniversary Date, as an Indigenous Mother in a Protest Encampment*
9. *A Response to My Followers re: Hurtful Comments re: My Marriage to a Kanaka Maoli Man, as an Indigenous (enrolled Cherokee Nation citizen) Mother in a Protest Encampment*
10. *A Response to My Followers re: Claims that I've Been Trying to Speak for Kānaka Maoli + a Recommitment to *Continue to* Amplify Kānaka Voices*
11. *Candid Campfire #22: Mark Wells, Kanaka Single Dad and Traditional Tattoo Artist, Answers "What's Your Why?"*
12. *Candid Campfire #23: Felicia Palakiko, Kanaka and Cherokee Teen (and My Daughter!), with an Update from the All-Nations Indigenous Youth Council*
13. *Teacher Tuesdays with @dianasaurusrex: Here's Everything We're Doing in Our Protest Encampment to Go Zero-Waste, and Why You Should Be Composting at the Very Least*

Comment from chloedonaldsonxx:

absolutely OBSESSED with the daughter's lack of enthusiasm like girl is so obviously over this??? #savefelicia

Comment from hannahharper:

Keep up the good work, Kayla. I'm proud of you! [heart-eyes emoji] [smiley giving a kiss emoji]

Comment from maddysullivanwrites:

This channel is cute (and tbh powerful) and I'm a longtime follower. But from everything I've been told in autonomous kānaka-led online spaces, kānaka activists and elders are now prioritizing the fight at nearby Mauna Kea (against construction of the 30m telescope) and they have been for a while. They are calling for land protectors to abandon the Mars hab fight and go help where it's most needed (mauna KEA).

↪**Comments from kanakakween:**

@maddysullivanwrites yep, can confirm. I was at Mauna Loa with Kayla for months (before we were encouraged to leave by our kūpuna). Kayla is an absolutely beautiful person and I have NOTHING but respect for her.

But I believe in the power of a gentle, community-led call-in (all love!). Kayla refuses to leave mauna loa's dwindling (ON PURPOSE) camp, or to explain any of this to the public, or even just to lift up kānaka voices AT MAUNA KEA with her platform to prevent the ***permanent*** construction of the TMT on sacred land.

The NYT profile was a disaster, total missed opportunity for a kanaka journalist to cover the story. Standing Rock has a bigger profile so I guess we're supposed to feel grateful that a white journalist even included HI? Insane that she interviewed 2 HI-based activists but 0 were affiliated with the Mauna Kea protest. Intentional erasure of Mauna Kea?? 1 of them (Kayla) is more of a mommy blogger and also, let it be said, NOT EVEN HAWAIIAN. obvi that article could have lifted up a kanaka activist with a smaller following, in her place.

↪**Comment from susanstark51:**

@maddysullivanwrites @kanakakween YIKES at all these videos Kayla keeps posting, trying to make a life-or-death protest look exotic and cute? classic white woman energy. anyone have contact info for her employer?

↪**Comment from dianasaurusrex:**

The fact that @susanstark51's bio says "skoliosexual settler living + learning on unceded Treaty 7 Territory" I hate it here!

Comment from susanstark51:

@dianasaurusrex Wishing you peace.
              @everybodyelse Have you seen this tweet??

Tweet from vsjakjthrowawayaccount:

@thatindigenousmama is this your husband? my
daughter was at temptations bar night club in honolulu
she said he went home last night w/ the girl in the pic

💬 Comment from **sarahjaan32**:
[big open eyeballs emoji]

💬 Comment from **arson615**:
[popcorn emoji]

💬 Comment from **kanakakween**:
lmao

STEPH

ALTERNATE

September 16, 2016

After what everyone insisted on calling "the attack," mission control would not repair our water tank. They would not move up our water resupply date. They knew we had thirty gallons of emergency water in the storeroom. They thought rationing under stress could provide helpful data, and encouraged us to document the experience in our hab logs.

We stopped cooking, cleaning, and doing laundry. We stopped exercising, to try to stop sweating. Our composting toilet couldn't function on the little water we poured into it, and the stench was unbearable.

I couldn't sleep. I lay awake hating myself, missing Nadia, weighing the chances I would still go to space. How could I have let myself risk that? What had I wanted, bad enough to be so weak?

I had chosen Nadia. Before that, I had chosen the chance that my sister might like me.

After dinner on the third day, Jed and Aziz tried to rally people to play dominoes. I started for my quarters. Allison caught my elbow at the foot of the stairs and pulled me into the storeroom. "We need to talk."

"About what?" I said. The storeroom was dimly lit and as small as the bathroom, four square feet of packed floor-to-ceiling shelves. We were surrounded by cans of protein powder and mashed potato flakes, a far cry from the space ice cream I'd yearned for as a child.

Allison folded her arms over her chest. Her uniform was ironed but dirty. "About what, *Commander*," she corrected.

"About what, Commander?"

"About your future with NASA. I realize how much a mission assignment matters to you, and that's a dangerous place for you to be."

"Oh. I think I'm entitled to want things, though."

"Of course you are," she said. "We all are. I had a baby at the Air Force Academy! You think I didn't study up on the protocol to make that workable?"

I knew this, of course, but the details of it felt irrelevant to my life. Every day at what was noon in the hab, twenty minutes before her daughter was due home from school in Texas, Allison recorded and sent a video from her desk. From the vague outline I knew, Allison had gone from a small-town childhood to flying planes to being a single mother at NASA. She had been to space.

Allison wasn't done. "The thing is, if I hadn't made commander, I would have been satisfied in the service. And if I hadn't gotten pregnant, I still would have been satisfied. I would have *brought myself* to a place of satisfaction—with an alternative outcome."

"Respectfully," I said, "it sounds like you got everything you wanted."

"Respectfully, Steph, you're in deep shit. I'm trying to help you. We call it PACE—primary, alternate, contingency, emergency. It's supposed to apply to setting up backup comms systems, but I use it for my life, and frankly, you should, too. Having Kristen on my own wasn't my primary plan, but I had an alternate and contingency in mind as circumstances changed. I had to be okay with that.

"You cannot want a mission assignment *this much*, to the point that you lose sight of everything else. If I report your unauthorized contact—"

I leaned back against a person-sized bag of rice.

"—and you better realize what even the *idea* of not reporting would do to my career, my moral code, and my identity as a serviceman. If I report it, you will have sabotaged us all. Months of work behind us! The sacrifice it was for Adisu and me, who both left kids behind? A year of their lives, *invalidated!*"

The room was too hot. I needed air. *Do not cry.*

"I'm sorry," I said.

I was. Not as sorry as I needed to be, or as sorry as I knew I would be later. But it was a break from feeling bad for myself.

I couldn't believe what I had done. I had no idea what I might do next.

Allison shook her head. "Yeah, well. I don't know if I'll report it. I should. I almost definitely will. But let me be clear—I *absolutely* can't recommend you for a mission in space."

It was like she'd knocked the wind out of me. The cans on the shelves blurred into each other. I stumbled past her to the door. Air. The rest of the crew laughed in the other room. Dominoes clicked against each other.

"I can fix this!" I said. "I messed up, I know, but I was loyal to my crewmates. I swear. I kept my suit on for my walks and maintained physical distance. I never missed a minute of scheduled time with the crew, I completed all assigned tasks, and I—"

Allison put a hand on my shoulder. Her brow was knit in worry, like my mother's had so often been. "This isn't about *loyalty*, Steph." Her voice was different, loose, like she'd let a layer of her learned accent fall. "We're accountable for the survival of a future crew on Mars. And you've compromised that work."

"Allison, please—"

She pulled her phone out of her pocket and read from the small screen. "Successful astronaut candidates *may not have* a history of poor or unstable work or interpersonal relationships or personality traits that interfere with functioning cooperatively with others. This may include personality traits such as self-centeredness, lack of concern for others, arrogance, entitlement, lack of empathy, insensitivity . . ."

She paused and looked up. "Do I need to continue?"

It was from the handbook, the section on medical standards for astronaut selection. I had read that page many times over the years, pausing over each disqualifying trait. *Is this me?* I'd ask myself, certain it was.

"You won't be assigned a mission," she said. "I need you to prepare yourself for that outcome."

I stepped out of the storeroom, almost falling toward the air lock. The crew looked up at me, concerned, from their little circle on the rug.

"Hang on," Allison said.

I turned.

She held a large cardboard box she'd pulled from a shelf in the storeroom, taped shut and labeled in black marker: *STEPH!* ♥♥♥

It was what Allison called a care package. What I'd called our emergency breakdown boxes. I was the only remaining member of the crew who hadn't yet asked for theirs.

"Here," Allison said. "Take this, open it in your quarters, and cool off."

It was heavy in my arms. Beside the air lock, I adjusted my grip and ran a finger against the rough yellow of my hazmat suit. It hung on the wall, a shade dirtier than the four beside it, and I knew I hadn't imagined it. I understood Adisu had known for some time. My suit smelled like campfires.

From the age of five, I'd imagined my footsteps on the moon. I'd only meant to run at first. To get as far away as possible. Then to be chosen, to stand on safe ground and belong. It occurred to me, looking out the porthole: I may never know more than this world.

Sprawled out across the floor, my crewmates seemed content. Even tired, frustrated, unshowered—they were laughing, reaching their hands across the circle and setting dominoes into place. They were at ease with one another. I turned toward the darkness that had chased me through childhood, where the world blurred and my ears turned the voices around me into a long, slow hum. Where I was totally alone, like I could reach out forever and never touch another person.

I sat on the floor next to Jed and put the box down behind me. Jed smiled and patted me on the arm, the first gesture of forgiveness. Either he or I felt alien and far.

I fell back into myself. I'm pulling up wild onions and Kayla's eating them raw, dirt-dusted. I'm cutting holes in a cereal box to watch the eclipse, and Kayla's standing proud-chested beside me, insisting she'll stare at it straight-on. I'm holding my head, shaking, remembering what Kayla doesn't know. But Kayla is there anyway, wrapping me in blankets and squeezing me tight. She won't let go till I'm okay again.

09/17/2016 sent at 8:22 from feliciaaaaaa1019@gmail.com

Auntie,

Before you're weird about it, I already saw the stuff online about my dad. I know you don't have social media this year but I'm hoping maybe my mom emailed you about it because she won't talk about it with me.

I'm worried about her, and my dad, and what's gonna happen next. Mom maybe wouldn't want to live in HI without Dad, especially with all the Hawaiians mad at her. Now the internet's involved. Yesterday people posted mean stuff about how I dress weird and have a bad haircut so I changed my account to private. When Dad came to visit for their anniversary, before any of this happened, he hugged me for so long I got scared he was giving me away.

The camp is really small these days (like 20 people) and my friends have left. Mostly their parents took them to the bigger protest at Mauna Kea, or back home. One girl flew all the way to Standing Rock, but her dad's rich and divorced and she said this was all just his midlife crisis. If my parents break up I hope my dad is normal about it, so I can stay in the same house and go to the same school. Not that I've been there in like half a year. I kind of forgot algebra.

Remember Mark? Mahina's dad, who does tattoos? He left yesterday for Mauna Kea. He tried to get Mom and me to go there, too. But he's spent *way* too much time hanging around us the last few months. He could never get the hint that Mom and I wanted our space! I'm glad he's gone.

Auntie Diana is leaving, too, on a flight next week. Back to the prep school where she lives and works, even though Mom says she doesn't *really* have to leave now because her sabbatical goes till December. (They had a tense conversation about that and I listened in.) Auntie D is way nicer than the people on the internet, but she agrees with them that Mom and I need to get out of here.

I'm sorry about your water tank thing.

I should get to the point.

Promise you'll never tell anyone this, or that I told you this, but I think there's going to be something big soon. It'll be around midnight, on September 20th.

The girl on Youth Council I was talking to heard it from her dad, who told her not to tell anyone because it's going to "wake people up to the desecration of Mauna Loa." I tried to stay casual, like hahaha is it gonna annoy the astronauts like blaring a siren at them all night, or hurt the astronauts like idk mustard gas hahaha?

And then the girl I was talking to was like hahaha beats me hahaha!! (I'm not talking to her anymore—she was kinda dumb but also I've decided to focus on Loving Myself in this new season.)

Please don't get my mom in trouble, or the girl I used to talk to, or her dad who means well but is 99% of the time All Talk. (Like his name is Tim but Auntie Diana literally calls him "All-Talk Tim," which should tell you not to panic.)

Remember, don't tell anyone. I just thought that if I emailed you, you could stay up late that night and read? If they even let you have books? And then IF IF IF anything more than a march happens, you'll be awake and can deal with it yourself. I know you have the mission control people on alert right nearby, lots of security, nothing bad could happen to you guys. So just PROMISE you won't call them unless something changes that night? Like, unless you don't feel safe?

Love,
F

A note pushed under the door on September 18, 2016

Steph—

Things got weird between us, *(YOU MADE THEM WEIRD)*, whatever, *(YOU GHOSTED ME IN A FUCKING DOME)*, whatever, but just hear me out—

Allison was talking to Jed in her quarters last night, on the other side of my wall. She's decided to report you.

Sucks, etc. You're probably sad + stubborn + pissed that I was pissed that you ruined our mission and wasted nine months of our precious few years alive.

But if there's a report submitted, they'll do an audit. Of everything, including the crew's tech use. I will not be brought down by, of all things, my one-time download of the Worst of the gay dating apps. I'm not ready to give up on *BEING AN ASTRONAUT* for my stupidest/most absurd three-day relationship. When everyone's asleep, I'm coming to your quarters and you will *FIX THIS.*

—Nadia, 36, ascan, for fucking now at least

CONTINGENCY

After Allison declared the end of my career, I imagined each life I might have had. I remembered each time I had loved or been loved, or felt myself pulled closer to Earth. Each time, I had run. I'd thought I had to.

Nadia came to my quarters in her daytime uniform, despite the late hour. A small whiteboard was tucked under her arm, and she'd erased our treadmill records. She sat on my bed with her shoes on, which she wouldn't stand for in her own quarters. She motioned for me to sit on the floor.

Nadia lectured me on the consequences of what I had done, and what we as a crew were now up against. How hard she had worked to get to this point, and what she had sacrificed. She told me her mother had cancer. Her mother had demanded, in a letter Nadia found in her box on the first day of our mission, that Nadia see this year through. She would not allow her daughter to give up on her dream. If Nadia did try, upon reading the letter, to quit the mission, her mother said she'd lock her apartment door and refuse to see her.

"My God, Nadia, I had no id—"

"Stop."

"I'm sorry, I—"

"Nope." Nadia pulled out the whiteboard and a blue marker, which she pointed at my face. Her hand shook. "There is nothing I want less in the world right now—"

A sharp breath. Her hand on her hip. "There is *nothing* I want less than to hear you talk about my mom. I mention her prognosis only because I hate you, and I want you to feel as bad as you can."

"I do. I'm sorry. I just—"

"No."

I nodded.

Nadia turned and bent over the whiteboard. She started writing, silently at first. Eventually, she asked whispered questions, logistical in nature. She made lists and took more notes.

Plan A. Plan B. Plan C. None would work. It was hard to convince Allison of anything.

"Think harder; this is your life," Nadia said. Hands out, exhausted. "*My* life," she corrected, a catch in her voice. I wanted to talk more about her mother, whose life made this scheming stupid in comparison. I knew I couldn't.

I could not make sense of my own life, I realized, without my mother in it. I should have emailed her over the many months of the mission so far. I wasn't sure why I'd been afraid to.

The marker fell and began to bleed onto my sheets.

I lifted the corner of my mattress and showed Nadia the notebook that held my camp log. The pages were full, folded over and scratched out. Scribbled details were everywhere. Names, positions, dates, and plans.

"Plan D," Nadia said, when she'd flipped through enough to understand. "Provide Allison with replacement data."

Well after midnight, Nadia moved to leave. At the door she paused, letting out a long sigh. She waved her hand over the cardboard box, still taped shut, that sat on the floor at the foot of my bed. "That's so dumb," she said. "I'll never understand what you've got against your mom."

I couldn't sleep. Nadia's plan wasn't enough.

I was grateful to have kept good data. It served a practical purpose, filling in any gaps in my hab log. Allison could answer questions of group cohesion with each crew member accounted for. She could quantify when I was absent, confirm that it was only a small number of hours across months, and decide for herself that its impact on our experiment would be marginal.

But Nadia's plan didn't prove loyalty or clarify how far I'd go for my fellow crew members in space. I would do whatever it takes.

I made up my mind on an alternate plan, a terrible one, and then I told myself: *you have no choice*.

I had whispered something similar on long nights in Moscow, missing Della soon after I broke up with her. But it hadn't been true. There had been no need, I now knew, to leave her the night before her graduation. To do it silently, cruelly, in the way that I had. That thought, waking up and showing itself all these years later, shook me.

After breakfast and back in the storeroom, I gave my camp log to Allison. She held it carefully between just her thumb and index, like it would tear. Or like she didn't want to touch it.

"You can use this," I explained, "as confirmation against your own hab data. It'll tell you exactly how many minutes I was gone, how many times, and then you'll know if that margin of error is enough to necessitate informing the research team."

"You want me to lie," Allison whispered. "Not just me, but the crew. You're asking us all to trust each other, forever, our whole careers—to put everything on the line. For *you*?"

I nodded.

"Steph, honestly. You're killing me. Except for maybe Nadia, who, if you ask me, might be a special circumstance, do you reckon you've made friends here?"

I was right. The camp log wouldn't be enough. I felt sick. I could smell the two of us, cramped in the dark storeroom, three days since our last per-mitted shower.

"I'm asking for something big," I said, steadying my voice. "I understand that. I can't ask you all to make a sacrifice for me without making one myself."

Allison looked at me, unimpressed. I thought of Kristen, the little girl in the photograph Allison kept in her cubicle. This year without her mother, a whole year staying with her grandparents in Houston—that time had to count for something. I had to bet on Allison wanting that for Kristen, as badly as I wanted space for myself.

"I have information on an incoming threat to the crew's safety," I said. "I know who's organizing it, and the names of most of the remaining protesters.

I know when it's scheduled to happen, down to the hour. I might want to share this information with mission control. For the sake of the crew."

Outside the storeroom, at a desk under a porthole, Allison picked up the direct line.

She watched me. Not like I had proven her wrong. She watched me like I was broken.

www.thatindigenousmama.com

It is with a heavy heart that I announce that my husband and I will be separating after many years of finding comfort, love, and joy in each other. My husband is, and will always be, a good father and a good man.

Someone once told me that in traditional times, this was easier. People didn't expect their partnerships to last forever. They stepped into them freely, with open arms. The Cherokee home belonged to the woman. When a relationship came to its natural end, there was calm. The woman would place the man's belongings outside her house, and he would know it was time to leave.

I do not mean to imply anger. I am not angry. I am not trying to put clothes outside a door, outside a home built on love. But I take from that story something that feels like, maybe, This is not the end of my life.

Or maybe, This has happened before.

I think about the ideas I struggle with, the unkind things I sometimes tell myself. This is the end of the only thing you know, *and* This is the ruin of a good woman, *and* This will destroy your child.

I was nineteen when I promised my life to him. A girl. How could I know, how could I imagine, all the women I was still yet to be?

This will not break our daughter, who is stronger and wiser and funnier than I have ever been. But it will hurt her. And her father, and me. It hurts. There is no natural end to a relationship, I realize, no shortcut to calm. There is no better or easier time.

I've been going on walks lately, at night. Here on the land of my husband and my daughter, the night sky is unlike anything I may ever see again. Only on these walks, far from my sleeping child, do I cry so hard I ache in my gut and my throat and I feel completely alone in the universe.

When I'm crying like this, like I might dry up and die and leave my daughter orphaned in a tent on a volcano, I think about the stars. I feel the presence of everyone I come from. I've been trying to learn more about them, to understand them not as the ancestors, but as people. People capable of harm and good. I feel them tell me that life is—that life is meant to be—long. There is time to decide the next part, and to forgive myself when it changes. Maybe I'm just telling myself that, but that's okay, too.

I didn't mean to share all this here. I thought this would be one of those posts, the kind with "conscious uncoupling," and then something bright just around the corner? Something happy and beautiful. But my life does not feel happy and beautiful. I'm trying to be accountable to the truth.

In the spirit of honesty, I owe my followers an update on what a lot of you are really here for—my content on Mauna Loa.

This is another ending for me. I regret that I wasn't up-front with you all earlier, when the elders and the leaders of this movement first made the decision to leave Mauna Loa and prioritize Mauna Kea. Over the last few weeks, the camp at Mauna Loa has been rapidly shrinking as land protectors honor that request and leave—either to assist in blocking the construction of the thirty-meter telescope at Mauna Kea, or to go home.

I stayed here longer than I should have. The longer I stayed, the more I felt an obligation to stay, or maybe even a right to? As if any part of this movement, led by Kānaka Maoli elders and community leaders and activists and teachers and youth, should, at the end of the day, center me. A guest. A woman who has briefly lived on this land, has loved this land, and who has a history of, maybe, caring too much how people see her. I've felt the weight here (at camp, but also online) of needing to represent something narrower than I am. (Than anyone is.) A certain kind of activist, Indian, wife, mother. Maybe especially Indian. Like if I didn't fight for that, for the image I had of what that meant, I wouldn't exist?

I am ready to do what was asked of me. My daughter and I leave camp in the morning.

To the Kānaka Maoli people who have too many times had to ask me to leave Mauna Loa, to help encourage others to leave Mauna Loa and to join them in solidarity at Mauna Kea—I am sorry.

To the Kānaka Maoli people who have fought to stay at Mauna Loa, who have asked me to stand by them, and who will no doubt feel betrayed by my decision to leave—I am sorry.

To my husband and my daughter, loves of my life—we are going to be all right.

Letter from Hannah Harper to Steph Harper

Written December 18, 2015
Opened September 20, 2016

Dear Steph,

HELLO UP THERE! Your mother is waving to you from back on Earth!
    Haha. Actually, while I'm writing this, you're still here "on planet" with us. I know you said you wanted to spend your first holiday season in Houston with your new astronaut friends, but it's not even Christmas yet and I'm already missing you. I wish you had come home. I can say that without that mother-trap of being a nag, because by the time you read this, Christmas will be long over. Rest assured I probably had a great time, all alone under the tree with nothing but my memories to keep me company. Haha!
    Anyway, it's a good thing your astronaut-boss Allison told me to put this together for you. That really impressed me, that she thought to reach out to all the families. It makes me feel good, especially when I'm all alone this Christmas, to know you're in good hands.
    Allison said in her email that they're thinking about doing the same thing on real-Mars, because these care packages are helpful for mental health crises on long-term missions. (I'll just say, I didn't like her implying that you'll be having a mental health crisis.) She said all I have to do in this letter is let you know that (1) I love you, and (2) everything is ok.
    Steph, I do love you very much.
    And as for the second ask, I wish I could be like the other astronaut moms and dads who write letters that say everything is fine. I just don't think I can.
    Everything you're doing this year is supposed to be make-believe. I know! I get it! But I'm scared for you anyway. I've always been scared for you.
    (I know I shouldn't be. Don't worry about me. I'm working on it. In recent years I've been thinking about how hard things were for you and for me, when you were little and Kayla was just a baby. I think about what you might have seen, and what I couldn't protect you from. I even went to a therapist two years ago for the first time, who said maybe it wasn't my best decision to never talk about this stuff with you. I know you've said you need to focus and do a good job on your first mission, and you don't

plan on talking to family much this year. Maybe when you're back, we can talk a little more than we used to. I'd really like to start over.)

I hope you asked Allison to give you this care package today just because, I don't know, you're a little sad. You miss the Earth, haha.

But I can't stop myself from thinking that there's the tiniest, tiniest chance you asked for it because you're in real trouble. Like a terrorist attack, or your volcano erupting. So here's what I've packed you:

- *Flashlight + 4 AA batteries*
- *MRE meals (expire Jun. 2021) x6*
- *Hand-crank radio*
- *First aid kit*
- *Aspirin, acetaminophen, calamine lotion*
- *Tourniquet*
- *Emergency blanket*
- *Whistle*
- *Surgical masks x10*
- *Matches*
- *200 dollars (in twenties, see yellow envelope)*
- *Hershey bars milk chocolate x3*
- *Books x2 (*The Big Bang: Secrets of the Early Universe *+* The Worst-Case Scenario Survival Handbook*)*
- *Swiss army knife*
- *Pepper spray*
- *Taser*

I know, I know. Please don't make fun of me. You and Kayla love making fun of me, but I'm doing the best I can. And if something bad really has happened, though I hope it hasn't—

I love you more than you will ever know. If things are bad, ever, wherever you are, I want you to know I'm with you. Even if I'm far away, or dead, or on the moon. If you're feeling alone or scared right now, and maybe you don't know what's going to happen next? I'm with you.

Love,
Mom

STEPH

EMERGENCY

That night, I heard sirens.

I waited to hear the others get up and do something, to hold me back from undoing what I'd set in motion. Allison knew what I had done. Nadia would guess. But to Aziz and Jed and Adisu, I hoped to appear innocent.

Downstairs, Allison stood by the door. She was dressed and alert, with her hair in a tight, low braid. She looked out the window, walkie-talkie in hand. She spoke into it, her voice firm and clear. Calm.

Lights flashed blue and red; they shot through the porthole and across our walls.

I ran for the porthole. I cupped my hands against the glass, like binoculars. Beside me, Allison described the scene to mission control.

Outside the hab, the protesters were outnumbered. The police wore armor and helmets, gas masks, and they looked out through the scratched polycarbonate of five-foot shields. They stood in front of the entrance to the hab, blocking our solar panels with a line of police cars, a fire engine, and a tanker truck. They walked into the line of protesters, forcing them back.

Where was my sister? What had I done?

I heard a door slam at the top of the stairs. Adisu. Soon my crewmates would be all around me, telling me what to think. His pajama shirt was wrinkled. He looked exhausted. "Steph, not again," he said, like I'd invited guests.

Outside the hab, the protesters faced the police. They held their hands up in the air and chanted, or sang, or maybe prayed.

An officer gripped a megaphone. He said, "Stand back, stand back. We don't want anyone to get hurt tonight! Stand back."

I looked past the police, at the people who gave most of a year for this. I saw the children they'd brought with them, and two elders in camping chairs sitting quietly at the edge of the crowd. I hated that they'd brought children, who hadn't really had a choice.

The protesters moved in practiced rows. Stepping forward, gaining ground, till the police pushed them back again. They fell back, then stepped forward again.

Someone threw a rock. It clicked against a police shield, low and heavy.

There she was, my sister, dressed for battle. Her arms were protected in a black leather jacket, her legs hidden in the folds of a red ribbon skirt. She had pinned her hair close to her head. The triangle of a floral silk handkerchief was tied over her nose and mouth. For a moment she stood quietly, touching foreheads with Diana.

I tensed at that, how Diana gave my sister a comfort I never could. But so many people had. It must not have been such a hard thing to do.

In another life, I could be standing at my sister's side, shoulders bumping on the front lines, watching over her. I could have a daughter, most realistically with the physicist; she could be six by now. Reading age. Safe at home. But if she *were* here, somehow, I'd take her elbow and hold her body behind mine. She'd look up at Kayla, her aunt; she'd hold the hand of Felicia, her cousin. We would all step forward together.

In this life, real life, I was a still, dark shape blocking yellow light from a porthole at the bottom of a dome. Allison was a few feet to my side, eyes focused and arms crossed, still speaking into the walkie-talkie. Adisu and Jed and Aziz and Nadia, even Nadia, huddled together on the other side of the hab. The farthest possible point from me.

I pressed my head closer to the glass. I held my palm against it.

A shadow passed over the blue-red light of the sirens. There was a firetruck, then the turning of a crank against its side.

I heard the roar of water, and saw it shoot through the crowd. People fell. They shouted for it to stop. They pulled one another to their feet and fell down again. They stood again. They ran in all directions.

My sister did not run. She linked arms with people who were strangers to me. The strangers screamed into one another's faces. Eyes closed, mouths open, chests pushed back with the force of water.

Behind my sister, behind a wall of women, I found her. Felicia crawled forward on her knees.

PART

FIVE

2016

October 10, 2016

Kayla Palakiko:
hi

Kayla Palakiko:
hi

Kayla Palakiko:
hi

Kayla Palakiko:
are you seeing my texts?

Kayla Palakiko:
call me

Kayla Palakiko:
still in HI?

Kayla Palakiko:
news says your mission ended early. you
should have cell service now.

Kayla Palakiko:
hey

Kayla Palakiko:
hi

Kayla Palakiko:
hi

Kayla Palakiko:
hi

Kayla Palakiko:
steph

Kayla Palakiko:
dad died.

Kayla Palakiko:
it was 3 days ago. Not in a car crash when we
were kids. I got a google alert for the obit

TO THE MOON AND BACK ✳ 329

Kayla Palakiko:
steph?

Kayla Palakiko:
steph?

Kayla Palakiko:
are you fucking kidding me

Kayla Palakiko:
come home

DAVID R. JAMES, of Dallas, Texas, passed away on October 8, 2016, after a long battle with heart disease. He was 55 years old.

David was born on April 5, 1961, to Robert and Andrea James in Little Rock, Arkansas. Two years after David graduated from Harris High School in 1979, he moved to Dallas.

In June 1987, on a road trip at age 26, David fell asleep at the wheel and swerved his car off the edge of a cliff. He suffered catastrophic injuries. The police were alerted by a call from an unidentified good Samaritan, and David was airlifted to Parkland Memorial Hospital. For the rest of his life, in his Testimony of Salvation, David would credit his long and painful season of recovery, following the amputation of his left leg, as the turning point in his walk with Christ.

At age 30, while working full-time as a store associate at Farmer Supply Depot, David enrolled as a part-time student at Dallas County Community College and then transferred to UNT Dallas. After graduating with a degree in Business, David became an assistant manager, a manager, and then a district manager. At the age of 48 he was honored at Farmer Supply Depot Headquarters in San Antonio, receiving a lifetime Farmer Supply Service Star Award for excellence in customer service.

David met his beloved wife, Lisa, née Baker, of Little Rock, in a science fiction book club in 1993. Last summer, surrounded by family and friends, they celebrated twenty years of marriage. David is survived by his mother, Andrea James, née Simons (75); his wife, Lisa (53); and their four precious children: Joshua (21), Faith (19), Hope (17), and Grace (14).

Services will be held at Woodside Fellowship Baptist Church on October 12 at two o'clock in the afternoon. In lieu of flowers, the family requests that donations be made to the Dallas Homeless Shelter, where David served every Saturday for twenty-six years.

STEPH

A WILDERNESS OF WAVES

October 16, 2016

In the days before we went under, I felt a dread in me, even as Aziz and Nadia took walks down the beach and ordered appetizers up to their hotel rooms and pointed out every color of the sunset like children seeing it for the very first time. We spent our days in training, preparing for two weeks in an underwater research station off the Florida Keys. The mission in Hawai'i had been promptly canceled after the incident, not forever but for our crew. We'd had barely three days off in Houston before we were here again, three ascans, assigned another mission that wasn't to space.

I dreamed of drowning. I saw our underwater hab filling with seawater. Quiet in the night, slow drips falling from a crack over the door. And then, all at once, a rush of water.

I tried not to think about my sister—what I had done to her, and if she knew it was me. I wasn't sure if I could be forgiven, or should be; and when her texts came in, I panicked.

I'd been dreading some future talk with her about Hawai'i. But when the texts were about our father, who had lived and then died again, I dropped my phone on the hotel bathroom floor. The screen cracked. My sister called, the phone buzzing hard and loud against the bright white tile. I hurried away from it and closed the door. Barefoot, I walked down the hall to Aziz's room. We watched his show about housewives yelling at one another.

I tried and failed not to think about our father. Who all this time had lived! Just five hours south of Tahlequah. I took Aziz's phone from his bed-side table and looked up the obituary, feeling the lives of four half-siblings and a grandmother. In the story they told of him, we did not exist.

On my previous mission, I had let myself get distracted—by Kayla, by Felicia, and by Nadia along the way. I had nearly lost everything, if everything was space. This mission was a gift. A second chance.

I didn't reply to my sister's messages. Our father was dead. I had always thought he might be. I had sat in my booster seat with his blood dark and heavy on my clothes, listening. Waiting to see who would live.

The day came. Our trainers waved frantically from the dock, our little motor-boat pushed out to open water. Aziz, Nadia, and I sat at the end, legs hanging down, with our support crew and their ropes and instruments and hard-cased computers. They had whistles and radios and orange vests glaring in the sun. Tom, our captain, called Aziz down first. He hesitated, clearly afraid. Nadia and I sat on either side of him, our finned feet slapping against the water's choppy surface. She caught me looking at her and turned away.

Nadia had been nice enough to me through training week, but was still distant. She had spent her entire three days off between missions at a retreat for queer Muslims, where she had hit it off with a woman from Boston named Daryan. I knew this because she'd said it, almost too casually, at brunch on our first day in Florida.

"But you're not even *religious*!" I said.

Aziz raised his eyebrows at me across the table like, *Get a hold of yourself.*

Nadia ignored my outburst. She said the best thing about Daryan was how the two of them hadn't just "fallen into it." (At this phrase, Aziz patted my knee sympathetically, making me suspect Nadia had described sex with me that way.) Nadia said Daryan was a math teacher. Kurdish, femme, crunchy, socialist, child-less, divorced but still "super cool" with her ex-husband. Wasn't it great how *aligned* Daryan and Nadia were, on what they both wanted in a relationship? They would move slowly, but they both ultimately wanted to get married. Aziz cut his waffle down the middle and silently slid half onto my plate.

The boat rocked under us. Tom said it was getting rough out; it was past time to descend.

"Now, don't y'all rush on my account," Nadia drawled. It was a decent impression of our last mission commander, and I cringed at the reminder.

Allison had written letters of recommendation for everyone on our crew, even for me. But on my last day in Houston I'd seen her at the grocery store with a little girl, who was alternately pushing and riding on the back of their cart. I raised a hand to wave. Allison looked past me, her face firm, and followed the speeding cart down the aisle.

It was unseasonably cold over the water, high winds and gray sky. I put a hand on Aziz's shoulder. I reminded him, and myself, of our training. We could swim twenty-five meters in one breath—maskless, finless. We could swim four hundred meters in under twelve minutes. We'd both done more than fifty dives at this depth, half of them in the black water of night. We'd twisted and fastened tourniquets on each other's legs, faking death on the ocean floor. We'd flooded our masks on purpose. We'd felt the seawater pouring into our faces, cutting off our breath and burning our eyes. We had vented, flooded, and vented again.

Aziz didn't move. His hands shook in his lap, and he held them still against his knee. "You've got this," Nadia whispered.

Tom said, "Any day now, Aziz," and Aziz said, "Yes, sir, just checking my equipment!"

"You know what might help?" I said. "There was this Nigerian man, a few years ago, who managed to become an aquanaut without any training at all. He was working as a cook on a tugboat, and the tugboat sank to the bottom of the ocean, but he felt his way to a part of the ship with a bubble of air in it and used an old mattress to keep his head above water. He stayed that way for three days till he was found. They had to put him in a decompression chamber at the surface, but then he was fine!"

Nadia looked at me, confused.

Aziz sighed. "He was the cook?"

"Yes."

"So there were other people on the boat, and they died."

"Well—"

"They died on the boat with him, I bet—drowned—and he had to tread water around their bodies."

"Aziz, buddy, you're holding up the team," Tom said. His paper checklist fluttered against his clipboard in the wind.

Aziz pulled on his eye mask. He gave a little salute and pushed forward. He slipped fast below the surface, and we followed him.

I was the last to swim down, and then up into the hab. I entered through the wet porch, an opening at its base. I heaved myself out of the pool of water at the center, called a "moon pool." I sat on the scratchy concrete floor, waiting my turn for the shower. I spent this time quiet, staring down at white light shining on water, processing the reality that I was on the ocean floor.

When all four of us were clean, dry, and dressed, our wet suits and scuba gear hanging from hooks above the moon pool, Tom led us on a comically short tour.

A hab underwater is like a hab on land. A hab is a hab, mostly in that it's cramped. After the wet porch was a small compartment called the entry lock. This was an air lock, a real one with real consequences, where we squished against one another in the closet-sized space and waited for the pressure to adjust to match the galley. We'd been told what to expect under pressure. The air would feel heavy. Sealed cans of snacks would collapse inward. We would all mostly lose the ability to whistle.

Being able to withstand that pressure was the whole point of a specialized underwater hab, what made us aquanauts and not just scuba divers. We could stay down for days without dying from the bends. Scientists used the hab for research. NASA used it, according to Nadia, because they liked putting ascans in weird, cramped, unpleasant environments before shooting them into space. Before our scheduled ascent in two weeks, the hab would be programmed to depressurize—slowly, over a period of forty-eight hours.

We climbed through the entry lock and into the main compartment. The hab was the shape of a wide and rounded tube; its thick walls made me think of a cement mixer. In the galley was a toilet behind a shower curtain; then a sink, a counter, a table, two metal bench seats, and four bunks. I took the top bunk, like I'd had as a kid. Nadia slept eighteen inches under me. Across from us, Aziz slept in the bunk above Tom.

· · ·

In the morning, we sat in the galley for our daily video conference with mission control. Which it was, for a few minutes. Then someone in Houston said to hold as they connected us to the International Space Station.

"Are you kidding me?" Nadia said. She hugged her knees to her chest, ready to burst through the walls.

"Just don't cuss," Tom said. "They want to stream it on NASA TV."

Tom had done this all before. His general demeanor was that of a middle-aged father on a bench, waiting for his children at Disney World. He took a big bite out of a granola bar, brushing the crumbs into a cupped hand. He leaned over a wrinkled checklist on his clipboard while we lost our shit.

The three of us waved and laughed and sputtered out questions, our body language shifting between straight-shouldered almost-astronauts and children first encountering Velcro, goats, dry ice. *What is it like, how are you, how long was the wait before your first mission, what are you studying up there, can we see this morning's experiments, can we see out the cupola, can we see what you usually eat for breakfast?!*

Mission Specialist Kat Rigani and Lieutenant Brad Anders had questions for us, too, but they were likely just being polite. Kat and Brad were both aquastronauts; they had lived both in space and underwater, in our very own hab. They had assembled coral trees in a nursery on the ocean floor. They had showered on the wet porch and peed behind the shower curtain. They had slept in our beds.

Before Tom closed the connection, Kat and Brad turned their camera toward Earth below them. Toward the Atlantic Ocean, where they zoomed in. Toward the Florida Keys, toward us. It threw me. Them looking at us, us looking at them. All the blue. Nadia grabbed my hand suddenly, and I breathed in sharply, in happy surprise. She let go. Aziz clapped a hand on my shoulder from behind.

I imagined Kat and Brad looking down at us, not through the video chat, but from the cupola, with its windows down to Earth. But we were on NASA TV, too, streaming live. Even though I hadn't known ahead to warn my mother, I hoped she'd been following the mission's Facebook account for updates like this. She'd taken to social media to follow my sister, so there was a chance she was watching us now.

After Hawai'i, I'd realized how much I missed her. How much I missed my whole family! But I was the reason the police had deployed water hoses, on my own sister and niece. Now that I might want to go home, I couldn't.

I leaned in to the computer monitor, past Kat and Brad. Through their window and down to Earth, to Oklahoma.

Two days later I suspected I'd feel differently. Maybe I'd heave myself up to the wet porch after a six-hour research dive in murky, pre-storm waters—cold and sore and exhausted, and so jealous of Kat and Brad doing summersaults in space I could scream.

But in that moment, space looking at sea, sea looking at space, fish flying past our window, the screen blue, and then black, and then stars, I thought I might make it. I felt close to space, even when I'd never been farther.

KAYLA

THE WESTERN HISTORY COLLECTIONS

October 17, 2016

Felicia and I hadn't planned on Oklahoma. But here we were, three weeks into living with my mom, with no idea when (or if) we'd leave.

Jason and I would share custody. The first thing I'd told him was not to worry about that. I said to think of me in Oklahoma as a vacation from our divorce proceedings, a period without pressure to figure things out. He agreed. The divorce exhausted him, his work life and home life creeping into each other.

I took Felicia out for ice cream on a Sunday afternoon. Mom had said to go along without her, which was new and weird. Part of her recent habit of leaving me alone. Not physically—she was always in the same room as me, following quietly behind like a cat. She asked for nothing. She read library books and wrote in a small journal. She drank coffee very slowly. She took two short naps a day, one of them in a hammock so she could watch the birds in the bird feeder. She cooked three meals a day on her own, until I decided to help. She didn't ask me hard questions about my life or tell me what was wrong with it. Every morning and every night she told me and Felicia she loved us.

When I was a kid and Brett left, and then Steph, too much was put on me. Not just dishes and laundry and meals, but waking Mom up for work, and setting her clothes out, and making sure the bills got paid even if she was sad. I wasn't sure if Mom knew what that had been like for me. It's no wonder I ran away to Hollis, no wonder I started the kind of family that owned a label maker and knew where it was. Only now, fallen apart at thirty-three years old, was I being more parented than ever in my life.

Felicia and I sat on the curb outside Braum's, far from everyone else. She wore a bright yellow sweatshirt and large beaded earrings, in the shape of neon rainbows falling from puffy white clouds. She'd put her grandmother's gel in her hair and it stood straight up, like she was being electrocuted.

Felicia said her grandmother was "kinda different this trip."

"Hmm," I said. "You think so?"

"Yeah. And don't tell me she's just older now." Felicia took two big bites, and got chocolate on her nose. I wanted to lick my thumb and wipe it off, but didn't. She was about to turn fourteen.

She was also right. Mom seemed extremely different, in just the year since she'd been laid off. She worked part-time now, behind the counter at a fancy new bakery. It was the first job to ever let her sit down, but it didn't pay well. Before Hawai'i I'd set up monthly auto-transfers from me and Steph. Maybe that had helped?

Maybe she was changed, maybe I was, maybe this was all just the shape of our lives switching around in those weeks. The mess of it! The divorce, the protest, the police. Me and Felicia at the airport, unshowered, deciding together where to go. The obituary too-bright white on the smudged screen of my phone. The unanswered texts to my asshole of a sister, who I then saw online had fucked off to the bottom of the sea.

Felicia looked up from her half-eaten cone. "Why did Elisi live with intimate partner violence?"

"Sorry, what?"

"It's an updated term for domestic violence."

I almost laughed. The older she got, the less she thought I knew. "Huh. Well. Did she tell you she lived with intimate partner violence?"

Felicia nodded. "When she couldn't come for ice cream! I just asked where she was going."

"What did she say?"

"A monthly support group for women survivors of intimate partner violence." She recited it carefully, with a lilt. I still wanted to wipe her face clean.

"Huh."

"It's not a secret or anything. I just was like, 'Hey Elisi, where are you going?' And she was like, 'A monthly support group for women survivors of intimate partner violence!' She would've told you, if you ever asked her stuff."

I crumpled a napkin in my hand. She could wipe her own nose.

"So?" she said. "Why did Elisi do that? When she could have, like, left?"

I scraped the edges of my paper bowl. "She *did* leave."

Felicia looked at me like I was a child.

"Okay, okay! I'm not sure what to say. Can I think for a minute?"

Felicia nodded. She chomped on her waffle cone and swallowed. She tried to lick the chocolate off the bottom of her nose and failed.

My spoon still scraped the bowl, which was empty. I gave up and set it on the curb. "Honey, I don't think anyone can know that but your grandmother. And I really don't think she likes to talk about it. I know that when she got pregnant, her parents kicked her out. Her and my dad, the one I was too young to remember, moved to Dallas together. And when women get in that kind of relationship, they can end up more and more isolated."

"When *people* get in that kind of relationship," Felicia said.

"Sorry. You're right."

"But why'd they kick her out? Just 'cause of the baby?"

"I think so," I said. "It never came up."

"Did you *ask* her?"

I tried again. "I think things were hard for your elisi's mother, too. Remember, she's the one whose parents left her in a—"

I stopped myself. I didn't really know.

If I were right, if my mom's mom had lived some super sad life, then what? Could I point to something bad enough and say *that was why*? Was that a thing to teach my daughter?

That night, I lay in the bottom bunk and let myself be pissed at Steph for not being here. It was all very blast from the past. Here I was again, left in charge of the family! The only one around to answer questions about Mom.

Someday, knowing Steph would be useless, it would fall on me to be the one to bother with our ancestors. I could almost picture them, hundreds of long-dead people; how they'd jump on my back and demand to be carried.

But then again, did I even want Steph's help? Maybe I preferred her in the fucking ocean. Maybe I'd prefer her in fucking outer space.

I opened Instagram. On NASA's feed, Steph and another woman wore wet suits and scuba gear. They stood way too close, Steph's arm around the woman's waist, and I wondered if they were having sex. She was Steph's type, wasn't she? Sciencey, driven girls whose careers she could ruin. They both waved at the camera from a part of their submarine that had a showerhead on the wall and a square pool of calm shiny water at the bottom—which meant the pool was *inside*, even though the submarine was underwater, which made no sense to me.

I got out of bed. I googled the physics of the pool thing on the toilet awhile, giving up when it made me feel dumb.

Standing at the sink I scrolled through Instagram again, looking at the friends I'd lost and the friends I might never see again. I commented a heart under a photo of Diana at some kind of faculty cocktail party at Exeter, *that* Exeter, home of the *one* time in Steph's life she couldn't bend the world to her will.

Diana was dressed up preppy like I'd never seen her, and so surrounded by friends that pieces of them were sliced out of the frame. Her purple glasses were gone, her hair was straightened and curled, and she held a tiny, quilted leather purse in one hand. Sometimes at camp, mid-gossip session, Diana and I would sit next to each other on two plastic, five-gallon buckets and shit into them. Now in my mother's bathroom, where she kept Steph's badly woven basket still filled with dusty potpourri, I massaged tea tree oil onto my scalp and breathed deeply and deleted the app from my phone.

On Monday, I enrolled Felicia at my old high school. I was in and out of the main office fast, mostly to avoid running into Brett. It would suck if he'd heard from the internet why I was in town, and it would suck if he hadn't and asked me to tell him.

"Starting her in school here is just for now," I'd told Jason on the phone. "We can figure out a real plan later." He suggested we have our first Values and Goals call at the end of the month. Values and Goals sounded more hopeful than custody negotiation, and for years I'd heard him call it that with clients over the phone. Then he'd press a timer button on an app, which divided his life into six-minute billable increments.

Our new lives fell into a temporary rhythm. In the mornings Mom and I would sit on the front stoop. Both of us were early-risers, drinking coffee in silence while Felicia slept in the house. Eventually, I was ready.

I asked Mom about everything that came before me, after me, and without me. She talked fast, excited, her mug unsteady in her hand. Suddenly, she seemed to have a lot to say. She had wanted to be a writer when she was younger, or a librarian. Maybe a social worker.

"I cared a lot about him," she said. She told me my dad had no one in the world but her, that he had so much pain in him and so much need. He would come home from work sometimes and lay his head in her lap and cry. She said she still remembered the feel of his hair in her fingers, how she'd hold his head in her hands and wait with him until it passed. "He felt things real, real deeply," she said.

"Not that I could have changed that," she added, "or that it excuses certain things he did."

One morning, I told her he had died. I said he'd been alive before, somehow, years after the car crash she'd told me had killed him. I said I'd found his obituary, and it was recent. It cited a car swerving off a road, not recent at all. "Why'd you tell me he died in a car crash?"

Mom squinted across the front yard, like she was waiting for the mail. "I never said car *crash*."

"What?"

She finished her coffee and put the mug down carefully at her feet.

"See," I said, "I thought we were out here really talking to each other. Like at least part of this family stood a chance."

She said nothing.

"Okay, fine," I said. "Car *accident*. Not *crash*, silly me. How'd you know something happened in a car?"

Mom closed her eyes.

"Was there a funeral? A death certificate? I don't know, a body?"

She kept her eyes closed a long time.

I'd let myself think she was ready to talk. She wasn't. We sat there. Here I was again, gentle-parenting her.

Then the alarm clock radio, Felicia in her new fluffy slippers, the pouring of cereal into bowls.

Midway through the day, as I passed Mom in the kitchen with a laundry basket on my hip, she looked up. "I *thought* he'd died in a car accident," she said. "I guess I was wrong."

I downloaded Instagram. Sandra, now vice president of corporate alliances for Subway, held a copy of *The New York Times* up to the camera. The newspaper was open to a headshot of Della Ericson about the size of my fist, accompanying an article too small to read. The caption said many things like "SO SO SO PROUD" and "Warrior!!!"—I skimmed over a wall of text to see that Della had published an op-ed. Something in support of the Indian Child Welfare Act, which was once again being challenged in court. After that I spent an hour scrolling through posts about the thirty-meter telescope and the protests building momentum on Mauna Kea. I deleted the app. On my way to pick up Felicia from school, I stopped at a gas station and bought today's issue of the *Times*. Then I deleted Instagram, downloaded Instagram, deleted Instagram, cut up a pear so Felicia would deign to eat it, and left the rolled-up newspaper in its plastic bag on the table.

We had spaghetti for dinner. When we'd all filled our plates, Mom slumped down at the head of the table like she'd been walking for days. "I want to talk to you two about our family," she said. Her face was serious, almost scolding.

Felicia glanced at me across the table, the look she sometimes gave me when she thought she was in trouble. She wasn't. I shook my head.

"Okay?" I said. I felt protective of Felicia, and wished Mom had cleared this with me before bringing it to the dinner table.

"When you weren't around," Mom said, just a little bit of bitterness in her voice, "I had a lot of time to think about things. And then when you told me David had died—"

"Who's David?" Felicia said, still chewing.

"Your grandfather," I said.

Felicia almost choked. "I have a *grand*father? On *your* side?"

Mom sighed into her dinner plate. She might have been rethinking the decision to include a kid.

"It's okay," I said. I reached across the table to touch my daughter's hand. "Felicia, you had one. Now he's dead. Mom, keep talking."

She did, but slowly. "A couple of years ago I started thinking about how I'd raised you and Steph. What kinds of stories I'd told you, what I hadn't told you, that kind of thing."

I'd waited so long for her to talk like this. Now I wanted her to cut to the chase.

"And, well, like I told you in that email. I talked to some researchers at the Heritage Museum. I kept going back, and I even made some friends there."

"And?" I asked.

Mom shot me a warning look. "And then I went to the archives. Turns out our family is in there."

"Cool," Felicia said. While the food on my plate was getting cold, Felicia had taken and eaten seconds.

"Some of what's in there I already knew," Mom said. "From what my mother had told me."

"Like what?" Felicia said.

"Like how we got to Indian Territory. I told your mom about that when she was a kid. Remember, Kayla?"

"You told me your great-great-great whatever helped sell the homelands," I said.

"I said he sold the land to save people's *lives*. He said he was willing to die for his belief that the treaty was what was best for his people."

"Wow," I said.

"But then he took his payment and hid out in Texas, while other treaty-signers were being assassinated by their fellow Cherokees for treason."

I nodded. Felicia's eyes were wide.

Mom continued. "Later on, when the tribe was split between Union and Confederacy, we have ancestors who fought with the Cherokee Confederates."

"What are the—" Felicia started.

"I'm going to tell you *everything* later," I said. "I promise."

"There's something else I didn't tell you about," Mom said, talking too fast. "On my grandfather's side—"

"Wait, wait, wait," I said. I was so tired.

"Yes?" Mom said. Her plate, like mine, was untouched.

"Mom," I said. "Thank you for this burst of honesty."

She looked hurt.

"I'm sorry. I didn't mean it like that. Thank you, for real. I just . . . still don't get it? I think it's important to me to know why."

"Why, what?"

I lowered my voice. "Why you told us the stories that you did."

Mom deflated. She picked up her fork, finally, and spun spaghetti around it. Then she dropped it. The click of metal on a plastic plate.

"The people in our family didn't stay long in one place," Mom said. "There was the move to Indian Territory, and Texas, and back to Indian Territory, and Arkansas, and then—oh, *before* all that, some of the white people on my mom's side of the family? They came from a man from Ireland who settled in the Nation. No clue about your father's people, though. And, anyway, with all these people—"

She stumbled. Felicia looked lost, almost bored.

"Mom," I said, harshly. The more she added to the conversation, the blurrier each piece of it became. If she kept going like that, heaping on more people and more time, none of it would matter in the end.

"I just wanted you to be safe," she said.

I wasn't sure what that meant.

"And home," she added. "I wanted you and your sister to know this land had a story that could hold you."

There was a long silence. Felicia asked to be excused, and I nodded.

That word, "safe," it was wrapped in the cloth of the story she'd never tell me. My dad, and that night. *I thought he'd died*, she'd said, only now I didn't believe her.

I realized there was more to learn. Stories to pick up and squint at— maybe to be scared of?—and decide to pass down anyway. Maybe there was no purity to yearn for, no better time or place. I had always hoped for—assumed, even—something better than this.

But at the kitchen table I held that word out for all the world, "safe," on the old wooden table and in the space between us. I sat with Mom while the sun went down. When we did the dishes, too dark to see through the window over the kitchen sink, I watched our reflections move together across the glass.

A week later, Felicia had a half day at school. Mom and I picked her up, passed a sandwich to her in the back seat, and drove an hour to the archives. Mom wanted us to see it. At the entrance she took her time chatting with her friend at the front desk, and Felicia raced across the room to a wall of metal filing cabinets.

I hurried to catch up, but she didn't need my help. Mom had already told her what to look for. A wide, shallow cabinet was labeled *Cherokee Nation*. In it, microfiche. We found my great-great-grandmother—Felicia's great-great-great—in no time at all.

Andromache Bell Shelton. "Ann." She was born in Georgia in 1831 and was about four years old during Removal. She was the daughter of Jane "Jennie" Martin Bell and John Adair Bell, who was one of twenty signers of the Treaty of New Echota.

Ann wrote many, many letters, sent from Texas to wealthy relatives in Indian Territory. "I think that's why she made it into the archives," Mom said. She joined us at our desk, skimming the writing on the screen.

Ann's letters were about, often, what she felt she deserved. Her own school in the Nation, where she could work as a teacher. Help and security, through her family and Cherokee political connections who were sometimes one and the same. Ann asked her relatives, over and over again, to send money.

The Nation was fast dissolving. *Being dissolved.* Ann wrote about her early career as a teacher, the struggle and thrill of it, and then it ended. Cherokee schools were shut down by acts of Congress.

Mom put her hand on my hand and asked to switch chairs with me. She sat in the middle, Felicia and I on either side of her, and clicked through the many pages. A kind of fast-forward button on the microfiche. She was looking for something, I thought, she had already once found. "Here," she said.

Ann wrote, again, about trying to move her family back to the Nation from Texas. She was frustrated by the need to plan and save for it carefully. How impossible it felt. "In this age," she wrote, "things are different to [a] long time ago. Each one of us has to take care of No. 1. We can't be as generous as when we had slaves to work for us."

I sat in my swivel chair in the archives; Felicia no longer spinning, my mother silent for once in her life. All of us bent over a wooden table, our sleeves rolled up to our elbows.

I looked at Mom, her hand still on my hand. I felt tempted to shake it off.

"I knew," she said. "My mom told me when I was a kid, once. Like a sidenote, I guess, to the Trail of Tears? I remember exactly the way she said it, that someone 'went with them' to Indian Territory."

"Mom—"

"I know. I decided ages ago not to pass it on. Let that part of the story end with me. I thought that made me better than my mom was."

She had given me something I didn't know what to do with. There were no instructions. I felt sick with it, almost angry at her for choosing to tell me. My daughter would have questions I couldn't answer.

When I was Felicia's age, I'd taken comfort in the clear answers of my mother's stories. Brett had tried to question them, sure, but it had felt good to have an outline of the kinds of Indians we'd been. That maybe, I had thought, we could be again.

"I thought I could start fresh when we came to Oklahoma," Mom said. "I didn't want to account for all the history I'd been told. Not unless it could help guide you, or unless it was part of the greater Cherokee story. But I've been alone a long time now—not just scrambling through your childhood, I mean. I'm starting to realize my mistakes."

"Like what?" Felicia said. "What mistakes?" I wasn't sure if she understood. Sometimes she was direct for the sake of directness.

"I built a story to serve you," Mom said. She looked at me. "You come from people whose lives were preserved in this room. That's not true of the people they enslaved, who I don't know a thing about.

"But, with my not-telling, I threw them out of the world. I told you a story that was only for you, that left them nameless and ageless and kinless."

The drive home felt long. No one talked. Mom had insisted on driving, and I stared at the road in front of us and tried to take in what I knew.

I remembered an old story about my grandfather, how Mom's white dad got her a plastic dreamcatcher as a joke. He'd bought it on a road trip, at a gas station. My grandfather thought my grandmother's family had been, but no longer were, Indians. As in "wild." My grandmother insisted she had come from scholars.

Sitting beside Mom on the highway, her taking us home again, I counted the years since she'd seen her own parents. Thirty-three? More time without them than with.

It was getting dark, a weird blue-purple that made me wish I hadn't quit painting. Sun and moon both fit in the wide glass of the windshield. I thought about the two stories Mom had been offered, Indians or scholars.

I thought about what we had been. Racist, and strategic, and violent, and manipulative, and hopeful. We were running, constantly, with blinders. And when we weren't running we were like people on steamboats, charging forward on an engine of our choice, churning up muddy waters.

The crops were planted by a person we enslaved. The treaty was signed for a profit. The seminary taught mostly what we'd need in the coming white world. My great-grandfather left his daughter in a barn, my grandfather locked his daughter out of the house, and my father drove from one life into another. And my great-grandmother stayed, and my grandmother stayed, and my mother stayed, until she didn't.

I felt I was home before I saw it. The jostle of gravel under the wheels. Mom opened the car door and turned off the engine and it smelled like fall, like campfires. The woods I'd tried to memorize as a kid, before I'd tried to draw them. Mom told me to go on in without her. I told Felicia we could talk if she wasn't too tired. If she had questions. We could go walk through the leaves.

DROWN

October 27, 2016

Tropical Storm Cynthia made an unexpected turn toward Key Largo. South Florida was evacuating, half of Miami parked in traffic, and here we lay at the bottom of it. Tom had come to NASA through the air force, where they made him spin upside down and jump out of planes and land on glaciers during ice storms. Being nearly impossible to alarm, Tom checked the levels on our air tanks and brought his radio to bed. He said we'd go if they told us to, fine, but what we really needed was to get some rest.

In the dream, I was in Star City, preparing for launch on a Russian Soyuz rocket. The American shuttle program was over. An Orthodox priest in long black robes flicked holy water onto my helmet. I stood behind a glass wall on a platform in a space suit, shouting something in imagined Cherokee that I couldn't understand, that no one could, and from the back of the room my father waved to me. He was in a space suit, too. I was a mission specialist. He was the pilot. The crowd parted, the glass shattered, and he took one step toward me.

I woke in the hab with a lurch and a gasp, like I'd fallen to Earth from many feet above.

As a child I had a Sunday school teacher who explained this. She said our souls went up to heaven when we were sleeping. It was a kind of temporary death, to talk to Jesus about what we'd done wrong that previous day. She said that if our bodies ever woke too suddenly, our souls would shoot back down into us from the distance of heaven. It would feel like we were really, physically falling—falling into ourselves—and that was proof of God.

Hearing this, I was terrified. I did not want to die in my sleep. I did not want to talk to Jesus, or to anyone, about all the things I thought might be wrong with me.

It wasn't until I was maybe eleven, that I finally asked for help. Brett took me to the library after school and read beside me from a little pile of reference books. I was not dying, he said. Above my bed was the roof and then the sky, the atmosphere and then space. Brett said that Jesus, if he was real, would not burden himself with performance reviews. That falling feeling was called a hypnagogic jerk. It was experienced by people everywhere.

I remembered this. I lay in my bunk, listening to the hum of the CO_2 scrubbers. I imagined a school of fish swimming past. All three of my crewmates were asleep, stacked under and beside me.

When I closed my eyes again, I pictured us drowning. Every creak or groan was a possible breach. I pressed my forehead and hands to the smooth metal wall, just inches between myself and the ocean. I listened to the little rocks, kicked up from the sea floor and thrown against the coral-covered hab.

Nadia took deep breaths below me.

I was aware of her body close to mine, aware of our shared, sharp-smelling soap from the shower and her legs curled up small on the mattress.

I opened my eyes. Her arm lay across the edge of her bunk, bony at the wrist. Just above that, the scrunched hem of the fleece she liked to sleep in. I reached down and, gently, took her hand.

Nadia's fingers jerked in surprise. She peeked out from the edge of her bed, looked at me, and squeezed my palm. She pointed with her forehead to the wet porch, and mouthed something like "need to talk?"

I shook my head no.

She shook her head back at me. "We're okay," she whispered, neither question nor answer. All of us, maybe, in the storm? Or, in another way, me and her?

Nadia lay back in her bed. I ran my thumb along the skin on the inside of her wrist, where the ulnar and radial arteries ran into her hand. Adisu had taught me that; we had been that bored together. Her veins felt warm and fragile under my finger, which ran slow, up and down between them. It was like I was following a path in the woods behind the house I'd grown up in. Pacing forward and backward, tracing familiar ground. I was always afraid to make sudden turns.

For years before we had met, from the time we were children with the same ridiculous dream, Nadia and I had unknowingly been competitors. Then colleagues, then friends. Then almost girlfriends, *briefly* girlfriends, before I disappointed her.

"I've been thinking about what you did," she'd said, on our third night underwater.

The two of us had been getting ready for bed on the wet porch, the pressurized door shut between us and the men. This time together was the only time we were alone, nightly minutes scheduled for showers and a change of clothes. We lingered. We brought snacks, tucked into our waistbands.

"It was shitty and selfish," she continued. "And when you *ghosted* me? Demonic."

I winced.

"But—how far you went for your rec—I guess some ascans might've done the same. Maybe me too. I hope not. Now that we're so close to making it, I kind of hate that we did this to ourselves."

"Did what?"

"Space?" Nadia touched her hand to the porthole, like we were already there. "There's this guy on Reddit who says the worst thing a person can do is set out to be an astronaut, 'cause they won't be one. Statistically, at least, they really won't. Like it's meaningless to try to figure out the right degree program to do *for NASA*, so we should just build a life we can be happy with and go from there."

"Nadia. We specifically? Like, me and you? We might very well be astronauts."

She held her hands up, exasperated. "We might. But I lost a lot of life trying to get here. Didn't you? Don't you hate that for us?"

I thought about her mother. And mine, too, how I wouldn't be able to call her till after this mission was over. How I'd said that all throughout our last mission, and after it had not called.

Nadia looked at me, expectant. I had a tendency to hide from things, to skirt around them and run. She didn't. If we left this mission as friends, for real, I couldn't hurt her again.

"I'm serious," Nadia said. "Astronauts or not! I want us to be better."

When she said that to me, the two of us cross-legged, pajamaed, looking down at the light shining over the moon pool, I immediately thought "better," like harder. Better, stronger, faster, etc.

Nadia leaned her shoulder against mine. She poured M&M's into my palm, from a small ziplock in the breast pocket of her shirt. Behind her, in the porthole, a goliath grouper bumped against the glass. A cloud of small gray fish raced out of sight. The grouper was bigger than me and likely older. It could have easily seen the hab's last thirty years, as well as the people who passed through it: oceanographers, marine biologists, geologists, and hopeful astronauts.

Had Della ever been here, maybe as a grad student? By the time we left Hollis she wanted to be a marine biologist, despite never having been to the beach. I'd never looked for Della online, too scared I'd learn she hadn't made it there.

Nadia touched my wrist. When she turned her hand over, I saw the flash of color leftover from the candies on her palm, bright reds and blues and greens. And I knew.

"Better" meant kinder.

PART

SIX

2016

THE SHORT DURATION
OF MY LIFE

October 28, 2016

Hours later, sirens. Mission control on the radio, static—voices blaring instructions through the dark.

The storm had knocked out our Life Support Buoy (LSB) with its air supply, as well as the hab's depressurizing system. The depressurizer was worse news than the LSB. Without it we'd have to evacuate to the surface painfully slowly, nineteen meters over eighteen hours. If not, we'd risk dizziness, pain, paralysis, and death.

Shouldn't I have known to fear the ocean? Wasn't it another kind of space? It had killed before. I thought of the Russian naval submarine that exploded when I was in college, 118 dead. I thought of a tiny parish in Ireland, where church bells still rang yearly for eleven residents killed on the *Titanic*. I thought of the three hundred migrants drowned off the coast of Egypt, just three weeks before: Egyptians, Eritreans, Somalis, and Syrians. How often that happened. How merciless the sea was, how many it held.

I held tight to a rope. It was daytime, I thought, sometime daytime fourteen hours in. Below me, Nadia gripped the same rope. There was a second one beside ours, with Aziz and then Tom. They were many feet and many hours below us, having delayed their ascent to secure the hab. I couldn't see them and didn't know when I would again.

Even Nadia's presence was only an idea. We were locked within our bodies—masked eyes screened against a silty rush of water, lips spitting bubbles through scuba filters. The tubes that held us to our air supply, and the ropes that held us to the shadow of a boat—they rocked in the storm above.

We measured our progress in inches, in hours. We couldn't sleep and couldn't speak. We held on to our rope, the bones in our fingers burning in their joints, and let the ocean pull us forward and back.

I looked down. Nadia held my foot. She squeezed it three times, hard. With one hand, she held two curved fingers to her goggles. The diving hand signal for *look*. She repeated the gesture. I followed her gaze.

Shark.

Huge. Nearly as long as I was tall, gray and wide and close. Maybe twenty feet away, and swimming closer.

My chest tightened.

My blood and tissues were filled with inert gases, under enormous pressure. If I rushed to the surface, without the monitored depressurization of a slow rise, my blood would bubble up with these gases and I would die.

My training kicked in. Do not panic.

I looked down at Nadia. I watched the bubbles on her filter and aligned my own breath with hers. I held one hand flat, palm down, and moved it slowly up and down. *Calm, slow, easy.*

Nadia joined her thumb and index in a ring, holding out three fingers. *I'm okay.*

I'm okay, I signed back. Briefly, I touched a hand to my heart, though it wasn't one of the dive signals.

I opened the small supply pack at my waist. I clipped a rattle pointer to my belt—it was like a long, metal screwdriver with a bell in it, and we were supposed to use it to point at interesting fish or to signal danger. Too late for that. I wrapped the braided cord of a small diving mirror around my wrist and angled it toward the shark. We'd been taught not to make direct eye contact.

The shark swam past the second rope and then our rope, past the second rope and then ours again. It swam five meters toward us and my breath stopped. Then it turned back and circled again.

I remembered the weight of the ocean on top of us. I imagined it pressing on my head and my back. The swoosh of churning stormwater and my fast-beating heart in my ears—the only sounds in the world.

Nadia moved slowly up the rope, toward me. Now we were one animal, a larger one. This was smart, if risky to her body.

Even these stolen inches of ascent would hurt her, shooting through her body with dizziness and pain. I reached my left hand down, holding the rope with just my right, and Nadia took it. She squeezed my hand with every breath in and out, and with this I felt I could calm my heart. I focused my gaze on the small half-braid she'd pinned at the nape of her neck. Its texture and color and light. I held the rattle pointer against my chest and moved it up and down with each breath. Another sign—*calm*.

The shark came back, far too close. The length of a body away. It swam left, then right. I rushed a breath and felt my chest freeze up again. That was dangerous. Dive panic killed far more divers than sharks did. If I let myself fall into it, I'd breathe so quickly as to feel like I was suffocating.

I concentrated on the right pace of breath. On Nadia's hand in mine. I remembered meeting her on the night of the house party before our swearing in. She'd appeared at the door in an ironed white shirt and navy pants, and shook my hand with such strength I caught a small gasp in my throat. Later that night, when the ascans were drunk and the party was collapsing, an alarm dinged on her phone. She stood on a chair and stomped her feet, herding us upstairs. We climbed through someone's bedroom window and out onto the roof. The space station passed over us, right on time. Cheers, applause. Aziz lay on his back and waved upward. Nadia held a flat hand over her lips and trilled. A cosmonaut threw a glass bottle onto the street and a neighbor called the police.

Down here, the shark moved back and forth in a straight line. Clipped turns, each leading it back to where we were. It was evaluating us. *Sideways-flanking*. I remembered it from a tenth-grade science class back home.

Suddenly a trick of memory.

I saw my teacher at the front of the room. Brett. The pang of missing him, from this strange place and time. Science vocabulary was still being developed in Cherokee, and we were only learning, so he used a basic, everyday language with many work-arounds. "Sideways-flanking," he said in English, waving his facing palms in the air in front of him—and then he spoke in Cherokee—"is when you stand your body across from his body, you stand like *this* and like *this*, you walk this way and you walk that way and you walk this way and you think—hmmmm—*can I kill you if I try?*"

A partial eclipse, seen in shadow through a hole at the top of an empty cereal box. I cannot see my mother, but I feel her at my side. In the memory I hear a familiar story. I know she is reading from the green, hardcover book, with a man in a turban on the front of it. *Myths of the Cherokee* by James Mooney. He was the son of Irish Catholic immigrants, sent to save our stories before we disappeared. The book gives the account of another Irish James, watching us watch an eclipse: "They all ran wild . . . like lunatics, firing their guns, whooping and hallooing, beating of kettles, ringing horse bells, and making the most horrid noises . . ." Many of my mother's stories come from this book.

In our story, the frog is hungry. Nothing in the world is enough for him. He jumps up from the Earth to the sun and bites down.

As the frog strains to swallow the sun, pulling more and more of it into the darkness of his mouth, we shout to scare him away. Brett and my mother and my sister and me. My mother puts a pot in my hand, and a wooden spoon, and I'm supposed to bang on it, to join in the sounds of my family. But I can't. I am mesmerized. It is only me, a small opening in the corner of a box, and the blinding light of sun and moon. My family shouts. I sit, very still, and wait.

Sharks don't know how vulnerable we are in open water. They don't know the utter uselessness of our teeth. In training they said this keeps our people alive, nearly every time.

We had no way to warn Aziz and Tom below us. No way to alert the crew in the boat above. They had a schedule of safety checks every hour, the next not due for another fifteen minutes. We could die in seconds.

The shark was close enough to touch.

It brushed past Nadia's face. She gripped my hand so tight it hurt. The back of the shark was short. The head was huge and curved and sharp. I kept my eyes down, on the mirror in my hand. No movement. No eye contact. We are not here.

The shark paused, mid-circle. Nose down, nose up, then *whoosh*—it turned upward and cut through the water. Mouth open, it lunged.

I wake to bright light, back in the darkness of my old room. Della has slipped out of our bed. In the corner I see the soft outline of her back, her shoulders leaning into the monitor on her computer. It is all blue. A shadow darts across her screen and folds back out of it, its body curling like an eel. Thirty-five seconds and it ends. She presses play.

She hasn't told me that she likes frilled sharks, or why. But I've caught it, quietly, in moments like this. I've read about them, enough to know they're living fossils. They're still here, somehow, descendants of ancestors gone eighty million years. One has been recorded alive—recently, and for only the first time. It's here, in the room with us, twelve years ago and three thousand feet underwater.

I could cross the room and join her, wrap a blanket over her shoulders and ask: Why frilled sharks, why the Mariana Trench, why the ocean?

I can't know what would have happened if I'd asked. If everything after could have been different or should have. The beach was two hours' drive from the bed we shared three years, and I still wish I'd taken her there.

The video ends. Della presses play, once and then again. She cries happy tears, both hands cradling the screen.

I threw my fist forward, aiming for the eye. I missed. My limbs were useless and heavy underwater and my hand grazed against teeth.

The shark pulled back once, returned, and dove forward. I hit it with my rattle pointer, swinging it like a baton. The shark opened and closed its mouth. I shook. At my waist, the rattle pointer made a small sound.

Nadia pressed her back to mine, covering me where I had been open.

The shark snapped its teeth at her. I swung around to her side and hit it again—this time in the gills. It pulled back, then forward; its mouth clamped down on my leg. I heard a crunch but felt nothing. I saw blood.

Its teeth were razors. It pulled at me. I held on to the rope even with everything in me screaming in fear, even when I'd spit out my mouthpiece, how had I spit out my mouthpiece, I couldn't breathe. Panic. I made the dive signal for *help help help help*. I tried to stab the shark in the eyes—too weak, too terrified—and Nadia was off the rope, she was untethered, she pushed my mouthpiece back between my lips.

The shark let go, and rushed at Nadia from the back. There was a cloud of red.

Nadia's body hung from its teeth, her body long and loose like a fish. With one fist, she fought. Weak punches to the shark's jaw that could only have hurt her hand. She looked at me, terrified.

I hit the shark repeatedly with my rattle pointer, and caught the time flashing green on my watch. Four more minutes, and the surface crew would come. They were going to save us. They were all that could.

There was a cramp in my arm, and Nadia swatted open-handed at the shark. There was blood in the water.

I couldn't save her, I realized, but I could live. The surface crew was coming for me. If I stayed here, holding my own palms tight around my wound, I could live. Three more minutes. The shark veered out of my reach, Nadia limp in its mouth.

Nadia blurred past me, red. The shark pulled her down.

Friendship. Many years of jokes about how she knew I used to love her. Watering her plants. Starving them, drowning them, replacing them. Picking her up from the airport. Washing dishes at Standing Rock in bins of soapy water, freezing our hands off, our laughter turning to steam. Me, Kayla, Nadia, and Daryan. A six-month prognosis for Nadia's mother. My Arabic lessons. Nadia's engagement. A funeral. A broken engagement. Nadia crying on my couch with a diamond ring in her fist. Nadia falling asleep on my shoulder. Red marks pressed in her palm from the ring, the empty white mug I dropped it in for safekeeping. The sound of her breath. How I stayed. How I sat up in the night and held her, how I watched our reflection in the window.

A short period of heightened devoutness. A short period of thoughtless sex. An apology brunch. An apology cactus. An apology bar of soap, with a tiny plastic astronaut trapped inside. Nadia stealing my old orange baseball hat. Nadia taking it to space.

"Can we try again?" I said.

We marry in the birthplace of her late mother, in a town on a mountain in Morocco. Her mother had left it before she'd had memories, but still she'd always hoped to return. Every house and street is painted blue, though Nadia doesn't know why. She reads to me from her phone that it was Jews fleeing Spain, or maybe an effort to prevent malaria. It is just the two of us at a small café table, seated facing each other. Our vows are written beside small tea glasses filled to the rim, then read to each other in low voices.

The paperwork marriage comes one year after the vows, six years after the law has come to include us. It is done by a Texas judge who takes walk-ins, early in the morning on our way to work. I drop my paper coffee cup on the courthouse floor and sob, unexpectedly, into the neck of my wife. It is not because she has chosen me, an old and comfortable fact. It is new to feel I'm part of my country, part of the world.

Hadn't we waited long enough? Couldn't any of this happen?

I turned away from the light at the water's surface, from the people who would save me if I stayed. I took one look at my leg, torn blue wetsuit and red cloudy water.

I dove.

The shark shook Nadia in the dark water below, blood pouring. Its teeth were inches from her heart. I reached first for her body, like I could take her in my arms and end this. Her neck fell to the side.

Her mouthpiece dragged, hanging from the tube connected to her scuba tank. I scrambled for it. My hands shook as I tried to push it between her teeth. I slapped her cheek, my fingers three inches from the shark's mouth at her shoulder, and her eyes fluttered open. I cupped my hands together before her face, signing *boat*. Like *the boat people are coming*, like *breathe*, like *don't leave me*.

I held the rattle pointer in my fist, firm, tip-down like a knife. I was losing too much blood and losing it too fast. I felt faint in a way that shot far past tired, like I was slowly floating toward a door. I was leaving a party late in the night, waving. It had all come to this, to the instant I'd known to follow her. My life expanded out, then balled up into the size of a fist.

I thrust the rattle pointer into the shark's eye, hard.

I pulled out. I pushed in and in and in.

The water was dark with blood, mine and Nadia's. The shark's? I was falling into myself, or past myself, gone. I pushed in and the shark thrashed, but I held steady, red red red from Nadia's chest. The blur of it, the color. I pushed in and in and in.

My mother asked me once, when I was a child, to explain the secrets of the early universe.

I told her everything I understood about the Big Bang theory, which wasn't nearly enough.

I think that morning she wanted to feel settled, a kind of settled impossible to anyone alive. Even to scientists, who were only people.

Yet I've known people like that, who wanted more. People who ask impossible questions. Not in moments of crisis alone, like my mother did that day, but as a permanent state of being. They're always looking back, theorizing, trying to understand the point of it all. Saying things like, *what if simulation?* Or, *what if holographic universe?* Or, *extinction event when?* The TA in college, in my first astronomy class. The physicist who asked me—begged me, on her knees—to follow her to Yale. And also, of course, my father.

He liked to read.

Sci-fi, mostly. He could sit for hours—studying the universe not as it was, but as it could be. And so failed to see what was right in front of him.

After we left, I wanted to hate it. Space. The universe. All of it.

My father had described it in a way that scared me. He'd even drawn pictures, to help me understand. After the sun is a red giant, it will become a white dwarf. After a white dwarf, a black dwarf. Trillions of years from now, all of us dead.

Unless.

Stories about travelers through gaps in the space-time continuum. Babies engineered in test tubes on Mars. The multiverse. The mycelial network. Black holes as time machines. He was constantly reading aloud to me. Terrible, terrifying stories. Stories I'd sometimes find again as an adult, surprised to still remember them. Something from Stephen King. Something about a little boy traveling outside the solar system. An accident during teleportation. Millions of years in a void, alone with his thoughts. The boy tore out his eyeballs with his own hands. "Fascinating, right?" my father said. I was five.

My mother called this a hobby. Later, a distraction. A Band-Aid. "His way of running from the world." She hinted at his upbringing, how it was "roughneck"—with "roughneck" people I never met nor learned anything about. They had not protected him from things they should have. She said it like an explanation, an unspoken plea for patience with him. And, maybe, for forgiveness of her.

The night we left, I saw the moon.

I had seen it before. But everything in the sky belonged to my father and scared me. The moon was to be conquered, colonized and fought over by the countries of the Earth. We had to be ready to get there first.

We lost most things that night. Our clothes and toys and books and beds. Our plastic boat and shark. Marine Biologist Barbie, with her tiny purple scuba tank and her glitter-pink flippers, sparkling in the tub water between my sister and me.

Only hours before, though already dark out, our father had announced we were taking a trip. He hadn't said where. An endless road, the car winding up and around mountains that must have really been hills. He was silent, after a long and loud evening. Our mother offered again—her voice lifting higher and higher, ever softer—to drive. Kayla was asleep in her booster seat. We took another sharp turn.

Our father pushed his foot down on the gas. The car flew forward off the edge of a cliff, slamming me back.

Our mother unclicked her seat belt and threw herself into the back seat. She crouched on the floor and held two arms up, one for each daughter, like she could catch us in her small hands.

I remember a tossing through many trees. Later I'd decide this had saved us. It took a long time, falling, or it felt like it did. I remember flying forward, my mother's palm against my chest. I remember the bruises from her hand and the seat belt, the month my sister and I would spend marked under our shirts.

I don't remember hitting the ground. But, after that, we ran.

The moon was bigger than before. Brighter, fuller. What would my life have been, if we'd left in the darkness of a new moon? Instead, this:

I saw the moon when we pulled onto the highway on the outskirts of Dallas, and again when we stopped for biscuits. It was impossible not to notice it. The landscape changed around us. As did the cars traveling alongside us, the white letters and numbers on green signs as we passed them. But I watched the moon out the window. It followed us.

All my mother said that night, when I dared to whisper questions from the back seat, was "a new world." "Starting over." "Home." I didn't know how Oklahoma could be all these things, or what had happened to us. Why had we raced through the woods, if he hadn't climbed out of the car to chase us? He hadn't even moved. Woods and then a car and then another car, the drive to Oklahoma. My sister slept with her head in my lap. I touched her hair with gentle hands, as our father had told me many times to do.

I came to love the moon. How it stayed with me through that night, and all the nights to come. As we drove I thought about going there, and in my mind there were no borders or minefields. Nothing to destroy, or to be destroyed by. Another place to exist.

I thought about a moon he had no claim to, natural satellite of Earth. A rock. Simple, stable, always there.

Later, every night before bed in our new home, my mother would help me climb up on the counter to reach the window over the kitchen sink. She'd hand me a thick bar of white soap, and hover her hand behind my back to catch a fall. I drew each phase of the moon night by night, the march of crescents carrying me through that first month. Later, Brett would take me out on the roof and pull the telescope from its case.

Close-up, the moon's surface was speckled. Something like ten thousand visible craters, something like four and a half billion years of asteroid and meteoroid bombardment. The same had happened to Earth, all those hits, but here you couldn't tell by looking. We had our atmosphere. Erosion. Plate tectonics. Water, covering most of our world.

Now, in the ocean. A few miles off from Key Largo, tethered to a rope. There's a tourniquet fastened at Nadia's shoulder—purple, my own—though the memory of tying it is lost. My leg is still bleeding. I hold her hand.

I sway back and forth in the current. I fall in and out of my life. I do not know the secrets of the early universe, or what there was before the Big Bang. I don't know if I'll live, or if we will, or what will come after us.

I want to love the universe, even if I don't know what it is. I do not have to know what it is.

Four divers circled us, their backs to our bodies, with long blades of knives glinting at their waists. Two wrapped Nadia in a space blanket, shiny like foil, and adjusted the tourniquet I'd placed. She had lost so much blood. The waves picked up speed and yanked us against the rope. A diver used a cord to fasten me to it. She twisted a tourniquet onto my leg through a pain I could not have imagined. The bleeding stopped.

The medics came. They checked us both. I had stabilized, but Nadia had not. She was unconscious. They brought her up to the surface, right away— the risk of her bleeding out was greater than the risk of depressurization.

They checked my pulse and my wound. They forced me to drink through a tube. Something thick, like a smoothie. They replaced my scuba tank and my diving fin and my rattle pointer, strapping a long-bladed knife of my own to my belt. And then, communicating through words written on a white-board, they told me they would leave. Everyone but the men with knives. The medics would monitor me. In shifts they would leave and come back and leave. Ascend another six inches, they said, like Tom and Aziz down below you. And wait.

The medics returned as promised, every half-hour now. To check my pulse and air supply, all my tubes and equipment. To hold up little boards that said *hang in there*, that said *just two more hours*, that said *are you experiencing any dizziness/itchiness/numbness/fatigue/pain/paralysis—point if yes*. To take my mouthpiece gently from my lips, press tablets onto my tongue, and then return it to me.

The pain had held off before, a fact that astounded me. My body had gone to such lengths to let me fight for it. I thought it must be very hard to die.

Now, though, I hurt. I had never felt such physical pain, in those pauses of aloneness. I drifted back and forth with the current, the rope swinging with me. I worried about Nadia. I worried about the shark returning, maybe with all its friends, though the diver with the whiteboard had written that this wasn't a concern. She did not specify if this was because of observed shark behavior, or because of the men with knives.

The divers watched over me, as they had said they would. At one point I thought to myself, the bad thing has happened now. I stopped looking for shadows in the water. I closed my eyes.

I remembered the adrenaline I'd had when I needed it, the merciful numbness behind small, sharp teeth. I stayed very still, wrapped in the knowledge that I had lived. I had been waiting. All these years of fear, a sureness inside me that something chased close behind.

I would be okay now. I would be safe. Wasn't that all my mother had wanted, the night she took us in her arms and ran?

A diver came down to me. This time, I could see outside myself. A woman, young-looking, like my sister had once been. Skinny arms and legs. A hot-pink wetsuit with a gold-colored zipper. They shouldn't have let her work that day, at sea in a storm. I wanted her safe with her parents, or somewhere far from Florida. I also wanted her to stay with me, to let me drop my weight against her and stop fighting the current. My sister used to do that for me—all my life that I'd let her. I ached to see her now, and our mother. I wanted to tell them that things—that I—could be different.

The diver swam closer. She read the numbers on my pressure gauge, wrote BREATHE in big letters on her whiteboard, and checked the straps and gauges and tubes that kept me living. She pulled gently at the neck of my wetsuit and checked my skin with a red flashlight.

She moved to leave. I pressed her hand against my shoulder and my cheek. Parts of me that couldn't feel anything, that hadn't felt anything in hours. She touched the cold metal of her dive regulator to my hairline, like a rough kiss on the head. She made the sign of index and thumb in a ring. *You're okay.* She swam to the surface, bright blue fins fading in murky water. I held on.

PART

SEVEN

2016

EMERGENCY CONTACT

October 30, 2016

In a small hospital outside Miami, a nurse said I was fine. I would be fine. After all, I was alive! It was early morning. There were blue wires dangling from stickers on my chest, and an IV port in my hand.

I asked to see my leg. A little roughly, the nurse pulled back the sheet. It was all there, bandaged, held straight in a black brace. Rows of Velcro pulled tight across it.

"You're alive!" she said again.

I asked her about Nadia. The other girl? She was alive, too.

Could I see her? No. She'd had surgery. She would need time to recover.

I fell back asleep. When I woke, my leg hurt. The nurse gave me a pill and said I'd be discharged soon. I said my leg hurt, and she said I was alive. I asked her about the rest of the crew, and she said they were in their own hospital rooms, with their own families.

"What about my family?" I asked.

The nurse sighed and unhooked a clipboard from the foot of my bed. "Your emergency contact was your sister, right? Kayla Palakiko?"

I nodded.

She squinted down at her notes. "We called her yesterday, and she had us confirm that you were stable. She said she trusts we won't discharge you until you're safe to find a ride home."

Huh. Was "almost killed by shark" not enough to merit a visit? Or a text?

I lay in my bed, propped up on pillows and hurting. I listened to the voices of Nadia's parents in the room beside mine. Nadia hadn't woken up from surgery, but they were already there. I imagined the call from NASA, the panic and concern, the rush to the airport with only their phones and wallets. Maybe they'd bought their tickets at the counter. Now they sat in her room. They laughed and talked loudly with harsh, warm Brooklyn accents. I smelled pizza. Like they were at a party, chatting away, and Nadia would join them soon.

I was doing it again, I realized. Sinking into myself, feeling sorry for myself, getting myself ready to run. I knew why my sister hadn't called me. Hadn't I wanted—back when I'd thought I was on my way out—to do better?

I had lived. I pressed the button on my bed for the nurse, who was less gruff with me when I explained what I'd like help with. She left and came back quickly with the wheelchair, but also a blanket, a red Jell-O cup, and a plastic spoon. She helped me out of bed.

As the nurse wheeled me into Nadia's hospital room, both her parents stood. They looked down at me, each of them holding one of Nadia's hands as she slept.

"I'm Steph," I said. "I'm friends with Nadia. Is it okay if I join you for a little?"

"Ha!" said her mother. "Look who the cat dragged in!"

"Imane, please," said her father. He sat down in an armchair by the bed. He was big and tall, slumped over the edge of the bed in an oatmeal-colored fleece. "When your daughter wakes up, she'll kill us."

"Let's try again," he said, turning back to me. "Hello, Steph. I'm Jim. Good to meet you."

"Hi," I said. "It's good to—"

"You know you're *famous* in her emails," said Nadia's mother. Jim had called her Imane. "Why pretend we don't know who you are?"

Imane looked older than Jim, but I wondered if that was a sign of her illness. Her hair was gone, her head was uncovered, and she was very thin. Her eyes narrowed, aware I was assessing her for frailty.

"Not infamous, right?" I said. I laughed awkwardly.

"Come here," Imane said, patting the space beside her.

I nodded, lowering my eyes, and wheeled myself up to the bed. Nadia looked serene, eyes closed, sheets pulled up over the shoulder that had been operated on. She wore a blue medical hairnet, and I badly wanted to push her curls back from her forehead.

If I were alone with Nadia, I'd want to hold her hand. I'd tuck her blanket a little higher under her chin. I'd want to sleep here, in the armchair by her bed, and wait for her to be okay. She didn't have to love me back. In fact, she had a girlfriend! But she did have to be okay.

"She's okay," Jim said. Gently, from the other side of her bed. He must have seen my worry.

I let out a breath.

"She scared the shit out of us, too!" he said, lightly rubbing Nadia's good shoulder. "Not sure how I feel about her launching into space now, ha ha ha. But she's out of the woods. So that's something."

Wordlessly, still looking at Nadia, her mother patted me twice on the hand. My IV port was there, and I winced.

"Want some pizza?" Imane said.

I was a little scared of what Nadia had said about me in her emails. Did Imane know I'd messed up as a friend, a girlfriend, or both? I almost wanted to defend myself. Something like, "I was the one with the tourniquet!" or "Nadia forgave me on the wet porch last week!"

But it wouldn't be simple like that. Not with Nadia, and not with Imane. But pizza was a start.

I stayed. The three of us sat close together, using the edges of Nadia's hospital bed as a kind of table for our paper plates. We talked, mostly about Nadia. They wanted to know how truly great an astronaut she was, and was it true that—as Jim had always suspected!—she was the best that NASA had ever seen? "The smartest and the funniest and the most beautiful," Imane said, "yes?" At that part, *most beautiful*, Imane stared down at me like she was holding a gun to my head. I held back a laugh.

"No offense," Imane added, almost smiling. "It's not so bad for you. You could still be—maybe?—their number-two astronaut."

For once, I didn't correct this with "ascan."

I wanted to know about the night Imane and Jim had been arrested together, how long it had taken them to know they were in love. Was it true that they'd been friends first, in the space between jail and elopement? Or had they been more like comrades in the anti-war movement? Imane broke down in laughter, finally, covering her face and shaking her head. It was like I'd asked about a long-past mission to another planet. Jim leaned in even farther across the bed, still holding Nadia's hand, and launched in. He told it like his favorite story, like the central text of his life.

Around eight p.m., a different nurse came in and wheeled me backward out of the room. Nadia hadn't woken up yet, and Imane didn't seem to know what to do with me. But Jim smiled, and waved, and said to come back in the morning. I did.

On the afternoon of the second day, I was discharged. Aziz and Tom (who had freed themselves from the sea without a scratch) brought a duffel bag to my room with all my clothes. Somehow, they'd been acquired from the hab by mission control. I changed out of my hospital gown in the bathroom, lifted my crutches from their place against the wall, and made my way back slowly to Nadia's room. Jim had fallen asleep in his chair, but Imane came to the door. She nodded at me, almost approvingly, and let me in.

On the morning of the third day, Imane told me I could leave for Oklahoma if I needed to. "That's where your family is. Right? They must be anxious for you to visit. You should send your mother a picture of your leg! We always like to know whether or not they had to amputate."

I told her I would book a flight to visit them, just as soon as Nadia was okay. Only after I said it did I realize both parts were true. I would wait for Nadia, and I would go home.

Imane smiled, for real this time, and asked for help with her crossword. Jim woke, left the room, and came back with a paper bag of biscuits and three cups of coffee. That afternoon, when Imane was starting a book of crosswords I'd found in the gift shop and Jim was telling me what was wrong with youth protest movements these days and I was nodding along, trying to be agreeable without being fake so that both her parents might respect me if things went south with Daryan and I stood a chance with their daughter someday, Nadia woke up.

STEPH

REMEMBER THE SKY THAT
YOU WERE BORN UNDER

November 2, 2016

Two flights, a rented car, and a drive at night to Tahlequah from Tulsa. I
was lucky to have injured my left leg and not my right. I hurt, but I could
drive.

On the highway I pictured Nadia's face when she'd woken up, how her
eyes had widened in surprise as she looked from Imane to Jim to me. How
she'd smiled. Later, her parents left us alone in the room, for some completely
made-up reason that involved Imane wiggling her eyebrows and nudging
Nadia's good shoulder, and Nadia groaning in response. Nadia waited to
speak till they'd closed the door behind them.

"So you stayed," she said.

"Um, yes," I said. I realized, too late, the intensity of the gesture. The
night before, after I'd been discharged, her parents had asked a nurse to bring
up a third cot for me.

"Wow," she said. "You didn't have to do that. I mean, I didn't think you
would—"

"Oh God, *please* don't worry about it," I said. "I just wanted to know you
were okay. I care about you, but I was just on my way out? To go see my family, but—yeah, I care. And you have a girlfriend and that's really good. I'm so
happy for you. I respect that so, so much."

Nadia fell back on her pillow and laughed. The sound was surprisingly strong and deep for what she'd been through, and I had missed it.

"Calm down," she said, still laughing. Over the hospital blanket she touched my hand. "I'm glad you stayed. Call me tomorrow so I know you made it home?"

I got to my mother's house around four in the morning, though I hadn't warned her I was coming. When I knocked on the door, each light in the house turned on, one room at a time. In the doorway Felicia ran at me. I dropped my crutches and my duffel and put my arms around her, only letting go to limp to the couch.

"What's wrong with you?" my mother said.

"*Elisi!*" Felicia said, tugging at her hand. She turned to me. "She meant to say, 'I'm so sorry your leg looks all messed up. What happened?'"

"If I told you," I said, "there's no way you'd believe it!"

"Shark attack," said Kayla, expressionless. She stood apart from us, half in the kitchen. She was wrapped in our mother's blue quilt.

"Very funny," our mother said.

That surprised me. I thought, even if she had no plans to visit me, Kayla would have told our mother. But I was here now.

"Like I said, you wouldn't believe it." Carefully, I pulled my sweatpants up my left leg. A bandage was wrapped from my thigh down to my knee, layered under a brace. Peeking out the edges were bruises, dark purple splotches down to the ankle.

Kayla winced.

Felicia leaned in so close, her nose bumped the Velcro fastener on my brace. "Cool!" she said.

I laughed and kissed her on the head. "Right?" I said.

"You should really be resting," my mother said.

I shrugged. "It hurts! But I'm alive. The whole crew is. Also, I've got four more days of medical leave."

"Oh. And you decided to come here, I guess, of all places." She looked like she was holding in a smile.

"I thought this might be where the party was," I said.

The toaster dinged in the kitchen, and Kayla muttered something about waffles. She hadn't hugged me, and hadn't even said hello. But she had started, apparently, making us breakfast.

"And," I added, quieter now, "I wanted to be with you."

The look on our mother's face then—it was like her heart exploded. A sudden burst of joy, of life, and then she caught it and pulled it back into a small smile. It struck me then how much time she must have spent as a mother, how much of her motherhood, pretending not to feel things.

I moved toward her, still limping, and brought her into me with both arms. I hugged her like I'd wanted to the moment I'd come home. I held her as close as I could.

When I let go, she went straight for the kitchen. She piled all the waffles on a plate, poured cups of milk and placed them on a plastic tray. She carried them into the living room and all three of us followed her, holding in our hands syrup and whipped cream and a full coffee pot that Kayla must have started before I'd stepped into the house. She had known it was me. Felicia had taken the blue quilt. She wore it like a cape now, trailing behind the rest of us. We were a parade.

In the living room, my leg propped up on the coffee table in front of us, we ate. We sipped from mugs and wrapped ourselves up close together. All the blankets were out now, running over this shoulder and onto that lap. Had it really been this easy? All this love just waiting for me, where I'd started, and I'd only had to knock at its door?

It was quiet, comfortable but quiet, and I could feel that my life had finally caught up to me. It was time.

"Mom?" I said. "I've been trying to understand something, if you're okay to talk about it. Why did you stay with our dad?"

"Steph!" Kayla said. "Oh my God!"

"I just meant—"

"Ma, you don't have to answer that," Kayla said.

"But Kayla, you sent me his obit. You're telling me that wasn't a request to talk it through?"

"You didn't freaking text me back! You didn't give a shit until *right now*—who cares why—and then you woke us all up to cater to you?"

"A *shark* was trying to *eat me!*"

"For two weeks? What, one toe at a time?"

"I find this tiring," our mother said.

Kayla and I looked at each other. Felicia seemed genuinely thrilled. It was a wonder no one had sent her back to bed.

"I'd been thinking we should talk about this," our mother said, "even before you all suddenly descended on this house."

Then she waited, long enough that I thought she might be stalling. Kayla glared at me, like this was proof I had pushed her too far.

Our mother put her mug down on the coffee table and cleared her throat. "There's a hundred good things I could say about your father—"

"What the *hell*, Mom!" I said.

"Shut up, Steph," Kayla said.

"—and a hundred more I told myself," she continued, "to explain the things he did. When I met him, he had one of the saddest stories I'd ever heard. Sadder than anything that had happened to me before that point. I used to think that was real important."

She paused and looked hard at Felicia, who was holding a waffle in two tight fists. "I hope you know it isn't," our mother said. "Don't you go thinking so little of people who suffer, like they don't have a choice how they treat you. Okay?"

Felicia nodded. She bit into the waffle.

"I'm preaching to the choir," our mother said. "Young people are smarter these days."

"Your parents kicked you out when you got pregnant," Kayla said, "so you didn't want to abandon our dad . . . 'Cause you knew how painful that was. Right?" Her voice was bright almost, clipped, like this could be tied up nicely and put away.

Our mother didn't answer. She turned to me. "I've wondered if you remember that night, Steph. I hope not."

"Which night?" Kayla said.

"You do, though, don't you? Is that what all this is about?"

Reluctantly, I nodded.

"Remember *what?*" Kayla said. There was alarm in her eyes. "Steph, what's she talking about?"

Our mother started to cry. There was a time that would have scared me, and she would have left the room. I'd been a kid afraid of adults with big feelings, and I had barely let her have them.

Now I leaned my head on her shoulder, and her breathing slowed. She wiped her eyes and cheeks with the corner of the quilt and tucked it back around Felicia's shoulders. She picked back up her mug—heavy, red, chipped on the rim. She held it to her chest, close, even though it was empty.

"Kayla," she said, "do some of us need to go back to bed? That's your call."

"No," Kayla said. She leaned Felicia back against her chest and laid her palm over her head.

"All right, then." Our mother took a long breath. "We were in your father's car, all four of us. You two were in your booster seats, thank God, and your father was mad—

"No," she said, interrupting herself. She held out a hand between us, stopping me before I could start. "It doesn't matter why. What matters is that he got mad, and we were driving along this ridge—"

"He drove off it," I said.

"*No,*" Kayla said.

"He did," our mother said. "He meant to."

I waited for her to continue.

"Kayla, you didn't seem to remember? I hoped, maybe . . . if I didn't let it turn into a story, Steph might manage to forget it, too. So I said nothing."

An old anger came back to me. I'd long since learned that my silence protected my sister—and that my mother wanted that from me. But she hadn't had the guts to ask for it. She shouldn't have put that on a child.

I tried to calm myself down. I worried that, at any point, our mother might walk out of the room.

"We left him there," I said. "I thought that meant he'd died, or was about to? Wait, Mom—Kayla must've shown you the obit. Right?"

She nodded.

I remembered the blood, pooling, and the twisted shape of our father's body. The way our mother took us up in her arms and ran.

I'd been certain he was dead, even as I'd been certain that he wasn't. That he was, somehow, chasing me.

"So, the story in the obituary. When he lost his leg," Kayla said. She spoke slowly, putting it together. "That was the night of the car—"

She had almost said *accident*. I was furious for her.

Kayla tried again. "That was the same night we left?"

Our mother nodded.

"Steph, how long have you known?"

I didn't want to say it. But she knew.

Always.

Kayla pressed her face to the top of Felicia's head.

"Excuse me," Felicia said, so young and polite. So desperate to stay. "Why's it matter so much that you left him in the car? Dead or alive, like, either way? It sounds like you didn't need to take him with you."

"Honey," Kayla said, "I think leaving him there means your elisi didn't think she could stay. Not for the paramedics, or the police, or any of the people we wait for when someone is hurt."

Kayla looked at our mother, checking her work.

"I didn't trust that I could leave him," our mother said, a shake in her voice. "If I didn't go *right then*."

Felicia slumped back against Kayla's chest.

"If we'd stuck around another hour," she continued, "with the police report, and the ambulance, and the chance of him waking up . . . I know I would have stayed for good.

"So I left him to die. That's what I thought I was doing—what I was *willing* to do—when I ran."

Kayla gently moved Felicia off of her and stood up. She walked to the kitchen with two mugs in her hands, and I listened to her wash them. Eventually, she came back to us.

Our mother began again. She answered questions, filling in details from that night. How she'd carried us through the woods and up to the highway.

How she called from a pay phone outside a gas station. Then she hid in the trees, watching the cars that passed.

Our mother talked about the middle-aged woman who picked us up on the side of the road. She'd looked long and hard at the wild state of us, but asked no questions and drove fast. She turned back toward Dallas, two hours out of her way. She was Choctaw from Durant, but her sister lived with a Cherokee boyfriend in Tahlequah. She said she'd heard they liked it there "well enough."

The Choctaw woman dropped us off outside the house we'd been renting. Our mother wouldn't even go inside. She put us directly into her car, which she had packed with clothes and food and money months before. Just in case. She drove us to Oklahoma.

In Oklahoma, now, our mother put her hands over our heads.

"I was always gonna get you out," she said. "I always, always, hoped I would."

I closed my eyes. I thought about starting over.

I might not make it to space. For once, the thought did not scare me. Whatever came next, I wouldn't be alone. I never had been.

I opened my eyes and let myself feel stillness. The warmth of my mother's palm, and the bright, fruity smell of Felicia's shampoo. The yellow light that hung by the window in the kitchen, like a sun to our small world. Between two fingers I twisted a blue thread loose at the end of the quilt.

Our mother had come here looking for our nation and ancestors, for the purity of a story to save her. Or to tell her who she was and then forgive her for it. It didn't exist.

But hadn't we lived? Hadn't she taken us home? Here we were, together. Starting everything, even ourselves, even meeting ourselves and one another, finally, and all over again.

STEPH

CONTACT LIGHT

We exhausted ourselves. The four of us talked for nearly three hours, with breaks to carry strange combinations of food from the kitchen to the living room. Macaroni leftovers and cookies. Frozen, microwave-steamed vegetables and a jar of pickles. A single biscuit cut in fourths.

At one point, midway through someone's story, Kayla leapt off the couch, shouted "the light!" and raced to our old bedroom. She came back with her film camera, which I didn't think she'd touched in years. She took a picture of the coffee table, every inch of it covered in cups and plates and little pieces of food. My bandaged leg rested on it, and beside me Felicia was half-asleep. Her head was on my lap, and over her shoulders was the old blue quilt. We hadn't realized it was our grandmother's. (We'd only just been told it was stolen, by our mother on the night she left home.)

I didn't have my sister's eye for light, but I could tell it had shifted in some way. It made me stand up and stretch and look out the window. There were leaves on the ground, the first I'd seen of the season. Fall, with the start of school, had always felt like the new year.

My mother set me up on the couch, my leg propped up on a small pillow. She gave me a hug and left the room. I called Nadia.

"Hi," I whispered.

"Why are we whispering?" she whispered back.

"My whole family is napping. I woke them up at the crack of dawn and made them talk through our deepest family trauma. I'll fill you in later?"

She laughed. "So, you called, but you can't talk."

"I told you I'd call, though," I said. "So I'm calling!"

She laughed again. "Okay. I like the follow-through. How's your shark bite?"

"I love it. I think it makes me look tough. Yours?"

"My mom thinks it's gonna scare away Daryan. She won't stop ordering me turtlenecks from Lands' End."

I smiled. "I'll call you tomorrow. Say hi to Imane and Jim for me?"

"Uh, okay?"

"Okay. Cool. I miss you."

"Bye, Steph."

"Bye!"

I pulled my laptop into my lap and leaned back. I started working on what I hoped would be, if I could get it right, an email to Della. Calling Nadia when I had said I would, as her friend, was a very small thing. But it had made me feel like it wasn't too late for this. I could try.

The email took every free moment when I wasn't with my family. That afternoon, that night, and again the next morning. I finished it in the kitchen, while my sister and mother enjoyed some new just-them routine on the front stoop.

If I was going to say anything to Della, to bring this all up again even in her head, it couldn't be for me. I didn't want to write to her in a selfish way, not to find her or claim her or keep her. I wanted to write to her like an old friend. She had known me before. When I knew nothing of anything that matters to me now.

Della,

I'm sorry. For wanting you and chasing you and trying to pin you down. For pushing you to throw yourself in with me so quickly. For all the department lectures and weekend museum trips and conversations about my own godforsaken college major!—how stupid to want to prove myself during nights we could have made each other laugh or I could have learned more about you or we could have been together, which I always, always loved.

I'm sorry I didn't ask you—not genuinely—about your parents (all of them), or about that hard time in your life. When we met, your background was like a story to me, something to learn the beginning and middle and end of. It kept going, though, your story kept going, and I was only interested in the parts that fit in my life. The parts that might let me keep you? I'm sorry for thinking "good riddance," when you lost your faith. I'm sorry for insisting I was first, for assuming you were second, for believing your dreams were less meaningful than mine.

I'm sorry for that night in our junior year, you know which one, when I said you weren't really Indian. I don't even know what I meant by that, why I tried to cut down what I knew was the most precious to you, the most vulnerable, the most endangered. Except that I'd seen other people do it—I'd seen the highest court in our country debate "how much" you were of who you are. I knew it would hurt you, and I knew, in that way, I could win.

I think, back then, people would look at the two of us and believe that I had the more straightforward history. The hard parts of my childhood had not been featured on the news, and I was ridiculously vocal about where I was headed. And those same people might think it was a wonder you knew anything about yourself, let alone your Indianness or your queerness or anything else you had to fight for.

I admire you for that fight. For all the different parts of yourself that you held close. I picture you in those quiet moments from our past. I'd come home from class some days to find you lying on your stomach in the sun outside the house, barefoot, a flowy patterned skirt spread out on the grass. Your legs crossed behind you, your head at rest on your hand. Your gaze down, your eyes racing across a page. You had so many things you were interested in. You were so interesting, yourself.

I picture you now as something like you were then, your hair and face and body maybe changed as mine have, but still with the science journals stacked on the grass beside you, dog-eared and highlighted. Still with large headphones over your ears, with a planner open to today's date, with a neatly written list of everything you want to do next. Purple ink. A graphic novel in your bag, a paperback thriller you've read once before. A jacket folded, just in case. In those moments you were so at peace, so happy to be alone, so happy to be with yourself.

I wish you that, always.
Steph

ON LEAVE

November 5, 2016

Three days passed, the longest I'd been in my mother's house in years. After the hab, the protest camp, and the chaos I'd brought to both, after the shark, the hospital, and how scared I'd been until Nadia woke up, time moved slowly here.

No one in the house woke at dawn to work out. No one tried to optimize their time or beat their personal best. They just did things, one after another, because they had to or wanted to. My mother made coffee and went to her job at a bakery. Kayla drove Felicia to school, then sat at the table with a notebook she said was for "figuring out her life." I didn't know if that meant a job, maybe, if she was looking for a normal kind of job, but I didn't push her on it. I called Nadia every morning, refreshed my email way too much throughout the day, and fought my insurance company over covering the physical therapy I'd start soon in Houston. I even felt bored.

A few times I made scrambled eggs. As a family we went to the movies and the grocery store, and sat on the stoop until the mailman came. We chatted with him, briefly. Felicia got very into the art of building bonfires, the controversy of log cabin vs tipi, and three nights in a row we had firepit time in the backyard after her homework was done. We made s'mores. My mother told us stories about our family, some of them strange and dark, and when I seemed surprised by this Kayla looked at me seriously across the fire. "We'll take you to the archives before you leave."

This sounded almost ominous. Like I had missed something, which I likely had. But it was the first thing she'd said to me, to me alone, since my first morning here.

Nadia had run out of patience on the topic. "Steph, duh! Stop telling me your sister won't talk to you!"

It was election day, and we were on the phone. Kayla and I had voted absentee. Felicia's school was closed. For the first time since landing in Oklahoma, she'd been invited to a friend's house. I'd called Nadia from the front stoop, my crutches splayed out across the steps, while Kayla accompanied our mother to the polls.

"I just can't tell if it's on purpose?" I said. "Maybe it's a coincidence that we're never alone. 'Cause of our different schedules."

"Oh my God, Steph. It's not a coincidence. You have no schedule. She has no schedule. You *called* the *police* on her."

"Yes, but *she* doesn't know that?"

Nadia laughed. In the background, I thought I could hear her parents bickering. "For the last time, *she knows*," Nadia said. "You can keep speculating to me—wait, no, I'm over it, don't do that!—or you can apologize. It's so, so stupid that you haven't apologized."

"I know," I said, to end it, because Nadia was right, even if I wasn't ready to say it. Despite our rocky start, she was the closest friend I'd ever had. I wished I could have met her sooner, or even just made more space for friends.

For the rest of our call, Nadia talked about Daryan. Truly, I didn't mind like I'd thought I would. I liked being close to Nadia and knowing her well. She liked it when I followed her through her thoughts, as she tried to tame the world into a sensible long-term plan.

"I don't know," she was saying. "Before our shark situation, I'd felt *so sure* about Daryan. Wait, I don't want you to think I'm crazy. We've met *once*; I wasn't gonna propose or anything. I just mean that things have a good shot if you're both aligned on your goals and values."

"What you're saying isn't crazy, Nadia," I said, smiling into the phone. "It's just lame."

"Good. So, I had a good feeling about Daryan, and Daryan had a good feeling about me—"

"What does our shark friend have to do with this?"

"I can't believe you blinded him," Nadia said.

"He was eating you!"

"See?" Nadia said. "Exactly my point. You and me, we almost got eaten. And, like I keep reminding you, they're announcing mission assignments in February. To space. We do our PT exercises—and I mean we do it like it's our job, which it kind of is?—it could be one of us."

"It'll be me," I said. "But I don't see how this changes things with Daryan? I'm sure you can find time to do both physical therapy and dating."

Nadia groaned into the phone, like she couldn't believe I didn't get it. "The issue is not my schedule," she said. "It's that . . . I'm okay with some degree of mess now? I thought I needed to find someone who was fully formed and self-actualized and wanted, like, exactly what I wanted. Down to the tiniest detail."

I stayed quiet, listening. I had felt something similar for a long time.

"And then, shark attack!" she said, with a small laugh. "Maybe life is a mess. Maybe people are a mess and they need to just grow into each other. Maybe I can chill out now."

Kayla pulled into the driveway and let our mother out. She looked happy. She was carrying donuts in a red, white, and blue paper bag.

"Hear, hear," I said. "Maybe I can chill out, too. And Nadia?"

"Hm?" she said.

"It could still be Daryan," I said.

For the first time in the Daryan conversation, which I'd otherwise experienced as only half-real, I felt a small pain in my chest. I wanted it to be me. But, in a feeling so new and stupid it made me almost sick with myself, I wanted Nadia to be happy.

"Thanks for saying that," Nadia said, her voice low. "Who knew you could be so mature?"

"I love that you think you're funny," I said.

My mother walked up to the stoop, put down the donuts, picked up my crutches, and held out a hand to help me to my feet.

"Really," Nadia said before I hung up on her. "I wouldn't have seen it coming in a million years!"

I did my PT exercises on the couch, stretching and bending my leg with a giant rubber band. The physical therapist at the hospital had told me not to call it the "bad" leg but the "affected" leg, which I'd rolled my eyes at before taking to heart. I made eggs for lunch for the three of us, again. I asked Kayla if we could go out together before Felicia came home from her friend's house, just us two. Kayla said she was busy.

Our mother, increasingly nervous about the election results, dragged a giant plastic box into the living room. It was the first of "several boxes, actually" of our old belongings, and she asked if now was a good time for us to sort them into keeps and giveaways. I hopped on one foot to the bathroom, crutch-less, nearly falling, and closed the door behind me. On the toilet, my affected leg stretched out over the rim of the bathtub, I refreshed my email four times. At the top of the inbox, newly arrived, was a message from Della.

DELLA

THE DEEPEST PLACE
ON EARTH

November 9, 2016

I waited at a café for, unbelievably, Steph Harper.

She'd started it. She'd sent me an email out of nowhere. I ignored it for a few days, maybe just because I could? But then I was in Tahlequah with the baby, visiting with Matthew and his family. (*Our* family; I was still working on that.) I decided I'd be curious to see Steph's mom and sister—*maybe* Steph herself—on one of my trips back here. At some point we might overlap, probably Christmas. I replied.

Steph wrote back in seconds. She said she was in Tahlequah, *right now*, recovering from a shark attack, which I found incredibly hard to believe. (She must have googled me, learned I was a shark expert, and thought I'd be impressed by that? The chance of that for anyone was 1 in 11.5 million. On Steph's eternal quest to one-up the whole world, she might have confused a shark with a mola mola. People did that all the time.)

Still, I was curious. We hadn't seen each other in twelve years.

I was also anxious for a distraction. The election results had come in at three that morning, in favor of someone who freaked me out. When the president-elect had given testimony against Indian gaming laws, and the tribal citizens they applied to, he'd said "they don't look like Indians to me." It edged too close to what they'd said about me as a child in a courtroom, how the justice had cited my blood quantum. It made me want better for my baby, who was Indian in a country still puzzling out what that meant.

The bell jingled at the entrance. I watched Steph through the wall of glass. She struggled with crutches in a way that shouldn't have been funny to me but *almost* was, her body stuck half in and half out the door. I stayed in my chair and made little sounds to quiet the baby. Steph kept her eyes on the floor—interesting—before ordering at the counter. Was she pretending not to see me? I did the same.

I looked back and forth at what was in front of me, the baby in my arms and the pile of student essays on the table. The fancy red pen, uncapped on its side. Like, *Here they are, my kid and my career!* Or, *I bet you thought you could stop me!*

"Della?" she said.

Steph stood across from me, tall even as she hunched over her crutches. She wore a white linen collared shirt and a pair of jean shorts, even in the fall weather. Probably to show off the bandage, which was, admittedly, cool. My own body had gone soft in the last year, in a new way I was slowly coming to like, but Steph looked like she'd come straight from army bootcamp. Not thin, but weirdly disciplined, all purposeful angles and lines. It was like she'd spent these years shaping each muscle to her will. In college she'd spent money she didn't have on monthly salon visits. She'd had short hair then, too, but was insecure about its style and shape. She'd agonized over it when she thought I wasn't looking. Now she had a buzz cut.

"Hi, Steph," I said. I didn't get up.

A man stood behind her in a black apron, holding two large mugs. He set them on the table and backed quickly away.

With some trouble, Steph sat down. Her bad leg stuck straight out on an extra chair she'd dragged over with the help of a crutch.

"Still drink caramel macchiatos?" she said, nudging the drink in front of me. It was topped with whipped cream, rising above the rim like a cathedral spire.

"Of course not," I said.

Her face fell.

"But I got here early and ate. Figured at least I'd have breakfast, get some work done?" I gestured at the pile of papers, at the very nice pen.

"*At least*, like, in case you regret the rest of it?" Steph said. She tried to smile. I'd forgotten what nervous was like on her.

"Exactly," I said.

"I meant what I said in my email," Steph said. "I'm really sorry. I should have treated you better."

"I appreciate that."

"Can I ask how you've been since then? Are you comfortable with me asking that?"

I laughed. "Steph. Please. I'm not here to march you to a public stoning."

She relaxed a little in her chair. "Yeah, I'd hope for a lighter sentence than that."

"I've been well," I said. "Want to ask about the kid on my chest?"

"Yes. Who *is* that?"

"My new baby."

"He or she is beautiful! I can tell from the top three inches of the back of their little head."

I smiled, gently turning the baby around to face her. I bounced him a little in my lap, and he reached out for the air in front of him. It made me miss the tiny person he'd been last month. I felt a silly ache for the week he'd discovered his hands.

Steph held out her own hands, either to mirror his or to ask to hold him. She caught herself, abruptly, and lifted her mug for a sip. She said, "See? From this angle you're even more beautiful."

"Did you read my op-ed?" I said. "Like, two weeks ago?"

Everyone in my life had read my op-ed. And of course, many thousands of people not in my life. The ones who hated it had emailed me to make sure I knew it. The ones who didn't hate it had also emailed, but I was taking my time in replying to them. They were kids like me, or parents and siblings and grandparents who'd lost kids like me. Reading their stories was heavy, now that I was both myself and someone's mother.

The op-ed was the first time I'd told my story, after more than two decades building back my privacy. I'd never had a social media account and never agreed to an interview. I'd ignored several emails from publishers wanting a memoir. But the Indian Child Welfare Act was being challenged at the Supreme Court this term, again, over the contested adoption of a three-year-old Osage boy. I had skin in the game. Now my baby did, too. This time, I'd said my piece.

"I didn't know you'd written one," Steph said. "Where can I find it?"

"So you aren't caught up at *all*?"

"I wish I were. I wish we'd stayed friends."

What an insane thing to say, considering the last time I'd seen her. I ignored it. "It's a lot to catch up on. You ready?"

"Ready."

"After you nearly destroyed my spirit—"

"Oh my God, Della, I'm *so sorry!*"

"—I went home and lived with my parents. Gave up being gay. Started dating poor Ethan again. Got engaged. Planned a wedding. Sent out invitations."

"Wow!" She was trying to sound neutral. For all she knew, Ethan could be the baby's father.

"Then Lucy sent me this obnoxious email about what a big disappointment I had been, how I'd wasted her time and made her look bad to the colleagues she'd set me up with. But she was also like, 'hey here's another rec letter; you should apply one more time!'"

"I *love* Lucy."

"Cute. I applied to PhD programs," I said. "*Secretly.*"

"Hey! Your signature move!"

"Got in. Broke up with poor Ethan two weeks before the wedding. Went to UC Santa Barbara."

"Wait, wait, what happened to Ethan?"

"He got married, maybe six months later? Three kids. He's fine."

"Cool."

"Maybe I'll email him someday," I said, laughing, "and beg forgiveness over coffee."

"Very funny. Then what?"

"I went in under an adviser I met through Lucy," I said. "And then, in my second year—"

I stopped myself.

So much time had passed. I didn't feel like talking through the rest of my résumé, and Steph hadn't asked me to. The six years of school didn't mean much, in the long run, compared to nights I'd spent listening to the ocean outside my window. Totally on my own for the first time and rewriting who I wanted to be.

I made very few friends in grad school, but that was okay. I learned to surf. I went on a research trip to Tahiti. I dated just enough to get to know myself, and to know I wanted more time alone. Once, in a miracle of place and time that has happened three times in history, I observed and recorded a live frilled shark in the wild.

Steph wouldn't understand what that meant in my field—the version of her I'd known could only process achievements in the category of *shoots self into space.* I realized, my hand warm against the mug of sugar-coffee I wouldn't drink if she paid me to, that I didn't care if Steph was different now. Or if she wasn't. I no longer felt that urge to impress her.

I smiled at her, gently, and meant it. "You remember Sam," I said.

"Of course," Steph said. "Are you two still in touch?"

I nodded. "He's a neonatologist in Kansas City. He got stuck in New York forever, becoming very fancy and sought-after, and then he moved to be near his family."

"Good for him."

"Well, that's why I moved, too. I told you I'm visiting Matthew this week, but I live in Kansas City, too. I used to teach at USC. Now I'm at Haskell."

"Wait. You *moved* to be near Sam?"

I almost laughed at her tone. Like we were all kids again, and she was still jealous. Sam used to complain to me that every time he tiptoed back toward a friendship with Steph, she'd get weird about me and him and be impossible all over again. He used to say Steph's whole vibe reminded him of straight male culture, a culture he had no patience for.

I said, "Yes. I moved to be near Sam's family. Our family. Our son is Sam's biological nephew."

I kissed the soft top of the baby's head, avoiding Steph's gaze. I knew the guidance on talking to the baby about our family—early, honestly, often. But I was still learning to steel myself for how other people might take it. By the time our son could be a real witness, I'd need to model an easiness I didn't yet have.

"Wow," Steph said. Again, her voice was too neutral. Like most well-meaning people, she didn't understand and seemed scared to ask for help.

"He's Prairie Band Potawatomi and Kickapoo," I said. "So that was a factor, too, for where we'd live."

Steph looked like she was straining to form a question, maybe workshopping it in her head, but I waved her off with my hand. It was easier this way.

I said Sam's sister wasn't in a place to parent right now. (The *why*, she and Sam and I agreed, was not our story to tell.) She had called him in New York last year, asking him to come home and consider adoption. He, immediately, had thought of me.

Since when was romantic love required of parenthood? That wasn't how it worked in the animal world—not that I still looked there all desperate for reassurance. Sam and I could live together, even as we continued to date other people. We could parent together.

What I didn't tell Steph was what it had meant to me, to hear Sam say I'd be good at this. The out-loud echo of what I'd known a long time—not just that I knew how to raise a child like this child, but that—apart from anything that had happened to me, or anything that had been done to me—I would make a loving parent.

I *was* a loving parent. I invited everyone in to love our baby, everyone I possibly could. Sam's sister. Sam's mother. Sam's giant extended family. My mother, who had lived with us for the first month of the baby's life. Matthew, and his wife I'd decided not to hate so much, and the three little siblings I was starting to get to know. If I ever found my own bio-mother—off and on I still looked for her—I'd invite her in, too.

Steph was nodding, smiling, amazed. It felt good to sit with her, and I realized I did want to know about her life. The shark bite was, I suspected, the least interesting part of it. I would stay here as long as I wanted. I'd order an early lunch. I had nothing to prove.

Back in college, Steph had made me feel known and wanted. It had been special at the time, a gift, but so many people had done that since. I had made myself knowable. It was the rule in my life now, not the exception.

I never thought I'd be an adoptive parent. I had been so literal back then, so punishing of myself, like my only ticket to the human family would be through genetic offspring. Last year, when Lucy and I met for drinks at a conference, I was finally ready to laugh at that. Lucy said she'd been almost scared to teach me about the parenting behaviors of hamsters and black widows. She said I'd come a long way since then. I said, sure, I turned out all right. But weren't we peers now? She raised one eyebrow, flagged down the bartender, and ordered me another drink.

My child wasn't the only part of my life that surprised me. I'd never expected the relationship I now had with my parents. Or the job that let me think and write and teach about the ocean. Ninety-five percent of it was still unexplored. I'd been so determined back in Utah, after all the things I'd been wrong about in college, to even just once stand at a seashore.

I've done that now, many times. The first time I saw it was my first night on my own, after dropping my bags in grad student housing. I thought of my mother, the one who'd carried me. She'd grown up near a beach, and had felt sand and cold water like I felt now. She'd made choices, one and then another, which didn't need forgiving. Standing alone, at the edge of an unthinkable volume of water, I saw stars.

Now there was a watercolor painting of the Mariana Trench at home, hung above the baby's crib. More blacks than blues. Abstract, unknowable, the deepest place on Earth. Mom said, on one of her first visits after the move, that the painting was spooky. Dark. Not for babies. I said I didn't want the baby to be scared of the ocean, or anything else we can't fully know.

STEPH

EVERY AUTHENTIC
GOOD ON EARTH

There was a long, narrow window in the hospital room door. I couldn't bring myself to open it. On the other side of it was another world.

In that strip of glass was my mother. Her eyes were closed. There was a long tube in her mouth. Small, narrow pieces of striped, white tape. A gray hospital blanket was tucked under her arms.

In a plastic chair beside the bed, my sister sat. She held our mother's hands in hers. I pressed my forehead to the glass. Then I lifted my crutches from their place against the wall, opened the door, and stepped through.

Kayla gasped and looked up. Her eyes were red. Maybe she'd thought I was a doctor, someone who could help. She sighed back into her chair, small again.

"What happened?" I whispered.

She looked at our mother and back at me. She shook her head.

I shouldn't have asked for more. She had said it all already, in a frantic and terrified voice message I should have listened to right away, when I'd first stepped out of the café.

Instead, I had sat in the car and called Nadia. The forty-fifth man of forty-five men had just been elected president, and he'd called for a "shutdown of Muslims entering the United States." Nadia's mother was scared, Nadia was scared, and I'd stayed with her on the phone till she felt ready to hang up. Only then did I listen to Kayla's voice message.

Kayla had taken Felicia to school. The drive home had come to include the gas station and the grocery store, and even a few minutes alone on a shaded bench in a park. It was hot outside, unseasonably miserable, and despite this our mother had gone for a walk before her shift. It was part of an exercise routine Kayla had started with her, another fresh start.

The mailman found our mother on the side of the road. He picked her up off the ground and drove her to the hospital in his truck. After she was admitted, he called Kayla from our mother's phone. A nurse took the phone from him and said it was a heart attack.

This hospital smelled just like the hospital in Florida. I was struggling to process that I was here. "Where's Felicia?" I said.

"Her friend's mom picked her up from school," Kayla said. "She said goodbye over the phone."

The word sent a jolt through me. "Wait."

She looked at me blankly. Our mother lay between us.

"Just, wait. I don't know the details here. What have they tried already? What if—wait—"

"I wouldn't let them do it without you," she said. Soundlessly, she was crying.

The meaning of it, and where we were, and what would happen to our mother—what had already happened to our mother—it pressed down on me. All of it had already happened. I'd been sitting in a wooden chair by a wall made of glass, drinking coffee with my first love.

There had been the ambulance and the operating room and the waiting room. A doctor and a social worker in a closed, peaceful part of the hospital with a small fountain on a desk. My sister, sitting alone on a couch. The doctor leaving. The social worker staying. A practiced, loving explanation of the brain without oxygen. A practiced, loving meditation on *quality of life*. A practiced, loving period of waiting through a stranger's despair, a fatherly kind of patience, like he will never in his life have another place to be. A decision. Many signatures on pages.

I took the chair from the other side of the bed and pushed it slowly across the room. What are you *doing*, Kayla hissed, and with my unaffected leg I kicked the chair into place beside her. I fell into it, my crutches heavy across my lap.

If our mother had been with us truly, if she had even a chance of that, I would have sat on the other side of the bed. My sister and I could each take one hand, could each lay our heads on her chest like two children before sleep. But I was needed as a sister. A better one than I had been.

We sat with the sounds of the machines. A nurse came in, looked at the screen, and dispensed something. She talked softly about keeping our mother comfortable. She said a priest was on his way. When he arrived, we would begin. I didn't know how many minutes or hours that left us, or how we were meant to use them.

When the nurse was gone, I asked what was up with the priest. He'd apparently been summoned through some kind of miscommunication. Maybe a computer error? Our barely Protestant mother didn't qualify for what he offered.

Kayla shrugged. "Whatever. I didn't ask for him." But she made no effort to stand up, to tell the nurse to tell the priest to stay home.

I wondered if maybe Kayla *had* asked. A priest would bring something from the Holocene, this flash of time with all our recorded history. He'd bring a story of comfort outside ourselves, whether or not we believed in it. We were in a current with so much else.

I thought, like I imagined I would forever, now: this was something our mother would have liked.

Kayla leaned her head on my shoulder. I kissed it and tried not to cry.

More time passed. Light faded out slowly through the slits in the drawn blinds. I wanted to tell Kayla I was sorry for what I'd done in Hawai'i, that I'd been an idiot for leaving it till now. But I couldn't bear to talk about myself. Instead I sent her to the cafeteria. She hadn't eaten all day, except for a cup of tea the social worker had brought her to hold while they talked. I promised Kayla nothing would happen without her. I would stay.

Alone with my mother, I sobbed into her lap. I wrapped my arms around her waist and held her hands. I had almost forgotten the feel of them.

Together we had run, sure that a dead man chased us.

But when we made it to Tahlequah, my mother had turned to me. And I had turned away. I had thought, I now realized, too much about my father. All that time, he had lived. I had feared—I had cared about—the wrong thing.

•　•　•

The door opened. Kayla brought me a paper cup of coffee and a sandwich wrapped in wax paper. Behind her was the priest. The social worker, the doctor, and two nurses. The nurse mouthed to us across the room, *It's time.*

I looked around, confused, both hands full and no idea how to change this. The social worker stepped forward, touched my shoulder, and introduced himself. He took the coffee and the sandwich gently from me and put them on a small table at the foot of our mother's bed. Kayla, crying harder now, took my hands in hers and brought them back to our mother's.

There were questions from someone in the room. Did we understand what was going to happen and did we consent, was this my sister's signature, was this my sister, was this my mother, and so on. Kayla must have heard this before, in the room with the small fountain and the cup of tea.

This time, I answered for us. I found a thread of focus; I borrowed a voice that was old and calm, that could be here and do this. This left Kayla some minutes to whisper in our mother's ear and tuck back her hair.

The priest was very young. He prayed. He said, ". . . for in meeting You, after having sought You for so long, we shall find once more every authentic good which we have known here on earth, in the company of all who have gone before us . . ."

I thought about how I didn't believe in heaven, and our mother wasn't Catholic, and the part about "lovingly accepting Your will" made me want to throw my chair out the hospital room window and scream, because our mother should have had better health insurance, should have gone to the doctor more often, should have gotten her heart checked earlier, shouldn't be dying in what my sister said our mother said was the happiest or at least the truest time in her life.

Then I thought about the holy oil on our mother's forehead, the gentleness of the young priest's soft and quivering hand, the image he spoke into the room of our mother now with her mother, our mother who we held in our arms. I tried to hold that image in my mind, our mother in the company of all who had gone before her. The mercy of what you want to hear, at the moment you hope to hear it.

In a chair in a room beside my sister, beside our mother, I felt the presence of others. All the people we had come from, people we only knew to look for in stories she had heard and held and told us. Little pieces of life.

Our mother's breathing slowed. A terrible sound, small gasps I felt someone should shield us from.

My little sister sobbed and shook against my chest. I held her. This was something I could do. I had been trained for this, in a way, to stay steady in a rocket as it hurtled through space. Even if it spun out. Even if it killed me. I could be very still and carry her through.

Hours later in the early morning, in what would be the last moments of my mother's life, a memory washed over me. It was the third and last night of the school play, the third and last time my classmates were dragged from the mountains to Indian Territory. Each night, as my character, I would fall on the edge of the stage. Broken, scared, unsure if I had what it took to start again. On the last night, I felt this as myself. I forgot my lines. Meredith squeezed my hand. I tried to look out at the crowd, for the comfort of Brett or my sister, but the spotlight shined in my eyes. So bright it hid everyone behind it, like a flashlight in the dark. Like a quasar.

I remembered my line and said it. We all held hands and sang. The audience clapped. Meredith and I kissed inside the curtain after the rest of the cast had gone, and then she told me it was over.

For a long time, I stayed where she left me. I was invisible, wrapped in the pitch-black of the backstage curtain. I felt alone in a starless space. I gripped the thick fabric in my fists and held it tight.

I was the last to leave the auditorium, and the janitor had to unlock the back door to let me out. I'd told my family I'd ride home with a friend, which meant Meredith. Almost an hour had passed since the curtain call. I would have to walk.

But my mother was waiting for me in the parking lot behind the school, alone, leaning against the door of the old car that had brought us here. Just a look at me, at whatever it was she could see within me, and her arms opened wide. She folded me into her chest, the world gone dark in the warmth of her neck. Small stars on the backs of my eyelids, a peach-sized universe. For a moment, my feet lifted just above the ground.

PART

EIGHT

2016–2017

OTHER PEOPLE

November 13, 2016

I got to putting things in order. The mortgage, the home insurance, and the bills our mother had kept in piles around the house. At some point I would leave, and Kayla and Felicia would stay. Jason had agreed to move for Felicia's remaining years of school. He'd be joining a small firm in Tulsa, and renting in a small town forty minutes away.

I wanted the house to be nice for them, like their lives hadn't turned out like this by mistake. Every room was full of things to be dusted and sorted and given away. The endless tasks—made slower by my injury—let me feel like I was needed, even in this way I had made up. I needed to do things for and with other people, and to remind myself that I was part of them. Everywhere, I now knew, adults walked the earth with a parent dead. With both dead, even. Orphans! It was unthinkable to me, still.

I said something like this to Nadia over the phone, the second night after my mother died. Nadia had been discharged and was recovering well in her apartment with her parents on-hand to cook and clean. My sister was in the backyard, alone by a bonfire and drawing something. I was in bed, barely able to speak.

Nadia said this was fine. She told me to put my phone on the pillow beside my head, which I did, and she did the same on her end. We slept like that.

A few days later she flew in for the funeral. She didn't ask permission, which saved us the argument over how she should rest at home. She simply appeared in the second row of pews, a rare sight out of uniform. She was dressed formally, in a dark suit that looked new. Even her hair was different. It had been parted neatly on the left side, then somehow manipulated into ringlets. Her left arm hung at her side in a sling.

After the grave site and back at the house, Nadia kicked Kayla out of the kitchen with a look. She reheated casseroles and refilled bowls of chips and French onion dip. She appointed Felicia her sous chef, tying an apron around her waist (one-handed!). She taught her to peel vegetables into roses, and they came out so pretty that no one would eat them. Felicia beamed.

The house was crowded with people I'd grown up with and then never seen again. My old Sunday school teacher, and a grocer I couldn't remember, and the mailman. He'd found our mother on the road, after years of summers of her carrying him water. He told us our mother had learned that from her grandmother, back that one summer she'd spent with her.

Our mother's grandmother had lived in Bell, a small Cherokee community with no running water till the eighties. Residents, with the tribe's support, dug the sixteen-mile waterline themselves. Before that, when water was something to be hauled in buckets, our mother had learned it was a precious thing to give. Kayla and I looked at each other, realizing we'd just learned the name of our grandmother's town. It was maybe an hour southeast, and just a few miles from Arkansas.

Even Beth came to the house. Beth, whom I'd loved and looked up to before all the drama with Brett. It all felt ancient and strange, like these were visitors from another planet. There was so little space to move in the kitchen and the living room, everyone bumping into one another and eating cheese and crackers off paper napkins. Nadia wiped sweat from her forehead with the back of her hand and dumped another bag of chips into a bowl, smiling at me across the room.

Under obviously different circumstances, my mother would have found this fun. People teased me ruthlessly, about my hair and my muscles and my shark attack. About what a nightmare I'd been as a kid. They squeezed my upper arms and pulled me into their chests, laughing loud. Will, who'd once fired me from my job at the museum, said my mom hadn't shut up about her astronaut daughter. So why the hell was I always on Earth?

Brett, married to Beth for many years now, sent her home without him. He took the dishcloth from Nadia's hand and told her to stop working, jeez, go sit down! "Act like you got bit by a shark, why don't you."

Brett cleaned the kitchen, took out the trash, left, came back with groceries, and put them away where they'd belonged in the nineties.

The rest of us, Kayla and me and Nadia and Felicia, sat in a row on the couch and watched him. Felicia barely understood who he was. After all these years, I wasn't sure how to describe to her what he'd been.

I had always believed it was a perfect set of circumstances, pure luck, my mother loving Brett and Brett loving space, which meant Brett could love me. Brett showing up right when I needed him. Brett with his beautiful telescope in the leather carrying case with the shoulder strap. Brett holding my hand when I crawled through the open window, sitting beside me up on our roof, angling the telescope just so and saying, "Ni! Higowatis sgina noquisi wedoho? Ananisdani anaseho." Me looking up, leaning against him, looking for Venus, finding it.

I said, "Brett? If you give me a minute, I can get you your telescope." I'd found it during my week of housecleaning. It was in a closet. I hadn't used it since grad school, when the physicist had bought me a new one.

Brett closed the fridge and faced me. "You should hold on to that," he said. "It was your mother's."

"It was yours," I said.

"No, it was hers," he said, shrugging. "She saved up for it. I wasn't that into space."

"What?!" Nadia said. I'd told her about Brett. I'd told her about everything.

Brett tossed the empty grocery bags in the cabinet under the sink and sat down across from the four of us. He leaned forward, elbows on his knees. "It was your mom's idea. I think she got it from *Star Trek*?"

I remembered. It was *Star Trek: Deep Space Nine*. My mother had found it for us. Our show, after Kayla's bedtime. There'd been popcorn, and sometimes ice cream. Halfway through the first season, she'd finally let Brett move in with us.

"Your mom said she wanted something to share with you," Brett said. "She said you loved it. And if it helped with all those weird space stories your dad had put in your head? That was something."

On the couch beside me, Kayla squeezed my hand. It was the first time we'd heard Brett refer to our father. Our father was—for a while, and maybe when we'd most needed it—supposed to be him.

Brett told us everything and answered all my questions. Yes, our mother had told him about our father. Yes, all of it, even the parts she wasn't ready to share with us. She told him about space, and me, and how I seemed to be adjusting since Texas (not well). She bought a telescope. She gave it to Brett and told him not to say where it came from. She asked him to please encourage the space thing.

I remembered the first time Brett had shown me the telescope. For a while I'd been afraid. Bad things could come from men with telescopes.

And then I wasn't. Then I saw the moon close-up.

Every night, Brett and I would sit on the roof and look up at the sky, shivering in the cold or burning our feet on still-hot shingles.

Every night my mother watched us from her bedroom window.

On the way to his car, Brett called out behind him in Cherokee. *Let us, you-plural and I, meet again.* Not quite goodbye. I remembered that.

Nadia's flight home was the next day. Her parents could stay one more week with her in Houston, before they had to get Imane back home for continued treatment. I understood, better now than I could have only days before, what Nadia had given up to be here with me. There was no adequate trade for remaining time with her mother. When I reached for it anyway, I felt the tiny uselessness of my humanity.

I stopped at the gas station for M&M's and zipped them into the side pocket of her suitcase. I made her shakshouka for breakfast, which the internet said was Moroccan (or Tunisian or Turkish or Yemeni). In the drop-off lane at the Oklahoma City airport, I got out of the car. I limped around it, motioning for Nadia to wait a minute, so I could hug her with both arms.

DUST AND ASHES

November 14, 2016

Strangely, in the days since our mother passed, the house was more full than ever before. Then the funeral guests left, and then Nadia. Felicia went to her friend's house for a sleepover, the same girl whose mother had taken care of her when we were at the hospital. The mother seemed nice and had brought us a tray of macaroni. The daughter had four piercings, at least that we could see, and this time Kayla didn't say a word about it. It was good that Felicia had a friend.

Kayla and I were alone. "Can I take you to a bar?" I said.

"No thanks," Kayla said. Her voice was calm but cold.

I went to the kitchen for a bottle of wine. I'd bought it days before, in hopes that at some point I'd have a chance to talk to Kayla. She must have run out of ways to avoid me.

I uncorked the bottle at the counter, knowing we'd both consider it a waste to not drink now. (I'd been thinking about drinking again, in moderation. I'd also been thinking about giving up the four a.m. workout required for maintaining abs but not, as it turned out, a strict requirement for space travel.)

"Kayla?" I said. I called her name as I returned to the living room, like she needed to be warned of my presence.

"Hm?" she said. She was looking down at a book, though I wasn't sure she was reading.

I put the wineglasses on the coffee table between us. I remembered the early morning it had been covered in dirty mugs and plates and waffle crumbs, the mess of it. The warmth between all of us, even in a conversation that had felt unbearable. I wished our mother were here.

"You don't have to drink it," I said. "And you don't have to go out on the town with me."

"Cool," she said, returning to her book.

"But can we talk?"

She looked at me, blinking. Her eyes were tired, her face flushed and puffy from a week of tears. She was in the same sweatpants and sweatshirt as the day before, her hair trapped under a faded handkerchief I remembered from the camp. She left her wineglass untouched.

"I sabotaged the protest in Hawai'i," I said.

Kayla leaned back in her chair.

"I wanted to tell you," I said. "I hadn't figured out when, or how, after everything . . . Well, after Mom. But—"

I couldn't make excuses. "I traded information about what I'd seen at camp, to up my chance at a mission assignment. I knew what I was doing."

Kayla nodded.

"I saw the water hoses that night," I added. The worst part. "I saw you, even. And Felicia. I'm so sorry."

Kayla leaned still farther back, away from me. "I knew it was you. It was obvious. But yeah, I'd hoped you'd say something."

"I'm sorry," I said again. "I'm so—"

"It's fine," she said. "Better yet, I forgive you. I'm unemployed, I'm getting divorced, and Mom's dead. I don't have the bandwidth to be the right level of mad right now."

"Oh." I hadn't expected this.

"But! I need you to get that it wasn't *you* who ended the movement."

"I mean, I'm the one who—"

"I don't care. I'm not trying to let you off the hook. I just don't want you to think you're, like, *such* a big deal?"

"What do you mean?"

"You're one person. One phone call, or whatever batshit thing you did that night. At one point there were *hundreds* of people building up that movement, putting everything they had into it. They're the ones who decided it was over."

I leaned in closer. What Kayla was saying was the reverse of something I knew to be true, which was that every person had a role in improving the world. Every action mattered.

For the first time in a long time, I remembered my old thesis adviser in college. How much we'd frustrated each other; how hard he'd tried to guide me when I wasn't ready to be guided. We were barely in touch now, but I'd remembered all his stories. There was one about a rabbi in Poland who'd carried two slips of paper at all times, one in each of his pockets. One said, "for my sake the world was created." The other said, "I am only dust and ashes."

"You couldn't have stopped us if you'd tried," Kayla said. She closed her book, put it face down on the coffee table, and lifted the wineglass to her lips.

"What you did really sucked," she said. "I'm glad you finally said something. But you aren't as powerful as you think."

STEPH

WHAT WE WERE

A week later, Kayla gently asked me to leave. Jason would be staying with her and Felicia for a few days, to help them move furniture before his new job started in Tulsa. The bunk bed, finally, had to go. My sister said there'd be no room for me in Oklahoma. Not in that house. Literally no beds, once Jason arrived.

"This is just the push you need," Kayla said. She was laughing. We both were. I went back to Houston.

Nadia picked me up from the airport. Her arm was out of its sling, my leg was out of its brace, and in the parking lot we both jumped up and down, showing off, waving our mostly healed body parts in the air. She bent down and tried to lift my bad leg with her bad arm, just for the bit, but we both screamed in pain and fell back laughing into the car. When we could breathe again, she turned the key in the ignition, grabbed my head in her hands, and kissed me hard on my forehead. It was completely over the top, a kiss one cartoon character might give to another. Clearly intended not to give me the wrong idea.

"Jim says hi," she said. Her parents had always gone by their first names, encouraging her to question hierarchies from a young age. Felicia had thought that was amazing.

"What about Imane?" I said. We both knew Imane was harder to please.

"She *doesn't* say hi," Nadia said, pulling onto the highway. "She says you're a distraction from my work here, and bad at crossword puzzles."

"Am I?"

"I don't know; I've never seen you do one."

I laughed. "So I'm a *distraction*."

"Impossible," she said. She was almost smiling, but her voice was firm. "Don't take it personally."

I decided to settle in. On the first day Aziz was free to help me, I assembled my bed frame. I stopped sleeping on a mattress on the floor. I bought a cactus, and started sending postcards to Felicia. I subscribed to a newspaper.

Together, Nadia and Aziz and I protested a travel ban against people from seven Muslim-majority countries. We protested the border wall and the deportation of immigrants. We protested our country pulling out of an agreement on climate change mitigation.

Every other weekend, Nadia went to visit her parents in New York. Sometimes she went to Boston, to see Daryan. I went to work, harder than ever.

Then, in February, Nadia was assigned a mission to the International Space Station. Six weeks later, I was, too.

I was undone. Like all my life I'd been building myself up for this moment, and it was here, and I was not who I'd expected to be. Now I was taking myself apart again, looking at the pieces, putting them back in a different order. I would go to space. And I held so many other things in my heart.

One morning I got up when it was still dark out, just to pee. Then another morning, just to turn on the space heater at the foot of my bed, and then again to boil water for tea. I found myself awake on purpose, every morning a little earlier. I stirred hot milk and Ovaltine, the kind my mother once told me her mother liked, in a chipped red mug taken from the house I grew up in. I sat on my balcony, even in winter, wrapped in blankets as the sun came up. I allowed myself to sit still. To pause and wonder and question my life. I had been too rushed for this before, and too afraid of my own thoughts.

It wasn't enough, I realized. The trip to space. I had finally been chosen, just when I'd realized it wasn't about me.

Since I was a child, I'd been *fighting* for space. No one had shown me how to get there, which I'd thought made them obstacles to beat my way past.

Now I knew that wasn't true. My mother had given me the telescope and kept me safe as best she could. Brett had learned the Cherokee words for astronomical bodies, even as they were still being developed, just to gift them to me.

I had played down the fact of my people. I'd had shame at first, like being Indian would limit me. I'd have to arrive in spite of it. Or maybe I'd have to use it, taking advantage of the stories people told themselves about us. I had acted like my ancestors at the Seminary, how they'd armed themselves with English and calculus and bustles under their dresses. When I was older, and I had changed but so had the world, I had thought I wasn't Indian *enough*.

But this was what we were. What, for now, one of us was. Mine was one story of many, as Brett had tried to teach me—one thread of a history that wasn't over. Before I went to space, I wanted to share it.

On the news one morning in March, I saw the new president on a lawn in a long navy coat. He was touring the home of former president Andrew Jackson, signer of the Indian Removal Act. At the time of Jackson's death, on the grounds of the Tennessee plantation I now watched on my laptop, one hundred and sixty Black people had been enslaved. Fifty thousand Native people had been removed to Indian Territory, freeing up twenty-five million acres for white settlement and slavery's expansion.

The new president hung Andrew Jackson's portrait in the Oval Office. He said he was "a big fan." Andrew Jackson was "an inspiration." The new president laid a wreath on Andrew Jackson's tomb.

In my apartment in Houston, somewhere between eastern and western Cherokee land, I stared at my screen, thinking. It was the two hundred fiftieth anniversary of Andrew Jackson's birth, and I remembered his legacy. I wanted to be with my people.

When I was growing up, I'd been so sure I didn't have people. I'd never even bothered to look.

Eventually, dozens of phone calls. A grant application, a map, a proposed schedule of events. I asked myself what I was doing, why I was doing it, if I was powerful and what was the point. A memory, the nights my mother had planned a summer camp for me. A call to my sister in the early evening, how quickly she had said "yes."

OUR MOTHER'S WILDEST DREAMS

June 24, 2017

Six weeks before my trip to space, I flew to Oklahoma City.

Kayla and Felicia picked me up, and together we drove fifteen hours east. We shared a hotel room in Bryson City. It was twenty minutes outside Cherokee, North Carolina, the first of two stops on the speaking tour we'd planned. We'd start here, in Cherokee homelands, and make our way back to Tahlequah.

The first event wasn't scheduled for two more hours, so I suggested we visit Kituwah. Our mother had once, years ago, wanted to pray there. In the passenger seat beside me, Kayla threw back her head and cackled. "Why don't we wait for our mom to die," she said, "and then go live out her wildest dreams!"

This time, there was a historical marker in front. We filed out of the car and sat in the grass, looking out at the mound. I felt a presence there, the knowledge of so many people dead shifting quickly to who had lived. I wondered how our mother had experienced this place—after lunch with Brett and Beth, after Duke, after Dr. Carson and the long drive home.

I placed my hands on the ground. Grass peeked out between my fingers. Kayla and I could finally talk about our mother now, mostly but not entirely without crying. The day before, in East Tennessee during Kayla's turn to drive, we had made fun of our mother for the first time since she'd died. Kayla laughed so hard she cried, till her new SPF-foundation got into her eyes and burned. She yelled in pain, still laughing, and squinted so hard she could barely see. It was a relief when she managed to pull over at an exit. Felicia, lacking context and alone in the back seat, looked at us both disapprovingly.

An ant crawled across my hand. I jerked away, brushed it onto the grass, and looked up. Kayla was squinting at the line of trees in the distance, as if searching for something. Felicia sat between us, eyes closed, praying?

In the parking lot outside the event I called Nadia, who despite her imminent departure to space had decided to start a vegetable garden. My own mission was scheduled for soon after hers, so we wouldn't see each other for a while. Ten minutes into the call, I told her I missed her. She didn't say it back, but she left a long silence after I said it. It felt like a good thing. Nadia talked more about her garden, how much time and money had gone into her harvest of two cucumbers, and Kayla rolled her eyes, making a "wrap it up!" signal as she held open my car door.

Kayla introduced me to a small crowd, from the stage of a school auditorium. It was here that the Tri-Council meeting had happened, where Brett had touched Beth's leg in an empty classroom. A memory from another life.

During the Q and A, I sat on the steps at the bottom of the stage and leaned into the audience. Someone yelled for me to hold the microphone closer, and I did. Someone asked me how astronauts could sleep in microgravity, and I told them.

Afterward, I handed out pencils and sticker sheets in the lobby. On the sticker sheets, each planet was illustrated in a nod to the diversity of tribal nations. They were woven and beaded, carved into birchbark and whalebone and gourd. Kayla's doing.

Meredith, of all people, took one set of stickers for each of her children, then introduced us to her husband.

"Oh my God!" Kayla said. She stood up and hugged her. I followed, more slowly.

Meredith laughed. "Yeah, I live here now."

"How?" The question was for Meredith, but I looked at her husband. He was handsome and smiling. He offered his hand for me to shake. From up on his shoulders, a little boy waved down to me.

Meredith shook her head, eyebrows raised, like even she couldn't believe her life. "Telling you would take too long," she said.

Kayla and I gave her a look, pushing, but she held firm.

The younger child started to cry, and Meredith said something to him in Cherokee. She had really kept learning it, in the years since she'd struggled with it in school? She knew enough to speak it to her children? I sensed the jealousy building up in Kayla beside me, and I told Meredith it was so good to see her. Her husband shook my hand for the second time. I gave their children extra sticker sheets and greeted the next person in line.

The next day, we drove back to Tahlequah. On the way we circled some streets outside Little Rock, trying to find the house our mother had grown up in. We couldn't find the address we'd seen on an old envelope. It wasn't online and no longer seemed to exist. We had no one to ask.

"I should've looked them up by now," Kayla said.

She meant our family, whoever they were. Our mother had had brothers, who like her ought to still be alive. The brothers might have had kids. I thought about our half siblings on our father's side, four kids in Texas with no context for us, but I hadn't yet asked Kayla how she felt about that.

Just as we'd decided to get back on the interstate, Felicia threw up in the back seat.

We pulled over at a gas station, where Felicia took her time washing and drying her shirt in the restroom. I sat in the vomit-smell of the car, sweating, fully ready to die.

I called Nadia. "Well if you died," she said, "it would double my shot at the next mission assignment. I'd love to beat you to the moon."

I laughed. Our upcoming missions were to the space station, and public opinion wasn't hot on a mission to the moon. The same could be said of most missions, even going back to the Space Race.

But at the school visit, just a day before, the kids had talked about Mars like I used to. Like we'd be there, boots on planet, soon.

"Nadia, please. If that happened, you'd be a wreck," I said. "You'd visit my grave, what, three times a day?"

"In Arkansas? Fuck no."

"In Houston?"

"Houston?" she said. "I'd get on my knees and bury you myself."

Late that night, we made it home.

Kayla showed me around the changes she'd made. The old things I'd cleared out after the funeral had been replaced, with new and different clutter. There were bright, saturated colors on the walls of every room, like pictures I'd seen of houses in Mexico. There was art everywhere, framed prints of pieces by artists Kayla admired. In our mother's old bedroom, now Felicia's, Kayla had painted jasmine and hibiscus by a window. It was the start of a mural, which would cover the wall with Hawaiian plants.

We showered. Kayla boiled hot dogs for a quick and late dinner, ran the miracle of a dishwasher I never thought I'd see in that kitchen, and started pushing Felicia toward bed.

Quietly, while they put fancy serums on their faces side by side at the bathroom sink, I slipped into what had been our bedroom. It was Kayla's now, barely decorated in comparison to what she'd done for Felicia's room and for the rest of the house. But by the window, where my telescope had once stood on a tripod facing out, something caught my eye.

An easel. Clipped to it were several pieces of paper with uneven edges, seemingly ripped from a sketchbook. Each held a separate version of the same drawing, either in pencil or in fast, smudged ink. I couldn't make out what the drawings were, or what they would become. Maybe trees, or shadows? But I was so happy to see them. I had missed my sister as someone who painted, before she had become someone closely watched.

In the morning, I gave a talk at my old school. I went alone. I wanted to know I could do it.

"Don't make me speak the language," I'd warned the administrator who booked me, "I can't remember how." I stood in the auditorium where I'd put on plays as a child, where over many years I'd been a singing raindrop, a brick-housed pig, and somebody's husband—breaking the neck of a mock-ingbird and roasting it over a fire.

I answered questions from children about how to eat and wash your hair and pee in space. I answered questions from parents about financial aid and college and careers in the sciences. I introduced a woman near what I still thought of as my mother's age, with a white plastic name tag on her shirt. She was from Cherokee Nation College Resources. She sat at a long folding table in the back, with flyers and clipboards and free planners for the coming school year.

After the photos and the handing out of stickers, I walked backstage and collapsed into a chair. It was here, still, the heavy black curtain. I grazed the fabric with my fingers.

Brett knocked lightly on the backstage wall.

We watched each other, his hand on the back of my chair. I felt awkward with him, in a way I thought I'd gotten over at the funeral. There we'd been surrounded by other people, the weight of my mother between us.

Behind us, we heard the banging of metal chairs swept out of rows, lifted and stacked against the walls.

"Thank you," I said to him. Like it was for the event, or the bottle of water left for me on a stool.

"Ahnawake," he said, "you did good."

Brett brushed his hand over my head, a leftover gesture from when my hair could be smoothed down. His hand was heavy and warm. I had missed him so much when he had left. And in the years after sometimes, too.

I had missed this father. And, in that way I would never have words for, the one before him.

Brett slipped back behind the curtain. I cried silently in the girls' bath-room by the auditorium, like I had many times as a child.

I walked out the back door of the building, leaned against the brick wall, and looked out at the parking lot. It was empty. My eyes rested on the place where I'd found my mother after the school play. Where she'd stood, leaning against the closed door of her car, waiting for me.

Instagram Post

July 6, 2017

kayla.harper

[A close-up photo of an easel standing by a window, holding an oil painting on canvas. A streak of sunlight blurs white across the corner.

At the front of the painting are Steph and Felicia, legs stretched out ahead of them and cut out of the frame. They sit in grass, plastic bags and wax paper crumpled beside them. Steph leans in close to Felicia, looking over her shoulder at the phone Felicia holds out to her. In her other hand is half a sandwich. The two of them squint down at the screen, laughing.

Behind them is a fence. A field. In the far distance, only meaningful to those who know it, the gentle slope of a grass-covered mound. Kituwah. Originally, it was fifteen or twenty feet tall, the center of a town that is no longer there. Now, after nearly two hundred years of being plowed for farming, it stands six feet in a wide slope.

Behind the mound is a line of trees. Mountains and woods reach for the top of the canvas, blocking the sky. At the bottom edge of the forest, peering outward, are the ghostly shapes of many people.

From such a distance, it's impossible to know who they are. We can't know who they once were, or the quality of lives lived. Their faces are blurred, and the edges of their bodies flow into one another. Behind them are many hundreds more—unknowable, standing together in darkness, looking out.]

TEN YEARS LATER

STEPH

FLIGHT

For a very long time, no one went to the moon. It was tired, done, no longer valued in the aftermath of the Cold War. We made no plans to return. And then, finally, we did.

People saw it as a step toward what was next, toward farther travel, toward an eventual mission to Mars. Everything is only a step. Science and exploration happen slowly, carefully. Like three thousand years of Polynesian wayfinders, mapping sea by stars. It's hard sometimes, on the voyage to the next island, to realize when you're there. Or that you're somewhere.

Before they sent me to the moon, I went three times to the International Space Station.

Up there the days are full of research, logging incremental changes on charts and tables. Jogging while strapped to a treadmill, washing my hair live for NASA's children's programming, looking down at the Earth below. I cannot possibly make sense of life, of this life, not as I still live it.

Sometimes I float alone in the quiet dark and feel the rush of a thousand moments as they fly through my memory. In bright flashes I see myself wishing on a potato chip that came folded over itself and reading a book with a flashlight; I feel the particular itch of the grass under my neck, on nights I lay under stars. Sometimes I think about the years I lived in my father's house, and the years I lived in my mother's house, and then this—what this is now—and all the years I can't yet imagine.

Sometimes it overwhelms me, like I've lived a life so full and varied that little drops of it splash out over the rim. I can't catch them in my hands. On

Earth I hear the soft, low laugh of my wife sprawled out on a couch beside me—a sound that is easy, that is good—and I could cry at how lucky I am to hear it. In space I lie perfectly still, my legs in the air stretched out behind me; I watch those same stars I watched as a child.

On my first night in space, years ago, the others slept. I stayed awake and looked out from the cupola.

When I was a girl, I read the memoirs of astronauts. They said the view had made them feel like the only person in the universe. Michael Collins, the only Apollo 11 astronaut to not touch the lunar surface, wrote about circling above his two crewmates while they walked on the moon. For twenty-two hours he piloted the command and service module, talked to mission control, and waited. Someone had to stay on the ship, and Collins was the only one who could get them safely home. Later, he said his time with NASA was the shiniest, best chapter in his life, but not the only one. He said the thing he remembered most was the view of Earth. "Tiny . . . Blue and white. Bright. Beautiful. Serene and fragile."

I already knew to look down, to fully see where I had come from.

My crewmates and I were alone up there. Just the beeping, and the whirring, and the uneasy protection of thick walls. Our own slow breaths, mission control on a screen, the four of us on the space station I had watched pass over my head. All those years I had looked for it, had waited for it, in my most lonely hours. At one point, I could now admit, the slow streak of white station over night sky had been like the wave of a hand over a forehead, like Last Rites.

But here, in this near-total isolation, I only felt a chorus of souls echoing up from the Earth and the station, and someday the moon, and from places we hadn't yet been to or found. From the galley beneath me I heard the creaking of the ship, the humming, the sigh of bodies turning over in sleep.

We circled the Earth every ninety minutes. But only once, if I was attentive and careful, would I find what I was looking for. I stayed awake. I waited.

Below, just over the Ozarks, the minutes before dawn. It was still dark, the land dotted with the yellow and white of lit streets and houses. Looking out on our home world, I knew that even as I hovered here soft in my aloneness, there were people sleeping and waking up, closing books and buttoning shirts, millions of hands moving in the dailiness of life. I checked my watch and tracked our coordinates.

There.

Two hundred fifty miles below me, in the light of a house, one of a hundred thousand lights—my mother had lived.

I knew Kayla stood at the kitchen window. She held her palm, still and warm, against a pane of glass. In the house our mother had brought us to, in a town in the foothills of mountains—where *eclipse* means a story, means a frog eating the moon.

My sister had promised to leave the light on.

AUTHOR'S NOTE

Whether through research, my own experience, or the generosity of others in sharing their knowledge with me, I have tried to portray history and politics accurately in most cases. When accuracy did not serve the story, or when accuracy came too close to the stories of living people, I used creative license.

All protests depicted in the book—with one exception—are real. Some dates of real protests, including the protests at Mauna Kea, have been slightly altered in order to serve the greater timeline of the novel.

The protests at Mauna Loa are invented.

The real first Native American woman in space is Col. Nicole Aunapu Mann, Wailacki of the Round Valley Indian Tribes. On October 5, 2022, Mann launched to the International Space Station as the commander of NASA's SpaceX Crew-5 mission aboard the SpaceX Crew Dragon spacecraft *Endurance*. The mission came twenty years after the first mission of the first Native American man in space, John Herrington (Chickasaw Nation). While on board the ISS, Mann answered questions from Osage children via remote video link. At the end of the broadcast, she demonstrated a zero gravity flip.

NASA's astronaut candidate selection program does exist, and it is highly selective. But in some instances, I have strayed from accuracy for the sake of the narrative. The comment on Reddit by a since-deleted profile—in which someone reported having had lunch seven years ago with an astronaut who advised they not plan their life around trying to be an astronaut but instead pursue a passion that would make them happy even if they weren't selected—is real.

Alicia Soderberg and Edo Berger are real astronomers, and they were the first to catch a star in the act of exploding.

The HI-SEAS (Hawai'i Space Exploration Analog and Simulation) research station, on the Mars-like site of Mauna Loa, is real. The NEEMO (NASA Extreme Environment Mission Operations) project, carrying out missions in an undersea research station off the coast of Florida, is real.

Steph's future mission to the moon is real, though it has not happened yet. NASA's Artemis campaign will land the first woman, first person of color, and first non-US citizen astronaut on the moon as part of a series of missions currently underway.

In Artemis I (November 2022), NASA completed an uncrewed lunar flight test. In Artemis II, currently scheduled for April 2026, four astronauts will fly around the moon. They are Commander Reid Wiseman, pilot Victor Glover, and mission specialist Christina Koch, from NASA; and mission specialist Jeremy Hansen, from the Canadian Space Agency.

In Artemis III, currently scheduled for 2027, two crew members will spend one week on the surface of the moon. Future Artemis missions will work toward the construction of the first lunar space station, which will serve future crewed missions to Mars.

The Bell Waterline Project, in which members of a rural Cherokee community dug their own sixteen-mile waterline system in the early 1980s, is real. Volunteers were assisted by community organizer Charlie Soap and the late Wilma Mankiller, first woman chief of the Cherokee Nation. To learn more, see the film *The Cherokee Word for Water* (2013).

The Cherokee Tri-Council meeting is real, but it was not held in 1997 as depicted. Leaders of the Cherokee Nation, the Eastern Band of Cherokee Indians, and the United Keetoowah Band of Cherokee Indians met in 2012 for the first time in history, with the goal of advancing tribal sovereignty as a united people.

Museums, schools, summer camps, and other community-based organizations and projects in Tahlequah are my own invention. Out of respect and appreciation for the real people who dedicate themselves to language revitalization and cultural preservation today, I have made no attempt to portray them or their places of work. To learn more about Cherokee language revitalization efforts today, see the film *Dadiwonisi: We Will Speak* (2023).

· · ·

All named ancestors in Steph's family born before the year 1860 are based on real people. Anyone born after the year 1860 is invented.

On Fictional Ancestors

Andromache Bell Shelton was the mother of a seminary teacher, and Walter Adair Duncan was the father of a seminary teacher, and these two teachers did marry each other.

But these teachers, Hannah's maternal grandparents, are the first in a line of fictionalized ancestors. They have no connection to real or living descendants of Andromache and Walter; no children were abandoned in barns. From these seminary teachers forward, all members of Steph's family are fictional.

On Real Ancestors

The Western History Collections and archival materials referenced in the novel, which quote Walter Adair Duncan (b. 1820) and Andromache Bell Shelton (b. 1831), are real. John Adair Bell (b. 1805), one of the signers of the Treaty of New Echota, is real. Jane Martin Bell (b. 1812), his wife, is real.

Walter, Andromache, John, Jane, and unnamed but referenced ancestors (in order of birth: "a man from Ireland who settled in the Nation," Cherokee Confederates, and two aforementioned and fictionalized teachers at the seminaries) are ancestors of my own.

As a young girl, Steph learns of Cherokee beloved woman and political leader Nancy Ward (b. 1738), estimated to have perhaps forty thousand living descendants. Accordingly, my ancestors are the ancestors of many.

These ancestors, whether mine alone or yours, too, were necessary to witness and question in the writing of this novel—though I'll specify "to question" and not "to answer." The conversations they raise surrounding identity, legacy, and accountability are relevant to many Cherokee people—and many Indigenous people, and many Americans. And, if you'll bear with me in earnestness and hope, many people around the Earth. Not only today, but as we move toward the far future.

NOTES ON SOURCES

5   *All That Is or Ever Was or Ever Will Be*
"The cosmos is all that is, or ever was, or ever will be."
Carl Sagan, professor of astronomy and space science, in his 1980 book *Cosmos*.

33   *Obstacles on the Road to Imminent Disaster*
"Theater is a series of insurmountable obstacles on the road to imminent disaster."
From Tom Stoppard, playwright and screenwriter of *Shakespeare in Love* (1998).

42   *This Dreary Exile of Our Earthly Home*
"If there is anything that can bind the mind of man to this dreary exile of our earthly home and can reconcile us with our fate so that one can enjoy living,— then it is verily the enjoyment of the mathematical sciences and astronomy."
From Johannes Kepler, seventeenth-century German astronomer, in a letter to his son-in-law, Jakob Bartsch.

155   *I Spent a Star Age in Flames*
From the poem "Stone Love," by Louise Erdrich, 2020.

167   *The Sky Beyond the Sky Beyond the Sky*
From the poem "How It Escaped Our Attention," by Heid E. Erdrich, 2020.

183   *I Have Loved the Stars Too Fondly*
"Though my soul may set in darkness, it will rise in perfect light; / I have loved the stars too truly to be fearful of the night."
From the poem "The Old Astronomer to his Pupil," by Sarah Williams, 1868.

201   *Where Has the Tree Gone, that Locked Earth to the Sky?*
From the poem "Going," by Philip Larkin, 1955.

332 *A Wilderness of Waves*
"The sea is a wilderness of waves, / A desert of water. / We dip and dive, / Rise and roll, / Hide and are hidden / On the sea. / Day, night, / Night, day, / The sea is a desert of waves, / A wilderness of water."
From the poem "Long Trip," by Langston Hughes, 1926.

355 *The Short Duration of My Life*
"When I consider the short duration of my life, swallowed up in an eternity before and after, the little space I fill engulfed in the infinite immensity of spaces whereof I know nothing, and which know nothing of me, I am terrified. The eternal silence of these infinite spaces frightens me."
From *Pensées*, by French mathematician and philosopher Blaise Pascal, 1670.

379 *Remember the Sky that You Were Born Under*
From the poem "Remember," by Joy Harjo, 1983.

386 *Contact Light*
First words spoken on the moon. On July 20, 1969, Buzz Aldrin said, "Contact light," meaning that at least one of the three probes hanging from the bottom of the lunar module had made contact with the moon's surface.

400 *Every Authentic Good on Earth*
"And when the moment of our definitive passage comes, grant that we may face it with serenity, without regret for what we shall leave behind. For in meeting you, after having sought you for so long, we shall find once more every authentic good which we have known here on earth, in the company of all who have gone before us marked with the sign of faith and hope."
From Prayers for the Health and Dignity of the Sick, United States Conference of Catholic Bishops. St. John Paul II, 1999.

ACKNOWLEDGMENTS

Immense gratitude to Meredith Kaffel Simonoff—agent, creative partner, and absolute champion in my life as a writer. She believed in the most ambitious version of this book, and gave me the confidence to reach for it.

Thank you to my US editor, Margo Shickmanter, for her tireless dedication to her work, her sense of humor, and her expansive and deep understanding of the world and its people. Margo believed in the deepest version of this book, and I'm grateful for the brilliance of her questions toward that aim.

Thank you to my UK editor, Bobby Mostyn-Owen. I was so lucky to have their insight as they brought with them an astounding attention to detail and a strong sense of these characters and their relationships to one another. They also, importantly, have always made me laugh.

Thank you to katherena vermette, my Canadian editor, and the team at Simon & Schuster Canada, especially Nicole Winstanley.

Thank you to Avid Reader Press, especially Amy Guay, Alex Primiani, Meredith Vilarello, Alison Forner, and Clay Smith. I'm so grateful to Jofie Ferrari-Adler for his early and full-hearted enthusiasm, and to everyone at Avid: Katya Wiegmann, Allison Green, Jessica Chin, Ruth Lee-Mui, Alicia Brancato, Sirui Huang, Rhina Garcia, Eva Kerins, Sydney Newman, Paul O'Halloran, Fiona Sharp, Lauren Wein, and Ben Loehnen.

Thank you to Doubleday UK, especially Sara Roberts, Millie Seaward, Milly Reid, Georgie Bewes, and Beci Kelly. Thank you to btb Verlag.

Thank you to the Gernert Company, especially Nora Gonzalez, Rebecca Gardner, Will Roberts, and Sophie Pugh-Sellers. Through the Gernert Company, I've been so happy to work with Caspian Dennis and Michelle Weiner.

Thank you to Lena K. Little of Lena K. Little PR, for introducing me to the book as it exists for readers, and for great kindness.

I'm grateful to many organizations for a decade of encouragement and support, beginning with the Sewanee Writers' Conference in 2014 (thank you to my teacher the late Allen Wier, and to dear friends Graham Cotten and Kat Gonso). Thank you to the Tin House Summer Workshop for far too much, including my first conversation with Meredith. Thank you to Lance Cleland, and my teachers there: Lan Samantha Chang, Brandon Taylor, and Megan Giddings. Thank you to the Vermont Studio Center and the Kimmel Harding Nelson Center, for the gift of time and focus during crucial final drafts of this novel. Thank you to Catapult's Queer and Trans Novel Generator, particularly A. E. Osworth and early readers E. R. Anderson, MJ Kaufman, and Brendan Williams-Childs. Thank you to the Lambda Literary Writers Retreat for Emerging LGBTQ Voices, and my teachers Jeanne Thornton and Casey Plett. Thank you to *CRAFT* and *The Masters Review* for their support of my short fiction.

Thank you to my earliest creative writing teachers: Thomas O'Malley, Catherine Tudish, and Evan Fallenberg. Thank you to the Stephens Family Scholarship Fund at Dartmouth College, and to Dr. Ryan Calsbeek for the enduring joy of his Animal Behavior class.

The start of a great shift in my adult life—as a writer and a person—came by way of the Iowa Writers' Workshop. I will forever be grateful to the people there, beginning with Lan Samantha Chang. The University of Iowa supports the Iowa Arts Fellowship, which is so meaningful for the program and its students. I'm also grateful personally to the Guthrie family, who supported this novel in its early stages through the Richard E. Guthrie Memorial Fellowship. Thank you to my teachers at Iowa: Kevin Brockmeier, Ethan Canin, Amber Dermont, V. V. Ganeshananthan, Margot Livesey, and Ayana Mathis.

I am better for knowing the following writers, readers, and most importantly friends from my time at Iowa: Melissa Mogollón, Emily Dauer, Sergio Aguilar-Rivera, Tameka Cage Conley, Jade Jones, Cinnamon Kills First, Afabwaje Kurian, Claire Lombardo, Sarah Thankam Mathews, Grayson Morley, Anna Polonyi, Tanner Pruitt, Kiley Reid, Angela Tharpe, Keenan Walsh, Dawnie Walton, De'Shawn Charles Winslow, and Monica West.

Thank you to Connie Brothers, Deb West, and Jan Zenisek. Thank you to Stephen Lovely and the Iowa Young Writers' Studio.

Since grad school, I've been lucky to have the continued and treasured company of other writers, particularly Lydi Conklin, Kumari Devarajan, Carson Faust, Autumn Fourkiller, Jon Hickey, Ilana Masad, and Eli Raphael. In Nashville, I'm especially grateful to The Porch, the Gertrude and Harold Vanderbilt Reading Series, and Parnassus Books for their work in building a community of writers and readers.

In writing outside my own knowledge, I relied on the extraordinary generosity of many. First and foremost, thank you to my brother Noah Ramage for his research and counsel through countless drafts. As I revised this novel, Noah was at work on his dissertation, "Phoenix on Fire: The Cherokee Nation from Reconstruction to Denationalization." It was a lucky break for me as his sister, as his project continued to introduce, complicate, and sharpen the questions that built this novel.

Thank you to Gregory Buzzard, for many years of conversation and fact-checking on the Indian Child Welfare Act and its importance. (Thank you, far more, for a friendship that would turn into family.) Thank you to Schon Duncan for his expertise and assistance in the Cherokee language—any mistakes are my own. Thank you to Owen Mostyn-Owen for his much-needed knowledge of astrophysics and scuba diving. Thank you to Benji Kessler for reading for biology. Thank you to Sean-Joseph Takeo Kahāokalani Choo for such kindness and direction regarding Native Hawaiian culture, politics, and overall context previously missing. Thank you to Pōʻai Lincoln for Hawaiian language translation—as always, in all of this, any mistakes are my own. Thank you to beloved childhood friends Mihret Woldesemait and Shohreh Daraei: for Ethiopian and Kurdish fact-checks, respectively; but really for coming of age with me.

In 2018, my student Maya Dasmalchi arranged for me to speak with her astronaut relative Dr. Janet L. Kavandi. Thank you for the generosity of your time.

Thank you to the Martino and Barbuto families for their constant support. Thank you to Jim Kelley, and to Rebekah Kelley, maternal aunt and second mother. Thank you to my brothers and their wives: Avram Ramage, Rebecca Bieber, Noah Ramage, and Gisselle Pérez León—your team is my favorite team to be on. As the oldest sibling Avram has answered many phone calls, including the call that made me write again. Thank you to Maow, my late grandmother, who lived with us and cared for us through childhood. Thank you to my mother and father, who read me books, told me stories, and are an absolute pleasure to know and love in my adulthood.

Finally, thank you to my husband for his deep kindness and friendship. To our child, thirty-nine weeks in-utero at this time of writing: Thank you for being a kind of light, through many years of hoping we'd someday meet. I'll be so happy to have you in the world.

ABOUT THE AUTHOR

ELIANA RAMAGE holds an MFA in fiction from the Iowa Writers' Workshop. She has received residencies and fellowships from the Kimmel Harding Nelson Center for the Arts, Lambda Literary, Tin House, and Vermont Studio Center. A citizen of the Cherokee Nation, she lives in Nashville with her family. *To the Moon and Back* is her first novel.